# ONCE
*again*

# "Once upon a time"

*is timeless with these retold tales:*

---

# ONCE

*Snow*

by

# LIZ BRASWELL

*Previously published
under the pseudonym
Tracy Lynn*

*Beauty Sleep*

by

# CAMERON DOKEY

## again

SIMON PULSE  NEW YORK  LONDON  TORONTO  SYDNEY  NEW DELHI

SIMON PULSE

An imprint of Simon & Schuster Children's Publishing Division

1230 Avenue of the Americas, New York, New York 10020

This Simon Pulse paperback edition November 2015

*Snow* copyright © 2003 by Elizabeth Braswell

*Beauty Sleep* copyright © 2002 by Cameron Dokey

Cover photograph copyright © 2015 by Mike Dobel/Trevillion Images

All rights reserved, including the right of reproduction

in whole or in part in any form.

SIMON PULSE and colophon are registered trademarks of Simon & Schuster, Inc.

For information about special discounts for bulk purchases, please contact Simon & Schuster Special Sales at 1-866-506-1949 or business@simonandschuster.com.

The Simon & Schuster Speakers Bureau can bring authors to your live event. For more information or to book an event contact the Simon & Schuster Speakers Bureau at 1-866-248-3049 or visit our website at www.simonspeakers.com.

Cover designed by Karina Granda

Interior designed by Tom Daly

The text of this book was set in Adobe Garamond Pro.

Manufactured in the United States of America

2 4 6 8 10 9 7 5 3 1

Library of Congress Control Number 2015932674

ISBN 978-1-4814-5164-2 (pbk)

ISBN 978-1-4424-0837-1 (*Snow* eBook)

ISBN 978-0-7434-2850-7 (*Beauty Sleep* eBook)

These titles were previously published individually by Simon Pulse.

# Snow

A Retelling of "Snow White and the Seven Dwarfs"

## LIZ BRASWELL

*Previously published
under the pseudonym
Tracy Lynn*

*This book is dedicated to:*
Mom, Dad, Scott, and Sabrina;
Geoff, for giving me *The Book of Three*; my sisters-in-writing,
Mara, Alexis, and Katherine; the good folks at Ciao for Now;
and, of course, Lisa—thank you.

# Prologue

A LONE FIGURE WALKED DOWN THE DARK AISLE of a church. She was dressed for travel in plain gray with a heavy wool cloak, which fastened around her head like a nun's habit, hiding her face. The stones beneath her were ancient and cold; her footsteps echoed off every stone column and arch. She pulled the cloak tightly around her as the shadows crept up her skin and chilled her to the bone.

Light struggled and lost here: It strained through dim stained glass windows, glowed from occasional candles, and glinted off a golden locket at the girl's neck.

She walked past the altar to one of the side chapels, where previous dukes and duchesses had been buried over the long centuries. Their bodies were encased in stone coffins, some of which had the likenesses of those within carved in relief on the top. She used to come here often, to run away, to spend time quietly, to look at the strange gargoyles and tombs, to pretend to mourn, to mourn, to think. The dead never bothered her—except that she wondered how they really looked, in life.

She took out the locket she wore and looked at the miniature within. From everything she was told, her mother did indeed resemble her painting—with a few exceptions. She had longer lashes and fuller eyebrows, and a face bent more toward smiling than serenity. She wore her hair down in a braid, not up in a chaste bun. She had looked very much like her daughter, people told her.

She willed the colors in the tiny oil painting to flow into the stone, to open the coffin and present her mother again, alive.

"Good-bye," the girl said simply, kneeling. "I love you, and will return someday. Please, watch over me in my travels. Keep me safe." She bent her head in prayer. Tears welled up in black eyes. Motionless she stayed, even at the sound of footsteps padding behind her.

"It's time to go, Jessica," the boy whispered.

She nodded and wiped her tears. He was older and dressed in a servant's uniform, complete with cap and knickers, but he put his arm around her like a brother and led her gently away.

They walked together through the church and out to the field. It was gray and damp and misting slightly; the grass blew with the possibility of a storm. A carriage was waiting, a wagon really, with two old draft horses and an old man with a pipe at their reins.

"Good-bye, Jessica," the servant said, and kissed her on the cheek. "Remember that I love you. Keep safe."

"Good-bye, Alan. I will miss you, and Kenigh Hall." She

said it bravely, like a queen, but tears kept running down her face. He helped her up onto the cart and threw a bag in after her. The wagon began to move at a pace slower than walking. The two horses ambled as if they had all the time in the world. The servant boy cast a worried eye on the church and estate behind them. Slowly the horses gained speed, and soon she was halfway down the hill, standing up and waving.

"Farewell!" he cried.

"Farewell," she whispered. Then she turned around and sat down so she could see the road ahead and what lay in store for her.

Part One

# Home

# Chapter One

ONCE UPON A TIME . . .

. . . there lived a duke and a duchess in a remote corner of Wales. It was a cold land, rugged and wild, known more for its strange weather than anything else. A sunny day could become windy and rainy and turn to snow just as quickly, then clear away to blue skies again, full of rainbows and bright golden sunlight. Fields were few and carefully tended; most of the land was hilly and overrun with half-wild ponies, shaggy and fierce. There was an abundance of nothing but landscape, sheep, and canal boats carrying coal from other parts of the country.

Yet the people of Kenigh lacked nothing; they had their pubs and their dances, their gossip and their holidays. They were an independent people beholden to no one, and only grudgingly did they acknowledge the queen of England.

The duke and duchess lived on a large estate in a positively enormous old house called Kenigh Hall, partly built into a real castle made from the same stones ancient invaders used for roads and temples. They had a proper staff, with servants, maids, cooks, butlers, and dozens of others. They had a huge kitchen in which feasts were occasionally prepared, libraries filled with old books occasionally read, velvet-draped studies decorated with French furniture, stables with expensive horses, game parlors, and dozens of bedrooms. Like royalty in the rest of the world, they passed their hours usefully: The duchess ran the house, wrote letters to friends, and embroidered and sewed. She spoke French with important visitors when they arrived and was as perfect a hostess as one could imagine. The duke managed the estate and the finances, spoke with his retainers, and invested in exports from the Caribbean. Their leisure time was spent mostly with each other, except when the duke went on foxhunts or the duchess made the long trip to visit a friend in London.

In the rest of the world far away, time marched on relentlessly through its new mechanical clocks, but at Kenigh Hall life went on much as it had for hundreds of years.

The only thing it could be truly said that the duke and duchess lacked was a child and heir. For many years they consulted doctors, midwives, priests, and spiritualists, all to no avail. Neither the duke nor the duchess had family, not even distant cousins with sons who could inherit the estate. The people of Kenigh were likewise apprehensive; as far as the whole business of royalty was concerned, these two were polite, generous philanthropists who employed almost half the town, from scullery maids to expensive orders from the butcher. Once they died the Crown might very well auction off the title to some rich nobody who would use the place as a summer retreat and spend most of his time in London. And where would they all be then?

But as the couple and their town began to lose hope, the duchess at last conceived a child. For nine months she was treated delicately, like the sickest of invalids, coddled and cooed over by the servants and lavished with kisses and presents from her husband. During the rare times that no one was around to keep her from leaving the bed, the duchess would rise and stand in front of her largest looking glass, hold her belly, and imagine what her son or daughter would look like. She herself was slender, with pale cheeks to her husband's rosy ones, and dark hair to the duke's mane of orange-gold.

"I hope he will be handsome. I hope she will be beautiful," she would say. Gazing out at the wintry landscape she would add, "With skin as fair as snow, lips as red as blood, and hair as black as shadow." Identical twins, boy and girl, played in her head. Then she would shake her head at her silliness. "I hope he is *brave* like my husband. I hope she is *kind* like—like I hope I am." She willed the baby inside her to be strong, to live out the nine months and be born healthy. The duchess knew the duke was expecting a boy, but she would be grateful for either, and secretly she would have been pleased with a daughter.

Finally, one chill winter morning, the duchess did indeed give birth to a girl. She had just enough time to cradle the baby in her arms and kiss her neck before slipping quietly away to the dark lands. "Jessica," she murmured with her last breath, her lips already gone cold.

The duke came running in, throwing aside the midwives and nurses. When he saw a maid gently removing the baby from her dead mother's breast, the duke howled in despair. "Mary," he cried, rushing over to his wife and kissing her hands. He wept and stroked her hair. Everyone in the room averted their eyes, allowing him some semblance of privacy.

He kissed her brow one last time and stood, shaky, spent, and almost as pale as her.

The baby made the softest noise, more of a sigh than anything else.

The duke turned to glare at it, all his anger at his wife's death directed toward the tiny thing.

"Well, what *is* it?" he growled.

"It's a girl, Your Grace," a nurse spoke softly as she curtsied.

"Even *that* is denied to me." His eyes flashed. "Not even an heir, a hope of the future now that my past is dead."

"My Lady's last words," an older maid spoke evenly, knowing the things that must be done even in unpleasant times, "were to request that she be named Jessica."

The duke's face went soft for just a moment at the mention of the duchess's last act on earth. Then he scowled.

"Jessica, Elizabeth, Constance—it makes no matter to me. Call her what you will. Just keep her out of my way while I mourn." And he strode out of the room.

* * *

A wet nurse was found for the baby Jessica. The first time she was brought outside, it was to attend her mother's funeral. A maid held her as she slept, woke, and made small noises. They stood at the back of the crowd where they would draw little attention.

But Jessica showed none of the sickness one might expect from the child of a dying mother; she was obstinately healthy and smiled early. The wet nurse and the other maids and servants doted on her; it could well be said that Jessica had a multitude of replacement mothers, fathers, uncles and aunts, and brothers and sisters. Her own father showed little interest in her fate or development. Once in a great while—on a holiday, for instance—Jessica would be dressed in long white clothes and presented to the duke. He would lean over and see her black hair and black eyes, so reminiscent of her mother, and his face would soften for just a moment. Then the baby would smile or gurgle, full of life, and he would send her away again.

Years passed.

The duke demonstrated no growing love for his own daughter; if anything, his bitterness grew with her as Jessica walked and talked. She was raised in the kitchen, sitting well-behaved on a stool in the corner when she was a toddler, playing with a wooden spoon or pot lid the cook gave her. Warm smells and big, friendly faces surrounded her early childhood. What mischief she made was little; at most, she would pretend to sneak out of the kitchen, only to be run after, caught up, and hugged in a fit of giggles by Dolly, the fat old cook.

Once in a while the local priest or a friend would come by and mildly suggest that the kitchen was no place for a child of royalty. For a fortnight thereafter the unhappy Jessica would be confined to a large, drafty bedroom near the duke, cared for by an equally unhappy butler. As soon as the duke stopped noticing or caring, off Jessica would go, back to the kitchen where she was happy again.

The problems of the estate, far from being a concern to the little duchess, were nonetheless strangely felt by the duke and the town. There was still no royal heir. Girls and women could no more inherit property than men could bear children. At the very least the old duke would have to live until Jessica grew up and married so the estate could pass to her husband if he were high enough royalty, to her own son if he was not. But that was many years off, and as the poor duchess was an example, there are no guarantees in life or death.

So the duke was obliged to find another wife—one who could still bear him a son. He was not inclined to do so; for all of his many other faults he had loved his wife dearly and had no desire to replace her. He took his time—some would have said dragged his feet—as secretaries and advisors suggested this match or that, and foreigners came from as far as France to offer their noble daughters and sisters as his bride.

Jessica was still a child at this time. But unlike many duchesses, by the age of seven she could bake bread, doing everything herself from weighing the flour to slashing the top for steam to escape. She could churn butter, make jam, carefully weave pastry lattices for the tops of tarts, and expertly carve a paper-thin slice of rare meat off a leg of lamb if required.

Her favorite kitchen task was turning meat on the gigantic spit over the kitchen fireplace. The fat would drip and sizzle, and the herbs would roast and fill the room with intoxicating smells. It was the warmest place in the drafty old estate house, and while staring into the fire Jessica would make up stories about the people and dragons she saw in the flames. Where other duchesses wore silk and velvet, she wore rough linen smocks; where they learned to sew and curtsy, she painted her face with flour and played catch-the-sack with the stableboy and the servants' children.

Little did visiting nobles, presenting possible brides to the duke, realize that their meals were prepared, and sometimes served, with the help of a duchess.

When she reached nine and ten the servants and maids who had been her family finally began to feel that a kitchen was perhaps, after all, not the most appropriate place for her. It had been a long time since any royal children had been in the castle—not since the duke himself had grown up, with his cousins—so the protocol was uncertain. Jessica was forced into a proper bedroom in the main hall near where her father slept, but not too close. She was lonely and scared the first few nights, and gathered as many of the hunting dogs as she could to sleep in bed with her. Maids tried to fit her with more appropriate clothes, switching from shifts to dresses, barefoot to slippers. They tried to make her brush her hair.

But exile from the kitchen meant freedom on the rest of the estate grounds. Soon—every moment she wasn't under direct supervision, in fact—Jessica was running wild, from looking out the highest gable windows in the attic to jumping in the hay in the stables, from catching frogs with the servants' children to tiptoeing about the great hall when it was empty, spooking herself with the empty suits of armor that stood guard there.

Her happiness was not to last.

The duke finally began correspondence with a woman whom he did not immediately dislike. She was Duchess Anne of Mandagor, from England and therefore at once distrusted by everyone. The duchess was, however, childless, which brought some relief, eliminating the fear of a complete invasion of the duchy. She was older than Jessica's mother would have been by a number of years, some said almost as old as the duke himself. The estate flew with rumors about her: that she was a spy for the Queen, that she was the most beautiful woman in Britain, that she had dark powers, that she had killed her previous husband, that she had just been considering entering a convent, and that she had a delicate hand and an unheard-of skill with the needle.

The duke traveled to see her with his most trusted advisors and secretaries. Jessica was only vaguely concerned about the goings-on regarding the duchess; the duke himself was merely a scary man she was supposed to like and who, having gone away, she wouldn't be forced to see for a fortnight or two.

Upon his return he announced his betrothal to Anne, who was making arrangements and would join him in a month for their wedding. Parties were planned, despite his annoyance. It had been far too long since his few friends and colleagues had anything to really celebrate. The stableboy, Davey, told Jessica that there were plans for cakes and great foxhunts. They were debating the various merits of the different kinds of possible cakes when she was summoned to the duke's presence.

Maids rushed to prepare her as best they could, combing her hair with their fingers and patting down her dress, removing ash and flour. A little frightened at the summons, Jessica entered the duke's private office with her head down, but remembered to curtsy and mumble "My Lord Duke" as she approached him at his chair and desk.

"My Lord *Father,*" the duke corrected. He looked her up and down as if she were a stranger, no fault escaping his eye. Her face was smudged, her stockings crumpled, and her dress the length of a child's—not the calf-length dress an eleven-year-old should wear.

"You are to have a new mother," he said, gazing at her levelly.

Jessica's mouth hung open in shock. Her mother, as everyone

told her, was dead and interred in the church. She had never known her. Dolly was the closest thing to a living mother she had, and Jessica loved her with all her heart. She didn't understand why she needed another.

"Close your mouth, girl. This will not do at all. Too long have I neglected your education, left it in the hands of incompetent and lally-minded maids. We shall have to shape you up before the duchess arrives."

"The duchess . . ." The realization came upon Jessica slowly that the woman who was to marry her father was also to be her *mother*. This was a connection she had not made before, listening to all of the servants' gossip. "Is she very . . . nice?" she asked meekly.

"She is very beautiful. And wise," answered the duke. "And she may be able to turn you into a real lady yet."

# Chapter Two

## The Duchess Anne of Mandagor

"STAY *STILL*."

Jessica, eleven and just beginning to be fully acquainted with the concept of *duchess,* mentally forgave the maid, Gwen, who dressed her and forgot to say "Your Grace" as she tied tight bows and brushed down the girl's dress. The little girl *might* have been responsible for making such a hassle of it; she strained on tiptoes and swung this way and that to catch a glimpse of her new mother, or at least her entourage.

"What kind of carriage does she ride in?" Jessica asked for what was probably the thousandth time.

"Not a carriage—she'll ride in a train as far as Cardiff, and the duke has bought her a pretty little Beaufort phaeton to ride here in. By herself!"

Jessica squinched her nose, trying to remember what Davey, the stableboy—now the coachboy—had said about such things. He and his friends were all mad for coaches, trains, and other conveyances. Maybe the phaeton was the one with the open roof? And the large—

"Ow!"

Now Gwen had the brush, the one with boar's hair spines, and was yanking it down Jessica's locks in back, which were perfectly black and mostly straight without the help of a maid, thank goodness.

"Mother cats are kinder when they groom their kittens, and they have long claws and teeth!" Jessica protested.

Gwen giggled.

"Oh, I think you'd be glad I'm no cat," she said.

There was some excitement in the hall beyond her bedroom, and Jessica managed to squirm out of Gwen's grasp just long enough to peek over the banister.

There was a crowd downstairs of porters, luggage carriers, drivers, servants, and more foreign wait staff. Piles of trunks and suitcases littered the front hall. The crowd parted for just a moment, and in the middle was the most beautiful, tall, and stately woman Jessica had ever seen, as regal and pale as an ice queen. She was delicately removing fawn-colored driving gloves and a matching bonnet when she seemed to sense Jessica's stare. The woman turned, locking eyes with her for a moment.

Gwen grabbed Jessica from behind and pulled her down the hallway. The little lady duchess did not object.

*Anne of Mandagor.* Jessica was positive that was the woman she saw—the woman who was to be her new mother. Maddeningly, she was told that the woman was exhausted from her travels and would be resting in private until the evening, when

Jessica would be formally presented to her. She found this horribly unfair; it was *her mother,* for goodness's sake. She sat and played as quietly as she could, trying not to mess up her outfit and require another horrid neatening by Gwen. Her own bedroom was huge and drafty, recently redecorated in honor of the duchess's arrival. No one had consulted Jessica on what *she* might like, however. The paint was a vomity pale green with white trim, and the bookshelves were filled with nasty little books about what happens to children if they are bad. The bed was the only real improvement; it was huge and high and adult, and like a whole other world when she was perched in the middle of it. She liked playing in the quilts, pretending that they were hills and oceans and that she was meeting and speaking with animals. Maids yelled at her for leaving bits of food out on the floor, claiming it would attract rats, but Jessica only hoped to see and tame a mouse.

Evening finally came; supper was brought up to her but she couldn't eat more than a bite or two. Bored and sick with waiting, she brought out her last defense: an absolutely giant book of ABCs with more than two hundred pages of illustrated, nauseating rhymes about the English language. She began at page one, reciting each poem aloud.

Jessica was deep in the middle of "Meditating Monkeys Might Mostly Meet Men" when she was called. Gwen and a butler formally escorted her downstairs into the sitting room traditionally reserved for the lady of the estate. A large fire was lit and roaring, as were a few gas lamps. The duchess sat in front of a silken screen that protected her from the extreme heat of the flames. The duke stood behind her chair, arms on its back, watching her intently.

Suddenly Jessica felt bad for all the trouble she had caused Gwen earlier with her hair brushing and wished she didn't have to walk the final few feet alone. But she did, even remembering to curtsy. She wrinkled her nose, distracted by the duchess's strange perfume, something like oranges, something from far away. *Exotic.* In the firelight the older woman was even more regal than before. Her face looked as though it had been carved from white marble, and her eyes were brown and warm like caramel. Her golden hair was put up severely and elegantly behind her. Her eyebrows arched elegantly; her cheekbones were high. She . . . was . . . perfect. *A queen.*

Jessica felt like a baby and wanted to look down or hide. She was small and ugly next to this creature.

The duchess sensed her discomfort and smiled slightly.

"Why, come here, child. I shan't hurt you." She offered a single white, long hand, beckoning Jessica to come forward. *I shouldn't touch her. I'll break her.* Jessica imagined herself stumbling forward and knocking into the duchess, causing her fine white skin to crack and her to fall into a pile of porcelain shards. She inched forward delicately, aware of being observed every step of the way by the caramel eyes.

"You're very pretty," the duchess said approvingly, turning

her head this way and that to see her better in the light. Jessica felt a warmth rush through her. "Very pretty. I am to be your new mother, you know that, child?"

"Yes, Ma'am," Jessica mumbled.

"I think we shall get along just splendidly. I've always wanted a daughter of my own."

Again Jessica felt thrilled that this woman was pleased with her . . . but it was strange to be called *daughter* by her. A mother was fat, dark haired, warm, and loving. Like Dolly or the picture in her locket.

"Let us see some of your work."

Jessica blinked; she immediately thought of the snowmen she had built in the winter, or the ravens she made out of straw with Davey.

"Here, My Lady," Gwen curtsied and came forward, handing the duchess a folded bit of cloth.

*Oh.* That.

Jessica frowned and stared at the floor while the duchess inspected her admittedly terrible embroidery.

"Oh, this won't do at all," the duchess said with a smile. "Proper ladies must know how to sew, mustn't they? And you *do* want to be a proper lady, isn't that right, child?"

"Yes, Ma'am." Five minutes ago nothing could have been further from the truth. *What* is *a proper lady, anyway?*

"We shall have to work on that. And you . . ." She reached a long, delicate finger out to touch Jessica's cheek. She turned her head this way and that in the firelight, inspecting Jessica's face. "Yes. You *are* beautiful. Almost. Well, you haven't anyone to properly teach you about your *toilette*. We will have good mother and daughter times together, I promise you that!"

Jessica was wondering what the word "toilet" was doing coming out of such an elegant woman's mouth when the duchess took both her hands in her own and squeezed them, with a smile that was not false, merely unpracticed.

"You may go now, Jessica," her father said with a faint smile.

He seemed to be pleased; Jessica had done well. She had known this was going to be some sort of ordeal, but she had no idea how or when she passed. She curtsied as prettily as she could, backed away, and then turned and left—that much courtesy she knew. *Court-esy. Court-easy. Curtsy.*

Within a few minutes she was playing in her bedroom again, making her fingers bow and dance for each other. But after she fell asleep, the duchess's golden hair and pale face haunted her midnight dreams.

The wedding was immediate and small, far smaller than the duke's distant relations and closest friends would have liked. The duchess herself had little family, and as a widow she thought it fitting to keep the ceremony close and elegant. Jessica could see a great number of the housestaff's fears relieved immediately. They had been terrified the duchess would be a spoiled big spender who would insist on luxuries the estate could ill afford.

Jessica's own opinions of the duchess were uncertain. She had imagined her new mother to look or be like any number of things, including wicked, and Anne had turned out to be nothing like she could have ever dreamed.

*She belongs in her own fairy tale,* Jessica decided as Anne walked down the aisle. *She is far too beautiful and special for Kenigh.* The duchess glowed silvery as white and shiny cloth reflected her pale beauty back at the candles and gas lamps. Her dress was just long enough to touch the floor and skate over it, pearls and trim making soft tinkles.

Jessica's own dress was itchy, but she kept as still as possible during the ceremony and tried not to fidget as the priest went on and on about the blessings of marriage. The only interesting and light-hearted moment in the solemn afternoon came at the end, when two altar boys released a pair of doves that fluttered to the ceiling. The duchess smiled in delight, and the whole room sighed at her beauty. My *stepmother's beauty.* Jessica was proud of that and walked behind the couple with her head held high. She only tripped once.

There was a proper fête and party afterward, but instead of joining the kitchen staff Jessica was now forced to sit at the head table. She looked longingly at the door where servants silently entered and left the kitchen with appetizers and main courses, where they secretly stared and gossiped in between serving the duke, the duchess, and their guests. The food was delicious, however, and deprived of good company she could at least dig into the roasted lamb and venison, terrines, and salads—and a glass of wine she managed to steal. Once the duchess looked askance at her, amused and chastising, when she caught Jessica sucking the marrow from a bone and smacking her lips afterward.

The lady used a fork.

Many hours later some of the guests were leaving, and Jessica was overtired but still refusing to go to bed. She was in her nightgown, practicing walking like the duchess up and down the hall, clasping her hands behind her back and not moving her head. Then she heard Anne and her father talking on the main floor below.

"Oh really, Edward, you shouldn't have—"

"But my dear, I know your passion for music, and we have so little in the country. . . . It's only fair."

"It is a frivolity."

"It is my *wedding* present to you."

"You are far too generous, Edward."

Jessica could barely contain her curiosity. What could they be talking about? Maybe an exotic pet; she had heard of some ancient kings and queens keeping nightingales or birds from the east that could sing twelve different songs. Perhaps it was a music box or *orchestrina* from Germany. She ran to the banister to look down just in time to see her father walking away and the duchess looking at a boy. Jessica was severely disappointed.

He wasn't even a foreign boy—he had the look of a Scotsman about him. He wore black pants that ended at his calf, a white shirt, and an old black coat that was clean and carefully mended. A cap was tilted rakishly across his red hair, and he carried a fiddle. He was not very tall for his age—fourteen or fifteen, she guessed. He stared at the floor quietly, neither meek nor proud.

"So," the duchess asked him once they were alone, "can you play very well?"

"Moderately well, I am told, My Lady."

"We are not as rich as you might think, boy. I have not married into endless money. We must economize; there is no room for people who would just play the fiddle. You will also help me with some personal tasks—nothing too onerous or unbefitting an *artiste.* In return I will act as your patron—buy you music, bring you to concerts, make introductions for you, and the like. Are you willing?"

"Yes, My Lady."

Still he kept his eyes on the floor; his voice never wavered. Jessica instantly wished she could be like him. *He's so . . . brave.* She could not think of a better word. He had none of the subservience or sarcasm the other servants possessed.

"Excellent. Follow me into my room then, Alan. I have some issues to attend to and would be entertained."

"Of course, My Lady."

She swept out of the room with a rustle of undercoats and

silks; the boy followed at a safe distance. He caught sight of Jessica and did not wink, the way another might have, but smiled—a genuine, friendly smile—before his face resumed its previous blank, polite stare.

Jessica had no idea what to make of him.

# Interlude

ALAN FOLLOWED THE DUCHESS SILENTLY through the halls; for all of the bustling around them the only thing he could really hear was the swish of her skirts sliding over the cold stone floor. She nodded her head at the few servants she had met already and the ones she had brought with her from her own household. *We're both foreigners here,* he thought. *Perhaps that's why she wants me close by.* He ran a hand quickly through his bristly red hair, which affected its appearance not at all. Ginger hair, orange and spiky, may have been bad luck in Scotland, but keeping it short meant he never needed a mirror.

He had already stowed his few possessions in his new cell-like room, all except for his precious fiddle. His parents had worked hard when they saw he had the gift of music and sent him to Glasgow to be properly trained. His dream was to someday play at the courts in Europe.

And yet here he was in Kenigh, another small town. *At least it's a new country.* And he wouldn't even have to learn French just yet.

They entered the duchess's bedroom, which in the manner of royalty was separate from the duke's. It was less feminine than he would have guessed, with just a few touches of the new woman's presence here and there: rose-colored velvets on the bed, silk robes piled on a chair, and boxes and cases of what looked like ill-packed toiletries. There was also a giant oval mirror, gilt-edged and covered with golden ivy, perched inconveniently in the corner. The duchess went to that first, ignoring Alan, and gazed at herself in it, brushing a finger over her eyebrows and pulling the skin back from her eyes. She sighed.

"Staying young and beautiful is a full-time job. Be glad you are not a woman, Fiddler."

Alan cleared his throat respectfully. "Being kind and wise is a full-time job, for anyone, My Lady. You are clearly beautiful, but I am sure people notice more than that."

She raised an eyebrow at him.

*Uh-oh.*

"You are full of wisdom, Fiddler. I do not think I like that. Here, pick this mirror up and hold it where I can see myself more clearly."

It was a huge thing, and it took all of his strength just to hoist it up so it could rest against his stomach.

"*You* try being wise and good and getting a second husband when you are forty. *Then* I will take advice from you."

While Alan struggled to hold the thing, the duchess went to one of her boxes and took out a golden necklace. "A gift," she said with a slight smile. Before Alan could object she fastened it around his neck and fixed it under his shirt. "*Very* manly. Maybe . . . maybe we'll get you a little charm for it—a violin, or the like. Something appropriate."

Alan started to say "Thank you," or "My Lady, you are too kind," or "This is a little strange," but the duchess hadn't finished. She backed up to look at herself in the mirror.

"From now on," she said, smoothing her hair and admiring her reflection, "you will speak to me only when I wish an answer. And you will find yourself unable to tell anyone about what we discuss or do."

Alan prepared a respectful bit of flattery, but when he opened his mouth he found he had nothing to say.

The duchess smiled.

"Good. Now, for instance, if I *ask* something—like, 'Mirror boy, of all you have seen thus far, who in this remote land is the most beautiful woman?' you would say . . ."

Alan found himself able to speak. "You are, without a doubt, My Lady."

"Excellent. We shall get along splendidly. Now put the mirror down and help me unpack my things."

Although he was worried about his sudden lack of wit—his teacher always said that musicians were almost like modern jesters and had to flatter as well as play for their clients—he was also just relieved to put the heavy mirror down.

# Chapter Three

## Alan

JESSICA WAS GIVEN A FORTNIGHT'S VACATION. "Time for the new couple to become acquainted," was what Dolly said. It was ridiculous thinking of them as a new couple since they were both relatively old, and previously married and everything. She overheard whispers and rumors of heirs and hopes for a child. Jessica, far more knowledgeable on the subject than her father would have liked, rather hoped she would get a baby brother, even if he would be really only half her brother. *If that's all I can get!* It would give her someone to play with; she strongly suspected her wild roaming about the estate was at an end.

She ran with the pack of kids in the castle these last fourteen days, climbing roofs, fishing in the stream, and stealing muffins when they thought no one was watching. Once, however, Jessica caught Davey planting a kiss on the cheek of one of the coachman's granddaughters and catching at her hand. The sight made her uneasy, and she felt like she was being left out of something.

She noticed the new boy, Alan, squatting on the steps of the driveway, frowning at a piece of paper in his hands. A perfect opportunity to subtly find out what his story was.

"Hello," she said, marching up to him.

Alan raised an eyebrow and cocked his head back to look at her, a smile playing at the edges of his mouth. His face was covered in freckles, like hers, but his were soft and red and all over, whereas hers were brown and sprinkled profusely around the nose. His eyes were a sunny blue, much prettier than her muddy brownish-black ones.

"Oh, hello there. And who might you be?"

"I'm"—she took a breath—"Jessica Abigail Danvers Kenigh, daughter of the duke."

"Oh, are you now?" he replied, nodding seriously. "Well, I'm Alan McDonald. Pleased to meet you." He stuck out his hand. They shook, very formally.

"Where are you from?" She figured such personal questions were okay now that they knew each other's names.

"Down the road aways."

She looked at him doubtfully. "I don't think so. Your accent is all wrong."

"Oh it is, is it?" he laughed. "You caught me. I'm from the Isle of Arran, Scotland."

"Is it very pleasant there?"

"It is if you like sheep and cows and heather and sky."

She thought about this, frowning.

"The cows are very shaggy," he added helpfully, "with long brown hair that hangs over their eyes, like a dog's. They're much smaller than your English or Welsh cows."

His voice had a lilt as he spoke, and he made everything sound like a question. She decided she could listen to him all afternoon.

"Is it true you can play the violin?"

"Word gets around, eh? Aye, I fiddle a bit. My mother and father would have sent me to music school in Italy if they had the money."

"Why didn't they?"

As soon as it was out of her mouth she realized this was probably a rude question, but Alan laughed. "Because, Jessica Abigail Danvers Kenigh, daughter of the duke," he said as he touched her nose, "I have six sisters, younger and older, and farming cannae get you much gold."

*"Six."* Jessica tried to imagine this. There were other children on the estate who she pretended were related to her, but it wasn't the same. If she had six sisters, she would always have someone to play with.

She noticed the paper in his hands.

"What are you looking at?"

"Among my other duties as servant and house fiddler of Kenigh Hall, I have to find all of these herbs for the duchess."

*"Herbs?"* She grabbed the list from him, again rudely, and again realizing half a moment too late. "Wolfsbane? Mugwort? Mountain mint?" The only people who used herbs like these were servants, who couldn't afford proper medicine or morphine from the chemist. "Is she a witch?"

Alan cocked his head at her. He opened his mouth, then scratched his head and tugged at something at his throat; Jessica saw a brief glint of gold. He opened his mouth a few more times, then finally said, "I think . . . it might have to do with . . . a baby." He kept smiling, but the words sounded forced.

His answer was enough to satisfy Jessica. Women always seemed to try mad things when they were trying to get pregnant. She was tiny and easily hidden, and heard many, many conversations.

"I don't even know where to start looking," he sighed. "Back in Scotland I could have found at least a couple of these."

"I can show you some places," Jessica volunteered enthusiastically. "I run around all over here."

"I'd be honored to have the company of such a fine young lady," Alan said, standing and offering her his arm.

Jessica took it with great seriousness, formally keeping a few fingers on his wrist.

They had a grand day in the woods, though Jessica wondered a little about why a boy so much older was being nice to her. As long as she could remember, all of the older kids on the estate never hung out with the younger ones and were often standoffish and mean. *Alan* always listened to her and was patient. Maybe he could be like an older brother—if he could stand one more sister.

*Seven, seven, lucky and heaven . . .*

## Chapter Four

# BEST years,
# a book of hours

**6:00 A.M. Rise**

True to her word, the duchess made Jessica follow her around like a small, occasionally disobedient puppy, starting every day as soon as she rose.

With the darkness of night not yet lifted and icy air not yet banished, the duchess washed. And so did Jessica. The duchess had a washbowl, a pitcher, and Turkish cloths; Jessica had a bowl and mug. The duchess applied unguents, oils, and creams at her vanity in front of a smaller version of the mirror Alan was often forced to hold. A high chair was brought in, and Jessica perched next to her, aping her actions. The duchess thought it charming the first time Jessica "accidentally" covered her face in too much sticky white cold cream, but after the fourth time, she smacked her.

**7:00 A.M. Beautify**

Cucumbers were applied to the duchess's eyes and a cold wet towel to her neck, and she lay back in her chair like the dead for exactly fifteen minutes. Jessica, not being old, did not require this treatment.

The smells at the table, the softness of the ribbons, cloths, and cushions in the duchess's dressing room, and the muted pink and cream colors reminded Jessica of something she believed she half-remembered, something warm and feminine. When Anne wasn't looking, Jessica would crawl up to the back of the ivory-striped silk divan and open the locket with her mother's miniature and stare at it. With the duchess simply lying there and not speaking, Jessica could almost believe it was her real mother in the room with her.

**8:30 A.M. Breakfast**

"A lady should not eat too much," the duchess instructed, "nor should she let the flesh fall from her bones."

Jessica was given porridge and cream, hot black tea, and a piece of fruit, often an apple.

"An incomparable aid to digestion," the duchess said.

**9:30 A.M. Traditional Lessons: French, Latin, and Sums**

A tutor was eventually found, which was a great annoyance to Jessica. Terrence *was* a young and good-natured man, however—if not as handsome or nice as Alan. She became excellent at sums and her times tables. When she wanted to do more, Terrence just laughed and said it wasn't necessary because she would never become a shopkeeper or a banker. Girls didn't do such things, especially one of her station.

When Jessica told this story offhandedly to the duchess, the older woman's face froze in a steely blankness Jessica hadn't expected. When Terrence was dismissed and a new teacher found, Jessica thought it was something *she* had done. This one was far less friendly, an older woman with glasses that pinched and an Adam's apple that stuck out so far it looked like she had permanently swallowed a cannonball.

### 2:00 P.M. Lessons of a Different Sort: Lying, Hiding, and Sneaking About

After her studies, Jessica had the afternoons all to herself. The duchess disappeared to her bedroom, to nap, read improvement books, or perform strange experiments, depending on who was asked. Jessica spent every scrap of these precious moments in the kitchen with her old family, or outside with her old friends or Alan, her best friend of all.

The duchess would have been appalled if she knew. But Jessica was perfect in her little frocks at dinner. Lying came as naturally to her as running. She never told the duchess she was catching frogs with Davey; she was always "picking wildflowers" or "getting some air." She was never running races with the servants' children; she was "playing with her hoop" or "enjoying the company of someone else's small dog." The duchess had taught her a key point in the importance of dress; Jessica very carefully kept her outdoor playclothes separate from her indoor, parent-approved ones.

### 4:00 P.M. Tea

Sometimes with stuffed animals and stories, sometimes with Dolly and extra sweets, sometimes with the duchess and instructions:

"A lady takes one lump, never two."

"Always offer to pour."

"Raise your finger—thus—while you sip."

"This is the correct fork for pie."

Jessica would nod sweetly, face scrubbed and tea frock on, and she scratched the scabs on her knees when she could.

## 6:00 P.M. Illicit Wanders, Dangerous Discoveries

The duchess was accustomed to spending this hour going over meals and groceries with the housekeeper and the cook. Jessica thought this a splendid time to go through the older woman's things in her other room—the one Jessica wasn't allowed to enter. Alan did not like this game at all, playing rarely, reluctantly, and only, he said, to keep her out of trouble. Jessica had been dying to see the secret laboratory everyone whispered about. The rumors of the duchess's being a witch doubled her curiosity.

The laboratory *did* satisfy any child's concept of a dangerous, mystical place. Where another woman might have had small paintings or statues, the duchess had strange machines with gears, knobs, and dials. Where other people might have stacks of favorite books or small bouquets of flowers, the duchess had racks of test tubes, some of which were empty and sparkled, some of which were stoppered and filled with strange, dark fluid. In a box that might have held correspondence with friends—like Jessica's mother had—the duchess had letters from famous scientists. She signed her own missives, Jessica noted, only with her initials, and her handwriting was distinctly unfeminine. *Is she pretending to be a man?*

In place of a shelf of favorite novels or Greek philosophy, the duchess had new science journals and treatises, and ancient tomes, some with locks and all with inscriptions in strange or foreign languages, by foreigners with names like Alhazred.

"Spells!" Jessica exclaimed delightedly, flipping through one of the older books. "Magic! I could turn you into a frog! Let's take one—"

"Jessica," Alan said nervously, ruffling her hair. "Magic isn't real."

She looked at him, raising an eyebrow at his tone.

Then he added, more honestly, "Ye shouldna mess with magic, Jess. A bad spell turns back on the caster times three, as my grandmum says. And . . . it does things to people. Or maybe the type of people who do it are of a sort, *touched. . . .*"

### 7:00 P.M. Supper

Before supper the duchess made sure the two of them got dressed together with the help of maids. Jessica had to admit that as much of a pain the bows, underclothes, tight shoes, and hair ribbons were, the new clothes the duchess bought her were the finest she had ever worn, and that she looked the perfect little noblewoman in them. Of course, she had to act like one too, which was an annoyance that involved careful eating, no talking, and more curtsying than she could stand.

### 8:00 P.M. Sleeptime

Before bed a toilet much like the one in the morning was repeated. Jessica thought her stepmother looked like an angel in the long, frothy white things she slept in.

The evening was grown-up time. Once in a great while Jessica would be called in after her dinner to recite what she had learned that day, or to kiss her father and the duchess good night, or, rarely, to share a cup of hot chocolate with them before they had their own dinner. In the books Jessica was now forced to read—though secretly she liked them—glamorous people like the duchess and rich people like her father threw parties and had giant dinners and constantly invited streams of guests through their houses, but no such events ever occurred at Kenigh Hall.

At first the arrangement suited both Jessica and the duchess. Jessica loved getting all of the attention of the beautiful and glamorous older woman, even if she wasn't *exactly* a mother.

Years passed. The duchess spent more and more time "napping" or "reading," and Alan was sent to gather stranger and stranger things, many of which Jessica was able to help him with, but some things he seemed unable to even tell her about. Otherwise, little changed.

Life at Kenigh Hall continued pleasantly for everyone, it seemed.

## Chapter Five

# Letter From Alan

*DEAREST CLAIRE,*

*I hope this note finds its way to you. While my dreams of playing in sunny palaces in Europe—in gardens filled with lemon trees and honeysuckle—remain undiminished, they are for a while delayed. I have managed to secure a position with some minor duke in Wales, of all places. You were right; making enquiries with about-to-be-married royalty has paid off. I am a "gift" to his new bride. No, no, nothing like that.*

*The place where I ended up—Kenigh, if you ever happen by—is almost as pretty as the Highlands. A pleasant little town not unlike where we grew up, removed from time. The estate is only middle-sized, I am told, but large enough for everyone back home. If there are any more Roman (or English!) invasions I have no doubt we will be quite safe—the weather and rocks are most forbidding. They gave me a snug little room in the servants' quarters, far away from everyone so I can practice. Ha! Remember when you and Elsie were mad because I got my own room at home?*

*The duke is, well, I suppose like all dukes—his prime pastimes are being dead stiff boring when he is not putting on airs.*

*Everyone is too busy bothering themselves about the new duchess to concern themselves with a violinist. I sort of take second fiddle—pardon the pun—around here next to the flurry over her. Which is good; they don't seem to be used to outsiders.*

*The duchess herself seems pleasant enough—cold, and beautiful in an older woman sort of way. Very polite. She has agreed to take me on and be my patron—yes, a real patron!—in return for doing other things for her as well. Minor things, like rearranging furniture to her contentment, and other tasks, hard to describe. No . . . I take that back. It seems I can* write *them, just not talk about them. . . . And those were her exact words:* "Tell *anyone . . ."*

*Claire, this is very strange—don't be telling Mum or Da. The duchess has me all over the countryside looking for strange things— she wants a baby and cannot, so far. At first it was herbs and roots and leaves, but now it's other things . . . animals, and—I fear to even talk about the others.*

*But that's just it, Sis—she gave me a golden necklace with a fiddle charm; it would be pretty if it weren't so strange. Since putting it on I cannot* talk *about the things I do for her. Almost like magic. She says it's not, though, something about magnets and mesmerism. Science, she says. Spiritualism, I say!*

*But she has bought me music and strings and done nothing improper. She plans on taking me to a real symphony this month! It is my first real job, and I'll take what I can get.*

*I hope you and Elsie are well, and Jo and Emma and Katherine, and do pass this on to Sabrina if you get the chance! I miss her so.*

*Tell her that her big brother thinks about her every day. I would send something for Mum and Da, but I trust the people carrying this message about as far as I can throw them. It's just as well that royalty doesn't expect a common fiddler to be educated in the ways of proper letters.*

> *Lots of love to the entire family,*
> *Alan*

## Chapter Six
# The Beginning of Bad Things

JESSICA'S LIFE WAS COMING TO AN END.

*Snow* could accurately count back to this time as the final days of her happy childhood.

One hot summer day, bored, she went to the stable to find Davey and his friend Michael, both of whom took care of the horses and, when by themselves, smoked and played cards like adults. "Do you want to go to the stream today?" she asked them.

"Oh, aw," Davey said, kicking some straw at his feet. "I dunno, Jess. I have t' do some stuff with the horses."

She frowned and looked at the other boy. "Michael?"

"I, uh, I dunno." He looked up at her and blushed, then looked down. "What if we get caught?"

"That never used to bother you!" There was something in the air, an embarrassment, a tension, that was new and undeniable. She looked hard into the faces of her old friends. They looked away.

"Is it because I'm a duchess?" she asked bluntly. "That was never a problem before."

"You're no duchess," Davey spat, with a little of their old

fierce friendship back. "Not yet, anyhow. Naw—it's just, you know, others might, you know, look funny."

"Oh." She had lost some strange little fight and hadn't even known there was one. "Well," she said nervously, "maybe another day, then?"

"Sure—when the master's away, maybe."

"And his witch," Michael added.

"She's *not* a witch!" Jessica stamped her foot, glad to have something real to argue about. "Everyone's always saying that. She's a *scientist.*"

"No such thing as lady scientists," Michael muttered under his breath.

"What's a *scientist* got Alan all over the countryside picking poisonous herbs for?" Davey demanded.

"They're not poisonous," she tried again. "You should see her laboratory. It's real, with tubes, and metal, and glassware—there's no cauldron or *anything* witchy."

"All I know is I wouldn't want her catching us together."

"You're a big coward, David Allen!" Jessica stamped her foot again and stomped off. As soon as she was out of the stables she thought of something better and meaner to say, and she turned around to deliver it with the cold haughtiness of a duchess. But when she turned around she saw Gwen enter the stables from the other way. Something made Jessica hide and watch.

She couldn't hear what was being said but could see the three figures silhouetted against the wide stable door. Both boys leaped up when she came in—*sauntered* in, Jessica realized, remembering the new vocabulary word. Gwen smiled and put her hands on her hips, tossing her long blond braids over her back. She laughed easily, high and ringing. The boys took off their hats and spoke eagerly.

Jessica wandered away, sad and confused. *They like her better.* But that didn't seem quite right. *They like* talking *to her better.* She thought about the way Gwen looked; peaches-and-cream skin compared to Jessica's freckly face, her rounded body glowing. Jessica's was more stout and muscled, and not shaped quite right. Breasts, yes, but like mushrooms, popping out and away from each other.

*They said they would never like girls.* She remembered a pact made by the stream years ago. They admitted that they didn't think of Jessica as a girl, something she had taken as a point of pride.

She wandered back to the estate, not caring if anyone saw her in her secret play clothes. She couldn't even talk to Alan; the duchess had taken him to a concert at the Edgars' that afternoon. It seemed as if the duchess liked Alan more than her—or at least paid more attention to him, a mere servant.

Jessica decided to drown her sorrows in a book, something juicy and French that she probably shouldn't have been reading. She went upstairs to change into acceptable clothes and went into the library. At least if she were caught she would be dressed properly. She pushed open the door as quietly as she could, dreaming of secret doors, which Kenigh Hall seemed to lack in prodigious numbers. She and her *old* friends had spent hours looking for them.

The library appeared to be off limits: Her father was present, in a gigantic chair in front of the dead fireplace. That was unfortunate and unusual; the duke never seemed to read, unlike Anne. Jessica peeped her head in as far as she dared to see what he was doing. The duke had his hand out and was staring at some object in it. Jessica leaned a little more and caught her breath when she saw what it was: a locket identical to the one she wore around her neck, with an identical miniature of her mother in it. As she watched, a single tear formed in the middle of each of his eyes, and they coursed their way silently down his cheeks.

Jessica watched with mixed feelings. Didn't he love the duchess now? If he missed Mary so much, why did he marry Anne? If he loved his wife, why couldn't he love his daughter? *Why does he hide this?* Closing the door quietly, she realized it was the closest she and her father had ever really been.

*I miss her too. And I never even knew her.*

Mixed emotions drained her mind and body; she spent the afternoon desultory on her bed. But when what began as a slight ache in her stomach progressed over the hours to searing, unbearable pain, Jessica was sure it wasn't just sadness. She ran, crying with fright, to Dolly. The old woman smiled when she first saw Jessica.

"Oh, Jess-me-love, I was just going to talk to you—"

"Dolly, it's horrible—I think I'm dying!"

The big, sweaty woman hugged her as she cried. When Jessica could finally speak she told her how sick she was, and sad and angry, trying not to double over in pain.

Dolly laughed kindly. "You're not dying, sugarplum. You're just becoming a woman."

*Becoming a woman.* Jessica had heard whispered snatches and phrases here and there about such a thing, about a curse, strange mysteries. Now she finally knew the truth—and it hurt.

Dolly gave her a raspberry tart, which Jessica consumed in three bites, still sniffling and wincing from the pain. Her appetite had been far from ladylike for the past week.

"You just need a lie-down and sommat good, a medicine," Dolly said soothingly. "Come now, stop crying. It's not that bad. . . . It means you're an adult!"

The duchess swept in at that moment, still dressed from the concert earlier. "Miss Margerson, I was wondering if you believe it's in the kitchen's capacity to—what on earth is going on here?"

Jessica looked miserably up at her, red-faced, sniffling, and covered in powdered sugar.

"The little miss just . . ." Dolly frowned, trying to think of a high-class way of saying it. "She's all grown up," she finally said.

"Oh." The duchess looked at the cook and then at Jessica, as if both of them had suddenly revealed that they were really cats, or French. "Well, I think that a mother should take this in hand, don't you?" she asked, a trifle nervously. Then she regained composure and put out her hand. "Jessica, come with me. We have to talk about this."

An hour later in the duchess's dressing room, a mug of tea cupped in her hands, still bent over from the pain, Jessica was even more confused than when the pain had started.

"Things will have to change, Jessica," the duchess was saying. "You are no longer a little girl. You are a *young lady*. A . . . *pretty* young lady. Women will begin to hate you and men will want to—men are just terrible. You have to start acting differently, Jessica. Let me inform you right now that boys and men are not your friends. They will never be your friends again. They will want to do improper things with you if you're *un*lucky, and to own you if you are. Marriage . . ." Her brow furrowed and she looked distracted for a moment. "I suppose you will get married in a few years. . . . I should start to work on that. . . . A *mother* would. . . ." She shook her head. "That is what you will be someday, Jessica. A mother. Society only has two uses for women, remember that. Beautiful young girls and mothers."

As the duchess spoke, she looked less and less at Jessica and more and more into the air between them. Her hand rose, seemingly of its own will, to touch her own cheek. "Be one or the other, or both, but not neither. No one wants an old hag. Or a trollop."

And then the duchess began to cry.

Jessica had little sympathy. *But* I'm *the one in pain. Has everyone gone mad today? Or is it just me?*

The duchess stood up abruptly. She didn't wipe her eyes; the tears dried rapidly. Her face was white.

"What was I . . . ?" She cast about, eyes flicking like a bird's, as if she really couldn't remember. "No matter. No more hanging out with the servants, or with boys, Jessica. Don't think I haven't been watching you. I just haven't had time to do anything about it. You are a woman now, and have to obey me and your father. Now go to your room and think about it."

"It hurts," Jessica complained feebly.

"What does?"

The duchess really seemed to have forgotten everything they had just talked about—as if she had had a fit. Jessica pointed to her belly and rocked back and forth to show her. The older woman's eyes widened, then narrowed.

"In some ways you are such a silly little girl," the duchess snapped. She went to her vanity and took out a little blue glass bottle, putting some droplets in her mug of tea. "Here. This will stop the pain. Go to sleep and think about what I've said." The duchess called a maid—not Gwen—to help Jessica to bed. Halfway to her room Jessica felt a wall of weariness and sleep slam her abused body; the maid almost had to carry her. Still afraid she was dying, Jessica fought it until she could do so no more, and blackness hit her like a rock.

# Chapter Seven

# A Pause Before
# the Storm

WHEN JESSICA WOKE UP, SHE WISHED SHE HADN'T.

Her head ached. Her whole body ached. Her throat was parched as if she hadn't drunk anything in days. She felt like vomiting, and the room spun.

A look outside the window confirmed her fear—somehow she had slept from the rest of the afternoon through the next morning. *Late* morning. Breakfast was brought to her in bed, which was a rare treat. Although she was sick Jessica found herself eating everything in sight.

She glared at the two maids who served her, indistinguishable from each other. They were new hires of the duchess.

"Where is Gwen?"

"Off to visit her mother, My Lady. She returns in a fortnight."

"Hmmmph."

For all the other pains she was experiencing, Jessica had to admit that the ones in her stomach had lessened some. Not a *great* trade-off, but at least she felt she could walk. "You may go. I will go see Dolly." Who, she suspected, might have less angry answers to some of her questions, and who wasn't likely to break down and cry in the middle of her explanations.

"You aren't to bother the kitchen staff today, My Lady's orders," one of the maids—the very slightly taller one—said promptly. Jessica could tell they would be no help. Now that she was a *woman,* she couldn't even have the sort of confidante maid and friend that she read about in books. Not until Gwen came back, at least. Even assuming she *liked* giggling and talking about men, which she didn't.

Men . . .

"Send me the fiddler boy," she announced, in her best grown-up voice. "Some music would improve my constitution."

The two maids looked at each other and laughed. "My Lady can't have a boy in her room. 'Twould be most unseemly."

Jessica was right on the point of telling them to go do something she had heard Davey describe once, but she decided to be a lady for the moment.

"Yes, of course."

She stuffed some more toast in her mouth and pondered escape.

"Is My Lady still feeling ill? Would she like some more medicine?" One of the maids held up the evil little blue bottle.

"Feed that stuff to me ever again and you'll both be on the streets before you can say *scat,*" Jessica promised—as high and haughty a thing as she had ever said.

\*    \*    \*

The few times throughout the day she tried to leave the room there was always someone to stop her and tell her that she needed to rest, that she shouldn't be up, and that they would bring her whatever she wanted. That she was *sick*. That everyone would understand if she wasn't at dinner, because she was having a "spell."

Bored quickly with her immobility and the maids' automatic responses, Jessica read books until they were gently but firmly taken away from her "because they strained her eyes."

The two maids didn't think sewing would damage her eyesight, however. Three days passed in confinement and misery.

"This is what being a grown-up lady is like," Jessica murmured to herself. "This is what the rest of my life is going to be like."

There was worse yet to come.

Jessica finally managed to sneak down to the kitchen by sending her new maids to find a book in the library whose title and author she made up. She stole a pastry, ate the whole thing, then took another and was just sneaking out, past the library, when she heard the maids gossiping.

". . . hasn't told her yet."

"My Lady is bound to have herself a fit!"

"Still, if *Dolly* can find herself a husband and move to her own house in Swansea, I suppose it means there's luck and love for *anyone*."

"Did you not hear? The duke himself is paying for part of the house as her wedding present for long years of service. It was the duchess's idea. . . ."

"What did she say the name of the author was?"

Servants and maids alike fell out of her way as Jessica ran through the house. She leaped up the back stairs to the wing with the bedrooms. Didn't it all sound a little too convenient? *Dolly never mentioned a gentleman friend before.* . . . And the weirdly acting, wicked duchess just *happened* to suggest that she move away?

But when Jessica knocked loudly and meanly on the laboratory door there was no response. She leaned her head on the wall in frustration, then screamed with fear and disgust.

A stream of black blood issued slowly from underneath the door.

Jessica turned and ran until she slammed into someone. She looked up, preparing either to excuse herself or to yell, when she saw who it was.

"Alan!"

"What's wrong, Jess?"

"Alan!" she cried in relief. She began sobbing again. Alan looked around quickly and pulled her into a nearby pantry. He held her as she sobbed, making soothing noises at her until she calmed down. Finally she spoke.

"Dolly—Dolly's gone away and it's all my fault. Everything changes. Anne was right. And there are these new maids, and they're horrible, like prison guards, and it's all because . . . because . . ."

"Because of what?"

She just kept sobbing.

"Oh! Is that what it is." Alan laughed gently and hugged her. She looked at him, shocked and surprised. "Jess, I have six sisters. There are few secrets in a house with four rooms. Dolly getting married, those two 'horrible' maids—those things have nothing to do with you, or with growing up. Dolly getting married is a *good* thing. She has a right to be happy, like everyone. Or don't you want that?"

Jessica sniffled, but nodded. "I just don't want her going away," she whispered.

"I know." Alan gave her a hug. "But you still have me."

"Barely," Jessica spat, thinking of the duchess. "What with you and the duchess, and concerts . . ."

"Jessica Abigail Danvers Kenigh, daughter of the duke!" Alan gave her a playful slap on the shoulder. "Lady Anne says that with practice I could join a symphony, maybe go to Europe and play—" His eyes shone. "Things are not so easy for those of us who aren't born duchesses, Jess. Even those two horrible maids—remember, they work because they have to and take orders because they are paid to."

"It just seems like everything bad happens when you grow up," Jessica sighed. "What are the advantages?"

\*     \*     \*

The advantages, at least for a young duchess, were revealed soon enough. She was summoned to the drawing room and presented formally to her father and Anne—later she would suspect some conspiracy among Alan, Dolly, and the duchess.

"You're a young lady now," her father began without preamble. "And you look . . . you look a lot like your mother." Jessica caught a quick frown on the duchess's face, an iciness that came and went in an instant. "It's time we started treating you like a young lady."

"Jessica, your father and I would like to throw a party for you. Not a—not a coming-out party, but a sort of introduction to the country gentry," the duchess said. "We shall hire some musicians, have a tea dance, invite some people your age. . . . How would you like that?"

Later Jessica would reflect that a *party* wouldn't really make up for being forced to abandon most of her childhood acquaintances, but at that moment the thought of a glamorous affair thrown for *her,* with guests and boys and food and drink and dresses—for *her*—well, it seemed wonderful.

She nodded mutely.

"Excellent," the duchess said, pleased. "We'll make a real lady out of you yet."

Jessica was sure she had heard those words somewhere before.

# Interlude: Mirror, Mirror

THE DUCHESS TURNED THIS WAY AND THAT IN front of the mirror that Alan held. She was wearing one of three possible dresses she had bought for the party. This one pushed her bust up very high, and cinched her waist so tightly she could barely breathe.

"So, Mirror," she said lightly, admiring herself. "When the people talk, who do they say is the fairest in the country?"

"Always you, My Lady," Alan answered, trying not to grunt under the weight of the gigantic glass. "People still discuss the blue outfit you wore to the concert, how you looked like a goddess of the sky."

"Mmmm." Her response was noncommittal, but her eyes narrowed approvingly, and her lips tightened to hide a self-satisfied smile. "And Jessica?"

"No one much talks about her being beautiful," Alan said honestly, as he was forced. "They say she is a growing beauty, but even more they talk about what trouble she is to the servants."

The duchess chuckled at this, then fixed her dark blue eyes on his lighter ones.

"And what of you? What do you think of our *little* duchess?"

Alan had known this question was coming. "As much as it may be permitted, I care for the young lady like she was my own sister."

"Mmmm." The duchess stared at him a moment, debating something internally. Then she went back to gazing at herself in the mirror. She touched herself lightly on the belly and frowned.

## Chapter Eight

# Thirteen, Fourteen: Princes Come Courting

THE FIRST GUESTS HAD ALREADY BEGUN TO arrive, a day early. Jessica peeped out from behind a bush to watch the coaches, carriages, and phaetons pull up and the splendidly dressed people step out: women in long gowns with large bustles and matching parasols, and men in dove-gray jackets and hats. Some of the dashing young men rode horses, cantering up the graveled path, gloved hands to their hats as they addressed the duchess.

Jessica was not to meet them formally until later and could hardly bear the anticipation. *This is for* me. *It's just a party that the duchess is throwing, but it's really all for me.* She watched eagerly for people her own age and thought she saw a couple, a pair of strapping girls who, despite their size, seemed young.

"Hey! Jess!" Davey whispered from behind her. She spun around.

"What are you doing here?" she demanded. This was *her* hiding spot. "Oh, and I suppose you've decided that it's all right to talk to me now," she added haughtily.

"Aw, Jess, c'mon." He kicked his toe at the ground. "I'm trying to make it up to you."

There was a long pause as Jessica glared at the boy and he tried to work up the courage to talk. "Me and Michael, we were . . . it's just . . . we're not wanting to get on the bad side of the duchess, yeah? I'm *apologizing* here."

That said, he sighed in relief. "Craddoc's bitch had a litter of puppies last night. Want to come see? They're playing with them now, in the clearing on the other side of the stream. You can choose one, as a birthday present," he added hesitantly.

Jessica's eyes lit up. A dog of her own! She was old enough. And from the looks of it, many of the girls and women arriving had small lapdogs that they or their servants carried in. Of course, she would miss the excitement of watching more people arrive, and she *was* supposed to get dressed and washed for when she was introduced later today. . . .

"Thank you, Davey!" she said delightedly, and ran off to see the old gamekeeper. Along the way she managed to rip her petticoat and step into the stream, something she would no doubt be in trouble for later. All worries were forgotten when she saw the scene in the small clearing beyond: Craddoc and a few children sat around a big mother hound with six squirming babies, brown and cream and white.

"Oh, they're *lovely*!" Jessica sat down in the grass next to the mother and tried to pet all of the puppies at once.

The old man laughed.

"Davey's keeping one for himself," he said, "but I guess he told you about choosing one."

It took her an hour to decide; they were all equally adorable. Finally she chose one with slightly more black than the rest. "I'll keep her until she's weaned," Craddoc said. "Come back in a fortnight, and she'll be all ready for you."

Reluctantly Jessica left. It was probably past time for her to go home, in case she was missed. She took the back way so she could sneak in by the stables and not be seen; her hair was down, her face was muddy, and her dress was not *quite* ruined.

She turned the corner to the muddy courtyard and there was a boy there about Alan's age, smoking a long, thin cigar.

He was handsome and well dressed, with brown wavy hair. His jacket fit him like a second skin. One shapely leg was propped on a barrel. He raised an eyebrow lazily in her direction.

"Hello," Jessica said, trying to think of something quickly.

"Hello." He looked her up and down. "Quite the preparations for a party going on there."

"It would seem so," she answered hesitantly.

"You're all a mess—all covered in mud," he observed. He pushed himself off the wall and sauntered over to her. She held her ground. Something wasn't quite right, but she couldn't put her finger on it. The boy was handsome. Her heart raced.

He came closer. She didn't move.

"Let me get some of that for you." He reached over, and

with a long finger he delicately brushed some dirt off her cheek.

"Sir," she began, uncertain of where any of this was going.

He put his hand around her shoulder and pulled Jessica in for a kiss.

Shocked, she let him.

*My first kiss! I wonder if this means we are to be married.* He was certainly good looking enough for her, and the kissing itself was pleasant enough in a strange way, although he pushed his face into hers a little too hard.

Then he reached up and grabbed her breast.

"Stop it!" She pulled his hand away. His response was to pull her in to him harder, a hand around her waist. One of his legs locked around hers.

"Come on," he whispered in her ear. "This might be your only chance for a *count.*" He grabbed her bottom with his other hand.

Wildly she tried to figure out what to do, what Alan would do, what one of Alan's *sisters* would do.

She kneed him between his legs.

He let out a long groan of agony and released her, both actions immediately satisfying. He keeled over on the ground.

The momentary triumph faded for Jessica. She felt like throwing up.

"Father!" she screamed, running into the house. "Duchess!" she sobbed as she ran through the house. She made her way to the entrance room where she found her father and stepmother, both greeting another well-dressed couple.

"What's the meaning of this?" her father demanded. The duchess's face dropped when she saw the state of Jessica's dress.

"This *boy*—he tried to *kiss* me—and then he—and then he—"

The duchess took control of the situation immediately. She called the two maids. "Lucy, Anna—take Jessica upstairs immediately. Edward, would you mind seeing about this boy? Felicia, Lord Belingham—forgive this little intrusion. Let me personally show you the rooms where you will be staying. . . ."

The two evil maids swept Jessica, sobbing, out of the room and upstairs before anyone else could see her. When they arrived at the cool silence of Jessica's room, she fell on her bed. The two maids left. Long after her tears finally dried up Jessica simply lay staring at the ceiling.

Hours passed.

The duchess finally came in. She closed the door behind her with a strange finality and approached Jessica with a predatory sway that reminded her of the boy.

On guard for the second time that afternoon, Jessica slowly realized she would get no comfort out of this woman.

"What," the duchess asked slowly, "happened?"

Jessica told her, and in doing so began crying again.

"Oh," the duchess said coolly. "You dress and act like a servant girl, and you're surprised that he treated you this way?"

"But he—he touched my—"

"And what did you *expect* him to do, you alone there with him? Give you a bouquet of flowers?"

"But he, *he's* the one who . . ." Jessica was terribly confused. She didn't think she had done anything wrong, besides making the mistake of leaving to see the puppy. The boy had hurt her, not the other way around. "But I am a duchess," she said finally, thinking the older woman would approve. "One doesn't treat a *duchess* that way."

"You *look* like a slattern!" The duchess slapped Jessica across the cheek. She said other things, too, but Jessica didn't hear them. When she put her hand to her cheek, her fingertips came away with droplets of blood.

"Behaving like a commoner—I have a hard time believing you are your father's daughter. Maybe you aren't," the duchess said pensively. Then her eyes filled with rage. "Do you know what you did, behaving in front of Lord Belingham like that? Do you realize the *embarrassment* your father and I will have to suffer for it? And Count Donhall—it wouldn't surprise me if his father never spoke to us again for what you did to him."

"I just wanted the puppy," Jessica said softly, knowing full well she sounded like a five-year-old. But in the end, that was the heart of it, that was what had caused all of this.

"Well, you certainly aren't getting a puppy," the duchess promised. "That, and your absence at this party except when I specifically ask for it, are just the beginning. You want to dress like a commoner? *Fine,* you can dress that way all the time, and do the job of one too. If you're not going to be a duchess, you can at least be useful. And one more thing," she added as she left, "if I so much as *imagine* you talk to any of the serving staff again, including Alan, I will have you beaten—the way I should have in the beginning."

And the duchess, if nothing else, was a woman of her word.

Part Two

# Snow

# Interlude: Reflections

"Mirror. *Mirror.* When people speak, whom do they say is the fairest in town?"

Alan held the looking glass up, as always; the duchess stared and primped into it as always. Some things had changed since the first time, however.

There was the smell, to start with. Burnt flesh cut with a clean, metallic scent like the smell before a thunderstorm. There were the cages of animals—all young, all babies—against the farthest wall of her hidden sanctuary. There was the basket with a bundle in it, a heavy burden that needed to be gone by midnight. There were the vials and pills—blue, blood red, and light purple—with medicines for the duchess's increasingly frequent fits.

And there was one more thing that had changed.

Alan ground his teeth and stammered, but the necklace bade him speak.

"For all her rags and dirt, those who catch a look at her face, the one called Snow—they claim she is the most beautiful, fey thing Kenigh has ever seen."

The duchess's eyes might have been hazel, but the look they gave Alan was the blackest he had ever seen.

# Chapter Nine
## Transfiguration

### 1. Spring

Davey sat on the steps of the stable, waiting to run an errand for the coachman, when a figure dressed in old clothes struggled by, barely able to drag the bucket of slop she was burdened with. He leaped up, full of the newly discovered chivalry that often brought smiles and blushes, occasionally even kisses.

"Here, let me help you with—" The pale girl turned her face to meet his.

He stopped short. "Jess?"

Deprived of sunlight, the starry freckles had faded from her face, and her copper-brown hair had grown in black. Her skin had whitened, becoming the pallor so many girls her age were trying to achieve by poisoning themselves with arsenic.

"I don't think you're supposed to be talking to me, Davey." Her voice was low, as if she wasn't accustomed to talk. "I'm being punished. They might dismiss you or your parents."

"I heard things, but didn't believe them—making you do all the chores, scrubbing, and cleaning, and locking you up? A *duchess*?"

She smiled wanly, remembering their last argument. "I'm no duchess. Not anymore, at least."

"I didn't even know it was you just now," he went on. "You're as white as a snowman. And taller than you were."

He shifted uncomfortably from foot to foot. "Is this because of the dog I was going to give you?"

"Oh, no." Her eyes crinkled at his guilt and concern, and it was painfully obvious it had been a long time since she had grinned. "It's because . . ." She shrugged. "It's not your fault. How is—the puppy?"

"The duke had a talk with old Craddoc and told him to give it to someone else. Jane Cooper, the bobby's daughter."

"I hope she takes care of it," she said sadly.

"I'll make sure of it," Davey earnestly promised Jessica, the only thing he could do for her.

"Well, I had better go before they catch me speaking to you."

"Well, be seeing you—*Snow!*"

He said it with a lopsided grin, like they were seven again. That was the last time she ever spoke with David Allen.

But the name Snow stayed with her.

## 2. Summer

She watched the seasons through the windows of her room. A pair of ravens had come in the spring and nested in the tallest pine, raising a family of fledglings who grew furry and then became slicked down with shiny black feathers and flew. Once she saw Alan climbing the tree toward the nest and was terrified for him. When she questioned him later he said nothing, only sweated and played with his necklace the way he sometimes did when they talked about the duchess.

From the start of her confinement, they'd had to pretend they weren't talking, but Alan had been even more silent to her than usual since that day. Snow was depressed, but she suspected something was up. He was always sneaking her little trinkets and things: a speckled robin's egg, a tea cake, a little carved whistle in the shape of a dog, small books of poetry by Robert Burns. A new *something* appeared one day when she came back after her lessons to change into her scullery clothes: a basket at her window, as if carefully lowered from above. This was the biggest prize yet: Carefully tucked at the bottom with a white string round its neck was a tiny white kitten whose eyes had just opened and who gave a huge, red-tongued yawn when she lifted it out.

Snow was very, very careful.

The kitten slept under the covers with her at night, curled between her neck and shoulder. Snow kept it in her pockets when she cleaned to keep it from mewing. She named it Katrina. She fed it milk and cheese and meat and cleaned up after it constantly.

One day she came back from lessons to change into her scullery clothes, and Katrina was gone.

### 3. Autumn

Captain Andy Campbell surveyed his colleagues and compatriots. Lieutenant Commander Murray was looking a little gray, but then again Colin always did before a campaign. He rubbed his hands together and through the hair on his head. Field Commander Nigel Kensington stroked his whiskers wisely, still refining the plans, always the strategist. The hill rose depressingly high above them, but they would take it. They had God on their side; they were fighting for truth, honor, and Queen Victoria. In a far-off tree his spies were taking account of the situation and updating orders on an hourly basis. Captain Campbell loved these complicated missions. Why, compared to previous adventures in India, this was nothing.

After their victory feast tonight, they might even begin planning the rescue of the Lady in the Castle.

### 4. Winter

The door flew open, and the duchess burst in. "I'll do it myself!" she cried.

Mice went flying. The tame—and carefully named—Andy Campbell, Colin Murray, and Nigel Kensington each scurried their separate ways from the hill pillow with the cookie on top, the towers made from novels by Sir Walter Scott.

Snow knew better than to watch them go; the older woman would follow her eyes and see her friends.

"My *daughter,*" the duchess said, towering over her. Snow

knew to never talk back but wouldn't have chosen to anyway. There was a strange look in the older woman's eyes. Her face was white, and blue veins throbbed on her forehead. She held a pair of sewing shears, Snow observed as the seconds stretched out. Pretty little silver ones, in the shape of a bird, something large and vaguely foreign. "'*My.' 'Daughter.'* How about a brother just like you?"

Snow's instinct was to look at the duchess's face and belly, but she didn't feel she could let her eyes stray from the other's for a second.

"Am I to congratulate you, My Lady?" she whispered.

The duchess threw her head back and laughed. One of her hands whipped out with praying mantis precision and grabbed a lock of Snow's hair. With a slower, slightly unsteadier movement, she snipped it off with the shears.

Snow didn't move.

The duchess held the raven lock up to the light and looked at it with a critical eye. Then she turned and walked out.

"Get Gwen to fix your hair," she said over her shoulder.

Spring came again, and still there was no heir for the duke, nor release for Snow.

# Chapter Ten

# A Rag, a Bone, a Hank of Hair

"IT SHOULD WORK. *WHY DOESN'T IT WORK?*"

Alan stood by the mirror, not compelled to hold it this time. Instead he surveyed the scene on the laboratory table from a safe distance, behind the duchess.

Machinery hummed: strange things powered by strikes of lightning baited and caught by rods the duchess had had him mount outside her window. A series of brass rods and gears wove their way from the machines to the table and through a mirror with a frame similar to the one Alan was often burdened with. This one was smoky and black and didn't reflect things properly. He tried not to look in it.

What the mirror was aimed at was more horrible still. Propped up like a doll in the middle of the table was a stuffed body made of pink muslin. A baby's skull, dug up from a cemetery—a memory Alan wished he could erase—was sewn to the top, and pearl button eyes were hammered into its sockets. Horribly familiar black hair was nailed to the skull. The duchess's own blood trickled down its body; a bandage was around her wrist, and there was plaster on the area above her breast.

*This is worse than the animals.*

"I have everything. *Everything!*" The duchess knocked aside a pile of books in a rare fit of rage. Ancient grimoires of curses and spells fell down among scientific treatises. None was dusty; the duchess was neat and careful through and through.

"The lock of a maiden, the blood of a mother, gold and electrum, and a spectral screen of mica . . ."

Alan said nothing.

The duchess's normally immaculate appearance had come undone. Her golden hair was out in wisps. She threw her head down on the table and began to sob.

"My Lady . . . ," Alan began quietly.

Her head popped up. There was a wild look in her eyes Alan did not like, a feral gleam unlike her usual ferocity.

"Of course," she said slowly. "How could I be so stupid? A *heart.* It needs a human heart."

# Chapter Eleven

## Away

TWO YEARS.

Two years and fifty-five days Snow had been a prisoner in her own home. Several generations of mice had come and gone; Andy, Colin, and Nigel had formed clans, houses, and lineages of their own, but still found time to play with her. They now ran up and down her arms, looking for treats.

She missed being outside. She imagined shoving her fingers into the dirt, during the rain maybe, shoving her fingers and hands in as deep as she could.

"Jess!"

She looked up, surprised. Alan was the only one who called her that anymore—and there he was, perched outside on her windowsill.

"Alan." She carefully put the mice on her shoulder and padded delicately over to the windowpane. "Whatever is wrong?"

His normally rosy face was beet red and sweating; veins popped out on his head as evidence of an inner struggle. His hand twisted at the fiddle charm he wore around his neck.

"Listen to me. You have to go. She's going to—you're going

to be—she will—she hired—a murderer—" His face went white with the effort of whatever he was trying to say, and he almost fell.

"Alan!" She grabbed his hand to steady him. Andy Campbell squeaked with dismay as her shoulder jerked.

"You're going to be killed if you stay here," Alan said finally, after he had rested a moment. His eyes were closed and his breath came in gasps.

"What are you talking about?"

"Please, just listen to me. You have to go. I . . . can't . . . *help* you. . . . She'll ask. . . . I cannot lie. . . . Meet me at your mother's crypt as soon as you can. Take very little with you so no one will suspect anything! Hurry! Wait for me there!"

And he was gone. Just like that, her world had changed.

Murder *her*? Who? The duchess? Why? Was she pregnant at last? Was Snow some sort of a threat?

Her next thought was for the mice. She carefully set them down and took all of the food out of her special hiding place and put it under the bed for them.

"That will last you awhile." She would ask Alan to look after them after she was gone. *How long will I be gone?* Snow quickly went through a list of her dearest possessions. She was already wearing her locket. She found a little bag and put papers and a pen and pencils in it, so she could write letters from wherever she went. She folded up one of her nicer—but not nicest—dresses and put that in as well. *Money.* She almost forgot, not having been out or allowed to buy anything since she had been first confined. She gathered up all the money she had and some jewelry to sell: a couple of necklaces and brace-lets, and a pretty little ornamented pocket mirror the duchess had given her their first Christmas together. She put in a scarf and a muff, unsure of the weather, wherever she would be going. Then she hid the bag as close to her body as she could and donned the black cloak she was famous for wearing down to the old church. Snow inspected herself in the mirror. There was barely a bulge where she wore the bag. Then she quietly slipped through the shadowed halls of the great estate.

"Mistress Talbot," she said quietly and deferentially to the old tutor, who was reading in the library. "I would go see my mother's grave."

The woman frowned at her over small wire glasses. "I think you grow excessively morbid, child, but do as you will. Be back before supper."

"Yes, ma'am."

Where would she go? Where *could* she go? She had no other family, no friends. . . . Davey, perhaps? No, he lived too close. Dolly? Was Swansea also too near? Alan would think of something. He would take care of her.

*But wait, didn't he say he* couldn't *help? What did that mean?*

People saw her, but no one really took notice as she walked quietly down the gravel-strewn path under the beeches to the old church. It occurred to her that she hadn't even thought of her father—then again, she saw him so rarely. She wondered if he would miss her.

The wooden door was hard to push, the air cold and damp as she entered. Alan was nowhere to be seen yet, so she sat by her mother's grave, to say good-bye and to wait.

Part Three

# The Lonely Ones

# Chapter Twelve

# London

SNOW WAS SURE SHE WOULD NEVER BE WARM again.

It was not just the rain or the evening air, but a sinister mix of the two that became fog here, patches of freezing darkness there, and icy rivulets going down the back of her dress everywhere. She tried to put thoughts of fever out of her mind; she was a healthy girl and in no danger yet.

The wagon and driver Snow had found eventually got her to Cardiff, with a change to a real coach at an inn along the way. No one would think to look for a young duchess on such a "measly" means of conveyance. In Cardiff she took a coach-class seat on the train. It was her first trip on a locomotive, but she was too scared and exhausted to enjoy it. She fell asleep, awoke, bought a cheese sandwich and a watery tea, and fell asleep again.

When she arrived at Paddington Station, Snow stood stock-still, staring at the crowds. She had never seen so many people in her life. Families, women, children, policemen—but mainly men, all hurrying in and out as if there were very important places waiting for them. The building itself was larger than any she had ever beheld and could barely have imagined; three

Kenigh Halls could have fit below its curved archways and domed ceiling. She craned her neck and stared, wondering at the tiny country life she had lived.

It was probably while she stood entranced that her purse was stolen.

She did not notice it until much later, when she had finally tired of wandering around and exhaustion had caught up with her, numbing her ability to take in more wonders. It was evening and she figured she had better find a place to stay, so her first thought was for a bite to eat and something hot to uplift her spirits. There were bakeries just outside the train station, bustling places as busy as the platforms themselves, and if it hadn't been for her look of hunger the proprietor might have forever ignored her standing meekly there.

"Dundee cake, please," she asked, thinking of Alan. A hard, heavy bundle was slapped into her hand.

"That'll be tuppence."

The fat woman had greasy, floury arms and reminded her a little of Dolly, except for the pockmarked face and impatience. Snow dug quickly through her skirts as a line formed behind her, and she suddenly realized the little purse was gone. All that was left was its ribbon handle with knife-cut ends. She fumbled some more in her larger bag for loose change, trying not to panic. A handful of coins slipped coldly into her palm, and she nearly burst with relief.

"Thank 'ee," said the fat woman who was not Dolly, but

before Snow could give her a proper "You're welcome" she was already taking money from another customer, forgetting the girl before her.

Snow wandered away nibbling her cake, shocked that something so dreadful had occurred so quickly. She was under no illusion about her ignorance of the city and its people; she *had* figured, however, that she would be granted a little time to find her footing. . . . She clutched her bag to her and counted coins through the cloth. *Four shillings and tuppence.* Not enough for a night at an inn, much less renting a room, even if she knew where to go.

She tried to keep a "stiff upper lip" like the men in her Scottish novels, but finally she sank down on a bench and cried. Pigeons swept up around her and people rushed by like shadows.

When there were no more tears, she sat for a little longer, wishing for someone to help her, for guidance, for at least some idea of what to do.

When there were no more wishes, she rose and went out into the streets.

The city was enrapturing even through her sadness. Shiny cobblestones and golden reflections of gas lanterns glittered on the ground. Hundreds of people hurried wetly on errands or on their way home; the streets were far from deserted even at this late hour. Snow was easily coaxed into a dream state, already hungry again and still worn out from her escape. She fell into sleepwalk step with the other pedestrians.

She passed under the windows of middle-class houses, having left the station district. In each home families were gathered, fires were stoked, and modest meals were prepared. *Surely happy and good people would willingly spare a scrap. . . .*

Snow thought vaguely about begging—*It's not like my position doesn't warrant it*—but she could not for the life of her think of what to say. *Tomorrow,* she promised herself, *if I fail to find employment.*

She was still stuck with the problem of the night and the cold, and sleep. Something, from a book or a story or a song, prompted her to begin looking down alleys. She had visions of hidden gardens or at least rubbish bins, maybe a dry stairwell to sleep on. Snow worked to convince herself not to fear strange people and city rats. This was easier than expected, as she was both exhausted and familiar with neither.

"I should like to see a nice, honest rat," she chatted to herself while picking her way through the tiny spaces and crawlways between buildings away from the streets and their lights. It was as black as a moonless night in the country; she often had to feel along the cold, wet brick and stone with her hands. "It would give me someone to talk to. I would share my bread with it—if I had any."

Her steps echoed far too loudly against the hard walls and pavement, making her feel even lonelier. She was just on the point of giving in and crying when she saw something so strange and fantastic she stopped still, certain she was hallucinating.

Down one of the twisty little turns she had almost missed, a first-floor walkway connected two adjacent houses, creating a little bricked arch and a snug, dry corner beneath. Under this was the scene that caused her to blink. Someone had spread an old, flowered tapestry on the ground and arranged odds and ends of furniture on it like a room accidentally out-doors. A small, broken-legged cabinet with a cracked wash-basin stood next to a stool with a threadbare cloth-of-gold pillow, and in the center sat the best thing of all: a worn red velvet couch with carved and faded gilt trim. Everything was reasonably clean and decorated with all manner of cozy, soft trinkets, such as tiny cushions, torn silk throws, and old painted dolls.

"Doesn't look like the owner is around," Snow murmured as she approached the fairy tableau. "I'm sure whoever saved all this has to be poor—but regal. A lady of the streets, perhaps."

Such speculation did not really matter; Snow was dead tired, and nothing was going to convince her not to lie down on the velvet couch, short of an ax to her head. She carefully pulled the covers back, removed her shoes, and snuggled down.

Before her third breath she was fast asleep.


"SSSssssst!"

Snow awoke with a start. It was the middle of the night; the rain had stopped and the sky had cleared, but moonless, it was even darker than before.

A pair of slit yellow eyes glared at her from the other end of the couch. Snow sighed in relief.

"You want a place to sleep too, puss?" She moved aside some covers and patted the couch to encourage it.

*"This isss* my *place!"*

The eyes came closer, and Snow realized they were proportioned all wrong; what rose up out of the dark had a *human* shape and cat's eyes. She opened her mouth to scream.

A small hand—*paw*—clapped over her mouth.

"Cry and I ssslit your throat." A claw was held menacingly against her neck.

Snow caught sight of more movement behind this creature— two others. They were silhouetted against the sky, so Snow could see nothing of their features.

"Whatcha got there, Cat?" one of them asked.

"Sssomeone who has been sleeping in my bed."

"Well, kick it out and let's get on with it then. We promised Chauncey we would split up by dawn."

"She looksss rich," Cat said, cocking its head. Snow could a see a brief flash of white, sharp teeth, but no fur; except for the eyes and the fangs it might have been a human face.

"Yeah? And I suppose that's why she's sleeping out here, on your flea-bitten old furniture."

Cat hissed angrily. "It'sss my place, flea-bitten or not."

"Oh, cut it out, Cat. Let's have a look."

This was an older-sounding voice. Cat pulled its face back and the two others drew close, but the claw remained on her throat. Snow could see little of these attackers other than that their eyes appeared to be normal, at least.

Somebody's *tail* waved behind their heads.

"She *is* awfully delicate looking, ain't she?" This came from the shorter, fatter one.

"Look at this, her cloth is like country wear—cheap," the older one said, picking at her sleeve. He had no claws, but something ran up the backs of his hands. Not fur—*feathers?*

"*This* isn't cheap," Cat said, reaching over and picking Snow's necklace out of her collar with short, stubby fingers. The dull gold heart glimmered like a dying flame.

"Take it—it's yours," Snow whispered, feeling her throat expand against the tip of Cat's claw. "But leave me the painting, please. You can have whatever you want, just leave me the painting."

"What else you got, then?" the shorter one asked. He began to rummage through her cloak, cackling triumphantly when he found her bag.

Cat opened the locket with a graceful snap of its claws and peered at the contents. It was still too dark for Snow to see anything, but apparently that wasn't a problem for these three.

"Who is this pretty lady, then?"

"My mother." Snow fought back tears. "She died when I was born."

At this the three creatures paused, even the one looking for coins.

"What's your story, little princess?" the older one asked,

not unkindly. Cat closed the locket but did not let it go.

"What d'ye mean, what's her story?" the short one demanded, resuming his pilfering. "She's some little rich thing who's run away. What—bad arrangement for marriage? Some rich old codger? Yer parents treat you poorly? *Not enough sweets?*"

Cat hissed in agreement.

Snow said nothing, tears streaking down her face. He was partially right, and treated her tragedy so easily . . . like it was a common story in the city. *What kind of people—or monsters— are these?* What would they do to her?

"That's *enough,* the two of you. She's alone, she's lost—and she's *seen us.* There is only one thing to do. We have to take her to Chauncey. Sparrow, blindfold her."

The last thing Snow saw was her locket, which Cat tugged at until with a snap it came off in his hands.

"Do as you're told, and everything will be fine," the older one said as a cloth was slipped over her eyes.

"Do otherwise, and your painting is the *least* important thing you'll lose."

# Interlude: Alan

THE DUCHESS WAS KIND ENOUGH NOT TO have Alan present while she made the necessary arrangements. All he heard was her muted whisper, referring to someone known as the Hunter, and all he saw was a tall, skinny man in drab black clothing slip onto the estate one day. Alan lay awake at night, imagining the Hunter looking for Snow, walking quietly up and down the hallways, the glint of a stiletto in his hand. *What will happen when he cannot find her?*

Alan needn't have worried, he saw, and should have trusted in the power of gold.

The Hunter eventually disappeared as silently as he had come, mission seemingly accomplished.

An ugly wooden box appeared on the duchess's vanity. Alan slipped out as she settled herself down and pulled out a tiny, golden fork.

These things were horrible, and true.

But this was also true: Thieves had stolen a sow from the

farmer Llanfred, and ravens feasted on something dead, large, and bloody in the woods.

And as long as the duchess asked him no direct questions about what really happened to Snow, then he, the Hunter, and the pig would never tell.

# Chapter Thirteen

# The Lonely Ones

SHE WAS NOT ABLE TO KEEP UP. EVEN WITH someone—or something—on either side of her, guiding her, they trotted and leaped, and she stumbled and fell. A couple of times she was grabbed by strong, short limbs and heaved. Then she was weightless, falling up and over. It was cold, and they were none too careful with her arms and legs; wherever they were taking Snow, she would arrive frozen and bruised.

Eventually they stopped. There were scratching noises like a key—or a claw—against glass. *Rap-rap, tap.* A secret signal? She was pushed down and inside, where the air was warmer and smelled. It stank of animals, Snow realized. Not badly, just powerfully, like stables. It was almost comfortable after the unfamiliar city smells.

"Well, well . . . what have you got there?" a new voice asked.

The blindfold was taken off her.

She was in a basement. A basement abandoned and seized, she realized, not rented. Tiny windows around the top let in a little bit of city light and moonlight, and a sputtering gas lantern lit the rest. It hissed and illuminated a large front room furnished with pieces of chairs and stools, worn rugs, and sheets and cloths mounded here and there in the corners. *Everything looks borrowed or left behind.* A cook-stove sat fetidly next to a couple of pots, caked with old food.

Before her was a person or creature she didn't think she had met yet, presumably the one who had just spoken. He was short and lean, tightly muscled and sinewed. Older than she, but hard to tell by how much. He had the friendliest face so far, with beady little black eyes but a comic, pointy nose and smiling lips that almost made her forget his large pink-and-gray ears and the long gray tail snaking down to the floor.

"She was in my place," Cat hissed. As it flung off its cloak Snow realized with a start that Cat was a young girl. But as this young girl flipped the rain out of her hair and slicked it back, Snow got a good look at the claws that had threatened to rip her throat out.

"So you decided to keep her?" the man—*rat,* Snow decided—asked.

"She *saw* us," another explained. This was the short, plumper one, younger than Cat. Was that Sparrow? He *did* have a round face, large brown eyes, and a beaky little nose.

"Obviously," the rat-man said dryly. "What I'm trying to figure out is why you decided to bring her back to our *hideout?* You know? *Hide*out?"

"We didn't know what to do," the tallest one admitted. He still had his cloak on.

The rat-man sighed. He cocked his head at her the way she had seen many rodents do when deciding to flee or investigate something more closely.

"I won't tell anyone, I swear it." She was trying to be brave but could not stop the tears from silently leaking out down her cheeks, or her chin from trembling, any more than she could help noticing his pointy teeth and nails. "I will forget everything I've seen if you let me go!"

There were snorts and growls of disbelief.

"Ah. Well. About that we shall see," the rat-man said, not unkindly. "But what's your story, Princess? Nice clothes like that, nice skin—you're not poor. What's a girl like you doing in the streets?"

And so, surrounded by a gang of half-human, half-animal people in flickering lantern light, Snow told a slightly edited story of her dead mother, her father, her stepmother, the fiddler and her escape, and the cutpurse who left her penniless. She mentioned no names or stations.

The members of the group became enraptured despite themselves. She could tell from their widening, dark eyes. Sometimes they fluttered, like the one in the back, and Cat's tail flipped back and forth slowly as if she were about to strike. Although Snow wasn't sure what telling the story would accomplish, she prayed it would at least soften their hearts a little.

"Fairy tale," Cat hissed. "Made-up stories."

"Highly unlikely," said another.

"Unbelievable," stated a third.

"Oh? And what are we?" the rat-man demanded. "I would be far more likely to believe that an insane old crone tried to kill her stepdaughter than in a pack of . . . of . . . *us.*"

"If you please," Snow asked, quietly but still surprising herself with her boldness. "Who *are* you?"

"We?" the rat-man grinned. "Why we, dear lady, are the Lonely Ones." He swept down in an elaborate and graceful bow that almost touched his head to the floor. "Castoffs and the swept-unders of the grand carpet of society. Thieves and poets, every one. And you have seen us, and that is very dangerous."

"But why? I could not harm you," Snow asked, eyeing his claws.

"No, but the authorities could. The Queen's finest. Fleet Street. Or, even worse, the *circus.*"

Everyone shivered.

The rat-man tapped his tooth with a claw. "Does your father still love you?"

Snow started. She had not expected the question, and now that it was asked did not have a ready answer. *Does my father still love me? Maybe, in a fashion.* She remembered him being particular about her introduction to the duchess, and the toys he had bought her over the years. It wasn't his fault that her mother had died, or that Snow looked like her. . . . "Yes, I suppose he does," she answered slowly, though no more certain of the answer than before.

"Excellent!" The rat-man grinned again. His teeth gleamed like bones in the light. "We shall demand a ransom for you. Besides our fat reward, your father will find out the truth about your stepmother and everyone will live happily ever after. Sparrow, come here and bring me a piece of parchment." He rubbed his hands together, very much like a rat, and sat down to prepare the note.

"No!" Snow cried out. "No, please! Don't make me go back." Despite her best efforts, she began to sob. "P-please, I beg you—she'll kill me, she's mad. . . . She locked me up for *two years . . .*"

The rat-man's eyes went wide with surprise and horror at her display. It was certainly not the reaction he had expected. Nor, Snow realized, was it the one she had expected, either.

"But certainly once you speak to your father, you can explain. She daren't try it again."

"You don't understand. She has some sort of hold over him. Over *all* of them." She thought about Alan and his strange devotion to the duchess, and the fear the other servants had of her.

All of the craziness inside her—the tears, the sorrow, and the horror of the last few days—crashed against the inside of her skull. *My stepmother was going to have me killed.* The craziness of it made her cry more. "Please don't send me back. I beg you." She fell to her knees, wracked with sobs.

"Is there anything we can do?"

This might have been said by the tall one; she could not be sure.

The rat-man tapped his tooth again for a long moment. "All right then. We shall solve both problems—ours (your having seen us) and yours (having no place to go)—at once. You shall stay here and cook for us and clean our place for us."

Everyone blinked at this, Snow and the Lonely Ones together.

"All right?"

"Isn't that dangerous?" the short, fat one asked.

"If she goes to the police there will be questions. About *her.* Resulting in a quick ride home and probably a fat reward for the bobby who brought her." He frowned at the thought of the money he was missing out on and gave her a hard look. "Besides, we're giving you a chance, Princess. You're not going to mess that up, are you?"

"No," Snow whispered. "Thank you."

Her mind raced. A couple of days ago she had been a miserable young lady of high estate. Then she had been a girl on the run. In neither situation did she imagine she would wind up as a maid for a pack of demons. It was the best, no, *only* option she could see at this point. *At least I know how to clean and cook,* she thought wryly. *And it's a good thing I like animals.*

"That's that, then. I think introductions are in order. What's your name, Princess?"

"Jes—" she began, then stopped and thought. "Snow," she said decidedly.

The rat-man stared at her, but did not question.

"Well, we are all in the big city together, and no one cares about your old life—that's fine. Choose whatever name you like. This is Cat; you've already met her." The girl—cat—in question didn't extend a paw to shake or say a "How d'you do?" She may have been part animal, but Snow could already see she was going to have problems with the human, girl side of her. "And Raven." He was the tall one. Raven took his cloak off and revealed pale skin with high, high cheekbones. His eyes were dark brown, and except for black, black hair he seemed to lack animal attributes. Snow reminded herself to thank him later for intervening and bringing her to their hideout. "And Sparrow." The other boy, short and plump, made a little bow. Soft brown feathers crested in place of his eyebrows. "The Mouser is on his rounds."

"And you are?" she asked, though she could guess.

"Chauncey," he answered, grinning.

# Chapter Fourteen

# Life with the Lonely Ones

SNOW WOKE UP LATE THE NEXT DAY. NO ONE had bothered to rouse her.

As to where she was, Snow was only confused for a moment. Even before she opened her eyes the smell confirmed what she might have dreamed. *I really* am *living with a gang of half-animal demons. Either that or I have gone completely mad.* But so far she seemed safe, safer than she had apparently been her entire adolescence. She fingered her locket, given back to her before she fell asleep the night before.

No one was in the main room. She waited for what seemed like a long time, and still no one came in. Deciding it was probably safe, she changed into one of the other outfits she had packed, a more roughly spun old dress that was more suitable for chores and for the company she now kept. *I wonder if I could hang a line up to make a private space for myself in the corner?* She smiled, amused at how quickly she seemed to be adapting to her new, alien situation.

A quick search of the room proved an absence of water basin and pitcher. *How do they wash?* She imagined Cat licking herself all over and decided not to think about it.

The floor was hard-packed earth covered with a layer of grime and filth at least a half-inch thick. Many of the rags on the bottoms of the piles strewn about the room were moldy and would have to be thrown out. There was no broom. She moved a chair to look at the table better; it had many years' worth of ground-in wax and stains.

"Here now, what's this?"

A bleary-eyed Chauncey stumbled in from his room, running his fingers quickly through his short brown hair like a— *like a rat.*

"I've begun cleaning." She wasn't sure whether she should say "Sir."

*"Now?"* Chauncey looked at the bright morning light that shone outside their tiny windows. "In the *day?*"

"I thought I would—"

"The first thing you should realize, Princess, is that the Lonely Ones work at night. Unless you thought old Chauncey would get up at the crack of dawn, have his cuppa tea, and stride briskly through the bright morning streets with all the other workday chumps, me ears sticking up and me tail hanging out back?"

She opened her mouth to apologize.

"Wake me when it's dusk." Chauncey yawned and stumbled back to his room. "And for the love of Michael, keep it quiet until then!"

$*$   $*$   $*$

It was a very long day. There was very little Snow could do that would not make any noise except sit quietly. She spent an hour or two sorting out the cloths and rags on the floor—a pile to be thrown out, a pile to keep. . . . After that there was nothing. Snow was used to long days of nothing, however, from her years of confinement.

She looked at the picture of her mother in the locket for a time. She thought over and over again about the last few days, her stepmother, the last few years. . . . She cried a little to herself, thinking about how it all went wrong—or perhaps how it had never been right.

How could her father have married someone that crazy? Didn't it show at all when he was courting her? *How could none of us see how crazy she was in the years that followed?* She thought about Alan and how he seemed unable to speak about what went on in the duchess's chambers. Surely he would have warned her, if he had known? His words came back to her from a day long ago: *"Ye shouldna mess with magic, Jess. A bad spell turns back on the caster times three, as my grandmum says. And . . . it does things to people. Or maybe the type of people who do it are of a sort,* touched. . . ."

Why hadn't he been clearer? *Why didn't I listen?*

She thought about her father and wondered if he had set up a search for her, and whether someone really would post a reward, as Chauncey had seemed to hope. Or would they both just be happy to be rid of her? Maybe the old duchess could have a baby now, or "find" one. . . . Where was Alan? Was he thinking about her?

She lay down and thought and worried, and half-dozed the day away.

The sun finally set and Chauncey reappeared, much more sprightly and awake than when Snow had seen him earlier. She was waiting for him patiently in a chair.

"Now then, *this* is a reasonable time for a body to be up and about!"

He stretched and grinned. Sparrow slunk into the room more sleepily. Snow wondered if it was hard for him to be awake at night, being part-bird of a type that was used to the day. He wasn't wearing a shirt, and when he flexed his shoulders grumpily Snow noticed with a start tiny wings fluttering off his back. They were like a cherub's, but brown.

She made herself look away. Sparrow didn't seem to notice her staring.

"Chauncey, I—I will need some supplies to begin keeping house properly."

Once she had exhausted her supply of memories and worries, she spent the remaining hours of daylight composing in her head a list of things she would need.

"Oh! Demands already! And not a day into the club! And what *exactly* would you be needin', Princess?"

"Well, *food,* for one, if I am to prepare your dinners," she responded archly.

Sparrow guffawed. "She's got you there, Chaunce."

The rat-man's eyes widened, but he smiled. "Fair enough, my sweet! Roasts and pigeons and lark's tongues for us all!—Sorry, Sparrow."

"No worries," the boy answered quickly, but looked like—*Oh goodness, it looks like he got his feathers ruffled.*

"Well, I don't know about lark's tongue, but I can make a good pie. Also, I shall be needing a broom, and soap, and a bucket—and water."

"Oh, aye, we'll get ye all that," Chauncey agreed, but looked a little lost, as if he hadn't quite realized what he had gotten himself into. Raven came out, barely visible as he slipped through the shadows and stood in a corner, tall, gaunt, and crook-necked.

"Will someone get that girl up?" Chauncey yelled, finding something he could get ahold of easily, his own territory again. "She'll sleep the night through if we let her."

"Just like a cat," Snow said before she could stop herself.

She covered her mouth in horror. The others stared at her in shock. Then Raven gave the faintest whisper of a smile.

"Aye," Chauncey said. *"Just* like a cat."

It was strange the way they seemed to both be perfectly accepting of their . . . *features,* yet also a little disquieted by them, as if they had been that way their entire lives but were the only ones they knew of like themselves. *The Lonely Ones.* It was more than just a cute name. She would find out about their backgrounds, she promised herself. *One of these days. Just probably not today.*

There was a rap on the door.

"That would be ol' Mouser now!" Chauncey said before disappearing into Cat's room.

Raven unlatched and opened the door.

Whatever Snow was expecting, it wasn't the Mouser. She was prepared for a short, fat little man or boy with a round face and kindly, cute features. She thought of the mice at Kenigh Hall.

What Mouser *actually* was: a young man almost as tall as Raven, skinny as a rail, with elegant, sharp eyebrows and an equally sharp and elegant nose. His eyes were gray and his cheekbones high; his hands were gloved so it was impossible to see if he had claws. *At least he has a tail,* Snow found herself strangely relieved to note. His ears were a nice mix of human and mouse, barely noticeable.

"Oh my," he declared, seeing Snow. "What is *that?*"

"That's Snow," Sparrow answered. "She's goin' to be our maid and cook."

"How splendid!"

With a graceful motion he swooped into the room and clapped his hands together. His clothing was much neater than the others, with real trousers and coat, Snow noticed, and his

107

hair was combed back properly, with perfect sideburns. "We shall finally make a civilized place of this mess. Oh, how *refined.*"

"Mouser's the gentleman," Sparrow explained needlessly. "'E actually talks to the Others. Keeps up on what's what."

*Others,* Snow thought. *Normal men and women.*

With another gesture too fast to follow, the Mouser had her locket in his hand and flicked it open—yes, there were definitely claws beneath his gloves. He studied the picture for a moment.

"Your mother?" he asked.

She nodded.

"She's dead," Sparrow again said helpfully.

"My sympathies," the Mouser said—genuinely, she was sure. He closed the locket carefully and let it fall gently back against her breast.

*Not what I expect in a mouse at all,* Snow thought.

Cat slunk out of her room, sleep still in her eyes and hair. Chauncey barred her way back to bed, crossing his arms and glaring at her.

"Well, the news is *most interesting* today, I daresay." The Mouser clapped his hands together and spun around, collecting the audience with his eyes. "It seems as if our fair section of Covent Garden is finally to get some gas lamps. Also, bustles are getting even larger, if that's possible. You should see the new line on High Street. . . ."

Sparrow rolled his eyes.

"The Mouser, he's a great one for talk and gossip," Chauncey said. "'Specially when he's the one doing the talking and the gossiping. Come on now, you lot. Off we go. Sparrow, you come with me. We'll get Princess her stuff and come back to a spic-and-span hideout in the morning! And, speaking of, my chaps, regardless of what you have heard, this is *still* a hideout." He raised one eyebrow for emphasis. "No more bringing home strays, you hear? We are not a charity house."

Snow tried not to smile. The others pretended to ignore Chauncey, but even the Mouser, who seemed to be the oldest, looked like he was really listening. It was obvious that their leader cared deeply about them, his gruff and comic exterior belying the deep, almost fatherly affection.

Cat scratched herself luxuriously all over and ran her claws through her hair. Snow wished she could take a good comb to it; it was thicker, blacker, and more beautiful than almost any normal girl's. *It would be gorgeous up in a bun. . . .*

The younger girl caught Snow staring at her and growled.

Snow didn't have long to wait before Chauncey and Sparrow came back with all manner of things for cleaning and eating, obviously unsure of what was appropriate, obviously never having done any cleaning or cooking themselves. There was a shoulder of pork, some carrots, and a few potatoes. The only seasoning they brought back was salt, but she was surprised and pleased that they even thought of it. Sparrow was laden with two buckets of water, just barely enough to get any job done. The rat-man wished her good luck, and once again she was alone.

She rolled up her sleeves and got to work.

And she found something miraculous—in the midst of a cloud of dirt, grime on her knees and hands, scrubbing furiously, Snow was the happiest she had been in years.

She was determined to do the best job she could so they would have no cause to throw her out. More, she wanted to impress them. Never in her life had she had to earn anything, never had she been needed by anyone. It was a good feeling to have to *work* to belong.

And dirt was something Snow could easily cope with and conquer; after all of the duchess's punishments, cleaning was something she knew without a doubt how to do.

At one point in the afternoon—no, night—someone rapped at the door. She stood still, clutching a rag to her chest. *Have they found me so soon?* The pattern was all wrong; it wasn't the Lonely Ones' secret code. There was another knock. She was both glad and terrified that they didn't have a peephole.

Eventually whoever it was went away, and Snow went back to work, convincing herself that it was Chauncey or the Mouser testing her. Or maybe a salesman.

It took a number of hours to get the main room to a barely passable state; her arms and body tired faster than she expected. *Probably because of the schedule change; my clock hasn't adjusted to this new life.* It would take a couple of days before she would become fully adapted. The floor sparkled as much as a packed-earth floor could be expected to, lit by two lanterns and rushlights that Snow constantly had to trim. The sky outside was just beginning to change colors, from black to dark blue, and she supposed she would have to begin making their breakfast—no, supper—soon. But first she spent a few minutes in Cat's room, straightening her things, fluffing her bed and remaking it as best she could. Interestingly, Cat's "real" room was far less feminine than the one in the alley, as though she was embarrassed by girlish tendencies.

Snow set to work on cooking when she was done. The only thing she could attempt was a stew, since she was lacking a proper oven. Perhaps she could improvise something later on. They were short a couple of bowls so she ate her own share before they came, directly out of the pot, and put the rest in hollowed-out pieces of bread. She tried to set the table—with no spoons, forks, knives, or napkins. She wondered if she should ask Chauncey about it; physical appearances aside, it was obvious they were from vastly different financial backgrounds. *When does being a maid slip over into a more civilizing role?* she wondered, seeing herself there for years, mothering them.

A knock on the door—*rap rap-rap.* Not the code, but almost. Snow ignored it. Another verson: *rap rap rap.* She sang a little song to herself. Finally: *rap-rap-tap.*

"Who's there?"

She undid the chain and opened the door a crack.

"Excellent. We'll have you trained yet." Chauncey's beady little eye gleamed. "Now open the door quick—we'd best not be seen, even coming and going."

They all trooped in. *No, not "troop." They make very little noise and spread out immediately, very much like mice investigating a place.*

"What smells so good?" Chauncey asked dramatically, nose in the air.

"A clean house?" Snow said timidly.

"No, it's supper!" Sparrow skipped over to the pot and peeked in. "We could smell it a mile away."

*They probably could, too.*

He started to poke a finger in for a taste, but before she could stop herself Snow had whipped out her spoon and rapped his knuckles with it, just like Dolly.

Stung, Sparrow put his fingers in his mouth.

No one seemed to notice or care. So, if Dolly she was to be . . .

She made her face look stern and put her hands on her hips. "No putting fingers in the pot. Ever. Sit down and I will serve you properly."

Sparrow looked chastened. Chauncey and the Mouser grinned. Cat and Raven quickly made their way to the table and sat down in chairs, trying to look proper.

"Mouser, I thought we'd hired ourselves a maid."

"Chaunce, I think we hired ourselves a *wench.*"

Snow served them as efficiently and carefully as possible. She put on a neutral face, but as soon as everyone was eating she sat by the pot and watched them, looking for the slightest hint of pleasure or praise.

She would be disappointed. There were no words, just slurps, burps, and chewing—all with mouths open, except for Raven, she noticed. He ate carefully, quickly, and quietly. In just a few minutes she was serving them more, and then more again. It wasn't until they were done that anyone spoke.

"Ah." Chauncey let out a big burp and pushed his chair back from the table. "What it is, to come home to a hot meal!"

"Not enough pepper," said Sparrow peevishly.

"I didn't have any to cook with," Snow replied.

"A splendid—if simple—meal, Princess." The Mouser stood up and stretched. "Not exactly haute cuisine, but . . ."

"I have neither an oven nor flour," Snow said, a little upset. "If you provide me with those I shall bake pies until they come out your ears."

The Mouser raised an elegant eyebrow but said nothing.

She cleared the table and rubbed it down as best she could. Chauncey took his usual seat at the head with a box of money he unlocked and a black ledger book. One by one each of the Lonely Ones came up and gave him money, or sometimes a trinket. Chauncey carefully wrote down each amount and put it away, sometimes giving something back.

"If you'll pardon me," Snow asked timidly, "what do you all do for a living?"

"What do we do?" Chauncey's eyes gleamed, and he smiled. "Why, Princess, we're miners!"

"Miners?"

She didn't know much about the vocation, but thought

they should have more equipment, like shovels, or picks, or hats with candle-lanterns on them.

"Aye, miners. The streets of London are *filled* with gold, if you know where to look."

Snow wasn't quite there yet, but she was beginning to catch on.

"Our quarries are the roads, our veins the dark alleys." The Mouser smiled. "We pick *pockets,* Princess, not dirt."

"Oh." Snow didn't know what else to say. She was certainly in no position to judge them. *But they are thieves.*

"What else do you expect us to do?" Raven asked softly. "Work in a factory?" He pulled back his sleeve to reveal black feathers that angled back from his wrist and continued up the backs of his arms to his shoulders. "Manage a bank?"

"I didn't . . . I just . . . I'm sorry." She looked down at the ground.

"You're not the one who should be sorry," the Mouser said bitterly.

Snow looked at the floor, at the wall, still unsure what to say.

"Hey!" The horrible long moment was broken by a cry from Sparrow, who had his head poked in Cat's room. "She made Cat's bed, but not mine!"

Cat yelped and ran into her room to look.

"I'm sorry, Sparrow," Snow said as contritely as she could since he was obviously still upset from when she had whacked him over the stew. "I ran out of time. I will do it from now on."

"You'd better." He stuck out a lower lip.

*"You've been in my room!"* Cat hissed.

When she came out of her bedroom there was very little of her human aspect showing. Her hair was on end and her eyes were so wide with upset that Snow could not miss how yellow they were, or how black slits cut down through the center of them. *"No one goesss in my room!"*

"I just did," Sparrow pointed out. Cat glared at him.

*No love lost between those two.* Snow wondered if it was because they were close, like brother and sister, or because birds and cats are enemies in the wild. How much did the animal they look like affect the way they thought and spoke?

"I'm sorry, Cat." *Apologizing again.* Just like the servants were constantly doing at Kenigh Hall: "Sorry, mum. Apologies, Your Grace."

"I thought you would like it if I got to your room first and neatened it a bit."

In answer to her apology, Cat deliberately stuck her hand in her pocket and pulled out a handful of things—coins, fluff, string, pocketstuff. Then she carefully dropped it all on the floor.

"Cat," Chauncey warned. She hissed and flounced into her room.

"There's nothing to be done with that girl," the Mouser sighed.

He and Chauncey stayed up late into the morning, talking and muttering about this and that. Chauncey smoked a clay pipe, the Mouser cigars. Snow shivered, the smell reminding her of the count who had grabbed her. Sparrow went to bed, Cat didn't come out of her room, and Raven disappeared.

She tried to stay up to listen to what the other two were talking about, but she had been awake for almost twenty hours straight and was completely exhausted. She sat down on her pile of rags, fully clothed.

She thought about Dolly and all of the pies, sweets, roasts, and buns she had baked. She thought about her own spoiled complaints to Dolly, and worse, her father's complete lack of comment, praise, or criticism. At least the duchess had said nice things occasionally, like after a particularly big dinner. "My dear Dolly, you have outdone yourself," she would say. And even if Dolly didn't like her—for Snow's sake—she would blush with pride. "Oh, it's just me job, Your Grace."

Snow wished she had said more. There were times she had, usually after a special treat or a holiday dinner. But not just on an ordinary day, for an ordinary meal that she loved, and now missed—not once. She wished she could say some things to Dolly now: "I'm sorry," "Your meals are delicious," and "I understand."

Eventually she fell asleep, sitting up.

# Chapter Fifteen

# Revelations

"I KNOW HOW YOU FEEL ABOUT ME LEAVING your hideout, Chauncey," Snow began tentatively one day. "But unless you or someone else wants to haul buckets of water back to the hideout every day, I'm going to need to do it myself."

Snow had been with them for a week and felt that she could finally suggest such a thing. She had settled in as comfortably as she could, considering her lack of a bed and their lack of any set routine. Chauncey tried to have them all get together for at least one night at home a week, but often they stayed elsewhere, out in the city. Raven and Cat had their own private, scattered hideouts in case they did not want to make a long trip home; Sparrow "perched," as he called it; and the Mouser found different places each time. With him it was usually gentleman's clubs—he was often misidentified as a regular patron who napped quietly in corners with a good book.

Then the Lonely Ones would return at all hours, expecting the hot food they thought they hired a maid for. She had finally convinced Chauncey that this was unreasonable.

"I understand there seem to be . . . ," she had said, looking for a politic turn of phrase, "certain . . . *resentments* because of who I am and who you are, and what you can and cannot do in society and what I can, but that does not make me your slave."

Chauncey had sputtered indignantly that no one felt that way about her and that that was certainly not the case, but he came down especially hard on Sparrow and Cat the next time they demanded the impossible of her. The Mouser eased off having her press every article of his clothing every day.

Snow felt that she and the rat-man could talk. The Mouser was nice, but too elegant and scary. Sparrow and Cat didn't seem to like her. And Raven—well, Raven didn't say much to anyone. He was gloomy; shadows hung off his features like black feathers. She thought they could be friends eventually, though, if he would just talk with her. She was determined to make friends with *all* of them eventually. She was a part of them now, for heaven's sake, and she had no place else to go. She had better make a family here.

Water was certainly important for her duties, but if truth be told, she was feeling a little stir crazy. She had been in the same three-and-a-half-room basement for more than a week straight, and though it was better than being killed by her stepmother, she began to wonder *how much* better, especially after the initial wonder of living with and working for a magical group of animal people had worn off. They were attractive, they were unusual—but in the end, they behaved just like anyone else, with very human faults and foibles.

"I could also take care of the market shopping."

She very carefully avoided any reference to the fact that she firmly believed they stole all their produce. "If you don't trust me with the money, I can write up a list of everything and keep an accounting book."

She could see he liked that. She thought he would. *Who knew rats were so punctilious?* They always seemed rather sloppy and broken-whiskered to her.

But still he said nothing, just looking at her, tapping his tooth.

"Chauncey, I'm going mad cooped up in here," she finally admitted. "I think I have performed more than adequately in my new position and have given you no reason to doubt me." The duchess's favorite tactic: When all else fails, be supremely polite. "If you distrust me so much, you can *follow* me."

"Aye, you do have a point there. I didn't think I'd become a water hauler, meself." He tapped his tooth one more time, for good measure. "All right. We'll give you a key. But you'll be under strict surveillance until we can be sure, Missy."

"*Thank* you, Chauncey."

After everyone fell asleep, she took the wooden yoke with its buckets and threw it over her shoulders, trying to remember how the dairymaids did it back home. She knew there was a trick to it and could already predict the blisters on the backs of her shoulders and neck. She carefully opened the door, trying not to bang the buckets against the door and wake everyone.

Snow stood blinking for a moment, enjoying the young rays of a morning sun on her face. In her pocket mirror the night before she had observed her clammy white face with some alarm. *Now they really could call me Snow.* The duchess probably would have been proud of her aristocratic paleness.

Snow shook her head, trying to clear the woman's face from her mind. She had no idea why she kept on thinking about her at unexpected times, and of almost-pleasant incidents and memories. At night before she fell asleep Snow would try to figure out what she would have said or done to the duchess if she had found out about the planned murder herself—if Alan hadn't been there and taken care of her.

Sometimes she imagined slapping the duchess, or hitting her across the face with something heavy, like a shovel. She tried to get rid of these thoughts as well, but there was a grim satisfaction in them she couldn't dismiss so easily.

She thought about Alan, too; he must have been worried sick about her. She must find a way of getting a note to him. For that she needed envelopes, stamps, sealing wax . . . she needed money.

Though she was doing quite well in her new role as maid and Chauncey had given her a few coins, she had no clue what things actually cost.

Cat had grudgingly told her about a market nearby and a public well. Snow went to the former and watched women conduct their business. This was no country market or farm stand, however; the end of a whole street was closed off, and there must have been more than a dozen tents and stalls selling everything from fish to flowers.

The cobblestones were slick with water that the merchants occasionally doused over their produce to keep it fresh. Those selling wore smocks and aprons over brown and black work clothes. Those buying were dressed in styles varying from servant's gear with caps, starched skirts, and aprons, to that of old crones bent over, all in black, complete with canes to point at things they disapproved of.

Occasionally there were real aristocrats, buying nosegays or putting in special orders. Snow gawked at them, having rarely seen real city gentry. *Their skirts are so wide . . . like gigantic bells from the belt down!* Tiny, tiny waists that must have been corseted plumed out and up into chests fluffy with lace and trim.

Unthinkingly Snow's hand went to her own breast and felt the plain, coarse fabric there.

The ladies' hats were indescribable. Some were so large and covered with so many feathers that the women they sat upon had to bend very delicately so as not to tangle them in the roofs of the stalls. All the rich women also carried pretty little parasols that matched their outfits, and pretty little purses that dangled from their elbows.

Snow smugly wondered what the duchess would think of these styles. *She has no idea how out of fashion she really is.*

The men were all handsome and well groomed, with perfectly even sideburns. They wore tailored jackets, striped trousers, and shiny, shiny boots. Tall hats finished them off, and some even had monocles and walking canes that they didn't seem to need. Some made a big deal of taking out gigantic gold pocket watches and looking at them *very carefully*.

Snow watched the parade of bright colors, fancy and poor dress, the assortment of accessories—including tiny dogs on long, thin leashes—so intently that she almost forgot to observe how they bought and haggled.

When she finally joined the crowd she was quiet, speaking politely and keeping her eyes down. No one took note of her. The dress accomplished that, she saw: The merchants were polite—some even smiled—but perfunctory, keeping their eyes out for the next, wealthier customer. She would not be remembered in their stories that evening as they met their husbands, wives, and children at supper and talked about the events of the day.

Jessica Abigail Danvers Kenigh, daughter of the duke, ignored and forgotten.

But she was Snow now.

Some of the younger ladies were her age, about to have their debut, she realized—their coming-out party—the first ball or tea dance just for them. This autumn would be their first season, when they would spend every evening at a different party, dinner, or theatre and be seen by the crowds and courted by young men. Jessica could have spoken to them about what it was like—what they wore, what kind of food was served at the dances, whether the dances were lit with candles or lanterns—but Snow could not, and speaking up would have been presumptuous.

As she picked through the onions and potatoes looking for good ones, she imagined Dolly looking on, approving or shaking her head.

And she thought about Jessica.

She had never spent any more time on her looks than the duchess made her, and she had never cared before what people thought of her. She didn't expect to be treated like royalty in her new position, but being a maid was harder than she thought, and it wasn't the work.

Still, she consoled herself, there was a whole world *they* didn't know about, where mice walked upright on their back legs, cats were snitty and girlish, and rats spoke like Irishmen.

She took out a stub of a pencil and the little piece of paper Chauncey had ripped out of his accounting book. She carefully wrote down what she had bought and for how much, and also where, just in case Chauncey wanted to know. She looked longingly at the buckets of flowers and tiny bouquets but decided against it. *Maybe later. After I have earned their trust.*

Once when she was debating the true value of a particular beet with a shrewish farmwife she caught a glimpse of black out the corner of her eye that was deeper than those of the suits around her—and was that a flash of tail?

She knew she would never really catch them, but at least

she knew she was being followed. *How long will they do that, I wonder? When will they trust me?*

The company was a little friendlier at the public well; unlike the frowning, snapping city folk at the market, the women filling their buckets were laughing and gossiping like any servants back home.

Their language was almost indecipherable, however.

"Ooow, d'ye see th' getup on Lady Farthington, then?" A fat, dimple-faced woman was speaking; her words went up and down like a screaming cat in heat.

"With the boat on her head, you mean?" another one replied.

"Aun' Katy works in th' kitchens there. *She* said 'twas the Baron Kingsley gave it her."

"Oooh! Ey!"

There were whistles and exclamations all around.

*This is like a book I have not read,* Snow thought as she took her turn setting the bucket that was free of vegetables under the pump and filling it with water. *But then again, I suppose most of life is like that.*

She listened to stories of boyfriends and man-friends, of husbands and laundry, of the habits of masters and mistresses. She heard suggestions for making gravy thicker, and unlikely gossip—tales of liquor and debauchery among the highest classes. She paid careful attention to the stranger, chilling stories about witches disguised as street-corner beggars, ghosts

124

that inhabited the attics of several well-known mansions, thieves and creatures who lived in the sewers, and the mysteriously named denizens of midnight London: the dead inhabitants of Number 50 Berkeley Square, Spring-Heeled Jack, the Clockwork Man.

No mention of people with the ears and tails of animals, however.

"Here now, they have you doing the shopping *and* the water?"

Snow looked up, surprised at being directly addressed. A girl close to her own age had her hands on her hips in indignation, but smiled. "You'd best have them get it delivered. I wouldn't work no household had me do *both.*"

Snow smiled wanly and shrugged.

*If only she knew that my "household" was run by a rat.*

Again, on the way home, she felt someone was watching her, and again she ignored it. As she had predicted, her shoulders hurt from where the yoke hung, and as the morning became early afternoon she grew sleepy. It was far warmer than she had expected for spring; besides the lack of ice and snow the temperature was far above freezing, and she had overdressed. It was only a few blocks before Snow entered the tiny alley with the hidden entrance to her new home, but Snow was sweaty and exhausted when she arrived.

She almost didn't find the door, a tiny thing concealed by

garbage and vines. She wondered if the people who owned the building knew what lived in the basement. Snow smiled at the thought of the real landlord hiring a ratter, an exterminator, to get rid of the Lonely Ones.

Once inside she carefully put away the produce and arranged the water buckets in the corner, resolving to take a sponge bath as soon as they had all left for the evening.

The Mouser came staggering dramatically out of his bedroom, stretching and yawning.

Snow raised an eyebrow. "Oh . . . just getting up?"

He wouldn't meet her eye.

"You're a *terrible* actor, Mouser."

At first he looked surprised, then he grinned sheepishly. No, wolfishly. *No—mousily?*

"You could at least play along. Make me look good in front of Chauncey."

"How long did you follow me for?"

"Long enough to see you drool over the latest fashions."

She blushed.

His look softened. "Don't be embarrassed, pet." He reached out and ruffled her hair. "You were from a *very* good house, weren't you?"

"It's not important anymore," she mumbled, staring at the ground.

"Your stepmother—she wanted her own heir, didn't she?"

Snow nodded, very slightly.

He seemed to care so much, and was gentle away from

the others—like a brother? No, maybe an uncle. He was too handsome to think about as a brother.

"Well, I think you're holding up extremely well. I'll talk to Chaunce about getting you an allowance—your *wages,* I mean!" He grinned.

A change had begun in that moment. Snow was never able to say exactly what it was, but it felt like a weight had lifted or a dam had broken. It had nothing to do with the possibility of receiving money, and everything to do with the Mouser's recognition of her feelings.

"Anyone up for a game of whist?" Chauncey asked the next morning, having finished with his pipe early. He slid a chair around and sat on it backward, shuffling the cards.

"I'll play all-fours," Sparrow volunteered, licking his fingers from the pudding Snow had made that evening. She had given him an extra-large portion, and his brown eyes, shy for once, flicked up to meet hers in surprise. She had smiled back. *Maybe he just thought that* I *didn't like* him.

"Oh, pish." The Mouser dismissed Sparrow's suggestion with an aristocratic wave. "Anyone up for a *refined* game?"

Raven joined them, quietly as ever. Cat was busy running a comb and claws through her long hair. She had been doing that more often, Snow noticed.

"I can play," Snow volunteered quietly.

"Excellent! You'll be *my* partner." The Mouser clapped his hands.

She pulled up to the table, the first time she had sat there with them as an equal, and took her cards as Chauncey dealt them. Some minutes into the game the Mouser cleared his throat and said casually, "So, Chaunce, are we betting?"

"Absolutely, Mouser."

"What can our pretty little maid wager, then?"

Chauncey thought about it. "I guess we can spare her a portion of the week's take."

"Nothing too much." The Mouser dismissed imaginary fortunes with a wave of his hand. "Of course, it's nowhere near what she used to have as a *lady*, but whatever we can spare I am sure will please her."

Snow blushed and stared at her cards.

"Oh, yes." Chauncey raised an eyebrow. "Our little gentle-woman. What's it really like, then, all bowing to you and gold forks?"

She smiled slightly. "Not out in the country."

When she was brave enough to look up from her cards, she saw that all the Lonely Ones had their full attention on her, eager to hear about a life they had never lived.

"What were you, then? A rich merchant's daughter? A lady? A baroness?" Chauncey tried to sound casual and stared at his hand, rearranging his cards, but the interest in his voice was unmistakable.

"A *duchess*, actually."

She tried not to grin when his jaw dropped.

\* \* \*

She told them about the maids, the fireplaces, the clocks, and the real beeswax candles. She told them about the rare parties, how they were held during a full moon so that country gentry could find their way in their carriages, chaises, and troikas. She told Sparrow especially about the food, the puddings, roasts, jellied consommés, platters of fish, punch, sherry, and toffee.

She told them more, about her clothes, her childhood, the things she liked, and the punishment the duchess gave her. She told them about her confinement, how she kept from going mad, and how she fed the mice.

"She fed the *mice*!" Chauncey slapped the Mouser on the back, laughing hysterically. "And now she feeds *you*!"

"I heard her, Chaunce," the Mouser said through gritted teeth.

"Where was this place that you grew up?" Sparrow asked.

"Kenigh Hall, near the Brecons, in Wales."

Chauncey and the Mouser exchanged looks, Raven sat up straighter, and Cat choked.

"But that's near where we're from!" Sparrow blurted out.

"Really?" Snow didn't know what to say. For starters, why did they have such strange accents? *All right, and while we're at it animal features . . .*

"We're from . . . the forest of the Brecons," Chauncey said quietly. "About ten miles south of you."

"Oh—what an incredible coincidence," was all she could think to say.

"Then we're *meant* to be together." Raven spoke up unexpectedly, his dark eyes burning. "We were *meant* to find each other."

Chauncey nodded slowly. "I think that could be agreed on." He fiddled with his cards as Snow did everything she could to remain polite and not question them about their origins.

"I'll bet you're just *itching* to know about where we're really from, aren't you?" he finally asked.

"It's your own business—"

Chauncey laughed. "Oh, yes. But it doesn't matter. We really don't know anything about our lineage or our mothers or fathers—or if we even had any."

Mouser jumped in as the role of storyteller quickly, eagerly, and dramatically. "We were left on the doorstep of an old widow who lived in the middle of the forest, in a basket, just like in a story. Ah, but unlike fairy-tale orphans, we came with *gold*." He rubbed his fingers together as if to make a guinea appear, but it didn't. "Tied up in our bundles. To provide for us. Chauncey and I were the first. After me and Chaunce came Raven. Then Cat, and finally Sparrow. There was another, when we were tiny, but she ran away.

"Anwyn was as loving a mother as any and treated us like her own children. She had no one; her husband had died years ago, and her son earlier on. She had her own garden and kept to herself. People probably thought she was a witch." Mouser sighed.

"She protected us and told us we were handsome, beautiful, and precious, and that we shouldn't trust other people who looked like her because they might not feel the same way. She taught us numbers. . . ."

"What happened to her?" Snow asked, knowing tragedy was near.

"We were out playing in the woods one day," Raven said quietly. "We came back and thought she was asleep in her chair. She was dead. Died in her sleep, I guess."

Sparrow's eyes were large and glistening.

"You're really too young to remember," the Mouser said irritably.

"I remember!" Sparrow said indignantly. "I remember being warm, and sunlight, and arms holding me."

The Mouser rolled his eyes.

"That was five years ago, more or less," Chauncey finished. "I suppose we should have stayed in the woods with the other animals, but we wanted to see the world, like normal young men. And girl," he added for Cat's benefit. "I suppose we thought we would find others like Mother Anwyn. We didn't," he added dryly.

They were quiet for a few minutes. Snow's mind buzzed with questions. Finally she picked one: "Where did *she* think you were from?"

The Mouser laughed. "She told us that we were sent by the fairies, that we were cousins of the fair folk, children of forest spirits—none of which I believe, by the way. We none of us can turn invisible, or make gold out of dust, or know how to get to kingdoms hidden under hills. We bleed and have to work like everyone else. Nor have we met a fellow forest dweller, that I know of—no nymphs or satyrs ever came round for tea when we were little."

"I should like to meet a beautiful young nymph, myself," Chauncey snorted. "Get one of them pretty young fairy things and"—he looked at Sparrow, Raven, and Cat and changed what he was about to say—"uh, *marry* her."

"Have you ever seen anyone else like, ah, yourselves?"

"Not once. Though to be honest, we haven't really tried. London is enough right now—the work is too hard and the nights are too fun!" The Mouser grinned.

"That fellow from the circus thought he had seen people like us before. Of course, he also thought you were a demon," Chauncey pointed out.

"No, no—you're thinking of that horrible priest with the dogs. The circus fellow—lion tamer, I believe—thought we were each the perfect, final version of our race, top of the evolutionary ladder, you might say. He was very taken with Darwin."

"This is from someone who thought we were overgrown monsters from the sewers." Chauncey indicated a scar on his left ear. "His bullet stung."

"Dreadful incident. I'm glad we got his purse *and* his whiskey."

They were being funny, Snow realized, tossing it off, but the Mouser was gripping his cards too tightly, and Chauncey was tapping his tooth. Cat's claws were out around her comb, and Sparrow stared at the floor.

"Your bid, Snow," Raven said quietly, getting them back to the game.

## Chapter Sixteen

# Meanwhile, Back at the Castle . . .

THE DUKE HIRED INVESTIGATORS TO LOOK FOR his daughter, who was presumed to have run away. Some were at the estate, looking for clues. Some traveled abroad. Farmers and locals were searching the forests and surrounding land. The kitchen staff was mourning, and gossiping. The duchess was doing her best to look like she was helping.

Alan was practicing Beethoven and thinking very hard.

*It's almost like the spell weakened.* He thought back to how close he came to telling Snow the truth about the duchess. It had hurt him; his head had hummed like a beehive for hours afterward. But despite the cursed charm around his neck he had been able to warn her. *Maybe love does have the power to break spells. Or at least* bend *them.*

The wretched bell rang. He sighed, put his fiddle down, and hurried up to the duchess's room. She rarely wanted him to play for her anymore these days, except to mask the sounds of things in her laboratory.

As soon as he entered her room, Alan almost had to turn around and leave.

"My Lady," he said in shock.

The duchess was clad in the lightest of cloths, the filmiest, flimsiest stuff; *probably inspired by one of those Italian paintings she bought,* he thought as he lowered his eyes. She reclined on her sofa, gazing into her mirror, but could only see her head and shoulders—hence the summons, he guessed. "Oh, don't be such a dullard, boy. Come in and pick up the mirror," the duchess said, rolling her eyes but keeping them fixed on Alan as he came over and lifted the thing. She was still quite beautiful, though she lacked the plump nubility of the oil nymphs she was trying to imitate. Her hair was rougher than theirs as well, though it cascaded nicely down around her shoulders.

Alan kept his head down as he raised her mirror and turned it lengthwise. *A beautiful would-be murderess.*

"Ahhh. Perfect." She narrowed her eyes and studied herself in it, playing with a tress of her hair. "Margaret Murray Huggins wrote me something of interest about mirrors in her last letter."

"She is a very fine and noble lady, My Lady."

"Yes. But rather plain, and boring in person, I am told."

Alan sighed to himself.

"So." She changed the subject. "Who is the most beautiful in the land?"

"With young Mistress Jessica gone," he answered, as carefully and as neutrally as he could, "there is no doubt but that it is you."

"Mmmmm. . . ." She flicked her lashes and peeped up through them, admiring the effect in the mirror. She ran her hand down to her waist and over her belly. "Still young," she murmured. "Again," she added.

The mirror was getting heavy. Alan shifted his weight carefully so he wouldn't tip the mirror. Her room was unnaturally cold and clammy for such a fine early summer day. Alan thought about apple blossoms and new hay and prayed she would get tired of admiring herself soon.

"I ate the heart of a young human girl," she announced unexpectedly. "What do you think of that?"

Alan tried to think of some other way of answering, some way of hiding what he knew.

"I think nothing." He tried to hold his mouth shut, but it finished his thought against his will: "Since you did not."

She sat up on her couch. "What do you mean? I think I know whether I ate someone's heart or not." She watched him very carefully.

"You ate the heart of a pig," he answered helplessly.

"How do you know this?" Her voice was torn, half anger and half curiosity. "The man I hired . . . ?"

Alan bit his tongue until it bled. Then he bit harder.

"He tricked me! He let her go!" She was furious. She stood up, pulling the cloth around her. "I shall see to him—"

"No!" Alan cried out.

The duchess raised an eyebrow at him. "Why should *you*

care? It was your little Jessica I thought to have killed, and the Hunter was willing to commit *murder* for just a little gold."

She did have a point.

"Did you help her escape?" The duchess came nearer, rounding on him. "Did you have something to do with this?"

"I am unable to speak of anything you do not wish me to, My Lady. You know that."

She narrowed her eyes, displeased by his evasive answer. "Did—you—*help*—her?"

"No, My Lady."

He thanked his lucky stars and his grandmum for her fairy stories that he was able to answer so quickly and easily. Getting the little duchess to think of hiring a wagon to take herself away had been a difficult game of charades and suggestions, but in the end it had been *her* idea. He had not really "helped" her.

"Hm." The duchess shrugged, satisfied. "I will attend to the Hunter shortly. As always, you will tell *no one.*" She fixed him with a stare, then retreated to her dressing room.

Alan stood a moment before carefully lowering the mirror back down to its stand on the floor. Her room was silent and cold.

As he thought about these things, the realization struck him: *I shall have to leave soon. She is bound to discover the truth eventually. But when can I leave? And how?* He couldn't lie to the duchess or leave the estate without her explicit consent.

He ran a hand through his ginger hair, grabbing it to bear the pain of his tongue. Three bright drops of blood fell from his mouth onto the wood floor. He took it as a sign, but did it mean he should leave in three days, three fortnights, or three months?

# Chapter Seventeen

# Understanding

SNOW WAS SCRUBBING THE DISHES AND PLATES; Raven was watching her quietly and building a castle out of cards. It was a warm night. Chauncey and the Mouser had gone out for a walk—*drink,* she knew—and Sparrow was snoring like a hive of bees.

Soon Raven was watching her more than his cards. She caught him once or twice, his eyes flicking back to his fairy building when she turned around.

"You're very good at that," he observed quietly after a while.

She laughed, thinking about what Dolly would say to the idea of someone complimenting her on her *cleaning.* "It's honest work," she finally said. She immediately wished she hadn't.

Raven looked at his castle. "You don't approve of us," he said quietly. "Chauncey, and the Mouser, and everyone."

"No! It's just . . ." She tried to think of a nice way of saying it.

". . . that we steal for a living," he finished for her. When he looked into her eyes like that, she couldn't lie. There was sadness there, but also a little bit of humor. He raised one eyebrow slightly, daring her to make something up. It was very much like what the Mouser would do, but more genuine.

She sighed. "Isn't there—anything—else you could do?"

"What would you suggest?" He grinned. It was probably the first time she had seen him do it.

"Well, I don't know, there must be *something. . . .*"

"To learn a trade you have to be part of a guild, Snow. Often that means working, living, and sleeping with the same people. It would be hard to hide how we look."

"Couldn't you . . . I don't know . . . open up a shop or something?"

"And what would we sell?" Was Raven actually *teasing* her? "Flowers, maybe?"

"I don't know!" She ran a hand through her hair in frustration. If she was still Jessica Kenigh, of Kenigh Hall, duchess and heiress-to-be, she could have done something to give them an alternative to their life of crime. Sell some of her jewelry, if nothing else. Maybe get them positions on the estate . . . she imagined the Mouser as a butler and smiled to herself. Then she imagined him stealing something, like her mother's silver hairbrush. "It's just—those poor people you steal from."

"*Those poor people?*" Cat was standing at the door, and from the disdain in her voice it was obvious she had been listening for a while. "We don't steal from *poor* people, duchess."

"No—I meant—but what about the people you do steal from? It's still their property; they own it. What's the difference, really, between stealing from the rich or the poor?"

"She's very quick to defend her own kind," Cat pointed out nastily.

"There is a *very* big difference between the rich and the poor in London, Snow. I cannot speak for the rest of the world." Raven shrugged; the smile was gone and he was as gloomy as before.

She tried very hard to imagine the real differences between Dolly and her father. It was true the old cook didn't get many days off, but her father worked all the time too, running the estate, doing business, or talking politics with the people in town. She seemed less unhappy than he did too. And Craddoc loved his horses and dogs like they were his own children. He seemed happy enough combing them.

"Let'sss sshow her, Raven." Cat's eyes lit up. "Let'sss give her a little tour."

Raven nodded mutely. And so they took her out.

It was strange being out, escorted by them. That hadn't happened since the first night they brought her back to the hideout. The streets were still dark; Snow looked to the east for the first faint signs of light, but the fog blanketed everything in the same ghostly gray. They passed the new gas lamps the Mouser had spoken of, and Cat snorted. Snow thought it was sort of beautiful, though—a single globe of light in what was otherwise a neighborhood far too dangerous and far too late at night for her to be walking around.

Cat and Raven moved quickly and silently; Snow was hard pressed to keep up. A couple of times they ran through back alleys and had to leap over piles of garbage. Snow gathered her skirts as best she could but still managed to trip and fall into a pile of wet offal. Raven put his hand out to help her up. Cat held her nose. Once they ran right behind the back of a policeman—a real bobby, nightstick behind his back and tall round hat. He didn't even turn around.

*This is fun,* Snow realized, her breathing ragged. *This beats out being a duchess by far.* Or *a maid.* She imagined herself running alongside her new friends and family, anonymous in the night, unseen by anyone. No rules! No chaperones! She felt perfectly free, and another piece of Jessica slipped away. She pictured her life back home, if she had continued living there with things the way they were before her punishment. Perhaps a season in the city, perhaps a month of balls, escorted by her tutor or some other old bat—escorted *every*where by someone. And then marriage, and confinement to another estate except for trips with her husband, a maid, or some boring female relative.

Snow said a breezy good-bye to mugs of expensive hot chocolate and fabulous jewelry, and wondered how she could become a full-fledged member of the Lonely Ones without a tail, claws, or feathers to recommend her. *Surely there is some way—*

And then she remembered what they did when they were out and about.

A pair of gentlemen walked out of the fog, talking loudly. In the thick, wet air, Snow couldn't hear a word they were saying clearly, just a lot of "tut-tut" and "I *say.*" They were middle-aged and had thick muttonchop sideburns and moustaches. They swung shiny black canes and wore tall top hats. They were so *loud*! Snow looked around the street. Didn't they realize they were alone, and in possible danger?

*"They just came from Madame Tumenca's."* Raven barely mouthed the words, but Snow heard him perfectly. She looked at him questioningly.

*"A brothel,"* he answered. *"And an opium den."*

Her eyes grew wide in horror.

Cat was nowhere to be seen until Raven touched Snow's hand and pointed. A dark claw reached out of the shadows behind one of the gentlemen and ever so gently snicked the catch on his golden fob. An expensive pocket watch fell expertly into Cat's outstretched hand. When the men vanished down the street—Snow could see they were walking unevenly, as if half asleep—Cat reappeared by her side, grinning and dangling the shiny gold watch.

At least, Snow *assumed* it was shiny. In the thick, stuffy fog nothing gleamed or shone.

"It's a good thing Officer Barnstable is patrolling," Raven said wryly. "Otherwise those two will never make it home. There's far worse than *us* out tonight."

It began to rain big, warm drops. Snow was grateful for

it; she felt the air was clouding her head. The whole scene had occurred so quickly and strangely it seemed like a dream.

Cat beckoned and they followed.

They moved through the streets, getting close to the water at one point. Snow could smell cool saltiness and hear seagulls. The sky finally seemed to brighten a little. The streets grew better and then worse again, cobbled and bricked and then back to dirt and large stones. Their footsteps, even Snow's, made no noise.

They appeared to be nearing their destination. A gigantic warehouse loomed before them, from which foul smelling smoke drifted.

"What is this place?"

"A poorhouse."

Cat pointed and they went around the back. Raven found a window some feet up and gave Cat and then Snow a hoist.

Snow had only a vague idea of what a poorhouse was: some place set up by the government to take care of people who couldn't find work. She looked through the window, wondering what the point of this outing was. What she saw was a nightmare.

It was cold. Breath froze in the air like spirits departing the inhabitants. Old people and young women, all wearing the same rough, colorless uniform, were shivering despite the fabric. A feeble coal fire burned at either end of the enormous room. Pools of flickering lantern-light illuminated groups huddled over work.

Snow sucked in her breath when she saw what they were doing.

They were grinding bones—piles and piles of all kinds of bones, large and small, blunt and sharp. Ivory, white, and yellow. Some with a little meat still on them. One small group pulled giant round stones like a hellish grain mill; pale-skinned women would carefully guide a bag of bones in on one side, and another pair filled a bag with the fine white powder that was produced. Bone dust settled over everything, and everyone, turning them into ghosts.

One old man, hunched over sorting a pile of bones, stuck one in his mouth and sucked at it, hoping for marrow. Snow had to work hard not to gag.

Everyone was thin and listless. The work was silent except for scrapes and grinding, and occasional groans.

"The powder is sent to factories." Cat hissed in disgust, as if she thought this an inappropriate use of bones.

"They separate families," Raven whispered. "When a poor family comes in, the old people and wives come here, the men go to a different section, and the children go to yet another. They're not allowed to see one another."

Snow felt weak, but she couldn't turn her eyes away.

"This isss what the rich do with the poor," Cat pointed out, smug and disgusted.

"They figure if you have no work that it's your own fault," Raven said, "that you must be lazy, or immoral."

"So you ssee, it is *hard* to ssympathize with the rich."

Snow felt as weak as the people in the poorhouse looked. The smell of burning bones made her feel faint, but it did not dampen her anger.

"So what do you do about it?" she demanded. "You just steal and that's all right, because the people you steal from are terrible? Do you ever do anything to help *these* people?"

"Sometimes I leave something in the charity box." Raven shrugged, a little abashed.

Cat hissed. "Would *they* do anything for *me*?" she asked peevishly.

Snow just glared at Cat. She had to control the urge to slap her.

The other girl must have realized this, and for once looked a little surprised, and unnerved. Maybe it was the fact that Snow was more than a head taller than she was, or maybe it was just the force of her emotion. *I'll bet she thought I was a milksop.*

Cat looked down at her hand, the watch still clutched in it. She growled, then pitched herself through the window, landing silently on her paws and toes. Raven and Snow watched as she scampered through the shadows to the old man who had been sucking a bone. She made a little noise and the man turned around, surprised and scared. Cat held up the watch, but he didn't react. She waved her hand in front of his face; he didn't follow it. He was blind. She took his hand—he flinched but made no noise—and wrapped it around the watch, pushing it to his chest. Then she scampered away again, back up to the window.

The old man waited a minute, listening by instinct to see if anyone noticed. Then, with a growing smile, he held it to his ear and listened to the tick-tocks.

"Someone will just take it from him," Cat hissed in disgust.

Snow realized that if she said anything Cat would just dismiss it, or ignore it, so she said nothing, letting the gravity of the act speak for itself.

Their trip back to the hideout was slower, each of the three lost in his or her own thoughts. Snow observed that even when they strolled, the two Lonely Ones had ways of making themselves unnoticeable.

They paused once to look in a wealthy mansion, partly for a comparison of opposites and partly because Snow was genuinely interested in how city gentry lived. The house they chose to peek in had its own tiny ballroom that had gilt ceilings and was tiled with silver mirrors from the previous century. The people who owned it were still asleep, but the maids and servants were already up preparing for the day. They wore uniforms that matched, all of them. Snow loved the dumbwaiter, the tiny hand-cranked elevator that allowed them to move silver-domed meals and less-fascinating stuff like laundry from floor to floor. There was a library with a small fire and thousands of books. Snow wondered what it would have been like to live there for a season, if she had a debut.

But as much as the wealth intrigued and distracted her, she was much more affected by the prosaic sounds of clinking glassware as it was being washed, and the low, whispered laughs of the help. She felt a pang of homesickness.

*I wonder if Gwen or Dolly think about me.*

Finally they left and wandered back home.

Snow was quiet the entire way, though her shoes rang louder against the pavement than theirs. In the living room she distractedly took off her cloak, staring into space, thinking of all the things she had seen.

"Are you all right?" Raven asked.

"Yes, I—" She shook her head. "It's just—the city is so *extreme*. Such wealth and poverty—and—" She didn't even know what to make of the brothels. "It's just a lot to think about." She smiled wanly.

"The roof is a good place for thinking. I mean, about things like that. It's where I always go. Would you like me to show you?"

She was exhausted and not a little bit sad, but he looked so eager, biting his lower lip, his brown eyes hopeful.

"Sure," she answered. "I'd like that."

They went into his and Sparrow's room. Hidden in the back was a rickety wooden ladder that led up to an unused closet on the second floor. From there they walked through a narrow tunnel between the inside walls of the house. It fed into a crawl space that led up to the roof at a fairly steep angle, probably beside a gable.

*How many other hiding places are there like this in London? How many people are there like the Lonely Ones, living shadow lives of the people who really live there?* She thought about her life piggybacking on someone else's life and wondered if anyone strange inhabited the walls of Kenigh Hall.

Finally they emerged in a dusty unused attic, which might have frightened Snow if she were alone, not so much from the eerie silence and cobwebs as the cracks in the plaster and the few safe planks to walk on without falling through to the floor below. Raven opened a window in the second-to-last gable and crawled out to the ledge, turning back to offer her a hand. Heights did scare her a little, but the space on which to walk was wide, and soon they were scrambling up the slate roof to sit on top of the gable, which somehow felt safer.

Snow gasped at the view.

They could see all of London just waking up. The streets had felt mostly flat when they ran along them, but from up there she could see slight hills and tiny valleys, houses descending one street and climbing up another. They looked jampacked; she would not have believed there were any alleys between them if she hadn't been there herself. Chimneys rose crookedly up in all directions like a field of strange, sick plants. Smoke drifted from them and joined the morning fog. The sky was patchy with stars, and layers of cloud were lit red from the lights of the city below. Everything glowed orange, like the whole city was slowly burning.

The sounds of morning were muffled. Occasionally a night watchman's call rose up to them, or the cry of a city bird.

"You can see the whole world from up here," she breathed.

"Yes." He smiled faintly. "None of the others really like heights. Sometimes Cat comes, but she talks too much."

Snow couldn't imagine it.

Raven looked out over the city, as if hoping to find words there. His pale brow furrowed. "It's almost like . . . I can fly up here, you know?"

She thought about the feathers on his arms and didn't say anything.

"I *dream* I can fly. Every night. With the other ones." He pointed to a raven arcing silently by on huge wings. "I can understand what they say, you know. I hear them talking about their nests, and food, and how wonderful the wind is on certain days." She thought about her own ravens, how much more pleasant her confinement would have been if she could have understood them.

He looked down at his feet, kicking a pebble off the roof. "I just don't understand it. Why would I think these things, or dream them, and not be able to do it? It's not fair. I feel like I'm . . . an accident, or a mistake."

"Raven." Snow put her hand on his arm. "It must be terrible. But—look at me. I'm just a person. I can't talk to the birds, I can't see in the dark, and I can't do anything the rest of you can. I wish I could." She had started out saying it to console him, but tears sprang to her eyes when she thought about it. *My life would have been so different. . . .*

"What do you dream about?" he asked softly.

"Home. And sometimes I dream that my father really loved me, and talked to me like a real dad. And there was no duchess. Those are the worst."

It was Raven's turn to be silent. They spent the last hour before dawn that way, watching the city wake up. When Snow grew sleepy she put her head on his shoulder, and he didn't pull away.

# Chapter Eighteen

# The Castle

"I MUST FIND HER, IF SHE STILL LIVES."

The duchess opened up a drawer of her vanity and began taking out all sorts of instruments—brass rods and gears, glass eyepieces and lenses. Two days had passed; perhaps the Hunter was dead. Alan could not think of a way to be gone by the morrow. He thought of the droplets of blood.

"Do you know how a mirror works, Fiddler boy?"

Though he had held it a thousand times for her while she gazed at herself, Alan had to admit he had never really given it much thought. He slowly shook his head.

"It's all about light."

With the careful diligence of a butler polishing silver, with the grace of a woman born to court, her slender finger began fitting pieces together, assembling the machinery. "Light bounces off of you, taking your image with it. When it hits a polished surface, it bounces back at the same angle, letting you see yourself in the same light." She chuckled at that.

Alan failed to see where she was going with all of this, but it had to be no place good.

"Mirrors, telescopes, microscopes . . . they all work on the same basic principle, gathering light and bending and shaping it so we may see better." She looked through a lens, blew on it, and fit it in a holder that looked like two angular hands clasping. "Light travels forever, Fiddler, until it is stopped by something. And if you have the right tools you can help it travel *farther.*" She erected a white silk screen stretched taut on a frame like a drum, then adjusted some knobs and screws. The whole contraption looked a little like a fair or a circus as it might be seen from above, Alan decided. *Or a clock and a telescope that had danced together and exploded.*

"I prepared for this day a long while past."

She lit a candle behind the screen and wound a key. A hazy image was sucked into view, and she turned some knobs and adjusted some rods until it came into focus. A blurry, unfamiliar face came into view, looking down into the screen, making faces and pouting her lips. As if—

*As if she were looking into a mirror,* Alan realized.

## Chapter Nineteen

# Clockwork Changes

SNOW LOOKED AT THE PRETTY LITTLE COMPACT the duchess had given her long ago. The silver filigree front had tarnished a little; she used the corner of her dress to rub and polish a particularly bad spot. She snapped it open in her palm, feeling the satisfying click of a well-made object. In the small round mirror her face appeared pale and grave. At one time she had been accustomed to make funny faces in it. She snapped it closed again with a sigh.

"Cat," she said.

Cat jumped. *Perhaps she thought the normal human couldn't tell when she was being watched.* She had a lot to learn, about many things.

"Here." She held out the compact. "I want to give you this."

It was a rainy fall night outside, and in their basement home it was damp, cold, and boring. *A thoughtful day.* Cat loathed getting wet and tended to spend the rainier days inside, sleeping or being grumpy. She always watched Snow when she brushed her hair, or cleaned or fixed her nails, especially when she was looking at the tiny mirror. Sometimes her claws came out and retracted again and again when she saw the pretty little thing, as if she ached to hold it.

So now of course she looked at Snow with suspicion. "Give it to me? Why?"

"Because you should have something beautiful and nice, just for yourself, and I know how much you like it."

*Because I am no longer the person who needs it.* Still, it was hard to give up, as one of the few emblems left of her former life. *Because I am a Lonely One now, and we share. Because once I was a girl who did what people told her, more or less, and was expected to stay pretty so boys would like me, so men would like me—but it's still my fault when they kiss me.*

*Because you don't have to steal it. It is yours by gift.*

She put it in the other girl's hand, closing her own hand around Cat's.

"Please take care of it."

Cat opened the mirror wonderingly, with a flick of the same claw that had loosened Snow's locket, what seemed like years ago. She looked in the tiny mirror, wrinkling her nose and touching her cheek, watching the effect.

"Would you like me to brush your hair?" Snow offered impulsively.

Cat hissed, as if she knew there was a catch to accepting the pretty thing. "Only girls—sissy girls—care about how they look."

*Spoken like a true sister in a family of brothers.* Snow smiled, remembering Alan's stories of all of his siblings. She frowned, deciding she was done with the younger girl's attitude.

"Don't be ridiculous, Cat. You can be beautiful *and* strong and scary *and* still steal like a thief. You have that choice. I didn't. Now come here and be *quiet.*"

Shocked, and still entranced by the pretty thing, Cat sat meekly while Snow went to get her brush and pins.

# Chapter Twenty

# The Castle

"NO, IT CAN'T BE!"

The image came into focus; the face became clear.

Alan gasped.

It would have been a pretty girl's face but for the yellow slit eyes and the sharp, fangy canines she kept running her tongue over.

"A demon . . . ," he said wonderingly.

"It can't be . . . ," the duchess said again. She fell back onto her couch in the least graceful movement Alan had ever seen her perform.

Alan kept watching; to his amazement the image shifted and he saw *Snow*. She was brushing the girl-beast's hair, smiling and saying something. He wished he could hear. She didn't appear to be in any danger, and from the way the picture suddenly shifted again and focused on the first girl's face, it was obvious Snow was forcing her to sit still. Like a mother or an older sister would.

"I must go," the duchess breathed, her hand on her head and reaching for her smelling salts. "As soon as I can without arousing suspicion . . ."

I *must go before she does.* His thoughts raced. He had to find a way to escape the charm on his necklace. *True love will break a spell, but my love for Snow was only enough to weaken it, not destroy it completely.* He sighed.

*I dinna love* anything *with* that *sort of passion.* And then he had an idea. . . .

# Chapter Twenty-One

# A Strange Visit

SNOW WAS FALLING.

She peeked through the window at her namesake, the white flakes that drifted down. Sparrow told her it snowed less in the city than in the countryside, on account of the pollution, factories, and warm bodies of tens of thousands of people. He had thrown a snowball at the Mouser on their way out that evening, upsetting the young man's dignity. Cat got him back in a flash, and they had all set out giggling and horsing around into the night.

Snow smiled to herself. It would be her first Christmas with her new family in just a few weeks, and she had been working on some surprises for them. First was a plum pudding she had made and set aside a month ago to age properly. Dolly used to add a spoonful from the one the year before—"Just like the Queen's cook does"—so in every Christmas would be a little remembrance of Christmases twenty, thirty years past.

She was also gathering presents. For Sparrow she had knit a striped scarf in red and yellow, his favorite colors. For Cat she had saved her wages and bought a pretty little comb for her hair that almost matched the mirror. For Raven, a book of poetry by Edgar Allan Poe. She had yet to decide about Chauncey and the Mouser. *A pipe, maybe, for Chauncey—a real meerschaum one . . .*

She was distracted from her musings by a knock at the door.

A regular knock. No code.

Snow continued sweeping. *Odd . . . most people don't even know this place is here.* Since she had joined the Lonely Ones, almost no one had called on them during the day. A brush salesman, once. Chauncey had let him in and the Mouser actually bought a boot brush, but they sternly told Snow to never do that herself.

Another knock.

*Very resolute.* Sometimes she saw little girls selling matches from house to house, or flowers . . . and it *was* Christmas . . . but she had made a promise to Chauncey, and besides, it was also for her own safety.

"Donations for the orphanage," called out a weak, feminine voice.

Snow felt her heart tremble. Ever since Raven and Cat had brought her to see the poorhouse she had set aside a portion of her wages for charity. Winter was coming, which meant the need for firewood . . . *and Christmas is coming. . . .*

"Please," the old woman called. "There's the consumption and fever we'd like to keep the wee ones from. . . ."

Snow leaned on her broom and waited, heart beating.

Eventually she heard the quiet crunching of footsteps walking away through the snow. She made a decision, throwing her broom down and putting her cloak on. She waited a few seconds so the old woman had a head start, then went out into the night.

After tiptoeing out of the alley, she spied an old woman dressed in dark clothes like a nun or a nurse padding up the street, heading toward the next likely house. *That must be her.* She waited until the woman turned a few more streets before catching up.

"Excuse me, Ma'am." Snow pulled the cloak tightly around her; she hadn't worn her mittens.

The old woman turned, a friendly smile on her face. "Yes, child?"

"Here." Snow pressed a few farthings into her hand. "For the children."

"Oh, bless you!" The woman counted them and put them into the wooden box she carried. They thumped against the bottom—apparently it was almost empty. *Poor things,* Snow thought. "The Kenigh Orphanage thanks you too."

Snow's heart stopped. "I . . . I beg your pardon?"

"That's our name, Miss. Founded by the generosity of Her Lady Duchess of Kenigh."

She felt faint. Silver stars appeared at the edge of her vision, mingling with the snow. *It can't be . . .* "Not from Wales," she said slowly. "Not the Welsh Kenigh. Surely someone else . . ."

"No, that's the one. If you know her, you must have heard the story." The old woman looked at her curiously.

"I . . . fear I have not."

"Sad it is, really." The old woman clucked her tongue. "Apparently the good duchess was mad—even went so far as to try to kill her own stepdaughter. Runs in her family's blood, they say. They got her treatment, though, at a sanitarium in France or some such place. She's better now, but weak in heart. The orphanage is just one of the many good deeds she has done to try to make up for what she did during her darker days. Are you all right, Miss? You look a trifle pale."

Hardly surprising.

*Could it be true? Does everyone know the story of what she tried to do to me?* And then: *Is she really better? This orphanage she founded, the sanitarium—could she be healthy now, and normal?*

"What happened to the stepdaughter?" she finally asked.

The old woman shrugged. "That's another sad part, dearie. No one knows. She must have fled for her life."

"What a . . . remarkable story." Snow cleared her throat. "Where is the duchess now, pray tell? Back in Wales?"

"No, she has an apartment here in the city, on Letheridge Street, until she finishes up with the administrative affairs of the orphanage and a few other things." The old woman leaned in closer and whispered, *"It's rumored she is looking to adopt. . . . Her stepdaughter was her husband's only child, and she is far past childbearing years.* If you ask me, though, it's another sign of madness—trying to adopt a commoner, and at her age!"

"It does seem a wonder," Snow agreed. *Letheridge Street.*

"How do you know of the duchess?" the old woman suddenly asked, sharply, Snow thought.

"My husband is from Wales," she answered promptly. "From near the Brecons. He's told me stories." *Every lie should hold a hint of truth.*

"Ah. Well." The old woman seemed satisfied. "Thank you again, kind miss. God bless thee," she said and tottered off down the street.

Snow watched her until she was a small, dark ball on a white and gray background, then disappeared completely into the snow and night.

She could not have said why, but Snow decided not to tell the Lonely Ones. Perhaps she was afraid they would worry, or lock her in—or simply make comments or accusations she wasn't sure she could defend against. She would see the woman herself, first, and verify what the charity beggar had said. *Then* she would tell them about her discovery.

It made sense, sort of.

The first thing she did when she had a moment alone was to write a note to the duchess:

> *My Lady,*
>
> *I have heard that things are different with you now. If people speak truly, I would be glad to*

*make your reacquaintance. Meet me at Trafalgar*
*Square, midday on the morrow so that I may see*
*for myself.*

*I remain,*
*Jessica*

She sealed it and paid a local child to deliver it.

*And after I see her? And if she has not changed?* What if the
duchess tried to kill her again?

Snow panicked for a moment at what she had begun,
images of the tall and frightening duchess looming over her
with knives and candy-sweet smiles.

She shook her head.

*I shall stay in crowded, public places with her, and if she should*
*try anything—I am a Lonely One. I shall run or fight and be gone*
*before she or anyone can follow.*

But what if she really were better?

That was harder to think about. She could go back. To her
father, and Alan, and Dolly . . . and maybe, just maybe, Anne
and she would get along this time. She could go *home*.

And leave the Lonely Ones?

She looked around at the tiny but snug basement, the
cheerful blue-and-white tablecloth that now covered the
old stained table. The pile of books she had been reading to
Sparrow, Chauncey, and Raven . . . the place where she had
been hiding the comb for Cat. The Mouser's waistcoat, due
for a pressing, hung by her iron.

She would be Jessica Kenigh again, a little duchess, heir to Kenigh Hall, with a fleet of servants, horses, hunting dogs, land, and jewelry. And her old room.

She shook her head.

None of it bore thinking about until after she had met the duchess. *Then* she would decide.

# Chapter Twenty-Two

# Alan

HE WAITED UNTIL THE DUCHESS HAD BEEN GONE a week.

It was obvious that even with all her skills and talents she had not been able to figure out precisely where Snow hid. Constant surveying of the reflection in the pocket mirror finally indicated a city—London—deduced from the smog and the buildings in the background.

"I shall move there for a while," she had announced, "and take all of this equipment with me. I shall say it is for . . . charity work. To . . . make up for my sins of being a bad mother. If I had been better, she never would have run away."

She smiled as she tried out this lie, but Alan found himself agreeing with her last sentiment wholeheartedly.

"Well, and who knows. I even have an idea—a gift, in return for forgiveness." She toyed with a piece of equipment Alan hadn't seen before, a golden ball. Then she shrugged. "She will still be useful."

She moved very close to Alan, gazing into his eyes so her order would have its full effect. "And Alan, no word of this to the duke. Or anyone else. *And stay here until I return.* I may have need of you."

He nodded. "Yes, My Lady."

The moment he felt it was safe, Alan cornered Gwen.

"Gwen—I have to go, for a while."

"Oooh, the Lady's not going to like that." She smiled down at Alan, taller than he by just an inch or two, and looked like she was barely resisting the urge to kiss him on the forehead. "What's the trouble, then?"

"Ah, a girl, Gwen. It's a long story. A lass from the pub the next town over."

The charm apparently made no effort to keep him from lying to *other* people.

Gwen grinned wickedly. "I *knew* it, Alan McDonald! I knew it! Your innocent face . . . but I knew you had something about you!"

"Aye." He grinned what he hoped was a wicked grin, then sobered. "I'm going to be staying with a friend o' a friend of mine, who owns a tavern in London; here's the address." He handed her a piece of paper, and she looked at it carefully, nodding, like it meant something to her. "Now this is very important, what I'm about to tell you. If Jess . . . ah, Snow, ever comes back, you tell her that's where I am, all right? And if anyone ever comes looking for me . . . anyone . . . *strange* looking, not like you or me, I mean, or is looking for her . . .

or me . . . you tell them to find me there, all right?"

She looked puzzled.

"'Strange,' Alan?"

"If it ever comes up, Gwen. You'll know if they come." He thought about the cat-girl's eyes and fangs and figured it would be pretty obvious. "Promise me, Gwen. Promise!"

"I promise." She said it slowly, but Alan could tell from her face that she was serious. Then she brightened. "Good-bye, then, Alan. You're a good sort. And good luck with that girl of yours!"

*Thanks. I'll need it—even if it's not the girl you think.*

The small town and estate of Kenigh never forgot the day Alan left, pack on his back, bow and violin in hand. He strolled over the hill and down the road, fiddling madly as he went.

## Chapter Twenty-Three

# Reunion

NONE OF THE LONELY ONES NOTICED SNOW'S
extra attention to her dress, the hours of ironing and fluffing; nor did they see her fix her hair using the bottom of a
pan as a mirror. *And hopefully they will never have to see the
note I left them.* It was hidden under the lantern, just a corner
sticking out.

*Friends,*

*Fate has served up what could be a most
strange and wonderful reunion. It seems there
is a good chance my stepmother has completely
reformed, emotionally and mentally. If this
proves not to be the case, however, please know
that I am to meet her in Trafalgar Square,
midday, in public. If I do not return by five
o'clock this evening then there has been trouble.
The duchess Anne has an apartment on
Letheridge Street.*

> *With any luck, this will prove all worries*
> *foundless!*
>
> > *Your sister,*
> > *Snow*

Her plan was to return no later than four o'clock and steal the note back before any of them woke up, which was usually around seven or eight.

*They'll never know.* It was just in case.

She checked her outfit one last time before leaving, and made sure everyone was asleep. Maybe she would make them something special tonight, to make up for this little deception.

*But it isn't really a lie, is it?*

It was a long walk to Trafalgar square, but she kept an even, ladylike pace, holding her head high and lifting her skirts to step up. She had never been to the famous plaza before, but she had read about all of the pigeons that inhabited it and the old women who sold bags of seed to feed them. Snow left early so she could do it herself, jamming a few crusts of bread into her clean dress pocket right before she left.

When she finally came to the square it was exactly as she had imagined it—just much, much bigger—with gleaming white pavement and a truly gigantic fountain in the middle. What she thought was a darkly paved area at second glance turned out to be thousands of pigeons. She felt elated, but small. Snow was just a medium-sized girl, a maid, standing timidly in a corner of this magnificent monument, whom no one would notice when they walked by.

Then Snow giggled. The expensively dressed pairs of men and groups of large-bustled ladies strolling across the square looked, in fact, exactly like pigeons. Men puffed out their chests as they spoke to pretty women, and fat women rocked and pecked, gossiping in the shade.

According to the clock tower Snow still had a few minutes, so she crept up to the closest patch of *real* pigeons and carefully took out a handful of crumbs.

She needn't have worried about stealth. Like everything else in this upside-down city, city birds were very different from their timid country cousins. Quick, greedy eyes saw her instantly and a dozen pigeons flew at her. Before she could react, three of them had landed on each arm, and one fat brown one roosted on her head.

Once she got over her surprise and fear—the pigeons' feet dug into her—she began to smile. Then, for the first time in a very long time, Snow laughed, out loud and uproariously. The pigeons continued to eat, cocking their heads at her as if they were trying to get the joke.

"Well, Jessica, I see your way with animals hasn't changed at all."

Snow froze, then slowly turned around.

She had envisioned her eventual reunion with the duchess a number of ways: a dramatic, eloquent fight between two well-dressed ladies as Snow told her off; a violent, bloody struggle in which Snow was forced to kill her; a pathetic, emotional scene in which the duchess apologized and wept. But never had Snow imagined it would be with a pigeon on her head.

The duchess was dressed simply and elegantly, in dark petticoats with thick trim that made the people around her look gaudy and clownish. Her hair was perfect and high off her crown like a Roman empress, and two expensive, simple pearl drop earrings swung slightly in the breeze.

But was there more steel and snow in her hair than gold this time? *And doesn't she look smaller, or frailer?*

The duchess had her eyebrow raised in the familiar mocking way, but her eyes were softer, and her lips had a faint smile.

"My Lady." Snow curtsied so gracefully and elegantly the pigeon on her head wasn't disturbed. She shook the birds off of her.

"Jessica," the old duchess said softly. "I'm . . . so *glad* you're all right." It was as if her face melted a little.

"No thanks to you." Snow raised her chin defiantly.

"I know, I know—I know I do not deserve your forgiveness." The duchess put a hand to her head and patted her forehead with a handkerchief in a gesture Snow did not remember. Maybe it had something to do with her treatments. "I have been *so cruel* to you. . . . When I received your note . . . it was like God was giving me another chance."

Snow didn't know what to say. This wasn't the way she had pictured their reunion at all.

"Are you . . . well?" the duchess asked after an uncomfortable moment.

"I'm fine, yes," Snow answered coolly.

"And you have found a . . . suitable situation?"

*She really thinks I'm a maid. I must play the part well.* "I am employed by—and living with—a most respectable family." *With furry ears. And tails.*

"Amazing." The duchess sighed, and sounded like she meant it. "I—I commend you for your strength. . . . I am not sure I could do such a thing. . . . Few . . . women of means could . . ."

Snow shrugged—a habit she had picked up from Raven. *And distinctly unladylike, speaking of ladies.*

"Jessica," the duchess tried again. "I understand if you do not trust me, but—let me at least have a chance to talk with you, to show you how I have changed. Spend the afternoon with me! We will . . . stay in public places, if you feel more comfortable with that, with the crowds around. We can spend a real day in London, as two ladies. We could start by setting you up with a . . . proper wardrobe." She held the handkerchief to her nose and looked Snow's ratty dress up and down.

For some reason this made Snow smile. *Just like the old duchess.* It shouldn't have comforted her, but it did. A little glimpse of the old, shallow woman somehow made the new one more real. *We're both two people now. It was the duchess and Jessica, and now I'm Snow, and she's . . . she's . . .*

She looked up at the woman's face. The duchess looked hopeful, and concerned.

*. . . Anne,* she decided.

For that one afternoon Snow was transported to the perfect, if somewhat occasionally uncomfortable, fantasy life she had always dreamed of. She could not think of the duchess as her mother, but she was getting much better at finding roles that fit now, both for herself as well as for other people. *Aunt,* she decided, or much older sister-in-law.

The first place they went was indeed a dressmaker's. The duchess silenced any snootiness or shocked looks directed at Snow's dress with a raised eyebrow and a cutting remark. The duchess sipped a cup of tea while Snow stood on a stool and they measured her. Snow talked about her present life—with major alterations. The Lonely Ones became a family with many children, with Chauncey as the father, and the Mouser as a favorite uncle. The mother had died, she extemporized.

Apparently the duchess did not feel comfortable discussing her own situation in front of the seamstresses.

Snow was fascinated by the free cup of tea, something she would not have thought twice about in her previous life as Jessica. Something she had taken as a matter of course before was often too expensive now; the Lonely Ones reused leaves several times before throwing them out, making weaker and weaker drinks with each cup. And lumps of sugar! Snow hadn't had any except a little to bake with since her "new employment."

The duchess picked out a matching hat, umbrella, and purse, which they took with them; the dress itself would be ready the next week. Snow felt special walking out of the store with wrapped brown-paper parcels under her arm; she was already planning to use some of the paper to cook fish in and carefully cut up the rest for letter paper.

They wandered some more, mostly just looking in windows; despite her insistence on keeping beautiful, the duchess wasn't, at heart, a shopping woman. She did take Snow to a little boutique where everything smelled good and had French names, and bought her cold cream that smelled like roses, powder that smelled like lavender, and toilet water that smelled like freesia.

"You're young," the duchess said. "You should wear floral scents."

Snow had no idea what she meant, but she already felt beautiful just holding the pretty little jars.

Finally they stopped for a *proper* tea in a lovely little salon that was so fancy no one looked at Snow or questioned her appearance next to the beautiful duchess. The two women were served a silver tiered tray of tiny sandwiches with the crusts removed, cucumber and smoked salmon and dill, and sugar-sprinkled scones with fresh clotted cream and strawberry jam, and on the top, tiny little tea cakes topped with sugared violets.

Snow had to pace herself; it had been a long time since she had eaten anything so good. She also snuck a chocolate and violet cake into her pocket for Sparrow.

"I suppose—I suppose I will tell you what has happened with me . . . ," the duchess said, nervously sipping her tea.

"I am interested," Snow said, a little more forcefully than she meant.

With one dainty, gloved pinky extended from her cup handle, the duchess told her story.

It was very much like what the old woman had told Snow, except for the breakdown Anne experienced soon after Snow disappeared. The duchess blushed as she told how she had raved like a madwoman and threw herself against walls and hurt herself until they brought a doctor, who immediately ordered that she be sent to a sanitarium in Bath—not France, as the woman working for the orphanage had said.

She was there for a number of months, taking the healing waters, listening to improvement lectures, and even being leeched. More scientific treatments were also administered, and magnets and the theories of mesmerism were applied, but it was one little old doctor from Prussia who effected a cure, using the most advanced electric techniques.

"Though sometimes I get the most infernal headaches," Anne admitted. "Anyway, after I was . . . *cured* . . . I realized the horrendous thing I had tried to do, through the calmer eyes of sanity. I put a reward out for you, advertisements in newspapers . . . I even sent agents all over the countryside and Cardiff, thinking you would have stayed with friends or some sort of relation. When it was apparent you weren't coming back, or you were dead, I decided to devote my life to as much charity as possible. If there was no way I could undo the evil my previous madness had wrought, at least I could spend the rest of my time on earth bringing good into other people's lives."

An inspiring story. If the duchess had looked Snow in the eye while she said it, and had wept, the younger woman wouldn't have believed a word of it.

But she finished the story dry eyed and trailed off, staring through the window of the shop at something far in the distance, or perhaps far back in her own mind. There was no look of sadness, just wonder and loss.

"It's getting late," she said suddenly. "Your employers must be getting annoyed."

"Yes, I should be getting back." Snow stood up. "Thank you for a lovely afternoon." Everything she said sounded too formal, but she wasn't sure what else to say. "And the tea, and the clothes . . ."

"Oh, they are nothing." Anne waved her fingers tiredly. "I shall not rest until I have earned your forgiveness, and re-earned your trust."

"I shall have a hard time forgiving what you attempted," Snow finally ventured, though she longed to say just the opposite.

"I . . . understand."

The duchess looked down at the floor for a long moment. From that angle Snow could see just how high and sharp the other woman's cheekbones were, and how age was making her skin taut and dry, like the life was being sucked out of her from inside. "Only—" She paused, hopeful. "Only—*do* come visit me at my apartment. When your dress is ready—a week Wednesday. You can try it on there. I'll have the seamstress come on the chance alterations will need to be made."

Snow didn't know what to say. The duchess was finally try-ing to—begging to—act like a mother, and the girl saw in her mind's eye another perfect, if somewhat strained, afternoon of chatting—Anne sipping tea, Snow telling her about things she saw . . . *Just like today, only better . . .*

She paused too long.

"I see you still do not trust me at all," the duchess said disappointedly. "What if you were to bring a maid friend? She shall keep watch for you."

*Well, that's out of the question,* Snow realized glumly. Even if she did decide to finally tell the Lonely Ones about the duchess and their reacquaintance, she had a hard time imagining Cat dressed up as a lady's maid, her tail going unnoticed by Anne.

"We shall see," Snow replied, uncertain. There was a telltale gleam in Anne's eyes that reminded her of the old duchess; she could tell that Snow's "maybe" was really more of a yes.

"Oh, do come! You won't be disappointed. I shall order the best sandwiches for us . . . and maybe some music . . ."

*Music.*

"Before I go," Snow said as casually as she could, "may I enquire as to the health of Alan?"

"Oh," the duchess said, surprised. "Well, I don't know, really. Apparently he stole some jewelry from your father—a locket that matches yours. I received a letter about it." Her eyes grew black for a moment. Then she smiled and waved her hand. "He ran off—something about a girl, another maid—not long after I came to London."

# Chapter Twenty-Four

## Discovery

SNOW WAS UPSET ABOUT THE NEWS OF ALAN. She couldn't for the life of her picture Alan with a girl, much less running off with one.

*Am I jealous?*

She turned the thought over in her mind. Thinking back on Alan's face, which was just beginning to fill out in a handsome, manly way when she left, made her smile. *Is that love, or affection?*

She frowned.

*More importantly, how did he meet this other girl?* She had only been away for half a year and had known all of the girls on the estate. Alan was friendly with each and every one, but not *too* friendly. And not as close as *she* was to him.

She had even written him a letter—all right, she had not sent it yet. It was difficult, and she wanted to go to a post office far away so it couldn't be traced. Now she had nowhere to send it. Could he have come to London?

In a peevish, pensive mood she returned to the hideout, almost forgetting to be quiet. She needn't have worried; it was four thirty and everyone was sound asleep. Snow was sleepy herself, having stayed up extra hours in the day to meet the duchess. She panicked for a moment when she couldn't find the note, but it was just pushed farther back under the lantern than she had thought.

She put the little cake she pocketed for Sparrow on the table; later she would think of some story about how she acquired it. *Maybe I just* bought *it.*

She took a quick nap, managing to awake just as the others were stirring in their own rooms. *I must be developing animal hearing, like them.* She grinned to herself as she began to cook. Maybe if she stayed with them long enough she would develop her own animal features. *I wonder what animal I would be.* Maybe a cat, like Cat; but she didn't have the personality. Maybe a raven—but did they all brood so darkly, like Raven?

*A seagull,* she decided. That was what she would most like to be. A pretty, playful bird, not too fancy.

She played with these thoughts to cover her anxiety during dinner, which nonetheless passed without a hitch. No one had noticed her absence, or mentioned her acting oddly. Chauncey complimented her on the roast quail while picking his teeth with a bone. Snow shuddered, remembering the old man at the poorhouse.

After dinner Chauncey and the Mouser went for a walk— the Mouser called it a "post-prandial constitutional," but

Chauncey used it as an excuse to smoke his pipe, which Snow had forbidden him to do inside after she noticed her clothes stinking of it. Cat was in her room, brushing her hair, and Sparrow went off "on a job."

So Snow was alone, sweeping the living room, when Raven confronted her.

"So. How was your little 'reunion' today?" His arms were crossed.

"What? I—"

"I came back early and found your note. And no, I haven't told the others. *Yet.*"

"It was fine," Snow stammered. "The duchess seems to have had a complete medical turnaround."

"Oh, has she?" It was the closest to sarcasm the usually stoic Raven had ever come. "And if she hadn't, you could have been hurt, or killed. Why didn't you tell us?"

"I'm not a complete idiot, Raven," she said, finding herself growing a little angry at his paternal accusations. "I met her in public, and made sure I was in—*public*—wherever I went with her."

"That doesn't explain why you didn't tell us. Why you couldn't have told *one* of us? Why you couldn't have told *me*?" His brow furrowed and his eyes flashed.

*Is that what he's really angry about? That I didn't confide in him?*

"Because—" She thought about it. He deserved an

honest answer, at least. "Because I was afraid you would have stopped me."

"Snow," he said, bewildered, "we wouldn't have kept you from going. A couple of us might have tagged along, hidden here and there for protection, but we wouldn't have *prevented* you. Who do you think we are? Your parents? The police? You're part of our family now, Snow. I thought you knew that. You're free to come and go as you please."

The tips of his pale cheeks burned red. Snow felt terrible; Raven was angry because he was hurt. They had taken her in, given her a job, accepted her among them, and her repayment was to not trust them.

"I'm sorry, Raven," she whispered. "All my life the people I've lived with have always tried to control me. 'Don't run.' 'Don't go out.' 'Don't play.' The duchess, my father, my tutor . . . I'm just used to lying and sneaking around people, I guess. It was the only way—for me. And *family?* When I was fourteen a boy tried to"—she still couldn't say it—"he tried to kiss me, and do other things, and for *that* I was punished. Told it was my fault. *That's* why they locked me up for two years. Not just because the duchess hated me. My father went along with it. The boy—the count—wasn't even given a stern talking-to."

Raven blinked in surprise. "I would have killed him."

"I nearly did." She smiled a little at the memory of kicking the boy in the groin. "But someday, if I was ever going to marry, there's a good chance it would have been to someone my father 'introduced' me to. That's the life of a duchess, Raven. I suppose I just assume everyone else will try to dictate my life as well."

"Even us? Even now?"

Snow just looked at the floor.

She thought she heard Raven's body relax, his arms drop as if he wasn't quite sure what to do with them.

"She's really all better?" he finally asked, trying to soften his tone some.

"She . . . seems it. They put her in a sanitarium and gave her all sorts of medicines. . . ." She told him about how she found out about the duchess's presence in town, the orphanage, her desire to make amends. She told him about the day they spent together.

"Anne—"

"Who?"

"The duchess. The duchess Anne. She wants me to come visit her at her apartment. Next Wednesday, at noon. I would like to go," she added carefully.

"Do you want to go back?" he asked, looking her levelly in the eyes.

"Well, of course I—" Then she realized he meant *back* back. Back home. To the estate. To her life, to Jessica Kenigh, duchess and heir of Kenigh Hall. To a new mother and an old father, to old friends—except for Alan—to dresses, money, servants, and animals who were pets or pests, not roommates. "I—don't know."

Raven gazed at her for a long, hard moment, then turned and walked away.

Snow felt a surge of emotions—confusion and sadness. Something was about to break, some decision had to be made, and she had no desire to do that just yet.

# Chapter Twenty-Five

# Return

RAVEN DID NOT TELL ANYONE ELSE. AT LEAST, none of the others approached her about it. Snow realized she was only pretending to debate with herself whether to visit the duchess again in her apartment; she *would* go, she would just feel guilty about it.

"I am going to see if she really is changed," she told herself. "I need more evidence."

"I want more news from home," she told herself as she scrubbed the floor.

"All right, maybe I want to see how I look in the dress," she told herself as she stirred the stew. But even this was a false admission.

Snow had a vision that she kept buried at the bottom of her thoughts like a golden guinea in a pocket, only taken out for brief looks. In it, the duchess really *had* changed. She would bring Snow back to Kenigh, full of apology and indignation at the life her stepdaughter had had to lead while in London. Her father would have missed her. Alan would hear about her triumphant return and come back. And, most secret and unlikely of all, she would introduce the Lonely Ones to everyone at home, and they would be rewarded for their care of her. They would be *welcomed* and could give up stealing. Cat could live with her like a sister or a maid. The Mouser could be introduced to the society he seemed to want to join, and Raven . . .

She knew this was close to being an impossible dream.

*But if the duchess* is *changed, why not everything else?*

The next Wednesday she took less care than she had originally planned for visiting the duchess at her apartment, not wishing to draw attention to herself. She smoothed the wrinkles out of her dress as best she could with her hands and brushed her hair a little more carefully than usual, but that was all. Raven walked through once and caught her eye, but she couldn't read what was written there; sadness, maybe, deep thought, definitely.

When the Lonely Ones were asleep for the day, Snow snuck out and made her way to the wealthier part of town. She felt strange and out of place. She tried to walk like a maid and pass unnoticed as a member of the servant class like many other young women around her, even though she was visiting the duchess, as a duchess herself, to try on elegant, voguish clothes befitting a member of the modern royalty. *Am I walking too loudly and slowly?* Her legs longed for the delicate, long strides of the Lonely Ones, the carefully balanced run of the night.

She watched all of the other people hurrying or strolling

down the streets. *Not a single one would guess I sit on rooftops, or occasionally run at night with a pack of half-animals, unheard and unseen.*

She felt like everyone was staring. But what would they accuse her of—being a duchess in maid's clothing? A maid pretending to be a duchess? A freak who consorted with thieves, unwelcome and uninvited in the daylight hours?

When she mounted the steps and slipped into the shadow of the duchess's apartment, Snow breathed a great sigh of relief. An old woman answered the door, a short, stout and stern house-motherly sort. One representative of a very familiar race. Snow didn't need to awkwardly explain why she was there; the woman immediately recognized her and brought her in.

The apartment was tiny but sumptuous; the hall, the waiting room, and the dining room were all miniature versions of the ones at Kenigh. The interior was very much like a dollhouse decorated by a fastidious and wealthy little girl. The walls had pretty painted stripes and designs on them, the rugs were rich and new, the furniture was smaller than their country cousins but burnished to a professionally butlered shine. Vases of exotic flowers stood on every open surface. *More kinds than at home in the country!*

She was led to a room that had no particular function, or maybe several; the only real features were two bay windows that stretched from floor to ceiling, whose long red velvet curtains created a pleasant nook with benches. *It could have been a dining room or a sitting room—what a waste of space.* Yet she envied it, thinking of the one common-room basement she shared with the Lonely Ones.

In the nook was a small table set with gorgeous little hors d'ouevres and niblets, a crystal decanter of sherry and two tiny glasses, and a steaming pot of tea. Another table, toward the back of the room, was put to a use so familiar it made Snow smile; it was covered with glassware, beakers, equipment, silk screens, and wire. *She takes her hobbies wherever she goes.* There was a quiet humming from a wood and metal box, and an occasional snapping sound accompanied by a small blue flash. Copper tubes ran from its back like worms, squirming their shiny way through racks of beakers and test tubes with pale golden liquid.

"You came! Oh, I knew you would." The duchess seemed unable to keep her initial excitement and glee out of her voice and expression before her face reset itself into its usual mask of courtly perfection.

Snow had not heard her come in; she was fascinated by one particular piece of the equipment that sat on the tea table, connected to the box: a golden orb with wires coming out of it, slightly tarnished and imperfectly symmetrical, just *begging* to be touched.

"Oh, you're looking at my latest experiment," the duchess said with a slightly arching eyebrow and smile. "I will show it to you later. Come, though; your dress came this morning.

It would be so much easier for us to talk if you were dressed properly."

*Same old duchess. Shallow to the core.* But Snow smiled a little herself as she was led to a changing room. The older woman was dressed less lavishly than usual; her dress and jacket were tight, so plain as to almost be utilitarian, and of dark colors.

Snow's dress, on the other hand . . .

A pair of maids helped her unwrap it and put it on—layers of crinolines, slips, and petticoats, which the teenage Jessica had hated, but which as Snow she kind of missed. The fabrics were expensive, rich red silk velvets. The underclothes were as soft as Raven's feathers against her skin.

She sat patiently as two silent girls did her hair, and she mused over the old woman who had greeted her at the door; even her voice seemed universal and familiar. It was nice to be taken care of. When they were done she looked in the mirror. Her hair was perfect, romantic and lovely, a half knot on her head with trails of hair falling down her back. *Almost as black and shiny as Cat's.* Tendrils fell over her ears like vines. She grinned despite herself, wondering what Chauncey, the Mouser, or Raven—especially Raven—would think if they saw her now.

When she was done, and sprayed with a splash of perfume, flowery and light, she presented herself to the duchess, walking in as dignified a manner as she could, head held high, neck unmoving.

"Oh, you look *beautiful,*" she said in admiration. "You could be my daughter." The comment hung in the air, awkwardly, until both women shifted in embarrassment.

"Let us—let us have some tea," the older woman finally said, indicating the table with her hand and sitting down smoothly in one of the stiff-backed, poofy-seated chairs.

*Mmmmm.* She could barely control her thoughts—almost as much as the dress, Snow had been looking forward to the edibles. Though she had eaten like a mouse—*no wait, I have seen the Mouser eat*—though she had eaten *very little* her last few years at Kenigh Hall, her appetite had grown considerably since she had moved in with the Lonely Ones. And the tiny sandwiches looked *so very* good. . . . She waited, though, until the duchess poured the tea and took a sip herself. From much experience she knew that the older woman would not indulge in any of the food. *More for me.* Snow was shocked to realize that she was actively wondering how she would be able to stuff a few sandwiches for later in her new dress, which had no pockets.

"I feel I should explain something to you," the duchess began hesitantly as she poured.

"Yes?" Snow wasn't sure she wanted to hear any explanations. As far as she was concerned, they were starting all over again.

"I . . . want you to understand some of the thoughts behind my insanity, what drove it. I feel it would be useful to you, and most instructive."

Snow still didn't want to hear anything, and was getting more uncomfortable by the second. She stuffed an entire sandwich into her mouth to hide her discomfort—worse, the duchess didn't notice.

"I wanted to give your father a child. If possible, a male heir."

Snow's ears burned. She was unused to anyone speaking this plainly about babies, especially the duchess. This was so different from the time she had coldly dealt with Jessica, when she was thirteen. . . .

"This probably would have been bad for you," Anne went on calmly. "English law doesn't deal fairly with female children and heirs. Nonetheless, your father wanted a son, and frankly, I wanted children myself."

So far, this all made sense to Snow. She suspected the insanity was coming soon.

"I am . . . an *older* woman, Jessica." The duchess sighed, as if this was a weighty admission. "I suppose it was folly for me to even try. Some would say that it has been my manlike tinkering in science, my hobbies, which has taken away some of my vital female essence."

Snow frowned. "That's silly. Just because you like, ah—" *Don't say toys!* She indicated the tubes, beakers, and boxes instead. "Didn't the Greek huntress Atalanta run and hunt like a man, and eventually marry?"

Anne chuckled. "An excellent classical reference. I thought you didn't take well to your studies."

"I like myths, and stories," Snow said peevishly, looking for a radish and butter sandwich. Those were her favorite. "Even math. It's geography and history I hated. Never understood the point—one is always changing the other."

The duchess chuckled. "So many things I never learned about you," she said distantly, almost to herself. Snow kept her eyes on the sandwich plate.

"Anyway, I suppose my desperation fed some incipient germ of madness that lay hidden somewhere in my spirit, waiting for the right circumstances to grow."

Snow thought the comparison a bit overdone, but it was interesting to hear the usually concise duchess wax eloquent.

"In my madness, I believed that eating your heart would enable me to have a baby."

Snow choked.

"And for that, I am terribly sorry."

The duchess could have been talking about how she had punished Snow unjustly, or told a vicious lie about her, or any one of a number of more prosaic things.

"But understand this: As mad as I was, there is some truth in what I am about to tell you." Anne leaned forward. Her eyes were cold. "My desperation to have a child, my obsession with my looks—these are merely a mirror for society at large. *Society* has only two uses for women: as young and beautiful things, and as baby machines. You are only wanted or useful as long as you fill one of those two roles."

"That's not true," Snow blurted out. "Women are wanted for the same thing as men—to be kind, to be wise, to work hard—"

"Maybe in a perfect world, Jessica, but not here. Not now."

"What about your experiments? What about yourself, Anne? You have done great things—"

"All of which I have had to keep secret or publish under a man's name!" the duchess hissed. "Like Georges Sand, Margaret Murray Huggins, Nettie Stevens—all in the shadow of their husbands or of fake masculine names."

"What *is* your latest work, there?" Snow asked pleasantly, trying to change the subject. She stirred her tea neatly and delicately, the way she knew the duchess liked. Inside, her mind was racing. *I don't think she is completely cured, after all. There is something broken there.* She didn't disagree with anything the other woman had said, but the look in her eye as she said it was mad.

She had chosen the right subject. The duchess's eyes lit up and she smiled.

"Ahhh. I'm glad you asked. This fits right into our discussion." She indicated the golden orb that had been sitting tantalizingly close to Snow. "Pick it up."

An inkling of doubt slowed Snow's hand, but she reached for it anyway.

"It's too late for me to have children, and perhaps too late to remain as beautiful as I once was," the duchess said. "But not for you."

"Why do you care about remaining beautiful?" Snow asked distractedly, turning the orb over in her hands. It was warm, not quite the temperature of flesh, and very pleasant to hold. *Rather like a skull,* she thought despite herself. "Father loves you."

"Perhaps. But you do not know your father very well."

"What do you mean that it's not too late for me?" Snow suddenly asked, looking up from the golden ball.

The duchess smiled, and hit a switch.

# Chapter Twenty-Six

# Falling Asleep

THE ORB GREW HOT, BUT SHE WAS UNABLE TO let go. Licks of invisible flames climbed up Snow's arms.

"My latest experiment—the *chronofin*. I realize the mixing of languages is a little gauche, *chronos* from the Greek for 'time,' and *fin* from the French for 'end,' but it has a nice ring to it, don't you think?"

The flames crawled up her neck, through her scalp and into her head. She felt her hair being lifted and separated by forces she couldn't see. Her mind slowed down and could not force her mouth to move, but one overriding thought was clear: *She is mad. She is* still *mad.*

"There are energies coursing through your body now, fixing it. They are putting a halt to the things that age us; they are cleansing your body of any traces of time. Your humours will be filtered, your muscles and filaments washed clean."

The duchess spoke casually, but her eyes were intently watching Snow for some outward signs or symptoms.

Snow concentrated on her hands, willing them to open, to drop the golden orb. She saw her fingers twitch, but that was all. She couldn't move her neck and had to strain her eyes to see.

"I really hope this works," the duchess said, with just a touch of nervousness. "Then you shall be always as you are now—a young, beautiful woman. That should more than make up for my violence toward you in the past."

While the thought of remaining young forever was of passing interest to Snow, still she panicked. A woman who thought that eating someone else's heart would confer upon her the victim's youth and abilities would obviously not make a very good scientist. Ever. Snow wondered if she was going to die. The licks of heat and tingles of things she couldn't see came down through her head like she was fainting, and cricked her neck. Horrible things like ants crawled over her eyeballs, which she was no longer able to move. She was forced to stare at the duchess.

"And if it *doesn't* work—it seems to be taking longer than it should—well, then at least you are a link in the chain of progress. Better you than me, as it were."

The duchess rose and moved out of Snow's vision. She could hear clicks and whirs as the older woman adjusted dials and knobs. She tried to scream, forcing herself so hard she thought she would wet herself, but nothing happened. The flames ran down her throat. In their wake they left a deep peace, a silence after the fire, buzzing, and storm. An absence of feeling.

The duchess moved back into her sight.

"It should be done by now." She clicked her tongue in exasperation, a habit Snow had never seen before. "Katherine!" she called.

The old house woman shuffled into view, and from her

walk Snow suddenly realized why she had seemed so familiar.

*The woman from the orphanage!* she realized. Her thoughts were muzzy and circuitous, like the moments just before sleep. *But the orphanage isn't here, is it? And shouldn't she be running it . . . ?*

*There is no orphanage. It was a trick. The woman is just the duchess's servant. It was all a trick to lure me here. There was no trip to a sanitarium, no doctor from Prussia. No one back home knows what she tried to do to me.*

*But* why *me? Why not some other victim?*

*How did she find me?*

*How did she find me?*

*How did she find me . . .*

The duchess was giving orders.

"We must go to their—*lair*—immediately. Whether or not this," she said, indicating Snow, "works, I can give her a cantrip that will cloud her mind and leave her a fuzzy memory of what occurred. But if it fails, this might be our only chance to catch them."

*Lair?*

The Lonely Ones? *She knows about them?*

Her legs burned with the remaining fires, but the rest of her was dead with lethargy. She could not even feel the orb anymore; her skin was dead. The cold followed, closing around her eyes with a will to sleep. . . .

The duchess turned to her.

"I think we can call this a failure. I was really hoping it would work, and you would thank me, and I could use it on myself safely; and we would all live happily ever after. Alas, I think we had just better make you forget about everything, just in case you actually ever recover." The older woman took a forked golden wire and stuck two of the ends into her own mouth so they hung out the sides of her lips. Snow couldn't see what she did with the other metal tail. The duchess's tongue stuck out a little, and she lisped a strange language.

Snow strained to listen, but she was already falling asleep. Her vision dimmed, but she couldn't tell if it was from her lids closing or from something scarier.

*Have to stay awake! Must warn . . .*

The duchess was rolling her sleeves up, and she put her glasses down on the table. "I'll be back in an hour. If you're dead," she said, frowning, "well—we'll give you a proper burial, back home. I promise. The streets of London can be so cruel. . . ."

And Snow was alone.

She thought; she silently screamed.

Minutes or seconds passed. She tried to blink.

Shadows flowed into the room.

Everything was still.

Cat's face appeared before her.

"She'sss not talking." Snow heard the familiar hiss. "Hey, wake up!"

Snow felt vague echoes of taps as Cat slapped her on the cheeks, and slight tremors as she shook her.

"Hey!" Cat began to panic. Her claws came out, and she scratched Snow across the face, near her mouth.

The pain finally came through. It wasn't as searing as the flames that put her to sleep, but it was enough to stir her.

"Stop it, Cat!" That was Ravens voice. "You'll hurt her!" His face appeared before Snow, pushing Cat's out of the way. The world spun; she was vaguely able to tell that he was cradling her in his arms. "Snow?"

"Hideout . . . danger . . ." It took all of her will.

"What? What are you talking about?" In the background, Cat was blurrily wrestling with the cords attached to the orb.

"Go *home,*" Snow wheezed. "Duchess . . . destroy . . ."

"Stay awake! Snow! Cat—go back. I'll take care of Snow. Warn the others—"

Cat looked unsure for a second, then scampered away, fully cat, little human.

"Snow . . . ?" Raven stroked her hair.

And the world went black.

# Interlude:

# A song overheard in a London tavern

*Hey diddle, diddle*
*I'm Alan o' th' fiddle*
*I play for a penny and a smile*
*Or buy me a drink*
*And I'll make you think*
*Your cares are gone for a while*

*Hey nonny nonny*
*From home I'm a long way*
*I look for a girl in a locket*
*Here, let me show you—*
*D'ye think that you know her?*
*The picture is here in me pocket*

*Hey moon and starshine*
*I'm in London a long time*
*I've no clue to her whereabouts yet*
*Dark haired and pale skinned*
*Black eyes and long limbed*
*Just like her mother, I'll bet*

# Snow

*Hey diddle, diddle*
*I'm Alan o' th' fiddle*
*I'll play you the sweetest song*
*I'll keep on looking*
*For her between bookings*
*And find her before it's too long!*

Part Four

# Sleeping;
# Waking Up

# Chapter Twenty-Seven

## Snowdreams

She slept.

*Once upon a time a queen and a king had a baby girl whose skin was as white as snow, lips as red as blood, hair as black as the windowpane. They named her Jessica, and raised her with wisdom and love. She never married, but took care of her parents when they grew old, inherited the kingdom, and ruled as wisely as she had been raised.*

*Once upon a time a woman bore a child whose skin was as pale as snow, hair as black as death, eyes as red as blood. The mother howled with pain and fury; the father did his duty and dashed the monster to the ground, grinding its head under his heel.*

*Once upon a time a wicked stepmother had a daughter who was not hers. Understanding the inevitable confusion, the king arranged to have the baby exposed on a nearby mountainside. Unbeknownst to him, however, the child was adopted by a family of woodland creatures: a cat, a sparrow, a mouse, a rat, and a raven. Together they lived in the wild until they were old enough to build a house. And there they lived happily until their end of days.*

*Once upon a time a girl got caught in a snowstorm.*

*"These snowflakes aren't real," she said, catching one and shaking her head.*

*"Come on," said her brother the fiddler, all bundled up against the cold. He held out his hand. "I'll help you. Mum's going to make us a big pot of stew when we get home. Rabbit, your favorite."*

*The girl took his hand, ignoring the white world and trudging along behind him. His hand was very warm.*

*A young woman sat on a rooftop, talking to a raven.*

*"As far as Constantinople, well, I've never been," it was saying.*

*"But we weren't talking about that," she said.*

*"I wish I could fly," the raven said sadly.*

*"Jess, look," the boy said.*

*He had dark eyes and eyebrows, and leaned in to reveal the secret the bird would not tell her. His lips were warm and brushed against her ear. Then he laughed, loudly—it was a prince with blond hair and blue eyes. She screamed and threw herself from the roof, falling . . . falling . . .*

*Once upon a time a girl was given a mirror by her two mothers. It was divided in three: a floor-length one, a vanity-sized one, and a tiny one hanging in a locket on one corner. The girl looked in each, seeing a wild young girl, an old dead woman, and something sad and gray. The room was a tower in the top of a castle and had five windows, each watched over by a giant gargoyle—half-human monsters with the heads of a cat, a mouse, a sparrow, a raven, and a rat. She ran from mirror to mirror, seeing nothing but sadness.*

*The door out of the room clicked and disappeared; she was locked in.*

*She ran from window to window but could not see out; a great snowstorm had blown in, drifts of white obscuring the landscape in every direction.*

*She finally sat in the middle of the floor for a very long time, regarding her reflections. The other versions of her had beautiful landscapes behind them—gardens, topiary mazes, and gently roll-ing hills and valleys stretched out as far as the eye could see.*

*Was she in a zoo?*

*Faces kept peering in at her, closely but not too close, as if they were separated by bars.*

*She wondered what kind of animal she was, but couldn't seem to move her hands, arms, or legs. Maybe she was a bird; she felt as light and silly as a sparrow. Maybe she was tiny and timid like a mouse—hence their pity.*

*"What should we do?" said one.*

*"She looks so peaceful," said another.*

*"Why?" said a third, miserably.*

*Their faces weren't quite right. There was something nightmarish about their features, something she couldn't put her finger on, but they seemed puzzled and sad, not threatening.*

*She realized they were on the other side of the mirror; she had become trapped in the glass.*

*She tried to scream, but her lips were frozen.*

*Once upon a time an old woman was telling a story to young children, about animals that could talk just like people. The children sat in front of a fire in a snug little house with thick wood walls and a thatched roof. The winter howled around them outside, but they were safe inside, listening to the words.*

## Chapter Twenty-Eight

# Beyond the Sleep of Reason

CAT RAN BACK TO THE HIDEOUT TO WARN THE others. Running, normally a joy for her, was now a necessity. She wished she had all four legs like her namesake. She used her paws to grab, climb, and leap, but down the streets it was two legs, just like the humans.

He and Cat had decided that he would take her to Cat's alley hideout. Cat would tell the others, and they would all meet there to figure out what to do. Raven tried to walk as gently as he could, cradling Snow in his arms. When he finally arrived, he laid her out on Cat's pretty little divan, the one Snow had slept on the first night she came to London. That brought a smile to the serious young man's face; he stroked her hair back and tucked an old silk blanket under her chin. Her skin was glassy and porcelain, but her colors were still healthy and vibrant.

One by one the others arrived by different routes, throwing off pursuers.

"Well, that's that," Chauncey said without preamble. "Hired thugs, all of them—with nets and bags and all sorts of nasty things." He came out of the night with a nimble leap and perched on the back of the couch where Snow slept. He balanced on the narrow edge against all reason, more like a rat than ever. They were all there, looking at Snow. "That duchess knew something of us, that's for certain. Prolly wanted to stuff us and sit us in a museum somewhere."

Sparrow made an angry snort, a whistling sound. "Trashed one, I did. Thumped him on the back of the head. Coming into *our* hideout!"

"Is he dead?" the Mouser asked anxiously.

"No. Wish he was, though. Hurting our Snow!"

"The last thing she did was warn us," Raven whispered, touching her cheek.

"Is she—is she dead?" Cat asked hesitantly.

"No—but she's not even breathing." The Mouser put his hand to her heart, and her head. "Her heart isn't beating, either. But she's warm, like there's still life in her."

"Magic?" Chauncey asked, astounded.

"Or science, or both." Raven sighed, standing up. "There was all this equipment around her, wires and golden balls and tubes. . . . We should go back and try to get them."

"Can't go back there anytime soon." Chauncey shook his head. "Place is surrounded by bobbies. And we can't go back to our old place again, I don't think. There's a place in the warehouse district, on Bank Street, that I had my eye on. . . . We should probably move our base of operations there."

"And?" Cat demanded.

"And what, Cat?"

"What about *Sssnow*?"

"Oh, don't worry, we'll find her a cure." The Mouser waved his fingers in the air as if it was no concern, but he looked worried.

"And how do *we* do *that*?" Raven asked. "Or where?"

The first thing they did was to break into the Olde Curiosity Shoppe and steal a glass cabinet in which to keep Snow. That way they could keep an eye on her while they were there, and throw a tablecloth over it while they were out. Not, perhaps, the best possible solution, but for the time being it would do.

Cat scampered around their new hideout—it was essentially half of a warehouse floor, all open.

"She would have loved thisss," she sighed. "All this ssspace."

When it was obvious that there was nothing more they could do immediately, they fell to arguing about what to do next.

"We should find the duchess and make her fix Sssnow," Cat hissed, extending her claws.

"I hardly think that the sort of woman who hires a private army to track Snow down is likely to be unprotected," the Mouser said mildly.

"Who else would know how to do the sorts of things the duchess did?" Raven asked.

"I suppose we had better find out. Ask around. Scientific circles and the sort."

"Aye," Chauncey agreed. "But except for you, and Raven on one of his good days, there's not a one of us who can interview respectable, normal people and all." He eyed Cat's lashing tail.

"We need help. But who?"

Raven coughed uncomfortably.

The letter Snow had been meaning to send, to a boy named Alan—Raven had found it and read it. His stomach had flip-flopped; she had told him so many stories about her fiddler friend. Nothing in the note was too intimate, but she was obviously quite fond of him. Of course, he *did* save her life, but still. . . . He shoved those worries and concerns aside; they were of little importance right now.

"I think I may know of someone who can help."

# Chapter Twenty-Nine

## Strangers

"AH, WE'RE LOOKING FOR A YOUNG MAN NAMED Alan," the Mouser said, smiling. Raven just stared.

The pretty young woman at the door stared back, scrunching her eyes and scrutinizing them. The Mouser shifted uncomfortably.

It had been a long journey for two unaccustomed to mixing directly with the rest of the human population. They had dipped into Chauncey's "Special Funds for Emergencies" box and had a semiprivate compartment on the train. But even with his suaveness, his passion for conversation, and his charm, the Mouser was grouchy by the end of the day, having to keep his tail tucked in and even sleep on it. And while Raven's feathers were hidden by his sleeves and not easily noticeable in his hair, he didn't much like the people, the crowds, or the Mouser's friendliness to strangers.

The bumpy carriage ride through the area where their mother had died did nothing to improve their moods.

And here they were, being scrutinized by this maid, exhausted from a trip which so far seemed to be unsuccessful.

"You don't look strange," the girl finally said, crossing her arms.

Raven and the Mouser looked at each other.

"I . . . beg your pardon?"

"Alan said I was to give his information out to people who looked *strange*. You don't look so strange." She cocked her head at one and the other. "You look like regular folks. Well, maybe handsomer than regular." She smiled at Mouser. Delighted, he opened his mouth to say something in return.

Raven sighed impatiently and pulled up his sleeve. Shiny black feathers sprang forth as he flexed his arm. "Is this strange enough?"

The pretty maid's eyes grew wide with shock.

"Aye, that will do."

Gwen didn't ask them any questions; she served them tea and biscuits and gave them Alan's address. Raven gritted his teeth through her and the Mouser's flirting, finally leaping up and demanding that they go; Snow needed them.

"Snow?" Gwen asked. "Is she in trouble? Is she all right? She ran away—I don't blame her, locked in her room all day— do you really know Snow?"

"We're taking care of her for now," the Mouser said carefully, "until it's safe for her to come home."

"Well, I'm glad she found some friends." From the tone of her voice it was obvious she was a little uncertain about the quality of friends who grew feathers on their arms. "You'll let me know, somehow, how it all turns out? I miss Jessica. . . ."

"Jessica?" Raven asked, startled.

Gwen smiled. "That's her real name. She got so pale Davey called her Snow, and then it stayed with her, at least to us downstairs folk."

"We'll make certain to let you know," the Mouser promised her.

Hours later, in a carriage back to the train station, the Mouser and Raven were silent for a long time, exhausted and bemused about suddenly heading back to London.

*"'Jessica'?"* Raven finally said, exasperated.

"It does seem a little plain," the Mouser agreed.

## Chapter Thirty

# Conversation Overheard
# in a Chelsea Tavern

"ARE YOU ALAN MCDONALD?"

The fiddler was just taking his first sip of a well-deserved ale after almost two hours of continuous playing. He looked at the three men who sat down unasked across from him and wiped the foam from his lips.

"Aye," he said slowly.

"We're friends of Snow," said Chauncey. The Mouser and Raven flanked him. Raven stared hard at the red-haired fiddler.

Alan choked.

"How did you know that 'strange-looking people' would come asking for you or Snow?" Chauncey continued before Alan had a chance to speak.

He started to answer but felt the familiar burning around his neck. The necklace sent little waves up into his head and mind, blurring his vision.

"I . . . can't tell you," he finally said, shrugging helplessly.

Chauncey gave him a hard look. "Yer friend's in trouble. The duchess did summat to her, and now she's like the dead, but not."

Alan was bewildered; this was some plan the duchess had not shared with him. What was it she said? *I even have an idea—a gift, in return for forgiveness. . . . She will still be useful.*

"We need your help, as a friend of Snow and a normal man." Alan was about to ask what he meant by that when Chauncey took off his hat to show his ears. "What we don't need," Chauncey leaned forward, showing evilly pointed teeth, "is a traitor and a looselips. Help us or not, but if you say anything to anyone, I'd sleep with me eyes open if I were you."

"I ran away to try and find Snow," Alan said calmly. "I escaped from the duchess myself. You have no worries from me, and ye have all of my help."

"Well and good, if you're saying the truth." Chauncey exchanged a look with the others. The Mouser shrugged; Raven glared at Alan. "Come with us."

They took him to their hideout, blindfolding him as they had with Snow, just in case. When they took the cloth off him, Alan opened his eyes to see all of the Lonely Ones regarding him curiously.

"You!" he cried, pointing at Cat. "I saw you! With Snow . . . in the . . . the . . ." But that was all the necklace would let him say.

Everyone looked at Cat, who for once in her life looked surprised and unsure.

Chauncey frowned. "Well, Cat *is* strange looking—for regular people," he added quickly when she began to hiss. "That's what you told the maid. . . . Strange looking . . ." He shook his head. "How you saw her is a mystery for another time. Here's your friend."

He pulled the cloth off the "table" in the middle of the room, and there she slept, like a curiosity in a sideshow or a chemist's shop.

"Snow . . . ," Alan whispered. He leaned over and touched her cheek, surprised as the Lonely Ones had been that it was warm.

Raven clenched his fists.

"Nothing wakes her up," Sparrow said quietly. "We tried everything."

"Someone must know how to cure her," the Mouser said. "The duchess couldn't have thought of all this herself. . . ."

They looked at Alan. He shook his head, shaking a little. "Books," he managed to get out. "Letters . . ."

"Well, that's it, then," Chauncey declared. "We all of us will start looking at books and scientific things—and gypsies, I guess, and magic people . . . ," he said, trailing off as he realized how ridiculous it all sounded.

"Alan, you can tell us if something looks familiar at least, can't you?" the Mouser asked hopefully.

"Oh, aye."

They made a place for Alan to sleep, though most nights he would be staying back at the tavern. One by one the Lonely

Ones went to their beds, worrying about the days to come. Raven gave Alan a curt good night; Cat remained sitting in a chair, staring sadly at the floor.

Alan went over to her, the most animal-like of his new set of friends. It was strange seeing her in person after watching her on the duchess's machine for so long.

"Don't worry, we'll help her," Alan said kindly, even if he wasn't sure he believed it himself. He resisted the urge to pat her on the head, like a cat, or one of his sisters, or Snow.

Cat nodded, but still looked sad, biting her lip. He said good night and went to his own bed.

She flicked open the mirror Snow gave her and looked into it.

"Am I really that ssstrange looking?" she murmured to herself.

# Chapter Thirty-One

# The Search

DAYS PASSED. WEEKS PASSED.

Five dark shadows and one bright bard spread out over London seeking a cure for Snow.

Alan caught Cat fixing her hair in the little pocket mirror that Snow used to carry when she was Jessica. As the girl surreptitiously pouted her lips, Alan made the connection.

"Don't!" he cried, swiping it out of her hands. He dashed it to the floor, smashing it into a thousand bright shards.

Cat hissed in dismay.

"Why'd you do that?" Sparrow asked curiously.

"The . . . mirror . . . ," Alan whispered, tugging at the golden chain round his neck.

Chauncey nodded thoughtfully. "You said you *saw* Cat. . . . It was the mirror you saw her through, somehow. But can you not tell these things, direct-like?"

Alan shrugged helplessly.

Months passed. Then a year.

Then two.

And still they searched.

And still Snow slept.

# Chapter Thirty-Two

# The Clockwork Man

THEY READ, THEY TALKED TO PEOPLE, THEY learned. They learned about metal, electricity, and chemicals; they learned about cantrips, drugs, and incantations. These were difficult things to research in this age; sometimes even Alan's charm and human features failed to get anything more than a door slammed in their faces—these were scientific times, didn't they know that? *There's no such thing as magic. . . .*

They searched libraries and questioned doctors, arcane bookstores and gypsies, curiosity shops, and practitioners of the black arts. No one had any answers for them. But one name kept coming up over and over again when they talked to the darker inhabitants of the city streets, the beggars, the fortune tellers, and the women who walked the night: the Clockwork Man.

"That's just a ssstory," Cat hissed.

"Like the one about the girl who slept forever without aging or waking up, and the five strange creatures who cared for her?" Chauncey asked archly. "We haven't found anything else; we might as well try to find him. They say he lives in the sewers and tinkers with things better left alone—sounds like our man, really."

"I'll go," Raven said. "The sewers don't frighten me."

"No, let me," Alan suggested. "You might scare him, or he might try to capture you."

"And *you* could by no means defend yourself down there!"

They glared at each other.

Although Alan saw how much the Lonely Ones cared for Snow, well, *he* had known her *longer.* And though Raven was determined to save her, he was disconcerted when he saw how handsome and cheerful the fiddler turned out to be.

"Ah, ye can *both* go," Chauncey suggested mildly, but there was iron at the bottom of his words.

The two young men descended into the sewers with a map stolen off a city worker, and hints and clues bought from shifty-eyed people. They walked for hours through large pipes and narrow tunnels, crossed incredible wide-open stone spaces and unbelievably foul-smelling streams of sewage. They argued over directions.

Things skittered around them in the darkness; once Raven thought he saw a human-sized form that moved with a rat's grace in the shadows.

"Maybe we've been living in the wrong part of town," he said ironically, indicating the parting figure.

"If you like the stink of sewers," Alan answered, wrinkling

his nose. "Though I dinna think these are *necessarily* of your kith and kin." He pointed at a mouse scurrying past. Raven started as he realized it was made of metal—a toy mouse, with cogs for eyes that moved as realistically as the real thing.

It even squeaked.

"I think we're getting closer," Alan said.

Not long after discovering the clockwork mouse, Alan and Raven came to what looked like a dead end on the map, just a big, empty blank space that seemed to be nothing, surrounded by smaller tunnels and pipes.

"Look at that valve," Raven pointed out. "It's dead, and none of the pipes around it seem to be carrying steam." Alan turned the ancient wheel; instead of hot air hissing through, low chimes rang softly.

"A doorbell?" Alan raised his eyebrow.

A panel in the wall in front of them slid aside, and they walked in.

They entered a strange octagonal room fashioned from piece-meal metal and bolts. Shelves and dark corners were filled with skulls and stuffed birds, test tubes and copper pipes, strange clocks that each told a different time, and books . . . hundreds of books—dusty, leathery tomes on everything from electricity to the dark arts. Nothing was in any order. Packets of herbs from foreign places lay next to piles of feathers from all over England. There were strange devices that whirred and clicked when shook, and did nothing more. Marionettes and tiny bottles of poison. . . .

"I welcome you," came a voice from the gloom.

Out stepped what at first appeared to be a fairly normal-looking—though pale—man, young and almost handsome. When he cocked his head to look at them, however, his glasses turned out to be something else entirely—one of the lenses was a thick brass tube that fitted over his entire left eye. The glass was faceted instead of being flat, and a tiny golden gear rested on the top. He adjusted them, spinning the gear, and the lens came out of the tube, as if he was mechanically focusing on them. The hand that moved the gear was also made of metal, like a brass skeleton. It clicked and whirred as it moved, and cloth-covered tubes ran up and down his arm under the sleeve. More gears spun inside his wrist.

"What brings you down to my humble abode, among the sewers?" He grinned as they tried to look away from his abnormalities.

Alan found his voice first.

"We seek a cure for a friend under a—a curse."

"Oh!" The man's eyes—his right one, at least—lit up. *"There's* something new. Sit down."

Over tea, which Alan sipped and Raven shunned, they told their story. Raven reluctantly filled in the parts about the Lonely Ones; the Clockwork Man seemed particularly interested in that. Raven rolled up his sleeves to show the feathers on his arm.

"Fascinating! An actual fusion of man and beast. . . . How extraordinary. Someone would have to be mad to even consider such a thing."

"Then . . . I am not a magical creature?" Raven asked slowly. "Not demon born, nor of fairy kin?"

"I'm afraid not, my young Sir," the man smiled. "You would have set off one of my alarms. You are human and animal, and nothing more—though that should be enough for most! As to the cure . . ." He tapped his tooth, much like Chauncey. "A very complicated thing, but not insurmountable. I should very much like to talk to this duchess; she sounds remarkable, if a little undereducated in the dark arts."

"She is evil," Raven hissed.

"So you'll help us?" Alan asked.

"Of course, for a price. I am almost certain the orb of which you speak is a *spiritus illuminatus.* She used electricity as a carrier, not just a power source, to open the veins for the *tempotus.* It might take me some time, but I believe I can reconstruct the more technical aspects of the machinery here. I will diagram the rest out for you—if any of you has the slightest ability it shouldn't be a problem."

"And your price?" Raven asked suspiciously.

"Ah, yes. In return I will take your feathers."

Raven and Alan exchanged glances.

"I suspect they will give me a clue as to how your origins were—originated, as it were. I should like to study them. I will need them all. And I warn you, I must have them whole—pulled, not clipped."

"Will they grow back?" Raven asked uneasily.

"I have no idea. It might be they were a one-time phenomenon." He cocked his head to look at the Lonely One; light flashed so that not even his normal eye could be seen. "But do you really want them to? You're a man caught between two worlds. With them gone, you could be fully human. No one could tell the difference."

He said it matter-of-factly, not like a demon offering a terrible choice, but rather more like a merchant explaining his options. The worst of it was that Raven could not answer his question.

"What if your machine doesn't work?"

The Clockwork Man sighed at Raven's distrust. "Young man, you know where I live. Simply come back. Bring her, even. It would be easier if I could work on her directly, as well as being a most instructive venture for myself."

Alan and Raven looked at each other and found themselves in agreement on one point: that would *not* be the best of ideas.

## Chapter Thirty-Three

# Revelations and Unwelcome Visitors

THEY SPENT THE NEXT THREE DAYS AND NIGHTS in the sewers with the Clockwork Man, though it was difficult to tell time with no sun and clocks that didn't work right. Sometimes he sent them aboveground on errands, to buy this or that component, or to pick up something from someone who met them on a street corner at midnight. Most of the time, however, was spent in the perpetual semidarkness of the sewers, talking or reading.

Raven thought a lot about the price of Snow's cure. He would do anything for her, of course. . . . But without his feathers, who would he be? *Will I look like a normal person but always dream of flying? Will I still be able to understand the language of the wild ravens?*

*Will Snow like me more, or is it Raven-with-the-feathers,* the Lonely One, *that she likes?*

"Once this is all over," he asked Alan casually, "will you go back to Kenigh Hall? Or stay in London and continue to play at the tavern?"

"I've been thinkin' a bit about that." Alan was lying down beside a clean-water aqueduct, hands behind his head, pretending it was a stream and a field. "This wee jaunt to London—and below it—has been simply amazing. And there's a whole world beyond this! I don't know, Raven. I always thought I might like to travel abroad—now I know it. Maybe nae as a young Scottish prodigy with a patron of the arts, but maybe I can find work once I get there."

Raven spoke carefully. "You would not wish to stay here, with Snow?"

"What, you mean Jess?" Raven flinched—he hated that name, the familiarity with which Alan spoke it. "She's like one o' my little sisters. I love her dearly, but I have to find my own way, yeah? Just like she does."

Raven felt a gigantic weight lifted off his stomach; his head went dizzy. "You love her . . . like a . . . *sister.* . . ."

"Aye, of course, Raven." Alan grinned at him, a mischievous twinkle in his eye. "How else?"

Two evenings later the Clockwork Man had the device ready.

"As my old grandmum used to say, good things come in threes," Alan said, winking at Raven and slapping the half-mechanical man on the back, perhaps a little too hard.

"What's the third one, then?" Raven asked. One was finding the cure, the second was his relief that Alan wasn't interested in Snow the way he was.

"That we sod out of this stinking hole!" Alan smiled.

Raven grinned.

"This 'stinking hole' is my *home,* gentlemen," the Clockwork Man reminded them. "Will you please sit down that I may explain this to you?"

It took a couple of hours and many drawings and notes, but Alan and Raven finally understood it.

"And now, *my* end of the bargain."

Raven refused the opium he offered; he refused a drink of whiskey. He rolled up his sleeve and gritted his teeth under the bright lantern. The Clockwork Man worked delicately, with a pair of silver tweezers. Each feather he pulled went into its own test tube.

Raven screamed twice, once each as two major pinions were pulled out of his arms. Tears of pain streamed down his face. He looked down at his arms in dismay: they were raw and pocked with holes; the larger ones leaked blood that streamed down to his hands.

When he was done, the Clockwork Man very carefully dressed the wounds, cleaning and bandaging them.

"Excellent." He held a bottle up to the light, admiring the iridescence of the feathers.

Alan had a thought. "Say . . . as long as you're in the fix-it business, maybe ye could try ridding me of this?" He pointed at the chain around his neck, unable to say the words.

The Clockwork Man looked at it over his glasses. "It's rather handsome on you," he pointed out.

Alan tried to say something, but couldn't.

"It has a spell on it," the Clockwork Man realized. "A charm. A coercion spell, I'll bet?"

Alan tried to nod.

"No trouble." The Clockwork Man shuffled around until he found a pair of iron shears and carefully sliced through the chain, holding Alan's neck so he wouldn't cut the skin. One quick slash and it was off.

Alan took a gulp and realized he could speak.

"I saw Cat in the mirror which is a device the duchess used to spy on you it projected images on a screen that's how I saw you all and how I saw Snow and I couldn't tell you that because she forbade me and the necklace made me listen and I had to do whatever she wanted and I ran away from the estate by playing my fiddle because I love it passionately and true love breaks a spell and I hate the bloody duchess she is such a bloody *bitch*!"

"Good heavens," said the Clockwork Man.

"Are those magic shears?" Raven asked, pointing at them.

"What, these? No. Just some cheap farmer's shears." He picked up the necklace and looked at it interestedly. "They're made of iron, which often breaks certain kinds of spells. . . . But the charm wasn't that strong to begin with, really. Not enough even to trigger my alarms. I'll just keep this if you don't mind—unless you want it as a souvenir?"

Alan shook his head decisively.

"Well, what a fascinating week it has been." The Clockwork Man sighed in contentment. "Now, Gentlemen. If you wish to leave my 'stinking hole' as quickly as possible, there's a ladder in the tunnel just north of here. It emerges outside of London, at the edge of a small wood. The road nearby will take you back to the city. Or you could just follow the stench."

Suddenly, Raven cocked his head, listening. "What's that?"

The Clockwork Man started to ask him what he meant, but Alan shushed him, used to Raven's superior hearing. A tapping and banging could definitely be heard, like someone was trying to find a false wall, or the door. The Clockwork Man turned to one of his machines and cranked it; an image flickered on a glass—like the duchess's mirror, Alan noted—but black and white and flickering. Two shadowy images, warped out of proportion, bobbed back and forth. Whispery voices rasped:

"It should be right here."

"Well, there's no bloody door."

"Maybe we should try shooting through."

"All right, all right! No shooting!" the Clockwork Man cried. He spun another wheel and threw a switch, unlocking the panel, which slid open. "Come in, if you must."

A pair of aristocrats was revealed, somewhat surprised, carrying pistols. One, the leader, was tall, blond, and blue eyed. His face was flushed with excitement. The other one was brown haired and stockier—neither one could have been more than twenty.

"How can I help you?" the Clockwork Man asked through gritted teeth.

"Are you—the—Clockwork Man?" the blond one asked breathlessly.

The man in question held up his machine arm. "Have you met anyone else like this? Now, ask me your question and be on your way."

"Oh, er, I have no—we only sought proof of your existence—"

"Well, you have it. You can tell all your gentleman friends you found the freak; discuss it at your next club or foxhunt. Impress some young lady or other. Good day, then."

Alan and Raven exchanged glances: their options were to fade into the shadows of the laboratory or to disappear past the newcomers as soon as possible.

"But wait!" The blond one held up his hand just as the Clockwork Man reached for the button to shut the door. His friend raised the pistol. "Oh, Henry, put it away. I am the duke of Edgington. This is Henry. I am a member of the Ghost Club . . . ?" The Clockwork Man rolled his eyes. "It is very prestigious, sir," the young duke said indignantly. "Charles Dickens himself was a member. We wish to find—I am on a quest for the strange and unusual, the exciting, the supernatural—"

"Who are these two?" his friend asked, gesturing at Alan and Raven with the pistol.

"*These* two came with a legitimate riddle and paid the price for their answer already. Actually, they *are* the unusual and exciting. Perhaps you all should talk. Leave, I mean, and talk on your way out. Actually . . ." The Clockwork Man's face turned thoughtful, and he looked at Alan and Raven. "You two should *definitely* take this man, and this other man, and their guns along with you."

"Absolutely not!" Raven snapped.

"My dear Raven," the Clockwork Man said gently. "You never know when you're going to find you have need of a duke. You have here a rich, powerful, and *trustworthy* young man—" The duke nodded eagerly and hopefully. "—who may be interested in your cause. Why not invite him along?"

Raven and Alan looked at each other uneasily.

"Have ye ever noticed," Alan said to no one in particular, "that lately, whenever there's trouble, a duke is involved?"

## Chapter Thirty-Four

# Snow

LIKE ALAN AND SNOW BEFORE THEM, THE DUKE of Edgington and Henry were blindfolded on their way back to the Lonely One's new hideout.

"Ye get used to it," Alan told them, winking at Raven.

"These two are not going to get 'used' to it," Raven said. "We bring them back, we wake Snow, they go away. They are only coming at all in case there's trouble, and there won't *be* any."

"We could take a carriage," the duke suggested eagerly. "I will pay."

"That's why you brought him along, isn't it?" Henry muttered under his breath.

"Ah, are the drivers nae going to be suspicious that we have ye both blindfolded?" Alan asked.

The duke frowned, or appeared to—it was hard to tell with the blindfold on. Then he brightened. "You could say it was for my birthday! You're taking me to a surprise party!"

Raven, Alan, and even blindfolded Henry exchanged weary glances.

"I think we'd better stick to walking," Alan suggested.

\*　　\*　　\*

When the four returned, Chauncey just rolled his eyes and went to get his pipe. "Is there to be no end of the stream of visitors we've been having?"

The Lonely Ones gathered and watched the duke and Henry remove their blindfolds as Alan and Raven explained what happened with the Clockwork Man.

"I say! So *this* is a hideout!" the duke exclaimed happily. Henry rolled his eyes, much like Chauncey had done, and threw himself into a chair.

Then the duke noticed Cat—and his eyes widened.

The Mouser quickly took Cat aside and nodded at Sparrow to make sure his wings were hidden. Henry didn't notice.

"This doesn't look so difficult," Chauncey said, puffing and looking at the diagram and pieces of the machine.

"It just requires some gold, for the bit here," Raven pointed. "About the size of the tip of your finger. Something to do with the way it never tarnishes, it isn't affected by time."

"Gold? That's easy then." Chauncey clapped his hands together. "Mouser? Sparrow? You feel like going on a jaunt?"

"You're *thieves,*" Henry suddenly realized.

"Then that sort of makes you our prisoner, doesn't it?" Alan said, pointing at Henry's pistol, which, with the duke's, was being worn by Chauncey.

"No, wait, here, don't do that." The duke fumbled with his watch. "Please, let me. I haven't helped at all yet." He wrenched a charm off the fob and handed it to Alan. "Will this do?"

Alan peered at it. "You're a Mason? Is there a secret club you *don't* belong to?"

"I'm going to see Snow," Raven said, leaving the room.

"Oh yes, let me see the sleeping damsel as well," the duke said as he jumped up and followed Raven into the other room.

Chauncey looked at Henry, who continued to sit looking at his fingernails. "Don't you want to see our *'sleeping damsel'* as well?"

"My job is to keep the duke from getting into *too* much trouble on his ridiculous jaunts," Henry replied. "Sleeping damsels don't really interest me. Seeing if you are planning to attack him from behind, however, does."

Chauncey nodded appreciatively. He and the Mouser then proceeded to ignore him and concentrate on putting the machine together.

Raven knelt next to Snow's sleeping body and took her hand in his. Alan, Sparrow, and Cat watched quietly from the door.

"Just a little while longer," he whispered to her. "Just a little, and—"

*"That's* your 'Snow?'" the duke cried, coming in.

Raven flinched. "Yes," he replied acidly. "She's our Snow."

*"That's* the young duchess of Kenigh Hall you have there."

The Lonely Ones and Alan looked at each other.

"I went to her fourteenth birthday party. Years ago." The

duke leaned over Snow and looked at her interestedly. "She didn't actually show up for very much of it. Some business with that nasty count what's-his-name. I don't remember—" He paused and looked up. "Ah, shouldn't she be older? Like, ah, me?"

"She ain't changed since she fell asleep," Sparrow said quickly. Raven looked like he was going to kill the duke for his nonchalance and familiarity. "Ever since the duchess cast her spell on—" Cat hissed at Sparrow to stop speaking; Alan slapped a hand over his mouth.

"Which duchess? Anne of Mandagor?" The duke stood up. "What on earth are you talking about?"

"*Chauncey,*" Alan called, "I think we have an information leak."

"Cor! Will ye all keep it down in there?" Chauncey shouted back. "Better yet, stop yer gabbing and come in and help us."

Everyone did wind up helping, each in his or her own way, long into the night. Cat's claws were invaluable for pushing bits of wire through and clamping pieces while Chauncey set them. Sparrow made tea and biscuits. Alan remained his cheerful and optimistic self, playing his fiddle to keep people awake. Henry kept Raven and the duke from interacting as best he could.

A day—and many scratched heads—later, an ugly lump of a machine sat next to Snow's sleeping body. It was a mass of tubes and jars of chemicals, wires of zinc and copper, and small bits of gold. A crank on the end had to be continuously operated during the process.

"This doesn't look like anything the duchess had," Cat said doubtfully.

"Just put the bits into her mouth, like the directions say," Chauncey sighed, scratching his head and rubbing his eyes.

Everyone looked at Raven.

Hesitantly he reached over, placing a green and corroded copper wire onto her lips.

# Chapter Thirty-Five

# Awake

SNOW AWOKE.
      Not with a kiss, but with a jolt of electricity.
      A voice spoke: "Wait, I want to see—"
      Her eyes snapped open in pain, and beheld
      Golden hair, blue eyes, a smile of wonder.

## Chapter Thirty-Six

# Awoken

SHE BLINKED AND SAT UP ON HER ELBOWS. People surrounded her bed, or coffin, or whatever it was. One was the handsome man who had bent over, and the rest were . . . were *wrong* somehow—strange shapes under hoods, eager feral eyes.

"Who are you?" she demanded, frightened. "Where am I?"

The people all looked at one another, apparently as confused as she.

*I know who they are,* she thought, putting her hand to her head. *They are—they are—*

"Who am I?" she shrieked, panicking. "Why am I here?"

A cloaked figure stepped forward to do something, restrain her maybe. *Its* eyes were all yellow and wrong, like a snake or something; when the figure opened its mouth to speak, sharp, evil little fangs showed.

She screamed and pulled away from the monster.

"Get away!"

She tried to get up, to run away, but her legs felt like they were made of stone; it took every bit of willpower just to back herself up into a corner.

"Easy," a black-haired, normal-appearing young man said, coming forward. "Don't you remember us?"

He had pleasant brown eyes but a very serious face. It was handsome, but inspired nothing within her.

She shook her head. Then she began to cry.

She sat with the man called Henry, ironically the only one in the group who didn't know her.

"Would you like some tea, or something?" he asked.

She looked around at the dingy room, the broken furniture, the piles of pots, and shook her head.

"Can I, ah," Henry sighed. "No, I don't suppose there *is* anything I can really do for you."

She was apparently a duchess. That was nice, since these people weren't. She had run away from home because someone tried to kill her. Maybe. The blond duke didn't seem to believe that her stepmother was capable of such a thing. Alan was a servant, but also her friend, which didn't make sense from what she thought she could remember about how classes and society worked. These other ones were . . . thieves, or something, who took her in when she was wandering London, lost. The hooded figure was a girl, sort of. She approached her later and whispered sadly, "You really don't remember me?" She kept her eyes lowered and lips covering her teeth. "You brushed my hair . . . ?" Snow—that was *one* of her names—couldn't imagine it.

The one called Raven had fierce tears in his eyes but a stony face; he was close friends with Alan, it seemed. Plump Sparrow sniffled a bit, trying to be grown up and not cry—she had no idea what her relationship with the boy was. The ones called the Mouser and Chauncey kept their distance, for which she was grateful.

Presently they were all discussing her.

"I mean no offense, but it is obvious she cannot stay here," said the duke.

Raven eyed him icily, but it was the Mouser who spoke and clenched his fists. "You mean to take her away? Absolutely not! This is her home."

"Easy there, Mouse," Chauncey warned. "This *is* her home, duke."

"Come now. It was very kind of you to take her in—many people would have tried to take advantage of the duchess in such a state. It is obvious that you have cared for her. . . ."

"*Love* her," Sparrow corrected.

"Well, all right, love her, but she has no memory, and nothing around here to stir it. She has been with you but two years asleep, a year awake—she *grew up* at Kenigh, with her father and mother—"

"*Step*mother," said Alan.

"*Evil* stepmother," said the Mouser.

"I am not entirely convinced that she tried to do as you suggested; certainly she was cruel, but—"

"For heaven's sake, man!" Chauncey cried, exasperated.

"We take you into our hideout, show you our girl-under-a-spell, and tell you her story, and you think we'd lie about something like *that*?"

"All he's saying," Henry broke in gently, "is that she is more familiar with her room, her things, the people from home. And they have the resources there to care for her, doctors and the like. And Alan, the duke, and I can stay in the area, making sure she is not . . . *abused* again. Alan, can you take up your old position there?"

"Ah, no." The Scotsman's brow darkened. "It would probably be best if I never set foot there again, where the duchess might see me."

"Well, then, at least he and I will be there. And if she regains her memory, she can always return, right?"

Everyone was silent; the two sides glared at each other.

Raven finally spoke. "Why don't we ask *Snow* what she wants to do?" he asked quietly.

They all looked surprised, then turned to her.

"Well, Princess?" Chauncey asked softly.

# Chapter Thirty-Seven

# Not Herself

WHEN SHE TOLD THEM SHE WANTED TO GO home, she had no idea what she really meant. She wanted so badly a mother or father she recognized, some warm and loving place and person she would know, and it just seemed more likely to find them at the place called Kenigh. The disappointed and sad looks on the faces of her old friends, whom she could not remember, was almost too much to bear; she pleaded to go at once.

The blond duke had Henry send word by post to Kenigh and swore to Chauncey that she would never be long out of their sight.

The journey was long and tiring. *Well, at least with no memory I shall be experiencing old places again like seeing them for the first time!* But the view outside the train was drab and rainy; she played checkers with Henry while the duke prattled on about all he could remember about Kenigh Hall and their somewhat shared life as privileged children.

". . . and, of course, Sunday tea was always different; I'm sure it was at your house as well. Sometimes we would get lemon curd, sometimes marmalade—I especially liked the marmalade, even if it wasn't freshly made—and spread it on scones. . . ."

She appreciated his attempts but kept thinking back on the people she left, and especially the dark, sad eyes of the one named Raven.

*Well, I'm heir to quite a fortune,* she thought upon her first view of Kenigh. She wondered if that was an appropriate thing to think, feeling somehow it was not. The duke and duchess greeted her first. Her father admitted to being initially angry at her running away, but now joyfully welcomed home his long-lost daughter. Jessica nodded mutely and accepted his embraces, not wanting to disappoint the kind-seeming man. Her stepmother wept and apologized over and over again for things Jessica did not remember. A fat old cook named Dolly had come back just for the occasion, but although her tarts were good, she made little impact on Jessica's memory, except for vague impressions of comfort. Jessica was shown her old things, her old friends. Jessica nodded her head and smiled— sure, sure, she was sure it was all right.

The duke—*my father*—employed the finest doctor to feel her head and look into her mind. The doctor suggested that perhaps the girl had a fit, an overheat of the brain. He foresaw no long-term effects, and suggested that time and familiarity alone would bring her back.

The blond man who brought her home was welcomed as

warmly as Jessica and was invited to stay. Everyone was kind to him and Henry. *Almost pandering. I'll bet the handsome noble-man gets that kind of attention quite a bit. Especially from people with a bizarre runaway daughter they would like to marry off as soon as it is convenient.*

And while it wasn't obvious how things at a place like Kenigh Hall could get so bad that she would run away from it, she was confident there had to be a good reason. Jessica could not remember much, but she was pretty sure she wasn't stupid.

# Chapter Thirty-Eight

## The Lonely Ones

THE BLOND DUKE WAS AS GOOD AS HIS WORD, and when Snow was delivered to Kenigh the old duke rewarded the Lonely Ones handsomely. They bought a proper house: The Mouser finally had his leather chair, shelves of books, and evening sherry. Chauncey had a master bedroom and a nice pipe. Sparrow had a kitchen, a pantry, and all the toys he couldn't have before. Cat had a beautiful woman's suite, with a vanity like the duchess's—though she didn't know it—and a pretty little chair, money for dresses if she decided to dress, and tiny silver daggers if she didn't.

Raven let the Mouser outfit him in new clothes but otherwise would not touch the money.

All they did was sit around their fancy new living room in their fancy new clothes and look at the bag of gold they still had left over, more than they ever had before—and rightfully earned—and kicked their legs.

"What's for dinner, Sparrow?" the Mouser asked, finally breaking the silence.

"Broiled salmon and pea soup for starters, then pheasant

with artichokes, and stewed pears with raspberry tartlets for dessert." He looked like he was about to cry.

"Oh," the Mouser said. "Not, just, ah, stew?"

Then Sparrow *did* cry.

Chauncey sighed and tapped his pipe.

Cat lay on her back on the floor, tossing a ball of yarn into the air. "Ssshe wanted to teach me how to knit. I sssaid no, it wasss sstupid. When she getsss back she can teach me, though. I'll let her. I will."

Alan came stumbling in; he played much longer hours at the tavern than he used to and practiced ceaselessly when he came home.

"Where's Raven?" he asked.

"Still on the roof," Sparrow said, sniffling. "He hasn't come down in two days now."

Alan turned to go find him.

"Ah, Alan," Chauncey cleared his throat uncomfortably and indicated the bag of gold. "You still haven't taken your share."

"What, this?" With a violence unnatural to him, Alan viciously kicked the bag, scattering the coins all over the floor. "I cannae make songs out of this rubbish!" he said as he stormed upstairs.

# Chapter Thirty-Nine

# A Ball

THE EVENING FELT STRANGELY FAMILIAR AS Jessica peeked through her curtains at the carriages that rolled up under the full moon. She watched for a while and then went back to looking at herself in the mirror. Her stepmother had come in earlier and exclaimed over her beauty. She *was* beautiful, no doubt about that. Her face was fashionably pale with excited rosy cheeks, her eyes and hair black, black, black. Her lashes were long, and she batted them at her reflection.

It was pleasing to look at her hips and breasts and waist under the pink gown and bustle, which had taken forever and four maids to get on. She just wished the gown was red. And bustle-free.

Her legs were pretty too, and well muscled: she stretched one forth and admired it. No one would ever see them besides her, of course, except for her future husband or a close maid. While her memories of social custom and ingrained habits were far more intact than her personal memories, she still had a hard time seeing the sense of exposing most of her chest while hiding the lower half of her body.

Her parents' latest attempts to fix their parental mistakes

included throwing a masked ball in the Venetian style. That way Jessica could be reintroduced to society, reintroduced to people she had known—the masks conveniently explaining away why she couldn't recognize them. Everyone would know what had happened to her but would play along, for politeness' sake. That's what being a duchess meant.

She appreciated the thought and looked forward to the party. She had sat with her kind-seeming, if somewhat over-eager, stepmother as they talked with tailors and artisans, shopped for masks, and chose the dress. Jessica wound up choosing not an animal or traditional *bauta,* but a simple white one, decorated with feathers and tiny silver six-pointed stars, held up by a slender wand and decorated with ribbons that flowed down like a drift of snow.

It would take more than a party to set her at ease, though. Whenever her stepmother wasn't looking, Jessica would watch her, looking for some sign of the murderess she might have been. The duke of Edgington and Henry found excuses to stay close by, but she wanted to know the truth for herself.

She slept on a bed she did not remember, on pillows with the impressions of their owner bleached, washed, and pressed out. When not formally dressed she wore resting gowns, pretty things, airy and with trailing ribbons. She preferred looking at them to wearing them, but somehow sensed that being caught asleep naked would have been frowned upon in this world she didn't remember well.

She found an urge to sit *next to* or *under* the bed, with crumbs in her hand, as if to feed pigeons or mice, but none came. *It's been years since I was last here; if I trained them they probably all forgot.* She found she could, if she desired, move so quickly and stealthily in darkened halls that no one, not even the butler, saw her. *Maybe I used to meet an illicit lover.* Jessica would ponder her skills while stealing cheese out of the pantry, where she was most comfortable—but not when people were there. She took the little gifts people gave her, jewelry and combs and things, and hid them under her bed for reasons she couldn't understand or explain.

"I'm a blank slate," she told herself cheerfully in the mirror. "I can be anyone I want."

But even this wasn't true.

It was expected that the duke would propose to her that night, like something right out of a fairy tale. And if that did not happen, well, she was going to be reintroduced to a number of suitable suitors. She was nineteen, for heaven's sake. She would be married in a year or two.

As if on cue, her stepmother knocked rapidly and came in. Jessica hated that. There was a lock on her door, but reversed so that she could be locked *in*. It was the first thing she had noticed about the room.

"Come dear, why don't you take off that locket and wear a real necklace tonight," the duchess suggested. She had an array of trinkety things in her hand, each probably worth a fortune.

Jessica shook her head and touched the locket she always wore. It was slightly beaten and scratched and held the miniature of a mother she remembered no more than the woman before her. But still she refused to take it off.

Frustrated, the duchess put on one of her fake smiles. "Well, it's up to you, but it just looks a little . . . common. I'll leave these here in case you change your mind."

She left the baubles on the bureau. Jessica might take one, for later, just in case—in case of what, she didn't know.

She descended the staircase in a grand entrance, the way she was expected. Her father took her by the fingertips and led her down to the floor, introducing her as he went. He held a mask but didn't wear it; his moustache was waxed until it shone.

Jessica had no idea of what kind of girl she was before her memory failed, but she thought that she might be wiser now. Perhaps her desperation to fill the void in her mind allowed Jessica to pick up quiet words and tense emotions that might otherwise be missed by those around her. A blank slate allowed Jessica to meet people she had known all her life as if for the first time.

With suspicion.

This man, for instance. The man who was her father was passably handsome, emotionless, boring, and, well, stiff as a prig. His wife, the duchess, was artificial and obviously scared of Jessica; probably because she was the only heir and was taking away everyone's attention. The duchess was obviously a very vain person. *It might be worth it to get married just to get away from those two,* she thought wryly.

The hall and ballroom were lit with hundreds of candles in little silver candleholders, the mirrors shining with their reflected light. Guests filled every nook and hall of the house. Ladies swished broad, elegant skirts trimmed with layers of silk and lace that cascaded in tiers, trains just skimming the floor. Long gloves covered bare arms; dark silk ribbons encircled bare necks and trailed down their blocks like streams of blood.

The young men were slim and elegant and serious; the old men were handsome and jolly. All wore similar black suits with white shirts, as if to better show off their peacock women, and all offered to kiss Jessica's hand.

The servants were beside themselves, also elegantly dressed and passing trays of goodies and drinks. She had overheard that this was the first party since her own fourteenth birthday—another mysterious occasion from her past about which she had yet to learn the whole truth. Waves of perfume hit her, musky and floral, light and overwhelming, and the sounds of laughter and music filled her head. It was all very, very beautiful—and she had the urge to grab a tray of food, a glass of champagne, and hide under the stairwell.

She had a little card to write down people's names for different dances; the blond duke had the first one. He bowed elegantly to her and offered her his hand; she took it.

Everyone watched as he led her slowly across the floor. Somehow her feet knew how to dance, and he covered for her when she didn't. His hair shone gold in the candlelight, his blue eyes were—*Well, all right, he's handsome. And obviously a decent sort for helping me out and bringing me home. But who is he?*

*And, while we're at it, who were those other people who he took me from? What happened to them?*

The blond duke leaned in and brushed his lips to her ear. "How has the duchess been treating you?" he whispered.

"I don't trust her," she whispered back.

Everyone admired the apparently flirting couple—or gossiped about Jessica behind their gold and crimson papier-mâché masks, looking away quickly when she glanced in their direction. She found herself scanning the crowd, thinking she might recognize someone. Ridiculous, she knew. One mask caught her eye; a black grotesque in the form of a raven. For some reason it gave her a warm feeling.

She kept her eye on the person wearing it through three dances, trying to work her way over to him. She thought she lost him at the fourth, a waltz, but he tapped her on the shoulder from behind her.

"May I have this dance?" he asked, ignoring her dance card.

"Of course." She picked up her skirt and took his hand, unable to keep her eyes off his ebon mask.

"This dance is mine," another young man interrupted, face flushed.

"Oh, Sir," a beautiful young woman in a cat mask approached the intruder, tapping him lightly on the shoulder. "My throat is parched. Would you kindly get me another glass?" She lowered her lids and looked up through her lashes at him.

"Of course," the man said, instantly smitten. He bowed and excused himself, leaving Jessica and the raven-man alone.

She dropped her fan and picked up her train as he took her in his arms.

"I'm sorry—I am sure you have heard about my . . . accident," she apologized, for the seventeenth time that evening. "I do not recall you—you were announced—the Earl of Sussex, I believe?"

"You do not remember me at all?" the man in the raven mask whispered. *"Snow?"*

*Why does that name sound familiar?* She lifted up his mask, and there were the familiar brown eyes and glossy black hair. The man from the group of thieves in London.

"I returned to the Clockwork Man—I have a cure for your memory," he whispered.

He spoke so intently. No one at Kenigh looked at her like that.

"What are you talking about? It was a fit, an overheating of the brain. . . ." But something wasn't right. The room spun. "The other room, the parlor," she whispered. "Get me out of here. Let us pretend we are trysting."

They danced off the floor and she laughed, loud and ringingly. He led her into the small study.

"I have the components here," Raven reached into his pocket. Jessica studied his face intently, less concerned for her memory at the moment. There was something about him that felt more like home than home. "The duchess put a spell on you, we think, so if you ever woke up you wouldn't remember who she was or what she did to you. The Clockwork Man said it probably wasn't that strong a charm, like on Alan's—you don't remember that, of course. You were asleep." He pulled out a nail with what looked like sheep's wool wrapped around the top, and an old black feather. "I'm afraid I have to cut your palm with this. . . ."

She reached up and kissed him.

Raven was surprised, but she put her hand around the back of his neck to keep him from pulling away. Her fingers entwined in his hair and feathers, and she remembered the ravens she used to watch from her window. . . .

*Remembered?*

*"Raven,"* the name came back to her, with all of its original meanings.

Her memories rushed in, hurting her head.

*"Raven,"* she whispered again. Her stomach turned; her head felt crazy. "What . . . happened? I was with the duchess. In her apartment. She *did* something to me. . . ."

"Snow? You remember everything? The duchess put a—"

Raven said, a little confused and very flushed. He touched his lips and looked at the strange iron nail in his hand. "I guess I didn't need this. . . . How . . . ?"

She smiled. "They say true love can always break a spell."

Raven opened his mouth. Nothing came out. He closed it again. Finally he changed the subject. "Do you remember visiting the duchess? In her house? She attached things to you. . . . It was more than two years ago. . . ."

Jessica—Snow—*thought,* and it was hard, like digging a hole. If she concentrated the hole widened a little. Layers of memory: her time with the Lonely Ones, two years of dreaming, her life before at Kenigh Hall . . .

"I slept for almost three years," she realized, sinking into a chair. "I lost three years of my life. . . ." She shivered at the memory of sleep: always dreaming, almost waking up, but never quite.

"You did sleep, but I don't think you lost three years . . . you haven't changed at all."

She looked up at him and realized he was right. Raven, once her height, was now several inches taller than she. His chest had broadened and he stood straighter. There were little creases around his eyes, not quite wrinkles, and a light in his eye that wasn't there before. He had a scattering of freckles, and some of his hair were actually feathers.

He was almost three years *older* than her now.

Jessica—*Snow*—opened her purse and took out a pocket

mirror. She looked at herself and realized she did look the same, and that should have been strange. Why had no one on the estate noticed it? "I *have* changed," she whispered. "Just not on the outside."

She still possessed the wisdom her erased memory had brought her; she still saw everyone at the estate as if for the first time, but now it was overlaid with layers of memory. The duke and duchess as people, not parents. *Flawed* people.

And, now that she matched up what she knew about the duchess with her revelation, *insane* people, she realized.

Raven knelt so that their faces were level. "You're all right now, you're safe with me. And the rest of us are here too."

"Cat. Chauncey. The Mouser. *Sparrow.*" She repeated them like a mantra, afraid of slipping away again. Raven helped her rise and led her to the door of the parlor so she could look out over the dancing crowds. At first, it just looked like a sea of silk, fans, and ruffles. Then she looked again, as a Lonely One.

In one corner a beautiful young woman posed, with black hair high on her head and a wicked, wicked grin, a cat mask held flirtatiously to her side. She was laughing loudly at something someone said. . . . She saw Snow and grinned at her. Candlelight caught her eyes just enough to show the slits; a flash of white revealed her fangs. The Mouser didn't bother with a mask; he was talking politics with some men in the corner, but he too smiled at her. Sparrow was strolling casually up and down one of the hors d'oeuvres tables, looking too intently at the treats to see her. Alan actually waved; the harlequin mask he wore didn't cover his smile, which she remembered like the back of her hand.

The blond duke was there as well, chattering inanely at someone; Henry looked bored beside him.

"Those two have been very kind to me," Snow said. She saw Raven tense out of the corner of her eye. "Oh, settle down. I can see you have a lot to tell me once we get away from all this. What happened to the feathers on your hands?"

Her fingers entwined in his hair and feathers, and she remembered the ravens she used to watch from her window. . . .

"Wait a moment," she said uncertainly. "It cannot be . . ."

A connection . . .

A *movement*.

She and Raven both turned at the same time, both realizing the presence of an intruder. She threw her mirror without thinking, at where she thought the person's head should be. It connected.

"You didn't learn *that* from your tutor," the duchess said wryly, coming out of the shadows and touching the blood on her forehead. "And who is this? One of your little thieving friends—"

The duchess stopped short. She and Raven were caught in each other's stares.

*With exactly the same eyes.*

"You couldn't have a child," Snow—Jessica—said slowly,

fitting clues from her childhood into place. "You tried all kinds of things. All of Alan's strange tasks . . ."

"*You?*" Raven cried. "*You* made us? Abandoned us? *You,* murderer?"

"My . . . son . . ."

"No son of yours!"

Snow was putting it together now. The kitten that disappeared. Cat? But *that* cat was white . . . maybe it failed the first time. The mice whose babies went missing. Alan, stealing fledglings from the raven's nest. The black blood leaking under the duchess's door. The fact that she and the Lonely Ones came from nearly the same place.

"Alan . . ." She knew she should do something about the murderous look in Raven's eyes, but one remaining thing bothered her. She remembered the day Alan helped her escape, his sweat and fainting. "You had him under a spell. . . ."

"Not a spell," the duchess said, never taking her eyes off Raven. "Not exactly. Mesmerism. His golden necklace resonates at the same wavelength as his brain. How many of you survived?" she asked Raven.

"You have five *children*, you witch," Raven spat, "who must hide from the sun and other people—five *outcasts*."

"Why are they so old?" Snow asked. "If you . . . made them as babies just a few years ago?"

"They weren't babies, exactly, when I . . . *operated* on them," the duchess answered slowly. "Animals age much faster than humans. That is also one of the reasons it had such a . . . high mortality rate."

"'High mortality rate'? And is that all Snow was, too?"

"Attempting to use her heart was ill-thought and probably a little mad," the duchess admitted. "But it might have worked."

And that was what made Raven leap for her throat; the simple coldness with which she spoke.

"Raven, no!" Snow leaped between them, pushing the duchess out of the way. "No good can come of this!" She saw her father sending for the police, imagined her Raven stained with murder. Her hand brushed the duchess's arm as she pushed the older woman out of the way.

*A bad spell turns back on the caster times three.*

She remembered Alan's words as sparks blew purple around the two women. *The spell on my memory—she cast it before I slept. What will it do to her?*

"What . . . where am I?" The duchess started to collapse; Snow caught her before she fell and lowered her gently to the couch.

The duchess put a hand to her head. There was something slack about her features, Snow realized. A dullness to her eyes that wasn't there before. *"Maman . . . ? Where is my maman?"*

She sounded . . . *old.* Confused. Her hair was still bright, and nothing physical had changed that Snow could see, but there was something missing in her face.

The duke appeared in the doorway with two men. "What the devil is going on here?"

Snow clasped the duchess's hand. "My stepmother started to say something and pitched forward. Her cheeks are burning up! Get the doctor!" *Where do such lies come from so easily?* She thought about the Lonely Ones, and then remembered her childhood, full of lies.

# Chapter Forty

# Endings

THE DOCTOR WAS CALLED. THE PARTY ENDED.

Alan's grandmother had been right—whatever mind-befuddling spell the duchess had cast on Snow had trebled back on the older woman. She could remember nothing except long stories from when she was a child. She had no short-term memory. The duchess had, in fact, turned into the somewhat lovable, scatterbrained grandmother type Snow had always wanted in her life.

At first Snow doubted it was anything but an act. To test her theory she threatened to burn one of the duchess's precious arcane books in front of her. Anne had shrugged helplessly and said she didn't care, but that it might cause a bit of a mess. Shocked but convinced, Snow was forced to swallow her feelings of rage; the old woman before her had little or no connection to the duchess of a few days ago.

The old duke had a manly breakdown over all of the recent mishaps in his family. He shed manly tears and was pitied and admired by all. When he emerged from his rooms a few days later he was a sadder but calmer man, who treated his wife carefully, but with a kindness and loving Snow could not remember witnessing before.

Snow pretended to regain her own memories over the next few weeks even as it was obvious Anne had lost hers. Some cheerfully said that it must be some sort of sickness in the household, and if the girl had recovered her mind so would the old woman. Expensive doctors privately told the family that they did not think this was the case; it was more like the old duchess had had a stroke.

Snow revisited with all of her old friends and people on the estate she had not remembered before: Dolly, Gwen, Craddoc, and many others who were glad to see her again . . . but who were changed from who they had been. She made the decision not to tell anyone about the duchess's attempt on her life; the old duchess was dead, and there was little point in troubling the new, feebleminded one about it.

Amid these pleasanter conversations, she forced herself to have a private conversation with the blond duke of Edgington, politely but firmly explaining that as a result of recent events she was in no position to marry.

"And," she added honestly, feeling the young man deserved the truth, "frankly—I have been asleep for the past two years. I have not—*lived* enough to make any sort of decision about the rest of my life."

"I . . . understand completely," he said, and gave a small smile. Snow looked at him, surprised. "My whole life I've searched for . . . another world, with adventures, and magic, and now that I've had a taste—I want to see *more*. I think highly of you, Jessica, but I must admit I am relieved. Proposing to you just seemed . . . what was expected."

She smiled. "I cannot speak for you, but I for one am tired of doing what's expected."

"Excellent. I am glad we agree. Also, I think Raven would have killed me on the spot if I had gone through with it," he added nervously.

They parted friends. Everyone in the estate and town was disappointed with her, resentful that she had spoiled their fairy tale.

Her own secret fairy tale of the Lonely Ones joining her on the estate and living with her was also revealed to be the flimsy stuff of dreams it always was. They didn't *want* to be servants, and there was no place at Kenigh for them, anyway—in a small town, someone would eventually discover the truth about them. And Alan, who was the closest thing she had to a brother, well, he couldn't stay forever either. He had a talent and a life ahead of him.

She took over some of the duchess's estate duties, which made her feel useful but left her bored.

Snow cried for hours, then found she couldn't cry anymore.

Snow was left wandering the rooms of the estate and the lawns, feeling let down. Her father had accepted her back and as his daughter now, but she didn't care anymore. The duchess had been defeated, but in a very sad, unsatisfying way.

Sometimes Snow read the duchess's old magic books and scientific journals and angrily wished that Anne could have been cured of her evil tendencies without losing her mind. Snow had questions about electricity, rituals, and chemicals, and now no one could answer them for her. *She could have been a great woman if she had not been so vain.* She imagined the good things the old duchess could have done with her equipment, knowledge, and intelligence.

"It's like it's all over, with a whimper. There's no perfect, happy ending. Nothing *fits* into a grownup life," she told Anne as she held a skein of yarn for the old woman. Snow found it very easy to talk to her stepmother now; it was like speaking to a wall that answered back occasionally with something meaningless but charming.

"I'm surprised you're still here," the old duchess said, slightly chastising. She thrust a needle for emphasis. "Turning down a handsome young duke! My word! *My* father never would have stood for it, I can tell you that much. What with all the scandals this family has had, you should have done it already, let things quiet down a bit. The whole bit with the ball. What nonsense. That's what we did in *my* day," she said, clucking her tongue.

"Done *what* already?" Snow asked, expecting something dull.

"Taken the Grand Tour, you silly goose. Of Europe. All the best lords and ladies who were victims of scandals did in *my* day."

# Epilogue

"HURRY, THE SECOND WHISTLE HAS BLOWN!"

Snow surveyed her entourage—entourages were allowed, even encouraged, she discovered, when people of the highest class were touring Europe to escape scandal. The ship they were about to board was large and fine; they each had a first-rate first-class cabin and their own chairs on the deck for sun, if they chose. They probably wouldn't, however. Currently it was night, and until such time as they found a place where they would all be accepted, the Lonely Ones—and Alan and Snow—would travel only by dark.

Porters scuttled up and down the gangplank, getting the last trunks and packages on. Sparrow, Chauncey, and the Mouser were already aboard, on deck high above her. Snow waved at them. The Mouser raised his glass; Chauncey tapped his cigar overboard in greeting. Sparrow jumped up and down. *He's going to get sick,* she knew as surely as the sun would rise. Alan and Cat were just about to board. Cat was dressed in a very modern dress with a low-cut bodice and sported an absolutely fantastic hat. Alan was trying very hard to pretend he was ignoring her—but grinned all the time she batted her eyelashes at him.

It was going to be an adventure no matter what they all ended up doing—*just taking this lot to a museum will be an adventure,* she thought to herself, visions of marble columns, kings, and foreign canals on her mind.

"Ready, My Lady?"

Raven held out his hand. He was dressed properly, with a black morning coat and trousers, with boots that shone, but with hair still wild. He wore gloves; the nubs of new feathers had just begun to grow back along his arms.

She smiled and took his hand.

*"Ready."*

# Beauty Sleep

A Retelling of "Sleeping Beauty"

## By Cameron Dokey

# Preamble

*(A FANCY WAY OF SAYING INTRODUCTION)*

I'VE HEARD IT SAID (THOUGH I CAN'T SAY whether or not it's true) that all good stories begin in the same way, with the exact same words.

Since I naturally want you to find my story a good one, one that keeps you reading as much for the comfort of familiar details as for the new ones that surprise you, I've decided to stick to tradition.

You know the words, don't you?

Of course you do.

*Once upon a time . . .*

There. Thank goodness that's over with.

Now that I've gotten the traditional opening off my chest, I'm free to tell my story any way I want to. Because isn't that at least part of the reason for telling your own life story? To tell the truth at last. Your truth, your way. Not the truth other people think you should tell in the way they think you should tell it. Which is really just another way of saying the way that makes them look best and feel the least uncomfortable.

Stories are tricky things, aren't they?

Because the thing about them is that the same events can be told any number of ways. It all depends on what you think is important, and, when the important stuff is happening, whether you're looking directly at it or looking away.

Here we come to my first true confession, which, coincidentally, may also be my story's first surprise. (By which I mostly mean that it surprises me.) Now that I've actually used those words (*once upon a time*) I have to confess that they don't seem so stupid and traditional after all. Actually I kind of like them. They have a certain ring. They conjure, like a spell. And I suppose the fact that I'm not the first to use them doesn't automatically make me unoriginal. Isn't it the words that follow *once upon a time* that make a story truly come alive?

All right. That settles it. If I'm going to tell my story (which I am), I want to tell it right. So I think this means I need to start over, this time really believing in *once upon a time.* Believing that it will draw you in, take you with me to a place you've never been before. (You only think you have—a thing that may well be my story's first surprise for you.)

I know.

Close your eyes. Now conjure up your favorite door within your mind. Perhaps it leads to a room you visit everyday. Or maybe it's for special occasions, the place you go to be safe and warm and comfortably alone. Perhaps the door is actually a garden gate, an entryway to a place filled with the mysteries of living things. Perhaps it's simply the front door to your own home. Are you going out, or going in? Never mind.

I'll tell you about the door I conjure. It is made of old, dark oak with iron handles and hinges. Not fancy, but sturdy and serviceable. A trustworthy sort of door. You know what lies beyond it, don't you?

That's right. My truth. My way. My story.

Can you feel its unseen forces gathering around you? The handle of the door slips from your hand and the door, my door, begins to open wide. Before you realize what you've done, you've accepted the invitation, put one foot across the threshold. That's all it takes. You're in for it now.

Begin at the beginning, the place where all good stories start.

You know the way. Of course you do.

# Chapter One

*ONCE UPON A TIME*

. . . and so long ago that the time I speak of can be remembered only in a story, a virtuous king and queen (my parents) ruled over a land that was fair and prosperous (though it wasn't all that large).

Their kingdom being at peace, and their people being well fed and content, you might think the king and queen would be so also. But alas, it seems they were not. (Content.) For they lacked the one thing which would make their happiness complete: a child.

For years, the king and queen had dreamed and waited. Long years, and so many of them that, one by one, their hopes for a child began to pack their bags and depart. And this stealing away of hope eventually took its toll. It compelled the king to do a thing he did not wish to do, a thing he never would have done, had he not lost hope for a child of his own. He named his younger brother's son as his heir apparent, the brother being deceased and therefore not available himself.

The boy's name was Oswald.

Not that anybody ever called him that. His propensity for skulking in corridors the better to learn other people's business (particularly their secrets), combined with his habit of playing nasty practical jokes based on what he'd learned, had earned him a nickname.

Everybody called him Prince Charming. Because he wasn't.

After many years of wishing for a child to no avail, a terrible day arrived. This was the day the king and queen awoke to discover that all their hopes were well and truly gone. But this turned out to have an unlooked-for benefit, for the absence of hope left a vacuum, a void. And now I'll tell you another thing I've heard said, and this I know is true: Nature hates a void. As soon as one occurs, something has to rush in to fill the empty space, for that is the way nature wants things to go.

And so it was that the void created by the desertion of their hopes turned out to be the best possible thing that could have happened to my parents. For in hope's absence, a miracle arrived.

On the very same day that she realized all her hopes had fled, the queen also realized she was with child. A thing that, when she informed her husband, caused both their hearts to fill with joy. So much so that all their hopes heard the ringing of it, halted in their flight, turned around, and raced right back home. Between their hopes, their miracle, and their joy and wonder at both, my parents' hearts were therefore filled to overflowing before I was even born.

Many great things were predicted for me. Naturally, I would grow up straight and true, for that is what's supposed to happen when you are born royal. I would be beautiful if a girl, handsome if a boy. Above all, I would do my duty. First, last, always. When I put in my appearance on the exact same day the royal soothsayer had appointed, this was taken to be a sign that I would fulfill all these predictions, plus many more.

Several years and many disappointments later, my mother would be overheard to remark that the day of my birth was the only occasion she could recall on which I had been dutiful according to her definition. When my father protested that she was being too hard on me, she settled for the unarguable statement that it was most certainly the only occasion for which I had ever been on time.

In spite of all that happened later, every account I have ever heard concerning my actual birth relates that Papa and Maman were so delighted that a child had arrived at last that they were willing to overlook the fact that I was a girl and not a boy, boys being the preferred rulers of kingdoms, as you must know. For reasons that my nurse once explained to me were largely reproductive, but that I don't think I'll go into here and now.

I was born on a bright but chilly day in late September. Nurse has told me that my very presence warmed the room, for, even then, my hair was bright as the dawn. It made such a perfect arc around my head that it resembled a halo, an aureole. A combination of circumstances that caused my mother to immediately proclaim that the only name which could do me credit was Aurore.

This though she and my father had discussed naming me after his mother, whose name had been Henriette-Hortense. But, as my father was not about to deny my mother anything in the moments immediately following my birth, that plan was abandoned and the deed was done. From that moment forward, I was called Aurore.

It was, and still is, the custom in the country of my birth to hold a christening when a babe has reached the age of one month old. How this period of time came to be decided upon isn't clearly remembered, but it's generally assumed that the reason is twofold. A month is long enough after the birth so that a baby no longer appears quite so wrinkly and red, thus sparing those who come to congratulate the new parents considerable worry in the way of coming up with compliments on the beauty of the child. A month is also thought a long enough period to determine whether or not the infant is a good match in temperament for the name bestowed upon it shortly after its arrival. Many are the girls who are born Charlotte but end up as Esmerelda. Or the boys who begin life as Wilfrid but end up as just plain Bill. Well, not many, perhaps. But some.

In my case, however, there was no possibility that I might, even yet, become Henriette-Hortense. My hair having apparently grown even more golden with each passing day, and my eyes even more blue and my skin more rose petal-like, according to the nurse, anyway, the matter was considered settled. I was to be Aurore. First, last, always.

You know about my christening, of course. Everybody does.

Or the bare bones of it, anyway. What went right. But mostly, what went wrong. Given the size and scope of the event, what seems most incredible to me is that my parents never saw the disaster coming ahead of time. It's been suggested they were dazzled by the gold of my hair. (Though, now that I think about it, I seem to remember that this suggestion came from Oswald.)

What I do know—what everybody knows—is this: When the invitations were sent out, for the one and only time in her life, my mother failed to manage a social engagement to perfection, and her list was one person short. Not just anybody. *Somebody.* By which, of course, I mean Somebody-Who-Proved-To-Be-Important, even if that wasn't how she started out.

Who she was has been greatly distorted. Most versions of my story say she was an evil fairy and give her some fantastic name, usually beginning with the letters *m-a-l*. *Mal,* meaning bad, which over time has come to mean the personification of evil, just as Aurore has come to be the personification of all that is beautiful, innocent, and bright. I am the candle flame snuffed out too soon; she, the years of impenetrable dark.

This is for the simple-minded, I suppose. An attempt to

show that she and I were opposites right from the start. All pure nonsense, of course. Not only didn't people think she was evil, they didn't think of her at all. And that, I believe, was the true heart of all the trouble that followed.

Her name wasn't "mal" anything, by the way. It was Jane. Just that, and nothing more. (And, for the record, there are no fairies in the land of my birth. They prefer the land just on the other side of the Forest, *la Forêt,* a place you'll hear much more about before my tale is done.)

After the big event, by which I mean my christening, people discussed Jane's life in great detail. Though I suppose I should say at great length, because there weren't really all that many details. Or none that anyone could accurately recall.

It was generally agreed that she was related to my mother, a distant cousin of some sort. And that she had been part of the entourage accompanying Maman when, as a young princess, she had come from across the sea to marry my father. There were even those who claimed to remember that Jane had been a member of the actual wedding party, that she had followed behind my mother, carrying her train. But when I asked Maman about this once, *she* claimed to have no memory of whether or not this was so.

When I remarked, very curious and a great deal put out, that it seemed incredible to me that Maman should be unable to remember whether or not a member of her own family had taken part in her wedding—been assigned, in fact, the important responsibility of keeping the bride's elaborate train straight and true during its long march down the aisle—my mother replied that she had been looking forward, not back, on her wedding day. In other words, her eyes had not been fixed on Cousin Jane. They had been fixed right where they should have been: upon my father.

Not long after, she sent me to bed without any supper for speaking too saucily, which was her way of saying I was asking too many questions, and furthermore that they were uncomfortable ones. This was neither the first, nor the last, time this happened. Nurse often remarked that I owed my fine figure not so much to all the time I spent outdoors, but to all the times I had spoken saucily to Maman.

Regardless of whether or not Cousin Jane actually took part in the wedding, on one thing everyone concurred. After the wedding, Jane simply dropped from sight and was forgotten. Or, more accurately, perhaps, she found a way to blend so perfectly with her surroundings that she became someone others completely overlooked. Everyone, in fact, except (perhaps) for Oswald.

Now we come to some important questions, ones to which we're never likely to have answers as only Jane can provide them, always assuming even she knows. The things I've always wondered are these: Did Jane *choose* to become invisible, or did it happen on its own, because of who and where and what she was? It's pretty plain she must have been unhappy for a good long while. But was her invisibility a cause or a result? Was it her unhappiness's root or vine?

Here's my theory: It was both.

I don't know how the world works where you live, but the place where I grew up is steeped in magic. This actually explains why ours is a place fairies don't call home. They prefer a more everyday place, where their own magic can have greater impact. There's magic in the air we breathe, the water we drink. When we walk, magic rises upward from the ground and enters our bodies through the soles of our feet, even when we have our stoutest boots on.

In other words, it's everywhere. In the wind and the rain. The feather from a bird that you find in a field during a country ramble. The hard, uneven surfaces of city street cobblestones. If you've grown up here, you're used to it. It's just the way things are. Almost everyone who's a native can do some sort of magic, even if it's something simple like boiling water for tea in the morning while you're still in bed, instead of having to crawl out of your warm covers to stir up the coals.

If you haven't grown up here but come to live, one of two things can happen, of course: Either the magic leaves you alone, or it doesn't. And if it doesn't, it does the same thing to you as to the rest of us: It makes you more of what you are.

This is a thing about magic that is greatly misunderstood. Magic isn't all that interested in change, which explains why things like love spells almost always backfire. And why those of us who grow up with magic don't use it nearly as much as people who haven't might think. (The boiling of tea water aside.) Nothing about magic is simple or straightforward, to be used lightly. And it's definitely not a substitute for what you can do just as well with your hands and your mind.

The people who end up with the strongest magic are the ones who are quickest to recognize this. Who see that magic's true power lies not in attempting to bend it to your will but in leaving it alone. Because if you do that, you'll discover an amazing thing. The will of the magic becomes your will of its own accord. For magic is a part of nature. It, too, hates a void. And the voids magic most wants to fill are the spaces that exist inside a person. It longs to strengthen that which is only waiting to be made strong.

Have you ever heard it said that somebody has shown her or his true colors? That's exactly what I'm talking about. The thing that interests magic is your true colors. Who you really are. And it can make you more powerful only if you first accept this. Which means, of course, that you have to be willing to accept yourself completely. Your virtues and your flaws. Most people shy away from doing this, another reason why magic doesn't get used as much as you might suppose.

But not Jane. She must have looked at herself without flinching. Unlike my mother, who has no time for magic, thereby making sure it has no time for her, Jane soaked it up, like a stunted plant in freshly watered ground. And herein lies magic's greatest danger. Remember what I said about the way it strengthens that which is waiting to be made strong?

If your virtues make up your true colors, that is well and good, for you as well as for the rest of us. But what about those whose true colors are comprised mostly of their flaws? These are the ones most likely to use magic for evil, even if they're not evil to begin with. For the things within them that the magic strengthens are like hunting knives: double-edged, wicked-sharp, and strong. They stick deep, cut both ways, are honed by power and pain alike. Such things cannot be held inside forever. Sooner or later, they must be released or they will slice their own way out.

What better way to release pain than to take revenge on the people you believe have wronged you? An eye for an eye. A tooth for a tooth. My power casts down your power, if only for a moment. Your pain replaces mine.

If Jane had been invited to my christening, who can say how much longer she would have held her pain locked up inside? Who can say what might *not* have happened? But she wasn't invited, and so something did.

"Little Princess, lovely as the dawn. Well-named Aurore."

This is what she is supposed to have said when, the last in a long line of wish-bestowers, she stood at my cradleside. By then, a horrible hush had fallen over my christening, a clotting sense of dread. Nobody recognized her, you see. Or (perhaps) nobody but Oswald. But her malice, that was an easy thing to recognize. Nurse has told me that the very air turned hot and tingled, the way it does right before a thunderstorm. You just knew that something bad was about to happen, she said.

As it happened, she was right.

"Yet even the brightest of sunrises must come to an end. *Tant pis.* Too bad," Cousin Jane went on.

Then, before anyone could prevent her, she reached down and scooped me from my cradle, holding me above her head so that her face looked up and mine looked down. I reached for her, my small fingers working to take hold of something, anything, for I wasn't all that sure that I liked my present situation.

At this, Nurse says, Cousin Jane smiled. As if I, myself, had provided the final inspiration for the pain she was about to unleash upon us all.

"Your end will come with the prick of a finger," she said, as she slid one of her own into my fist and I held on tight. Though everyone but Nurse has told me this is impossible, I swear I can actually remember this moment, what her finger felt like. Smooth and cool, but not the smoothness of skin. I know that now, though I didn't at the time.

Several years later, when I was judged old enough not to choke myself on it, I was given a chicken drumstick as a special treat at a picnic we were having on one of the many palace lawns. Any opportunity to get messy always delighted me, according to my mother, and all went well, until I'd gnawed my way down to the bone. At the first touch of it, I became hysterical, and it wasn't until several hours later that Nurse finally managed to calm me down enough to tell her what was wrong.

That's what Cousin Jane's finger had felt like. Not smooth skin, but the smooth caress of cool, hard bone.

"The prick of a finger," she said again, giving hers a little shake, as if everyone hadn't heard her the first time around. "One sharp wound. One bright drop of blood. That's all it will take to cut your life down. Sixteen years, I give you, *ma petite Aurore,* lovely as the dawn. The same number I was given before I had no choice but to follow your mother to this gilded prison, so far from my home."

There was a moment of stupefied silence.

Then, *"Jane?"* my mother gasped out. A question, an uncertainty, even now.

At which point Cousin Jane tossed me high into the air and swept my mother a bow. "Well met, Cousin," she said. "You will remember me from now on, will you not?"

With that, she vanished in a puff of smoke, through which I plummeted straight down into my nurse's desperate arms. Behind her, she left just the faintest tang of sulphur, and the ghost of a laugh that never quite died. It lingered in the air, like an elusive smell. Vanishing for days, for weeks, on end, only to creep around a corner and assault you when you least expected.

Haunting us all for more than a hundred years to come.

# Chapter Two

MAMAN SWOONED, OF COURSE.

She always does what a lady is supposed to do, though, to be fair, on this occasion even I must admit her behavior had good cause. For many moments, all was pandemonium. But at last, I was restored to my cradle, Maman to her senses, and the guests to relative calm.

Interestingly enough, it is Nurse's recollection that the person largely responsible for the return to order was Oswald. This in spite of the fact that he was only ten years old. Whether he performed this good deed out of the goodness of his heart, or from some other motive, I cannot say.

Though the goodness of his heart theory seemed doubtful to me for many years. Before you can act out of the goodness of your heart, it helps to actually have one.

But it was after order was restored that the next dreadful thing happened, because it was then that Maman said: "Do something, someone."

A thing which probably doesn't seem so bad, unless you understand that what she really wanted wasn't for somebody to *do* something, but to *undo* it. Specifically, of course, to undo what Cousin Jane had done. And even this probably makes perfect sense to you—why not do everything you can to undo a great evil? Why not just erase it if you have the power?

The thing is, you can't just go around undoing other people's magic. In the first place, it's considered terribly impolite, not to mention impractical. If you do it to someone else, what's to stop them from doing it to you? Before long, you'd have absolute chaos.

There is a more important consideration, of course.

If you start undoing magic, *any kind of magic,* you run the risk of undoing everything else. That's how tightly magic is bound up in the way things are where I come from.

And so my mother's request, so reasonable on the face of it, actually contained within it the seeds of the direst consequence: the unraveling of the way our world is woven. Because, as even the world's clumsiest weaver can tell you, you can't pull on one thread without affecting all the others.

Everyone who heard her plea knew this. Indeed I think she knew it herself. I also think she simply didn't care at that point. She'd never been comfortable with magic. Always, it had seemed unnatural to her. As unnatural as having your wish for a child snatched away almost as soon as it had been granted, for example. If that was the way the world worked, why not unravel it and start again?

*"Do something, someone."*

At least she didn't ask my father. To have begged a king to make a choice between saving his daughter or saving his kingdom would have been a dreadful thing. One that had the power to tear his heart apart without any magic at all. And I think my mother knew this, and wished to spare him. For she truly loved my father. Their long years of waiting for a child had drawn them closer together, not pushed them farther apart.

So it wasn't to my father she turned in her desire to erase what Cousin Jane had done. It was to her closest friend and number one lady-in-waiting: my godmother, Chantal.

No, she was not a fairy godmother. There aren't any fairies where I grew up; how many times must I tell you? But it is true that Chantal was generally acknowledged to have the most powerful magic in all the land, stronger even than my father's. And all of it good. Her true colors were as bright and clean as the colors of a rainbow. If anyone had the power to undo what Cousin Jane had done, it would be Chantal.

I often wondered, as I grew up, what her answer must have cost her. And the thing about understanding yourself, knowing your true colors, is that you have to be true to them. For if you don't, they change, and so do you. And so there was really only one thing my godmother could reply.

"I cannot do what you ask, Mathilde. What is done cannot be undone. You will know that if you think reasonably for a moment, just as you will know how sorry I am to answer you so."

But my mother was beyond reason. "For pity's sake, Chantal!

This is my *child*. Your godchild," she cried. "Does that mean anything to you?"

"Of course it does," my godmother answered in a voice that Nurse told me once sounded like an old piece of wood. "But this child is not worth unraveling the world for. No one is."

My mother struck her then. In anger, in pain, and in despair. If Chantal would not save me, no one could. And how much worse must it have been for my mother to hear my doom pronounced not by an enemy, a stranger, but by someone she knew well. Someone she trusted and loved.

"Leave me," she said, in a voice that sounded as if she had something hard and sharp stuck in her throat. "Leave this kingdom and don't ever come back."

Nurse has always maintained Maman took another breath, intending to say more. To proclaim a dire end should Chantal disobey her, should she dare to show her face anywhere within our borders. If she would not commute my fate, then hers would be to suffer a death sentence of her own.

But at that moment, Papa intervened. Not with words, for that was not his way. He simply placed a hand upon my mother's arm. As he did so, my mother swallowed the sharp thing inside her throat and her words choked off.

My godmother showed her true colors to the last. She gave my mother one perfect bow. Then she slowly walked down from the dais where she had been standing behind my mother's throne, toward where my cradle rested at the bottom of the steps. As she did, there occurred something odd. She began to weep. Not that that is strange in and of itself, but as her tears struck the marble steps, they made a clatter. All looked, and were astonished at what they saw.

For Chantal was weeping pearls so lustrous and fine their match has never yet been brought up from the depths of the ocean. At a signal from my father, attendants gathered them up. To this day, I have a necklace of them as tall as I am. But every time I put it on, the urge to weep becomes so overwhelming that I have never worn it.

When she reached my cradle, my godmother stopped and turned around, and bowed again.

"Your Majesties," she said. "All others here have given their gifts to the Princess Aurore. But I have not yet bestowed mine."

Though she had made a statement, my father understood that she was asking a question, and so he nodded his head, tightening his hold upon my mother's arm.

"If what is done cannot be undone, then let it at least be done again," said my godmother. "This child shall prick her finger at sixteen, but this need not bring death. Instead she will sleep for a hundred years, and be awakened by a kiss at the end of that time. If it's true love that awakens her, so much the better, but this is a thing I cannot promise. For true love comes when it will, not when it is called."

She ran a hand over my cap of golden hair, then leaned down low, as if her next words were for my ears alone. They weren't quite, of course, for Nurse heard them, which is how I know.

"May you keep what you hold in your heart safe and strong, *petite Aurore.*"

Then Chantal straightened and looked right at my mother. "That's the best that I can do, Mathilde," she said. "Whether or not it is enough, only time and Aurore herself can show."

I've often wondered what my life would have been like if Maman had answered, if she had called Chantal back to her side. But she didn't. The sharp thing she had swallowed slid down her throat to her belly. There, it mingled with her pride. And so she let Chantal turn and walk away. None of us ever saw her again. Perhaps she found her place in another story, one with a happier ending. I hope so.

And this was Cousin Jane's greatest accomplishment, I sometimes think. More than the pain the threat of my death caused. By her desperate actions, she drove others to desperation, and so we came to be deprived of our brightest light, our purest colors. Our truest friend and best ally.

And, with Chantal's banishment, it may be said that I truly embarked upon the first ten years of my strange and unusual childhood.

# Chapter Three

DO YOU HAVE ANY IDEA HOW CHALLENGING IT is to live your life deprived of sharp objects? To live each day as if the presence of a butter knife constitutes a threat?

Of course you don't.

Unfortunately, I do, so let me tell you this. A good time is *not* had by all. In fact, by hardly anyone. Sometimes I think the only person who really enjoyed those first years of my childhood was Oswald. And why should he, you might well ask. I know I did. *He* wasn't the one being reminded every day that *he'd* had two spells cast over him when he was only one month old.

The truth of the matter, as he often found occasion to mention, was that, in spite of my birth, Oswald's situation really hadn't changed very much. He was still my father's heir. For, as the years passed, Papa did nothing to change the decree of succession. In fact, contrary as this might seem, my birth might even have improved things for my cousin. I was only going to be around till I was sixteen, after all. At that point, something nasty was going to happen in spite of all my parents were doing to prevent it. Somehow or other, I was going to manage to stab myself. (Oswald was particularly fond of this word. *Stab.* It had such a healthy, gruesome sound.)

The resulting wound didn't have to be very big. One bright drop of blood was all that was required to activate the spell(s). After which, I'd probably just fall right down on the spot. Saved from death, that much was true. But, in its place, condemned to the nap from hell. A hundred years is a long time to slumber. More than enough to give Oswald *and* his heirs time of their own. Time to consolidate their hold upon the kingdom that should, by rights, be mine when I awoke.

And then of course there was a possibility that could not be dismissed, according to my cousin anyway, and that was that I might not wake up at all. Who in their right mind was going to want to kiss someone who'd been sleeping for a hundred years? Would I still be young? Or would I age as I slept and so grow old? Chantal's counterspell hadn't been very precise upon that point, even I had to admit.

Not a very promising future for me, all in all.

Which brings me to a second set of things I've always wondered: Did Oswald and Jane know each other? How much of what happened at my christening did my cousin know about ahead of time, even though he was just a boy?

There is no proof they knew each other at all, of course. Or none except the way the certainty of it, the rightness, seemed to ring in my heart like a great bronze bell.

Here is what I think happened: They met by accident, Jane and Oswald, in some musty little-used corridor. Or perhaps it was in Oswald's favorite hiding place, the one that enabled him to overhear the most secrets. He simply turned around, and there she was. For it has always seemed to me that their magic was complementary. A perfect fit, like the way Oswald's hand looks in one of his immaculately tailored kid gloves.

His great talent in those early days was for uncovering secrets. Hers, for being a secret in and of herself. What could be more natural than that they should discover one another? And that they would be drawn together having done so? It made no difference that he was young while she was grown. Kindred spirits are what they are. Their talent lies in recognizing their own true colors in another, and this recognition forms an unbreakable bond.

Perhaps Cousin Jane did what she did for love of Oswald. Who can tell? Certainly not I. Or perhaps she simply saw a way to hurt my parents and at the same time benefit the only person in all those years to have seen her truly. Perhaps it is even the case that her motivations aren't really all that important in the long run. She did what she did, then left the rest of us to deal with it. But there is no denying that the one who came out best was Oswald.

I probably don't have to tell you that I did my best to stay away from him. Most of the time, it wasn't really all that hard. In the first place, he was much older than I was. Eight when I was born. A gap that pretty much guaranteed we'd never have much in common, even if we were fond of each other.

Which we were not.

But about the time I turned ten and Oswald turned eighteen, a funny thing happened. The only way I can describe it is that Oswald grew up. My best guess is that he simply awoke one morning and realized that things might be better for him if he was known as Prince Charming for a reason other than the current one.

Not because he was so obviously *not* charming, but because he so obviously *was*.

I think it was right around this time that my nurse began to tell me bedtime stories featuring the adventures of various leopards who tried to change their spots. Unsuccessfully, I hardly need add.

Oswald had better luck. So much better that, before too long, everyone at court forgot that his nickname had originally been a cruel joke. Now the nobles called him Prince Charming because that's what they thought he actually was. Maman remained unconvinced. What Papa thought, he kept to himself. Chances are good I would have followed my mother's lead, had it not been for one thing:

It was Charming Oswald (as I preferred to call him) who finally convinced my mother to turn me loose in the great outdoors.

For years Maman had argued (with success) that the best

way to hold the spells that threatened me at bay was to keep me indoors, as far away from unexpected things as possible. It was true that I wouldn't be able to engage in any of the more traditional forms of princesslike activities, including the thing at which she excelled: painstakingly boring embroidery. But there were other ladylike tasks I might pursue, such as painting bowls of fruit or braiding rugs to set before the fire.

No matter how many times I ate the fruit instead of painting it, usually getting juice all down my front, and no matter how many times my rugs contained gigantic and mischievous bumps that threatened to send anyone foolish enough to tread upon them hurtling headlong into the fire, Maman insisted that indoors was safer than out. For me, at any rate. There were simply too many surprises out of doors. And after all, as she was fond of saying, usually as a way to end one of our inevitable arguments, even a simple stick, properly wielded, is capable of drawing one bright drop of blood.

In vain did I vehemently protest and my father gently suggest that she was being just a tad over-protective. The spells spoken over me in my cradle weren't supposed to be fulfilled until I was sixteen years old. Couldn't I at least go out from time to time till then? Well-supervised, of course.

Her answer was always the same: No. No. A thousand times, no. And that was the way things stood, until Oswald managed his amazing transformation and became genuinely charming. And no sooner had he completed one transformation, than he performed another: He changed my mother's mind.

"Well," he said one day, a particularly fine one, as I recall. So fine it had provoked an unusually impassioned plea on my part to be let out, and an equally impassioned denial from Maman.

All this happened shortly after lunch. We were in my mother's solar, a bright room at the top of the tallest tower, the room in which we always sat when the weather was fine. The fruit that had not been consumed at luncheon was now arranged into an improbably artistic pile and prominently displayed in a dish on a sideboard. My paints and easel stood nearby. Maman glanced significantly at them both from time to time, while her fingers worked her current piece of embroidery.

I wasn't about to do what she wanted, of course. Instead, I sat on the windowseat beside my father and tried my best not to pout. Not that I held back from this as a rule, but I did not want to pout in front of Oswald. My father reached over and tousled my hair in an attempt to cheer me up.

"Really, Philippe," Maman protested at once. "You'll make her all mussy, and she does that often enough all by herself. You were saying?" she asked, switching her attention back to Oswald. Not that she really wanted to know what he would say, but giving him her attention was an excellent way to show she was put out with me and Papa.

"I was saying that I'm sure you know best, Aunt Mathilde," Oswald said with an engaging smile. He really was astonishingly handsome, particularly when he smiled, a thing I may have neglected to mention before. His hair was everyday enough: dark brown. But his eyes were gray and flecked with gold. Like the ocean on a stormy day when the sun breaks through and flashes across the surface of the water for just a moment. When you looked at Oswald, you didn't want to look away. There was a thing about him that captured you and wouldn't let go.

At the moment, he was standing in front of the fireplace on what was, perhaps, the most unfortunate of all my rugs. Fortunately for him, there was no fire, as the day was so warm and fine.

"I refer, of course, to the matter of Aurore being allowed to go outside," he went on. "I might pursue a different course, if she were *my* child." Here a look of horror crossed his face, as if he realized he might have gone too far, and his words broke off.

"What different course?" my mother demanded at once.

A thing that might seem strange, on the face of it, considering she disliked Charming Oswald. But she disliked the thought that he might have considered something she hadn't even more. (A thing I'm absolutely certain Oswald knew quite well. My cousin was many different things, but stupid wasn't one of them.)

"It's just that it occurs to me," he said. He paused to flick an imaginary piece of lint from his sleeve and Maman leaned forward as if spellbound. "If Aurore's activities were more . . . varied, she might actually be safer in the long run. Naturally, as her mother, you would not notice such a thing yourself, but the truth is—"

Here he paused again, this time to poke at the biggest lump in the rug with the toe of one perfectly-polished boot. "The truth is that Aurore can be rather clumsy at times." He raised those strange eyes to mine, the gold in them shimmering with mischief. "No offense, cousin."

I bared my teeth, wishing I could sink them into his leg. I might have been only ten, but I could tell that he was up to something. Usually this resulted in me being in trouble.

"None taken, cousin."

"Of course I know she is clumsy," my mother snapped, at which my father made a sound. "Surely that is all the more reason to keep her indoors."

"Well, yes," Oswald said slowly, this time paying great attention to the little finger of his right hand on which he wore the signet ring that had once belonged to his father. "If you say so. That is one way of looking at it, I suppose. But surely you'd hate for her to grow up ignorant as well. Anyone may be either clumsy or stupid by birth, but it's really too bad for a person to be both things at once. Unless they simply can't help it, of course."

My mother's eyes narrowed and I held my breath. Of all the signs that my mother was becoming angry, this was the most dangerous one. The one most likely to result in an explosion. Beside me on the windowseat, I could tell that Papa was holding his breath, too.

"Are you trying to say that my daughter is a dullard by birth or that I am raising her to be so?" Maman demanded softly.

"Oh, my dear Aunt Mathilde!" Oswald exclaimed, his expression horrified. He moved to her swiftly and got down before her on one knee. "Now it is I who have been dull and clumsy, for I have failed to make you see my point. I only meant that the more of the world Aurore knows, the less chance it will have to surprise her. For isn't that what we all fear the most? That her fate will take her unawares, and so overcome her?"

"*C'est exact.* That is so," spoke up my father.

"Well," my mother sniffed, with a sharp glance in his direction. "If you're going to take his side . . ."

"But surely it is not a question of sides," Oswald protested, at his most sincere and charming. "It is only a question of what is best for Aurore."

A silence fell as we all looked at my mother. I could see her turning Oswald's words over and over in her mind, the way a fast-moving stream tumbles a stone. Seeking out the rough places, scouring them smooth.

"You think that Aurore will be safer if she is allowed to go outdoors."

"I do," Oswald answered promptly. "Children are curious, Aunt Mathilde. They mean no disrespect to their elders in this. It is simply the way they are. Since this is so, why not let Aurore indulge her curiosity? Let her go outside if that is what she desires.

If you don't, she'll only find ways to get into trouble where she is."

And it was this argument, so undeniably true, that finally won my mother over and changed her mind.

"Very well," she said at last. "Aurore may go out as long as she stays within the palace walls. But I really must insist . . ."

I never did hear what it was she wanted to insist I do. Or not do, more likely. Because by then I was off and running, out the door and down the long curving staircase that led from the solar to the great hall. Across the hall and through a side door I knew led to the kitchens, though I had never been allowed to spend more than a few stolen moments there (too many sharp objects such as skewers and knives).

And then, finally, there it was: the great oak door that lead from the kitchen itself into the kitchen garden. As it was a sunny day and the kitchen was warm, the door was standing wide open. Through it, I could see the sunshine running over the garden like honey. For as long as I could remember, I had wanted to walk through this door. To pull radishes and carrots as I had seen the gardeners do from my bedroom window. To eat them with the dirt still clinging to them, not even pausing to wash them off.

A pretty mundane place to want to begin my exploration of the great wide world, you may be thinking.

I can only say, with all due respect, that you would be wrong. There can be no better place to begin your exploration of the world than by stepping out your own back door.

The kitchen staff was well familiar with my longing to go

out into the garden. They also knew it was forbidden, a thing that had always made them shake their heads and cluck their tongues. As I edged toward the doorway I heard Cook's voice say, "You'd best stop right there, now, Princess Aurore. You know how your lady mother feels about you going outside."

"It's all right," an unexpected voice said. "Let her go." I jumped, for the voice was Oswald's. *"Madame la Reine* has changed her mind," he explained. "From now on, the princess Aurore may go into the garden."

At this, a spontaneous cheer swept through the kitchen, and I shot through the open door as if fired from a slingshot. I was so eager to explore everything at once, I ended up standing stock-still instead, simply inhaling the heavily scented air of the garden.

A thousand smells seemed to rush toward me at once, as eager to welcome me as I was to be among them. That one was rosemary, with its medicinal tang as sharp and pointed as its dark and shiny leaves. This, the musty pungence of oregano and thyme. Beneath them was a thick, rich smell that I imagined must be the earth itself. A scent that seemed to me to be the same as its colors, green and brown.

And over everything there lay a scent so sweet it made my head spin. Later I learned it was orange blossom. Just being able to stand in the sun and breathe it all in made me want to run around in circles and be still as a stone at the same time.

Though in the years that followed I went farther and farther afield, farther than I could dream was possible at that moment, in those first seconds of freedom, I had everything I'd ever craved. The kitchen garden was world and free enough.

When I finally did begin to move about, so engrossed did I become that it took me some time to realize that Oswald had followed and was watching from the arch of the open kitchen door. And there was in his face a thing for which I have no name even now, after all the years that have come and gone.

"Cousin, come and look at this!" I cried. And so he moved to kneel beside me in the garden, not caring that his perfect clothes got dirty in the process, a thing that, until that moment, I hadn't even noticed about mine.

I had found a plant whose leaves were pointed on both ends and broad in the middle. Bumpy top and bottom, colored green and purple all at once. I rubbed them, sniffing my fingers, and Oswald followed suit.

"That is sage, Aurore."

"Sage," I breathed. A word I knew meant wise. "Do all the names of plants describe the hearts of men, then?" I asked.

And Oswald answered, "No, not very often. I think you've found the only one. Beginner's luck."

I pointed to a plant with leaves as green as spring itself, long and pointed as the tips of spears. "What is that?"

"That is tarragon."

Twice more I pointed, and both times, he knew the answers. "You know them," I said, and even I could hear my voice was filled with awe. "You know them all."

"No," Oswald said. "Not all, just some. If you want to know them all, we must get the head gardener for that."

I gave him a sidelong glance. "Or perhaps the gardener's lovely daughter."

Her name was Mary. I'd seen her from my window and knew she was every bit as beautiful as her father's garden. Her hair was the rich dark color of the fertile soil. Her eyes were as green as the first leaves of springtime. I'd heard Nurse and my mother's lady's maid clucking their tongues over her and Oswald. He had his eye on her, they said. I wasn't sure what that meant, but it sounded suspicious.

Oswald reached out and tweaked the end of my braid which had, of course, begun to come undone.

"Very well," he said, neatly calling my bluff. "Shall we call her?"

"Not today," I said swiftly. "Tomorrow." For tomorrow would be different. Still wonderful, yes. But not filled with this same wonder. You don't have to be a grown up to understand the way things change. To understand that a thing can be truly new only once, and precious because it came to you when you did not look for it.

"Today, tell me what you know. Please, Charming Oswald."

This time, he gave my hair a tug. "I hate it when you call me that."

"I know."

At that, the thing in his face for which I'd had no name

became a thing I recognized, and that thing was a smile. "Just for today," I begged. "I won't ask again."

"Of course you will," he contradicted. "You're always asking for impossible things, Aurore. It's one of the very few things I like about you."

I sat back, intrigued. "Why?"

He was silent for so long I thought he would not answer, but finally he replied. "I guess because I want impossible things too, only I have never dared to ask for mine aloud."

"It doesn't do much good," I said, surprised to discover that I was drawn to console him. "I never get any of the things I ask for."

"You did today," said Oswald.

"Because of you," I answered. "Thank you, Charming Cousin."

At this I could tell that, for perhaps the first time in our lives together, I had surprised him. Pleasantly, I mean.

"You are welcome, *ma petite Aurore*. Very well, just for today then. I will tell you what I know. But don't expect me to be so nice to you every day."

"Don't worry," I said. "I won't."

At this, Oswald laughed and stood, not even bothering to brush off his dirty knees. He extended one hand down. I reached up to take it. He wrapped his fingers around mine in a grip that was at once gentle and strong, and together we set off to explore the rest of the garden.

Though things between us would never be simple, there was

a change from that moment on. He no longer tormented me quite so much, nor made quite so many mentions of my inevitable untimely end. And I no longer pointed out to him that, though he was my father's heir, he was still his second choice.

And there were many who remarked upon the fact that, when I discovered some new thing that I wanted explained or simply wished to share, I took my treasure first not to Papa or Maman, or even to my nurse, but to my cousin. And they remarked also that, whatever he might be doing, Oswald excused himself from it at once and remained with me until I had all the answers I wanted.

Whatever would come between us, sooner or later, nothing would ever be able to erase the thing that had been that day engraved upon my heart: It was Oswald who had won for me my freedom, the thing that I desired most.

And in doing this, he also brought about the third and last of his amazing transformations, for such things always come in threes, as you must know.

First, he changed himself. Second, he changed my mother's mind. And, finally, with my first step out of doors, he changed the inside of me, for he rewove the very fabric of my heart.

It still beat with a trip and a hammer, for that is the way a heart must go. But, whereas before it had woven only dark things when it dwelled upon my cousin, now within the fabric of my heart there ran, for him and him alone, one single strand of pure, untarnishable gold.

# Chapter Four

THE YEARS THAT FOLLOWED WERE THE HAPPIEST of my life. Though I suppose I should say the happiest until now. But the *now* that has but so lately come to pass was *then* so far away as to be almost invisible. The thinnest wisp of white cloud in a sky the same color blue as Maman's favorite china cups. I couldn't yet even imagine that *now* would ever be.

So I'll say it again:

The years that followed were the happiest of my life.

Oh, I still did plenty of things I didn't particularly want to, such as painting trees and wildflowers, for instance. Though even I had to admit this was an improvement over the never-ending parade of fruit still lifes. And there was one area in which as far as I was concerned Maman took Oswald's words a bit too much to heart. She now insisted that I learn to embroider, reasoning that the more familiar I was with my needle the less likely I would be to jab myself and so draw one bright drop of blood.

But, on the whole, things were so much better there is really no comparison.

Except for the nightmare, of course.

I suppose I should have expected there would be a price to pay for my newly acquired freedom. But I didn't. You don't really stop to consider these things when you're only ten years old. I didn't yet perceive the way everything that happens is connected—didn't realize that opening a door that led to outside exploration would inevitably open a door to the unexplored places inside myself.

And just as exploring the outside world brought new words to my vocabulary (*hyacinth, chamomile, mugwort*), so did exploring my inner world give me new terms to ponder. *Fear, confusion,* and *ambiguity* above all else. For, though I had certainly heard these words before, I didn't truly understand them until the nightmare began.

The dream was always the same, and I had it once a month. The day of the week varied, but the date stayed constant. The twenty-eighth. The same date on which I had been christened. This might not seem so bad to you. Just twelve nights out of a possible three hundred and sixty-five. But believe me, those twelve were more than enough. And the fact that the dream was always the same didn't make enduring it any easier. It actually made it worse, more inescapable, somehow.

From the time I was ten until I turned sixteen, the thing I dreamed every month, year in and year out, was this: I dreamed that I was someone else.

It unfolded gradually, like swimming through deep water, the way dreams so often do. In images that, from the moment they first occurred, always reminded me of a kaleidoscope. Clear one moment, distorted the next, until they finally settled into clarity again, having rearranged themselves into something else entirely.

I begin the dream by walking through the palace. A thing I've done every day for as long as I can recall. But a new, keen-edged sense of wonder and anticipation fills me. A sense of discovery seems to beckon me on. This is how I first come to realize that I am not myself in the dream. For I have never felt these things about the place where I grew up. For me, it has never been new, but always, simply, home.

No sooner do I realize I am not myself than the kaleidoscope of my dream performs its first revolution. The wonder of discovery begins to distort. It becomes a need, an insatiable hunger so strong I must obey it. And what it wants me to do is to run. As I do, I begin to weep. For it comes to me suddenly that I am searching for a thing I have lost. A thing that, though I cannot name it, I know in my heart matters more than anything else. But even as I wear myself out in the search for it, I know that it is lost forever. I will never be able to find it. It is irretrievably gone.

And as the kaleidoscope begins to turn again, I have one agonizing thought: that somewhere, in all the rooms through which I've traveled, I have lost myself as well.

Now there comes the part of the dream I hate the most. The part where I wish desperately to be awake, so that I could put a stop to everything simply by closing my eyes. But, as they are closed already, I am trapped. Try as I might, I cannot open my eyes and awaken, and so put an end to things that way. The dream is not yet ready to let me go.

For now the kaleidoscope revolves unceasingly, the images forming only for as long as it takes them to dissolve. I feel as if I am tumbling head over heels through the sky. It is dark one moment, filled with colors the next, until I lose all sense of space and time. But one thing always stays with me: the sense of pain, of loss. And as I suddenly see the ground rushing up to meet me I am filled with one desire: to make the whole thing stop, no matter what the cost.

I have heard Nurse say that, if you dream that you are falling, it is very important that you wake up before you hit the ground. Either that, or you must dream you land upon your feet, whole and unharmed. Since this is a nightmare, I do neither of these things. Instead the kaleidoscope turns again and, when it stops, I am lying flat on my face in the dark.

As I lift my head, light and color begin to return. I am in a room full of courtiers dressed in their finest garments. They pass so near that I fear they will tread upon me, but somehow, they do not. I recognize many and I call out to them. Not one replies. But it isn't until I reach out to catch the silken hem of a passing dress that I realize why.

They cannot see me. I can no longer see myself.

I know that I exist. I can feel my churning stomach when I

press a hand against it. Feel the hot stickiness of my own blood run down my face when I slam my head, hard, against the wall. But I can see none of these things. They are invisible, just as I am. Somewhere in the midst of my whirling tumble, I have been whirled right out of existence. Or, at the very least, right out of sight, of heart, of mind.

At this, so excruciating a pain fills me that an extraordinary thing happens: I wink back into being, as if this pain alone is the thing that gives me form. In that moment, I know I must carry it with me always, nurturing it like a child. Feeding it and tending it. I cannot afford to let it die.

For someday, I will find the way to make those who overlook me see me truly. Find the way to make them see the things I long for in my heart. And when I do . . .

I probably don't have to tell you that this is the moment when I always woke up, tears upon my cheeks, torn between relief and disappointment. Happy that the dream was over, it is true. But frightened by an outcome I could never see, and by a puzzle I have never been able to solve.

Who was I?

I can practically hear you say it. Surely the answer is obvious. I was Jane, of course.

This is what my nurse thought, for she said this is the way of strong magic sometimes. Nurse said that the strongest magic doesn't simply act upon us, it *becomes* us. Running with our blood, holding us upright from the inside out, just like our bones.

Two of the most powerful spells ever cast in the whole history of my father's kingdom were made over me. Now, according to Nurse, they lived inside me, constantly at war. One seeking my destruction, the other, my salvation. My nightmare was the inevitable result.

It made sense, I suppose.

Naturally, I tried not going to sleep on what I knew would be a dream night. It never worked. No matter what I did, sleep always came for me sooner or later, bringing the nightmare when it did. I suppose when the things that give you bad dreams live inside you, there's no point in trying to stop them. They're going to come out whenever they decide it is their time. Better just to close your eyes and hold on tight, the faster to get the things you fear to go back to sleep themselves.

I think the worst part is that when you know you dream another person's dream, you can never truly feel at peace. Never truly trust yourself. If you carry around somebody else's nightmare, who knows what else your insides might hide or when it might come out?

Now, where was I?

Oh, yes, the happiest years of my life.

They were, really. Nightmare aside. I got to go outside every day, usually for as long as I wanted. I started by exploring the closest places first. The kitchen garden, and then the other, more formal, palace gardens. Naturally, my favorite one of these was the one devoted entirely to roses, though it always gave Maman fits when I went there. All those thorns.

But finally, after several months, the day came when I had explored every single inch of the palace grounds to my satisfaction and was ready to take the next step: the world outside the palace walls. I wanted this so much it made my bones ache. So much it kept me awake on the nights the dream didn't come. Not in the same way. Not in fear, but in anticipation. As if the wide world had a voice and I alone could hear its call.

I was pretty sure I knew what Maman's reaction to my going outside the palace walls was going to be. As it turned out, it was Papa's reaction that provided the surprise.

I've already told you three important things about Papa and Maman. How they waited for many long years to have a child. How they loved one another in spite of this trial. How Maman preferred to define her world with words, and Papa his with silence. When Papa did choose to say what he thought, however, his words carried a weight Maman's did not. This was not simply because he was king. It was because everyone around him knew that, if he spoke a thing aloud, it was because he had thought it over thoroughly and made up his mind.

So when the day came when I could stand the anticipation no longer and announced at dinner that I wished to broaden my horizons, to go beyond the palace walls, a look of horror crossed Maman's face and she pulled in a breath to give the answer I expected, which would have been: *"Mais non!"*

But before she could, Papa uttered this sentence. "Why do you wish to do such a thing, Aurore?"

At this, I became so astonished every thought flew from my mind. I had been prepared for a battle with Maman, not a discussion with my father.

"I don't know," I stammered out. "I just do, Papa."

Oswald's face assumed the expression it carries when I have done something particularly stupid, a thing that made me want to kick him under the table.

"But you must have a reason," my father urged gently. "I would simply like to hear it. There's no right or wrong answer. Take your time. Not everyone expresses an interest in spending time outside the palace, so I'm curious to know why you wish to. That is all."

*Take that, Oswald,* I thought.

I don't know how things are in the land of your birth, but in mine there is a division, *the great schism* Papa calls it, between those who live at court and those who don't. Those at court are mostly nobles, except for the servants, while those they refer to as the *common people* live outside the palace walls. In towns and villages. In the countryside. The nobles think as little about them as they can afford to, but in this they overlook an important fact of life: It is the ones outside the palace who perform the tasks which keep our country prosperous.

The nobles find no fault with the current arrangement. It's the way things have always been or at least for as long as they care to remember. Why should things not continue the way they are? The common people have come by their name for a perfectly good reason. Doing common labor is what they are good for, the only thing they know. Besides, it's so difficult to tell one from another. With their dirty faces and hands, they all look so very much alike. Better to pay as little attention to them as possible and let them get on with their duties. Better to stay within the palace walls.

Papa disagrees. He's the first king in nobody knows how long to do so. He goes out among the people, which is what he calls them. Either that or *my subjects*. Regardless of which it is, he never calls them common. He knows them by name, at least the ones in the village nearest to the palace. He takes time to listen to their sorrows and their joys. In short, he treats them like what they are: necessary and important, even if they aren't high-born. And the inevitable result of this is that, among them, he is greatly loved.

When Oswald was younger, my father often offered to take him with him when he left the palace. Always an opportunity, never a command. One which Oswald always declined. When it became clear that he would always do so, that his allegiance was to the nobles, my father stopped asking. And that is the way that matters stood during that dinner when Oswald was eighteen and I was ten years old.

"Aurore?" my father prompted softly.

"It's hard to explain," I said. "I think because it's so simple,

Papa. I just know I want to go outside. It seems the right and proper thing to do."

"Yes," my father said patiently. "But why?"

"Because it does!" I exclaimed, feeling my face begin to color. This was becoming more dreadful by the moment. How did you explain a thing it had not occurred to you to question? A thing you just knew, clear through to your soul?

"The palace is wonderful and I love it," I said. "But it isn't everything. I know that there is more. The outside world calls to me, Papa. I *have* to go. I think it's because . . ."

I paused and took a deep breath. I'd said this much. Better just to get the rest of it over with quickly so Oswald could laugh and Papa could say no.

"Going outside is what I was born for. I can't explain it any better than that. I'm sorry, Papa."

During my ragged speech, my father had grown very still. Indeed, it seemed to me that for the space of time it took me to explain, he did not breathe at all, but sat with his head bent and his eyes closed. When I had finished, he exhaled one long, slow breath, sat up straight, and opened his eyes.

"I believe that explanation will do just fine, Aurore. Very well, since going outside is what you wish, you may accompany me when I ride out tomorrow."

With that, he signaled for the majordomo to serve the carrot soup that was the first course of our meal, Maman having been plainly rendered incapable of doing so.

I could hardly believe my ears. "You mean it?" I cried.

"Are you questioning me?" asked Papa. A thing that was unheard of. For a moment I feared I had offended him, for his tone was serious. Then I caught the twinkle at the back of his eyes.

"Absolutely not," I said. "I don't know what came over me."

"*Bien,*" he replied. "That is much better. Now, eat your soup, Aurore. Carrots are good for you, and you will need all your strength in the world outside the walls."

For several moments, we all ate dutifully. No sound in the dining room other than the scrape of spoons against the bottoms and sides of bowls. But, little by little, I felt the air grow thick and heavy, as if, above our heads, it was filling up with storm clouds.

"There is one thing I would have you promise," Papa said, as the soup bowls were removed and a roast chicken was placed in front of him to carve. "Remember that to go into la Forêt is forbidden. You must promise me never to go there, Aurore."

"Of course I promise," I said promptly. A thing that was easy, for, in truth, I'd forgotten all about la Forêt until that moment. I'd have remembered it sooner or later, of course. Who wouldn't remember an enchanted forest? A thing Papa had obviously realized, for he knew me very well.

"I cannot help but wonder, Philippe," Maman said quietly, as if my father's mention of the Forest had given her the opening for which she'd been hoping, "whether taking Aurore outside the palace is such a good idea after all. The world is a very big place. There are many . . . unknowns."

*"Mais oui, bien sûr,"* my father answered, as he calmly picked up the knife and began to carve. "Of course there are unknowns. And the sooner Aurore begins to meet them, the sooner they will cease to be unknown. That is the point. Besides . . ."

He paused and set the knife down. I all but felt my ears prick up, the way the palace dogs' do when they hear an unfamiliar sound. *Something important is coming,* I thought. *Something Papa has been thinking over for a very long time.*

"For many years now we have let the spells spoken over Aurore in her cradle tell us who she is. Now the time has come for her to tell us who she is, as well. For we must never forget that, even if the worst happens and she sleeps for a hundred years, Aurore is a princess. She is royal, with a claim to the throne."

"But you have an heir," I said without thinking. "You have Oswald."

"That is so," my father replied, turning his eyes upon my cousin. "And I have been content to have him be so. But tonight you have done a thing Oswald has never done. You have shown a desire to know *all* those you might rule one day, not just those who are noble-born. More than that, you have told me this is a thing you *must* do. That it was for this that you were born. In this you have spoken like my true heir, for this is how I have felt, also."

By now the air in the room felt so thick, I was surprised

I could still see through it. Across the table from me, Oswald clutched his fork so tightly his knuckles were white as mother-of-pearl buttons.

"You don't want me," he said, his voice tight. "You never have. You want Aurore."

"It is not a matter of what I want," my father answered. "It is a matter of what is best for the kingdom, best for all. Therefore . . ." He took a breath, and I knew in that moment we had come to the heart of what he wished to say. A thing that, since my christening day, he had been holding in his mind.

"Tomorrow, before Aurore and I set out, I will have you and your heirs proclaimed Aurore's stewards, Oswald. She will be my heir from tomorrow forth. It is Aurore who must succeed me, even if it takes a hundred years. Tonight, she has shown this must be so."

I heard Maman's swift intake of breath even as I felt my jaw drop open. It was a sign of her complete surprise that I managed to get it closed again before she could remind me that a lady never shows she has been taken unawares.

"For heaven's sake!" Oswald exclaimed. "All this simply because she wants to go outside the palace walls? She'll probably take two steps and fall into a mud puddle. Think what you are doing, Uncle!"

"What makes you think I have not?" my father replied. "If I had let my heart rule my head in this, I would have proclaimed Aurore as my heir the very day that she was born. But

I did not. I waited—to see who you both would become. You have been content to see only what is before you. Aurore is not. That is all I need to know."

Papa's words were making my head spin, and not just because this was about the longest speech I'd ever heard him utter all at once. He was saying he thought I was worthy to be his successor. Even more, that he *wanted* me to succeed him, a possibility that had never occurred to me before.

And in that moment, I realized there was a thing inside me I had never thought to notice, probably because it had been there all along. And it was, greater even than my desire to see the world, the desire to be worthy of my father's faith and trust.

"All those years," Oswald whispered, and now the devastation was plain in his voice. "All those times you asked me to go with you when you left the palace, but I said no. You never urged me to change my mind. Not once."

"But surely you can see that I could not," my father said. "You had to wish to go for yourself, as Aurore does. Because it was what you wanted, not I."

"You tricked me!" Oswald protested. "You played a game with me, but never told me its rules. You played me false, Uncle."

"No, Oswald," said my father. "And I am sorry that you think so. When you are calmer, I think you will realize I speak the truth. But I suppose it is too much to expect you to think so at this moment."

A thousand painful things seemed to chase themselves

across my cousin's face, each one hard upon the heels of the one before it. Then, as if he had seized a curtain and yanked it across a scene he had never intended to reveal, his face went blank, though his eyes continued to smolder. I was glad he did not turn them upon me, much as I wanted him to know that I was sorry for what was happening. I had not known what Papa intended any more than Oswald had. But I greatly feared that he would blame me for it.

"Madame," he said to my mother. He pushed back from the table, tossing his linen napkin onto his plate. "The dinner you provide is excellent, as always. But I fear I may have suddenly become unwell, for I find I have no appetite for it. You will excuse me, I hope?"

My mother cleared her throat before she spoke. "But of course," she replied.

Oswald rose from the table, his back as hard and straight as iron. He bowed in turn to each of my parents, then gave me the lowest, most elaborate bow of all. He departed without another word, the heels of his boots striking so hard that sparks flew up from the flagstones.

"Well, that's that," my father said, when he had gone. "I suppose there was no way to avoid hurting him, but even so . . ." He broke off, shaking his head, then picked up the knife and began to carve the chicken once more.

"I hope you know what you're doing, Philippe," my mother said.

*"Bien sûr,"* my father answered simply. "I am doing what must be done. It will be all right, Mathilde. You must trust me."

"I do. You know I do. But I hope to God you're right in this, Philippe," Maman replied. Her eyes stared at the door through which Oswald had departed. "He has the nobles' love. He has made it his life's work."

"He is like his father in that," Papa replied. "It may be enough for the son of a younger son. But not for one who will govern. The one who will do that must see beyond the palace walls."

"He would make a dangerous enemy," my mother cautioned.

"Then we must take care that he does not become one," answered Papa. "He is angry now, but his anger will pass. He is too smart to hold on to it for long. Now, if it's all the same to everyone else, I'd like to finish the rest of my dinner in peace and quiet."

"As you wish, Philippe," Maman said. And she held out her plate for some chicken.

But I said. *"Merci,* Papa."

At this, he smiled. "You are welcome, Aurore. But, I think it is I who should thank you."

"For what?" I asked in surprise.

But it was Maman who answered, and in a way which brought tears to my eyes.

"For growing up the way we hoped you might," she said.

After which none of us felt the need to say anything more.

## Chapter Five

AND SO THE NEXT SIX YEARS OF MY LIFE BEGAN, with a proclamation read aloud the next morning from high atop the palace walls. In it, all my father's people learned that I would be his successor, no matter how long it took, rather than my cousin, no matter how great his charms, though naturally the proclamation itself was more diplomatic on these points.

The reactions to the announcement were predictable. Dead silence from the nobles inside the palace; wild cheering from the people outside the walls. For apparently the fact that my father loved me dearly and had cherished high hopes for my future was well known outside the palace. As well known there as it was little known inside. (Not because he had said this to anyone directly, I think, but because, to the people, this was the natural order of things. What should be so.)

When it was further announced that the king and his daughter would shortly be riding forth, the cheering from outside grew so loud as to be almost deafening, while the nobles simply faded back inside the palace like so many bugs crawling back into their holes.

If I had been wiser in the ways of the world, I might have been more concerned about this. But I wasn't. I was only ten years old. Besides, I already knew the nobles did not love me. They had already given all the love they had to Oswald.

He stood just behind my father as the proclamation was being read, the counterbalance to the fact that I stood just in front of him. What my cousin was thinking, I could not tell. The curtain was still drawn across his face and now even across his eyes. If he was angry or hurt, dissatisfied in any way, he did not show it.

I hardly need tell you this day marked another change between us. I no longer went to him with things that interested me, questions to be answered, puzzles I needed help deciphering. For what else could they do but remind him of what he had lost? All the things he had not chosen? I caught him studying me from time to time, as, indeed, I sometimes studied him, though I tried not to show it. Save for the times when functions of state required us to be together, we stayed apart. It was simpler all around if we avoided one another.

But I was not thinking of such things. Not on that first bright morning. For it was after the proclamation was read that my father gave the signal for the palace gates to be thrown open. Then, seated before him on his great gray horse, he and I rode through them together and out into the world beyond the palace walls.

I can still remember the quiet. The way more people than

I had ever seen before abruptly fell silent at the sight of me. Voices beyond my ability to measure suddenly hushing all at once. And twice as many eyes as that, fixed on the place where I sat before my father. I remember gripping the horse's mane so tightly the coarse hairs cut into my hands.

And then Papa said: "My friends, I give to you my daughter and heir, the Princess Aurore."

At that, a great shout went up. The women fluttered their aprons; men tossed their caps into the air; children jumped up and down. And I did a thing that surprised everyone, myself most of all. I tossed my leg over the horse's head, slid to the ground, and dashed straight into the crowd.

Years later, in a particularly cross and cynical moment, Oswald asked me how I had known to do this. For he claimed it was the best, most perfect thing I could have done. To run to them, my people, my subjects. To fly to them with outstretched arms. *I want to know you,* my action said. *There is no difference between us. We are the same, you and I.*

My only answer was that I hadn't truly known anything, not in a way that lets you plan things ahead of time. I simply did what my heart demanded. And, in this way, I answered the demands of my people's hearts as well.

The years that followed are one bright blur, in which I spent as little time inside the palace as possible. Instead, I learned to do anything in the world outside I could. No task was too menial, too dirty, too hard.

I learned to plow and plant the fields, not letting the fact that I sunburned my face and blistered my hands stop me. I held on until I developed calluses and my skin settled down to the color of toasted almonds. I learned to cut peat for fires and the proper way to thatch a roof. I fell off. Twice. The second time I broke my arm.

While recuperating, I spent time with the herbalist, learning which plants could bring down a fever, which could purge a stomach, which were best for the dying of cloth. I even learned which plants could be used to bring about a death, though I swore to keep this information to myself.

When my arm had mended, I learned to shear a sheep, to card and spin its wool. Lest I become too domestic, I also learned to shoot an arrow from my very own bow and to throw a knife. Accurately in both instances. Though I never revealed these particular talents to Maman. Just as I never revealed the fact that, if I was doing particularly dirty or heavy work, I tied my hair back, stuffed it underneath a cap, and wore a tunic, boots, and breeches, just like a boy.

In short, I pretty much stopped behaving like a regular princess altogether and had the time of my life. But there were two things I never forgot: la Forêt and Oswald.

My thoughts on my cousin, I kept to myself. For, though not precisely secret, they were certainly confused, a thing which kept me from asking him about la Forêt as I might once have done. After thinking it over for quite some time, I finally decided that the person who could give me the answers I wanted was none other than Papa. For had he not been the one to remind me the Forest was off-limits in the first place?

I waited until he was alone. Maman had still not quite forgiven me for the broken arm, and if she learned I was interested in la Forêt, I half feared she'd shut me in my room and bolt the door. Papa often spent time in his study at the end of the day. It was there I sought him out one night when I was supposed to be in bed, being careful to first knock on the door. No one entered my father's study without his permission, not even Maman. It was his only private place.

"Come," my father's voice called.

I turned the heavy doorknob and pushed open the door. My father was sitting in a far corner of the room in a great chair made of dark brown leather. He had a book in his lap and spectacles perched upon his nose. He pulled these off and tucked them in a pocket as I came in.

"Why, Aurore. I thought that you had gone to bed."

"I can't sleep, Papa," I blurted out. "There is something I would like to know and not knowing is keeping me awake."

"This sounds serious," my father said, but I could see the way his eyes smiled. He took his feet from a low footstool covered in the same leather as the chair and gestured for me to sit down. "Have you come to tell me what it is?"

I nodded, and he gestured for me to continue. "Why is it forbidden to enter la Forêt, Papa?"

"Oh, Aurore." He closed his eyes for a fraction of a second, as if marshalling his strength, then opened them again. "I don't suppose it would do any good to mention how sincerely I have hoped you would never ask that question?"

"But you've made me your heir, Papa. I will be responsible for la Forêt myself one day. Don't you think its history is a thing that I should know?"

"You want to watch saying things like that," my father remarked. "It will make people think you're too clever for your own good. Not that you aren't right, of course. Very well. But don't tell your mother. She'll have my head."

"It shall be our secret," I vowed.

"La Forêt has been as it is for as long as I can remember," my father said. "Some would say for time out of mind. In my grandfather's time, there was a woman in the village so ancient none could remember her right name and so she was called *la Vieille,* the Old Woman. It was la Vieille who told my father what I am about to tell you.

"La Forêt is cursed, Aurore."

I felt something cold skitter down the back of my legs. "Cursed?" I said. "By whom?"

"According to la Vieille, by two great sorcerers," said Papa. "Where they came from originally, I cannot say. But they ended up here, in our land that is steeped in magic, for no other reason than to use it for their own purposes. To try to turn our magic to their will in a great contest."

"But why? What for?"

At this, my father shrugged his shoulders. "To prove who was strongest, perhaps. No one really knows."

"That's an awfully stupid reason," I said. "And if they were sorcerers they ought to have known better than to go messing around with magic that way."

My father's lips twitched, but he nodded gravely. "That is surely so. It is said that the one who triumphed realized his folly in the end and, with the last of his strength, he cast a spell. One that contained the destruction, the unraveling, that had been wrought inside the boundaries of la Forêt. He could not heal it, but at least he could stop it from spreading any more."

"But what's wrong with the Forest?" I asked.

My father cocked his head. "I'm not sure *wrong* is quite the way to describe it," he said. *"Different* might be a better choice. The magic of la Forêt isn't like magic anywhere else. And remember it is contained. Folded in upon itself with nowhere to go. Even time moves differently there. For the magic of la Forêt doesn't need human minds to work its will. Instead it has a mind and will of its own.

"I've seen it snow beneath the trees on a warm spring day. Placed a marker opposite a sapling one week, then returned the next to find nothing but a gnarled and rotting stump. La Forêt makes its own rules, Aurore. But what they are, it alone knows."

"Does no one ever go in?" I asked, for it seemed to me that, though he had warned me away from it, Papa himself had come very close.

"From time to time," answered my father. "According to la Vieille, if you enter the Forest with goodness in your heart, it will pretty much leave you alone. If you're lucky, it will even let you come back out again. But those entering it bent on mischief or destruction are never seen again. I hope you can see now why it is forbidden to go there."

"Of course I do," I said. "Thank you for telling me, Papa."

"Do you think you can sleep now?" my father asked.

I slid off the footstool. "Yes, Papa. I think so. And don't worry. I'll remember my promise." With that, I gave him a kiss good night.

"See that you do, Aurore."

And so my curiosity about la Forêt was satisfied, for the time being. And the tale my father had told me was enough to make even me leave the Forest alone. But I would be lying if I said that I forgot about it. Indeed, it sometimes seemed to me that the more I tried not to think about la Forêt, the more it took shape within my mind. It called to me, just as the world outside the palace had. Someday, it whispered, when the time was right, my moment to enter it would come.

And that is the way that matters stood when my childhood ended on the day that my sixteenth birthday arrived.

# Chapter Six

NATURALLY, MY PARENTS INSISTED ON THROWING me a party. Equally naturally, I wished that they would not. The fact that I was turning sixteen might not be much cause for celebration, particularly when one considered what was supposed to be the year's inevitable outcome. But my parents were adamant, even Papa. It was important to honor this birthday, he said. Not only for itself, but to show that we were not afraid of whatever was to come.

Finally we compromised. They threw me two parties. One in the village, one in the palace. The first I enjoyed. The second I did not. For it was at that party that it finally came home to me how completely unlike anyone else at court I truly was.

Not surprisingly, this revelation had to do with Oswald.

He was twenty-four now, well past time to be married. For obvious reasons, his choice of wife was considered of some importance and now, perhaps, time was running out. It was probably Maman who decided that, as long as we were throwing a party anyway, it might as well be used to parade as many eligible young ladies in front of Oswald as possible. But this decision produced an outcome Maman did not expect. Actually, two outcomes.

It showed Oswald to advantage, making clear how at ease he was among the nobles. What a catch he would be for any of their daughters. And it showed me to be his opposite. Out of place and frankly miserable. An odd duck in a sea of well-dressed swans.

I had attended court functions over the years, of course. I wasn't entirely ignorant of how to behave, though I was better at cutting peat than dancing a pavane. But the banquets or balls I had attended prior to this one hadn't been about me. For me. I'd been able to put in a brief appearance, perform what duty required, then escape to my room to plan my next day's adventure outside the palace walls. But this was an approach I could hardly take tonight, as the whole evening was in my honor.

It wasn't that anyone was rude. They wouldn't have dared, for one thing. If anything, they were incredibly polite. But it was this very politeness that finally first began to grate upon my nerves, and then to cause despair to rise up within my throat and threaten to choke me. For, no matter how smooth and correct the words issuing from the courtiers' mouths were, they couldn't quite hide the scorn or laughter in their eyes. And so, on the night of my sixteenth birthday, I saw myself as they saw me for the very first time.

My fingernails were clean, but my fingertips were stained a

faint blue. I had been helping the village weavers dye wool for winter cloaks. There were calluses upon my palms.

My hair didn't gleam like polished wood or stay perfectly in place as the courtiers' daughters' did, though it was true that it was still an almost impossible shade of gold. But all those years of being stuffed inside a cap had given it a horror of being confined and, over time, it had developed a will of its own. No matter how many pins Maman and Nurse jabbed in to hold it in place, my hair insisted on going wherever it wanted. Usually at unexpected and inopportune times.

On the dance floor, I forgot the steps and trod upon my partners' feet, though, naturally, they were too polite to comment. My new shoes, which Maman had proclaimed were the height of fashion, were just a shade too tight and pinched my toes. The whole evening was like suffering through the clumsiest moments of my childhood all over again—this time with the whole court looking on.

Finally, after a number of dances that seemed interminable, it was deemed time to take a break for refreshments and I sought a respite behind the column in the ballroom's farthest corner. What I really wanted was to make a mad dash for my room, but I knew there wasn't any point. Even if I would allow myself to give in to such behavior, Nurse never would. She would simply complete the evening's humiliations by sending me right back down.

So I settled for tucking myself away, leaning my hot face

against the cool stone of the column and praying for time to speed up so that the party might be done. And that was when I heard a woman's voice I did not recognize say:

"But where is the guest of honor, the princess Aurore?"

I straightened up. It would never do to let anyone catch me moping. But, in spite of the defects the evening was making so clear, it was apparently easier to overlook me than I had thought. For a moment later I heard a voice say: "I do not see her." And this voice I knew, for it belonged to Oswald.

"How odd," the first voice said. "Surely she must wish to be the center of attention. I know I would, if the party were in my honor." Here, she gave a laugh like the tinkling of silver chimes in the wind. "But my father says there is no point in such a comparison, for I am not the least bit like her."

"In that, he is correct," answered Oswald. "You are nothing like Aurore."

Again his companion laughed, though this time I thought the sound was not so pleasing. "Tell me," she urged. "Has the princess grown as . . . unusual as they say? I myself have not seen her since we were both young girls, for I have been among my mother's people and have but lately returned to court."

"She is like no other," Oswald replied. Which only goes to show how good at court word play he truly was, for it wasn't really an answer at all.

"You must be such a comfort to the king and queen," the young woman said, at which point I began to wish I could edge around the column without being noticed, the better to discover who she was.

There was a tiny silence. In it, I suddenly felt a lock of hair tumble around my shoulders.

"What makes you say that?" asked Oswald.

"Well, I mean, since their daughter is so . . . unusual," said the young woman I was beginning to think of as *l'Inconnue,* the Unknown. I'd never really minded the word *unusual* before. I'd rather liked it, in fact. But from her mouth, it sounded like an insult. What word might she have chosen if she were speaking to someone else? I wondered. One she had no wish to impress, and furthermore, one who was not my cousin.

"Surely the king and queen rejoice in knowing one as suitable as you will one day sit upon the throne," *l'Inconnue* went on.

There was a second silence, during which I felt another lock of hair come down.

"I regret to inform you that you are mistaken," Oswald said, and there was something in his voice I could not quite decipher. "I will be steward, not king. It is not my destiny to sit upon a throne."

"You think not?" *l'Inconnue* asked softly. "You seem to me to be no fool, my lord. Therefore, I think you know what all smart men do: The title means nothing. King or steward, it will amount to the same thing. You will be the one to rule, for the only one who might object will be in no position to stop you."

"*Mademoiselle*, you quite take my breath away," Oswald replied after a pause during which the hairs on the back of my neck stood up, even as most of the rest of it came tumbling down.

"But might I, perhaps, suggest that you have been too long away from court?" my cousin went on. "This is a place where one may think whatever one wishes, but there are still some things it is not wise to say aloud. Now, I believe I see your father trying to get your attention. Will you do me the honor of allowing me to escort you to him?"

"No, I thank you," *l'Inconnue* answered. "I am capable of crossing a room all by myself. Indeed, my whole family is considered capable . . . of many things. When you ponder the things of which it is not wise to speak, you might wish to keep that fact in mind."

"Mademoiselle," said Oswald.

I heard a sweep of skirts as *l'Inconnue* moved off. I counted to twenty, then to thirty just for good measure. "Who was that?" I asked as I came out from behind the column to stand beside my cousin. I actually had the pleasure of seeing him start, for I had genuinely surprised him.

"That is Marguerite de Renard," Oswald answered shortly.

"So that is the Fox's daughter," I said. For that is what her family's name meant. Fox. *Renard*. Though, for all of that, I'd always thought her father had a face more like a ferret than a fox. Cunning and sharp. Le Comte de Renard was a distant relation of my father's, which meant that royal blood flowed through his veins, though not enough of it to put him on the throne. Apparently, he was hoping to place his daughter there instead.

I remembered her, of course. Marguerite de Renard was just a little older than I was. She had been perfect, even as a child. And her embroidery as well. From what I could see from across the room, she had lost none of her perfection as she had grown. She had raven hair, and dark, lustrous eyes. Her face didn't look like a weasel's at all. By anyone's standards, she would be considered a beauty. I hid my stained fingers in the fold of my gown.

"I think that you should marry her," I said, and felt my cousin go very still at my side.

"Indeed, and why is that?"

"So that you may have children who are attractive and sharp-witted," I answered. "Are those not desirable attributes in the children of rulers?"

"But you forget. I will not rule here, Aurore."

"I forget nothing," I said, and was surprised to hear my voice come out like a sob. "I am not a fool just because the whole world thinks I look like one. Marguerite de Renard is right and you know it, Oswald. I thought you got resigned to being steward awfully quickly. Now I see the truth. You're only biding your time. What does it matter what you'll be called when the time comes? There will be nothing to stop you from doing whatever you like, once Papa and I are gone."

Oswald had gone white to the lips. "You think not?" he replied. "What about duty and honor, Aurore? Or don't you think I possess those attributes? No, wait. Don't answer that. Your opinion is plain enough."

By now, I was sobbing in earnest, a thing I despised but couldn't seem to stop. "I hate you. I've always hated you," I choked out. "You twist everything all around. Do what you like! Why should I care? Marry her. Don't marry her. Don't marry anyone."

At this, Oswald turned so suddenly I had no time to step away, and took my shoulders in a grip tight enough to snap my bones. "And why should I not marry her, *ma petite Aurore?* Give me one good reason. Can you do that?"

At that moment, two things happened. The musicians began to play once more. And, as if from a great distance, I heard my father's voice say:

*"Aurore."*

Oswald's hands fell from my shoulders as if the touch of them burned him. I stepped back, and bumped into Papa, who had come to stand directly behind me, a thing Oswald and I had been too wrapped up in ourselves to notice. Oswald brushed past us and vanished into the crowd without another word. He didn't even bow to my father.

"Aurore, what is it?" my father said, as he turned me to face him. "You're white as milk. Are you unwell?"

All of a sudden, I wished to be a child again. To be able to crawl into his lap and rest my head against his chest to hear the way his heart beat, the thing that had always comforted me the most when I was small.

"I'm fine, Papa," I said, though suddenly I seemed to be crying harder than ever. "It's just—my shoes pinch, and my hair is a mess. I can't seem to do anything right, and I—all I want to do is go up to my room. Nobody will miss me. Please let me go up. *Please,* Papa."

"There now, that's enough. Calm yourself, Aurore," my father said, and though he did not gather me in with his arms, he did so with the look in his eyes. At this, my tears slowed, then ceased to fall altogether. "Tell me what passed between you and your cousin just now."

"No," I answered simply, and saw surprise replace the compassion in my father's eyes. This was the first time I had denied him anything, and we both knew it. And it was over Oswald. "What happened isn't Oswald's fault, it's mine. I can't think straight with all these people around, Papa. They muddle everything."

Ruin everything.

"I see," my father said. "Very well. If it is truly what you wish, you may go up to your room, Aurore. Though you will give these nobles a hold over you if you do. They have been trying to cow you all evening. If you go now, they will know that they have won."

It was either the best or the worst thing he could have said, of course. For now it meant that I must stay at the party, no matter how much my heart cried out to be alone. For there was something in it that was clambering to get out. A thing I had not known was there until now. A thing with claws, teeth, and a temper, though I still didn't know what it was called.

The musicians ended one dance and began another. My father cocked his head. "They are playing a waltz. Will you dance with me, Aurore?"

"I'll only step on your feet," I said. But I took a deep breath. *Duty and honor,* I thought. Stern and difficult taskmasters, but I must obey them both now.

"What lady wouldn't wish to dance with the most handsome man in all the room?" I went on. "And don't worry. The stains on my fingers won't rub off."

"What stains on your fingers?" asked my father.

I smiled. I'm pretty sure it was for the first time that evening. "I love you, Papa."

"And I you, Aurore. Come, let us show these over-bred nobles how to dance a waltz with spirit."

"Just don't hold it against me when we fall."

At which my father laughed and plucked the few remaining pins from my hair, letting it stream down my back like a river of spun gold. I gave my head a shake, causing the river to shimmer as if struck by the sun. Then I kicked the shoes that had been making my feet miserable into the far corner of the ballroom, and let Papa lead me out into the center of the dance floor.

And so we were together when word of the first of the catastrophes was brought.

In the midst of the dance I felt a strange ripple pass through the ballroom, like an unexpected changing of the tide. A moment later, I heard a woman scream. My father spun toward the sound at once, thrusting me behind him. Before he could do anything else, the dancers parted to reveal a man dressed in the livery of the palace guards, his chest rising and falling as if he had just run a race for his life.

And his clothes . . . his clothes were covered in . . .

"Your Majesty," he gasped out. "Your Majesty, I must report—" Here his breath failed him. He collapsed to his knees and his voice choked off. At once, father knelt to support him.

"What is it?" he commanded. "Who is it that attacks us? Tell me swiftly, for God's sake, man! You are covered with blood."

At this the guard began to weep, his tears making flesh-colored rivulets down his red cheeks.

"I do not know who attacks us, Majesty," he whispered. "Or what. The blood . . . it is falling from the sky."

# Chapter Seven

HOW SHALL I TELL YOU OF THE DAYS THAT
followed, of the strange events that seemed to come upon us from
all sides, threatening to tear the very fabric of our land asunder?

It rained blood for five full days, after which the sun came
out but refused to go back down. Day and night it burned
in the sky like a torch, till those crops that had not already
drowned burst into flames in the fields where they stood. And
any that survived the sun were knocked down in the hailstorm
that finally put the sun's torch out, for the hailstones were as
large as grown men's skulls.

Nor was that all.

Cook's favorite white cat gave birth to a red-eyed raven,
then flew away with it. One of the noble's hawks hatched a
litter of mice that devoured it on the spot. Wolves roamed the
streets of the town at midday, their great tongues lolling from
their open mouths. Flocks of larks lined the boughs of trees
and sang their hearts out at deepest midnight. Stars streaked
across the heavens and fell to earth. Bolts of lightning shot
from clear blue skies.

The royal soothsayer was kept so busy with dire predictions that he ran out of adjectives to describe how bad things had become. And would become.

Then, as unexpectedly as they had begun, the terrible events that had plagued us stopped, and there began a series of days when nothing happened. Nothing at all.

I probably don't have to tell you that those days were the worst of all. For though things seemed normal again, none of us believed it in our hearts. We knew it for what it was. The calm before the storm that might carry us all before it.

But it is hard to do nothing when you have been doing something. You can work to put out a fire. Smother it with blankets. Carry buckets of water from the well. If it floods, you can build a dike to hold the floodwaters in check. But how do you protect yourself against an enemy you cannot see? How do you combat a thing that only threatens but never really comes?

And so it came to pass in those days of quiet that we ceased to fight an outside foe and began to fight ourselves.

It was the nobles who caused trouble first, for they had the most time on their hands and on their minds. Time to place blame and to hatch plots. And I'm sorry to say that Papa and I may have made things easier for them, for we were both away from the palace for long periods of time. For Papa saw, as the nobles could not (or would not), that it was the everyday people who were our country's true lifeblood. If they should fail, so would we all. And so he was much among them, and so was I. And so was Oswald, somewhat to my surprise, though it was impossible to predict just where or when he would turn up. Repairing buildings, furrowing and planting the fields for a second, even a third time.

It was after a day of working in the fields until my very bones ached, a day on which Oswald had not put in an appearance, cleverly, I thought, when I had the energy to think at all. At the end of such a day, Papa and I returned to the palace to find a delegation of noblemen waiting for us in the great hall. Le Comte de Renard stood at their head, so I knew there would be trouble right off.

"Your Majesty, we crave a word," le Comte said with a bow, as my father and I staggered into the hall. "The royal soothsayer has important news which you should hear at once." His eyes flicked to me, then away. "It concerns the fate of all."

Tired though he was, my father's mind was quick, much quicker than mine was. He knew, even then, I think, what was to come. "I trust you will not mind if we bathe first?" he inquired, his voice deceptively mild. "For Aurore and I have done a hard day's work while you have been communing with the stars."

At this, even le Renard had the grace to blush, and the nobles at his back dropped their eyes and shuffled their booted feet from side to side. None of them had so much as lifted a finger outside the palace, though the most virtuous and far-seeing among them had gone to the aid of their estates in the countryside. But even that virtue proved to be a danger now.

For it meant that the nobles left at court were the ones who cared the least for others and the most for themselves.

"We meant no disrespect," le Renard murmured. "Of course, you must refresh yourselves. Then, perhaps, we might beg a word in private?" His voice rose into the interrogative, a strange combination of demand and request combined. "We are all agreed this would be best," he said, at which the nobles stopped shuffling their feet and stood up straight, looking stern and grim. "What must be said touches upon the princess Aurore."

Beside me, I felt my father stiffen even as my own heart began to race. *Now I see,* I thought. For a terrible fear had been growing upon me, day by day, as to the cause of the dire events that had befallen us. A cause I had not yet dared to speak aloud.

"There is no need for secrecy," Papa replied. Though his voice retained its mildness, all could now hear its core of solid iron. This was the voice of a king. Even in the midst of my fear, I felt a sudden surge of hope.

*You have taken a false step, Monsieur le Fox,* I thought. For in his dealings with others, my father hated subterfuge above all else. Even a fool could become dangerous when armed with a secret. I had heard him say this many times. Suggesting I be excluded from matters that concerned me was the worst thing le Renard could have done.

"Let the princess Aurore hear what you have to say. Pronounce what concerns her to her face. Do not whisper it behind her back like a gossipmonger," my father went on. He ran his eyes over the nobles standing at le Renard's back, and I noticed how many of them dropped their eyes.

"Furthermore, since you are all agreed, there is no need for many to deliver your message when a few will suffice. Choose those you trust the most and wait upon me in an hour."

"But, Majesty," sputtered le Renard. "Surely the princess Aurore . . ."

"Enough!" exclaimed Papa. As if they had one body, the entire group of nobles stepped back, including le Renard. "You know my will. Come prepared to speak before the princess, or do not come at all. The choice is yours. Now get out of my way."

With that, he swept by them with me scurrying along like a terrier at his side. Neither of us looked back, though I could feel my father vibrate with tension until we turned a corner and were out of sight. He did not slacken his pace until he reached my room. There, at last, he stopped. He pulled in one deep breath, scrubbed his hands across his face as if to clear his mind, then took me gently by one arm.

"Le Renard is clever, but he thinks so highly of his own cleverness he turns his strength to weakness," said my father. "Do not fear him, Aurore. But come to me as soon as you have bathed. I would have us all together before these loyal and concerned noblemen arrive."

Somewhere in the passages between the great hall and my bedroom I had begun to shake. I could not stop, no matter how I tried. But I knew that now was not the time to burden my father with my own fears, so all I said was:

"It shall be as you wish, Papa."

At this, he sighed and took my face between his hands. "Someday," he whispered. "Someday it shall be as we both might wish, Aurore. Though not, I fear, for many years yet. Until then, I pray you, remember the words your godmother spoke on the day you were christened: Keep what you hold in your heart safe and strong."

Then he turned and left me, hurrying on to the rooms he shared with Maman. No sooner had he departed than Nurse swooped down upon me, fussing and scolding over the state of my hair and clothes. Not that she wasn't prepared, of course. The water for my bath was already steaming, the great copper tub set before the fire. I was clean in next to no time.

But, no matter what I did, how many times hot water was added, how many minutes I stood before the fire to dry, I could not get warm. For my father's words and my own fears were like two cold fists clenched around my heart.

The catastrophes had returned, and this time they came from within, not from without. Bad as what we had already endured had been, I knew the worst was yet to come.

# Chapter Eight

"WE GREATLY REGRET THAT CIRCUMSTANCES compel us to intrude upon you at this most difficult time, Majesties," purred le Comte de Renard.

He bowed low, then straightened, his glance somehow managing to linger on Maman and slide over me entirely. This, though she and I were sitting in my father's private audience chamber, side by side on the same straight-backed sofa. A piece of furniture I was usually careful to avoid because it was so incredibly uncomfortable. That night, however, anything I might do to demonstrate the strength and straightness of my spine had definitely seemed to be in order.

Le Renard had been clever to address Maman, I had to admit. She was well known to appreciate flowery words in matters of protocol. I doubted she would be swayed by them tonight, but the Fox was apparently taking no chances. *He has used his hour to regroup,* I thought.

"But when, in great agitation, the royal soothsayer came to me with what he had learned, I thought it best to bring the matter before you without delay," he went on, switching his attention to Papa, who stood just beside us. "In this . . ."

"You are all agreed," my father broke in. "I know."

At this, le Renard bowed again, though I could see an angry red blush begin to creep along his cheekbones. *Don't antagonize him, Papa,* I thought. *A cornered animal is almost as dangerous as a wounded one. Did you not teach me this yourself?*

At that moment, I caught a strange, intent expression on Oswald's face out of the corner of my eye. He was standing to one side of the room, before the fireplace, a location that put him almost precisely halfway between the groups comprised of our immediate family, and that of le Comte de Renard and his allies. A position I couldn't help but notice was ambiguous at best. Though we had never spoken of it again, I was certain neither of us had forgotten what had passed between us the night of my birthday party. I had not forgotten the words of Marguerite de Renard. Was he already in league with the Fox? Did that explain his absence from the fields today?

*"Duty and honor,"* he had said on the night of my party. Could he speak so and then betray us?

*No,* I thought. *Please, not Oswald.*

But when I followed the line of Oswald's eyes I discovered a curious thing. It was not le Renard he studied so intently. It was the men who stood behind him.

*Select those you trust the most,* my father had commanded. Apparently, they were five in number. Between them, they represented some of the most powerful families in all the land.

At the very back stood the royal soothsayer, looking as if he'd rather be somewhere else. And suddenly, as if Oswald's attention had shown me the way, I saw what it was that Papa had done. He had forced le Renard to make a choice.

If the Fox brought men below him in birth, he would be proclaiming himself the clear ring-leader of whatever this was. If he brought his peers, he would be revealing his closest allies. He had chosen the second course, and had thereby given my father the advantage. For the fact that le Renard was the spokesman had already revealed his prominent place. Now my father knew the identities of his key supporters as well.

"Naturally, we must appreciate the swiftness of your actions and the depth of your concern for our daughter as well as our kingdom, Monsieur le Comte," I heard my mother say to Renard, and, at this, I pulled my attention back to the Fox himself. "Perhaps you will begin by explaining why the royal soothsayer felt unable to come to me with what he learned."

For this is what he should have done, the thing that made le Renard's actions smack of conspiracy as much as anything else. In my father's absence, it was my mother who stood for him, not le Renard. A thing the royal soothsayer, indeed, the whole kingdom, knew perfectly well.

"It was considered a matter of some delicacy, Madame," le Renard replied, and he did glance at me now. As if trying to calculate my strength, my weakness. "It was felt, perhaps, a mother's love . . ."

"Would make me blind to the needs of my country, while you and these others, having only love for country and none for my daughter, must be considered neutral?" queried Maman. "An interesting contention, Monsieur le Comte," she went on, not allowing le Renard to respond. "And one I will not soon forget. On this, you have my promise."

I saw Oswald's eyebrows raise in appreciation even as I bit back a smile. The Fox was learning that it was not so easy to sway my mother with pretty words.

"Let the soothsayer come forward," my father said. "I will hear what he has determined from his own mouth and no one else's."

There was a moment of shuffling feet, and then the group behind le Renard parted. He stepped back and the soothsayer stepped forward. He was dressed in a long black robe which concealed everything but his hands and face, making him look like some enormous and bizarre puppet. His hands were long and very white. His eyes were huge and watery. As if the years he had spent interpreting signs that no one else could even see had stretched him, pulled him out of focus.

"Well," said my father. "What is so important you must tell others before waiting for my return when you know full well where I am?"

The soothsayer's huge eyes darted from side to side, as if seeking for a means of escape. Not finding one, they came to rest upon me as he answered:

"You must send the princess Aurore away. As far away as possible."

For an instant, no one spoke.

"Your reasons?" said my father. Not because he wanted to, of this I am certain. But because he felt he had no choice. It was a king's job to get to the bottom of things. To ask questions others would not.

"But surely the reasons must be obvious, Sire," said the soothsayer, relaxing a bit now. Perhaps he felt relieved that my father had not simply ordered his head lopped off at once for daring to suggest that the king send away his only child. Not that there had been a beheading in more years than anyone could remember. Still, a custom that has not been strictly outlawed may always be revived.

"You have only to think of the great calamities which have lately befallen our kingdom," the soothsayer went on. "The signs have shown me that they have the same root, the same cause. Furthermore, they suggest . . ."

"Are you by any chance trying to say," my cousin Oswald interrupted in a very soft voice, "that the dreadful hardships that have lately come upon us are because of the princess Aurore?"

Now a second silence filled the room, even longer than the first. *Of course that is what he is trying to say,* I thought. Someone had been bound to say it, sooner or later. It had been only a matter of time. Had I not told myself the same thing in the dead of night, when the sleep I so desperately needed had refused to come?

"Augury is not an exact science," the soothsayer blustered, wringing his long, white hands.

"True," Oswald responded. "In fact, I think we may safely say that it is not a science at all. But surely you must have some basis for what you have come to believe."

"Of course I do," the soothsayer snapped. "My reasons come from the very events themselves. Wet contends with dry. Fire with ice. Predators give birth to prey and are devoured by it. Lightning strikes out of a cloudless sky."

"Opposites," I said, speaking aloud for the very first time. Slowly, I rose to my feet and faced the soothsayer. "You mean opposites contend, just like the spells spoken over me in my cradle. You mean that they are the root of our present calamities, and I am their cause."

"No!" Oswald said swiftly. Vehemently. "You must not say such things, Aurore."

But the soothsayer never took his eyes from my face. "I am afraid the princess is correct, my lord. For remember this, also. It was when she turned sixteen that the calamities began."

"The year the spells will be fulfilled," I said.

And the soothsayer answered: "Even so."

"Why should I send Aurore away, then?" my father asked. "Will she not simply carry calamity with her wherever she goes? Or are you suggesting I set out to conquer what few enemies I have by sending my daughter to visit them, one by one?"

"Let her at least go from the court," le Renard spoke up. "She enjoys the outdoors, does she not? Perhaps a habitation in the countryside could be found."

"A fine suggestion," Oswald put in. "I'm sure she'd enjoy your properties, my lord, particularly the ones nearest the ocean. Unless you fear she'd cause too many storms and sink all those ships of yours with their fine, rich cargoes."

"If I might suggest," the soothsayer murmured, as le Renard stepped toward Oswald, his color high. "There is another course of action we might pursue. Though I fear, Majesties, it will be even less to your liking."

At these words, a third and final silence fell upon us. A terrible silence. A silence like a blight. In it, I seemed to feel all joy within me wither, as the crops that should have grown and sustained our people had so lately done. I sank back down onto the straight-backed couch.

I knew what the soothsayer meant. We all did. If the spells spoken over me in my cradle were fulfilled, the war within me would be over. The calamaties which threatened to destroy us all would stop. All it would take was the prick of a finger. Followed by one bright drop of my life's blood.

I heard a rustle of garments as my father moved to stand behind me and my mother. Exactly between us, framed by the curve of our heads and necks as we sat upon the sofa. Connecting us, turning the three of us into one as he laid a hand on each of our shoulders. Though I could not see him, for I did not turn, I had some notion of what was in his face, for I saw it reflected in the eyes of those who stood before us.

And the thing in my father's face was so pure and fierce that, strong though they were, the noblemen cried out and shielded their eyes, all save the soothsayer and le Renard. Oswald stood to one side as he had throughout, so still it seemed to me he had been turned to stone.

"We will speak no more of this," my father said, in a voice that I cannot to this day describe. For it contained so many things it was like a thousand voices speaking all together. A single voice and yet a chorus. "Leave me now, if you value your lives."

At this, even le Renard looked shaken. "Your Majesty, we only meant . . ."

"Oh, keep talking. Please," said Oswald.

At this, le Renard's face blanched. Without another word, he and the nobles with him bowed as if they had a single body, then backed out the audience-chamber door. As if they feared my father might yet change his mind and slay them on the spot if they turned their backs upon him. The royal soothsayer scuttled out behind them all.

"Well," Oswald said when the door was safely closed. "Something tells me that little worm will soon be looking for another job."

"You can't call him little," I contradicted, though how I managed to speak through a throat that had suddenly become so constricted I could hardly breathe I do not know. "He's way too tall."

"True. But let us both at least agree that he is low."

"Oh, how can you?" my mother exclaimed suddenly. "How can you joke at a time like this, the two of you?"

A sentiment that was somewhat undermined when my father laughed aloud. Not that he sounded all that amused.

"Let them joke, Mathilde," he told Maman. "They remind me to keep my perspective." He moved to the front of the sofa and knelt down before me, taking my hands in his, rubbing them when he found that they were cold.

"I want you to go back to your room and get a good night's sleep, Aurore. Don't let the ramblings of frightened fools keep you awake. In the morning, we will decide what must be done." Then he released me and stood. "You will see her to her room, Oswald."

"With pleasure, Uncle."

"Good night, then," said my father.

And though he turned away swiftly, he was not swift enough, for I saw the thing that was in his heart. The thing that the others had seen in his face. That had made them cry out and cover their eyes.

Grief.

For his own fate. But even more, for mine.

## Chapter Nine

BY THE TIME OSWALD AND I REACHED MY rooms, I had made up my mind. Not that I mentioned this to him, of course. Some things are best kept to yourself. Particularly when you're not sure whether or not other people will approve, but you're pretty sure they won't.

So I simply thanked him for seeing me safely to my room, went inside, then dismissed my nurse, who had waited up for me as she always did, drowsing in a chair before the fire. Though my heart hammered that I should *hurry, hurry, hurry,* for a moment I stood still in the center of my room. As if the rules of the universe had suddenly changed and the racing of my mind and heart had unexpectedly resulted in my limbs becoming frozen.

And then I realized that the reason for my paralysis was this: I had absolutely no idea what I was about to face. I only knew that, for the first time in my life, I would be all alone.

Though I might need new skills, there would be no one to teach them to me. No one of whom I could ask questions, from whom I could learn, as I had done for so long. I would have no mentors. No teachers. No one to guide me. What I was about to attempt was a thing that only I could do. And I would do it on my own.

And so, even as my mind and heart raced on ahead, my body paused, wanting one last moment in familiar surroundings before embarking into a great unknown. One last moment of solid ground before leaping straight out over a bottomless abyss. Then the moment passed, and my limbs began to obey the dictates of my heart and mind.

Near the alcove where my bed lay were two identical wooden chests, sitting side by side. The right one held what Nurse referred to as *garments befitting a princess.* Of the contents of the left chest, she preferred not to speak at all. It was this chest that I now opened, for it contained clothing much more suited for what I was about to attempt.

From this trunk, I selected a homespun shirt, a leather jerkin, and my favorite pair of breeches. Followed by warm socks and my sturdiest, most supple pair of boots. These I put on, being careful to fold the *garments befitting a princess* I was taking off and put them in their proper place. Nurse was going to be upset enough as it was. There was no sense in adding to her distress by not taking care of the things she valued.

Then I took out a second set of work clothes nearly identical to the first and put them in a knapsack I could carry upon my back, leaving both my arms free. To this, I added my knife in its sheath, though, after a moment, I took it out again and strapped it to my right leg so that the hilt just protruded above the top of my boot. I didn't know into what kind of danger I might be going, and I could hardly defend myself with a knife safely tucked away in a knapsack on my back.

From the kitchens, I could acquire provisions. From the stables, my bow and arrow, which I kept hidden behind a bale of hay in my horse's stall so Maman would not come to know about them. My mind whispered that I should take the horse as well, for I would make better time if I did. But my heart rebelled. I had no wish to take him into unknown danger, for I loved him well.

So I would go alone, and go on foot. Go without further delay. Go now. *Out through the kitchen gardens,* I thought, as I hoisted the pack upon my back, then covered it by tossing on my warmest cloak. A thing that seemed right and fitting, for had I not taken my first steps into the world through the same door?

Not only that, if I went that way, I could stop at the healer's cottage on my way to the stables. She slept in the palace, so she would never know until after I was gone. And taking with me what I might need to bind a wound or treat a fever seemed a wise and sensible thing.

If I was going to go haring off, I ought to be wise and sensible about one thing at least.

Sucking in a breath, I blew out my candles, then waited until my eyes had adjusted to the room being lit by the firelight alone. The palace corridors would be much like this as I made my way along them, illuminated by torches set at regular intervals along the walls. Earlier in the evening, they would have blazed brightly. But by now, they would have burned down low. When I was satisfied that my eyes would serve, I moved to my door and eased it open, then leaped back, startled.

Oswald stood on the other side.

Arms folded tightly across his chest as if to keep his heart from bursting out of it. His eyes hot and furious, a thing I could have discerned even had the room been much darker than it was.

"I knew it," he said. "You're going to run. You're so predictable, Aurore."

Before I quite realized what I intended, I took two steps forward, seized him by the front of his shirt, yanked him over the threshold, and closed the door behind him. How I managed not to slam it, I have no idea.

"I am not running," I hissed. "At least not running away."

"What does that mean?" he shot back, though he did keep his voice down. "That you're running *toward?* Don't be stupid. Running is running. Don't do it. You'll be giving that weasel le Renard exactly what he wants."

"So what if I am?" I said. "Even a weasel is capable of seeing the truth, Oswald. If they have nothing else, they have sharp eyes."

"And teeth," said my cousin.

"It doesn't matter! Don't you understand?" I cried. "He's right! You know it. I know it. Even Papa knows, though he doesn't want me to see that he does. All the terrible things that are happening to us—they're all my fault. They'll keep on happening as long as I stay. I have to go away. Don't try to stop me. Please, Oswald."

We stared at each another, and I realized both of us were breathing hard.

"I sincerely hate it when you do that," Oswald said at last.

"Do what?"

"Say please. Appeal to my better nature."

"It shouldn't. I'm not so sure you have one."

"Oh, Aurore." As if suddenly incredibly weary, Oswald crossed the room and sat down on the edge of my bed. After a moment, I went to sit beside him. "You really don't think very much of me, do you?"

"It's not that," I protested. "It's just—I don't understand you, Oswald. I never have. Not really."

"What's so mysterious about me?" he asked, his voice as sad as I had ever heard it. Actually, I don't think I'd ever heard Oswald sound sad before. "Why should we be so different, you and I? Do you think I don't want the same things you do?"

"To wear my father's crown, you mean," I said, and heard him draw in one swift breath.

"That really *is* what you think, isn't it?" he asked, and now his voice was bitter. "It's what you've always thought. Devious, scheming Cousin Oswald. So devious and scheming it never occurs to you I might want something simple and mundane. So simple and mundane you don't even see it when it's yours.

"What about, to be a part of a family? To be wanted. To be loved. Did you never think I might want those things, *ma petite Aurore?*"

"But," I said, then found the words I'd been about to say simply die away and slide back down my throat. For the truth was that such a thing had never occurred to me. Not even once. I don't think it had occurred to any of us, not even to Papa.

Oswald turned his head. I could feel his eyes upon my face. "You might as well just admit it," he said.

And so I told the truth and answered, "No."

He sighed, as if I'd placed and lifted a great burden on his shoulders all at once.

"Wait a minute. You are part of a family," I said, sitting up a little straighter. Angry all of a sudden. "We're a family, aren't we?"

Oswald gave a derisive snort. "Don't insult my intelligence, Aurore. Having relatives isn't the same as being part of a family."

"But you never said anything," I protested. At which he snorted once again.

"What on earth would you have had me say? One cannot simply ask to be loved. To be included where one is not. 'Please pass the marmalade, Uncle, and, oh, by the way, could you see your way clear to think of me not as your brother's son but as your own?'"

"You could have tried giving it," I said.

"It isn't as simple as that, Aurore."

Now it was my turn to snort. "Don't *you* be stupid. Of course it is. How many people do you think have the courage to love all on their own? It's really much easier when you do it in groups."

"You make it sound like a herd of cows."

My lips twitched. "I prefer the image of a flock of birds, myself."

"Crows?"

"Snow geese. I'm sorry, Oswald."

To my astonishment, he closed one of his hands over mine, then raised it to his lips and pressed a kiss into my palm. Then he kept my hand in his, resting it lightly upon one knee.

"So am I, *ma petite Aurore*. I kept telling myself that, someday, one of you would see me, see the things for which my heart longed. But you never did. There were days when I thought I knew just how Cousin Jane must have felt."

"Invisible," I whispered, and felt my whole body begin to shiver as fingers of ice walked down my spine. "It's you in my dream. Not her. It's been you all along."

"What dream? What are you talking about?" asked Oswald.

"I have nightmares," I answered. "Nurse is the only one who knows."

"Nightmares," he echoed, plainly bewildered. "How long has this been going on?"

"Since I turned ten," I said. "Since I first went outside. Once a month, on the same date as my christening, I dream that I am someone else. Someone lonely and in pain, searching for a thing they treasure, but have lost. They search so long, they become invisible. No one sees them, and so no one recognizes they're the same as everybody else. They have the same desires, needs, and wants. Until the day comes when their desire changes, and being rid of the pain consumes them. This becomes the only thing they want. To do that, they're willing to do anything, even inflict great pain themselves."

"Jane. You are dreaming of Cousin Jane," said Oswald, but his voice had suddenly gone hoarse.

"So I have always thought."

"But now you're not so sure, is that it?"

"I don't know," I said. "I don't even know if it's important." At this, we both fell silent, as if trying to decide where to go next. And then I heard myself ask one of the questions to which I'd always wanted an answer. "Did you know her?"

"No," Oswald answered. He toyed absently with the fingers of my hand. "Not really. Not in the way I think you mean."

"But you saw her," I persisted. At which he nodded.

"Yes. The first time it happened, I was so young I didn't even know who she was. She scared me half to death. After that, I got used to coming across her from time to time. We rarely spoke. But seeing someone is not the same as knowing them."

"I know that."

His lips curved up, though it wasn't really a smile. "It won't do any good to run, Aurore. Your father will only come after you. Have you thought of that?"

"Yes," I said. "That's why I'm going where no one will follow: to la Forêt."

At this, Oswald dropped my hand as if my fingers scalded and shot up from the bed. "For pity's sake, Aurore!" he exclaimed. "Have you gone mad? You can't go there. You mustn't."

"It's the only way," I said. "Whatever my destiny is, it's mine and nobody else's. And I—I can't explain it, but I think that la Forêt is where I'll find it."

"Is this another one of those things that you just know?" my cousin asked.

"Something like that," I replied.

No sooner did I admit this than a great urgency seized me. My limbs became restless all at once and I stood up. As if my very bones and muscles had come to the same conclusion my mind suddenly had: If I didn't leave now, I might never have the strength of heart to try again.

I moved to stand before my cousin, gazing straight up into his face. "Promise me something, Oswald."

"What?" he asked, and though his voice was steady, I could see the turmoil in his eyes.

"Look after Papa and Maman when I am gone."

At this, a strange combination of hope and fear came into

my cousin's face. "I'll do my best," he said. "But they won't want me. They'll want you. You are going to break their hearts, Aurore."

"No," I said, my voice calm and certain. "Their hearts were broken long ago. Cousin Jane did that. They have just been waiting for the proper time to come apart."

To my amazement, Oswald reached down and gently grasped my chin, angling my face upward as if he wished to see it more clearly.

"When did you grow up?"

A second surge of urgency flooded through my veins. This time, for him.

"Tell them, Oswald. Tell them that you want them. Better yet, *show* them. Maybe you haven't been invisible your whole life. Maybe you've just been hiding."

"Oh, so now I'm a coward, is that what you're trying to say?"

"Worse. You're a scheming, devious coward."

He gave a strangled laugh and pulled me against him. "Shut up, Aurore. Any more declarations of affection like that and you'll break my heart too."

We stood for a moment with his arms around me and my head cradled against his chest. I could hear his heart beat against my ear. A different sound from the one that Papa's made, but, to my surprise, just as strong and comforting.

*Seeing someone* isn't *the same as knowing them,* I thought.

And, for the first time, I wondered about all I had seen but never known about my cousin.

"I promise to look after them," he said at last. "I can't promise that they'll love me, just that I'll love them. Or your father anyway. Your mother may present more of a challenge."

"I understand perfectly," I said against his chest. "Thank you, Cousin."

And suddenly, I knew that it was time to step away. To this day, that single step back is the hardest thing that I have ever done. I had thought leaving Papa and Maman would be the most difficult, but it wasn't. It was stepping out of Oswald's arms.

"There's just one more thing," I said as I stepped back.

"You're awfully full of demands, all of a sudden," Oswald said. His tone was light. But I could see the way his hands clenched and unclenched at his sides. "What must I promise this time?"

"Promise me you will never marry Marguerite de Renard," I said.

I just had time to see his mouth fall open before I spun around and sprinted for the door. I had one foot across the threshold before I heard his answer.

"I promise. Fare you well, my little cousin. I will wait for you, Aurore."

## Chapter Ten

AND SO I BEGAN MY JOURNEY TO LA FORÊT.

I traveled all that night, walking swiftly. I walked on the roads when they would take me where I needed to go. When they would not, I walked across the open fields or whatever else lay before me. There were no signposts, but then I needed none. The call of the Forest itself was all I needed to guide me.

I reached it just at dawn, stomach rumbling, legs aching. I came to a halt at the place where the grass ended. A strange patch of barren earth edged the Forest on what I assumed was all four sides, for it extended in either direction as far as my eyes could see. My toes extended out past the edge of the grass as if over a bottomless pit.

*Just half a dozen more steps,* I thought. That's how many it would take to cross the patch of ground that marked the transition between the world of la Forêt and the world in which I'd grown up. The world comprised of everything I knew and loved. Six little steps to leave it all behind and enter who knew precisely what.

As I stood, hesitating, the sun came over the horizon

with an exuberant leap. And, as the light struck the trees, it seemed to me that the Forest came to life. Branches trembled and swayed upward, as if taking a morning stretch. Trunks gleamed like polished mother of pearl in the soft, early light. In that moment, it seemed to me that I could actually see the magic of the place, shimmering like a soap bubble over the tops of the trees.

*You can do it. It's only six steps,* I thought. *You've come so far, you can't stop now, Aurore.*

My body refused to cooperate and remained motionless.

The sun inched higher and now it seemed to me that the trees began to converse with one another. Each leaned over to its neighbor, first on the right, then on the left, in a great rippling motion, as if passing some vital piece of information from tree to tree in a great chain of knowledge that would soon be spread throughout the Forest. Then, as I watched, trees in the foremost line waved their branches in my direction, the very leaves curling forward, then back, as if beckoning me in.

I felt a breath of air pass over my face and, in that moment, I knew what it was the trees of la Forêt whispered to one another.

*Aurore.*

*Aurore,* they said. *Welcome. We have been waiting for you.*

At this I might not have been able to move at all, had not an unusual thing happened at almost the very same moment. A great gust of wind struck me from behind, strong as a hand in the small of my back. One. Two. Three. Four. Five steps I stumbled forward before I regained control of my limbs and brought myself to a teetering halt. Now I stood so close to la Forêt I could almost hear it breathing. One more step, and I would be beneath its boughs.

Now there was no wind at all, as if, instinctively, the Forest knew the same thing I did—that this final step must come from me, and me alone. It must be my will that carried me forward and no other's. For only then would I truly have chosen my own destiny, embraced no matter my misgivings, whatever it was that la Forêt might hold in store.

I pulled in five deep breaths. On the sixth, I took the final step. And so the deed was done.

How shall I tell you what going into la Forêt was like? Though I moved through the air, passing beneath the trees for the first time felt exactly the same as wading in a pool of deep, clear water. As if the magic of the place had given the air a texture and substance it did not possess in the world outside. It pushed against me as I moved through it, as if in silent challenge. Then, over my head, I heard the branches begin to stir once again.

*Aurore,* they said. *Aurore. At last. We've been waiting for so long.*

At that, I made a decision. We had to come to some sort of arrangement, the Forest and I. I couldn't let things continue as they were, with la Forêt being magical and mysterious and my heart beating just a little bit too hard.

"I hear you," I said, deciding my best course of action would be to speak out boldly, beginning as I wanted to be able to go on, even if that was the opposite of what I actually felt like doing. "I do have ears." To demonstrate, I pushed the curtain of my hair aside. "I'm sure I'm very sorry to have kept you waiting, though I had no idea that I was doing it. If there's something you want me to know or do, you might as well just come right out with it. Being all mysterious will only make me cross, which neither of us will like."

At this, a gust of wind swept through the branches like a sudden laugh and blew into my face with such force that I threw a hand up to cover my eyes. When I brought it down again, la Forêt was quiet and still. Even more, the air was now the consistency to which I was accustomed, though it was so clear and pure it brought tears to my eyes.

Now I could see that the trees, which from outside the Forest had pretty much all looked alike, were in fact as different from one another as people are. Some were smooth-barked; others had rough skins. They had shades ranging from the black of ebony, to the red of cherry, to the papery-white of ash and alder. The air was so clear that I could see from many feet away a thin line of black ants marching in single file up the burnished copper bark of a madrona.

The everyday rules regarding the habitats of trees did not seem to exist inside of la Forêt. Spruce and figs grew side by side, embracing one another. *It is a study in opposites,* I thought.

*Just as I am.* And I heard the Forest sigh and rustle. As if a question that had troubled it had been answered, and a course of action decided upon. And that was the moment I lost what remained of my fear, or most of it, for it seemed to me that la Forêt had reached our agreement, even if I didn't yet understand quite what it was.

Naturally, no sooner did I have this encouraging thought than overhead there broke out the loudest clap of thunder I had ever heard and it began to storm. To hail, to be precise. And though the hailstones were only as large as a grown man's fist, and not his skull, they were more than large enough to make me scurry for shelter.

The first place I tried was beneath the boughs of the biggest evergreen I could find. But the wind gave it a mighty shake, causing all the hailstones that had been trapped among the branches to rain down upon my head at once. Next I tried crawling beneath some low-growing shrub, only to be chased off by a fox who had taken shelter there along with her cubs. Finally I tried clambering up into the branches of the madrona, but instead slid right down its smooth copper trunk.

At that, I gave up.

"Must we play twenty hiding places?" I shouted at the storm. "Three is more than enough. I can take a hint. I'm not stupid. Just show me where you want me to go."

As if in answer, the wind snatched at my cloak, tugging until I turned around. Through the driving hail, I could just make out the outline of a cottage, a thing I had somehow failed to notice before. This so surprised me I was incapable of moving for several moments, completely oblivious to the fact that I was growing colder and wetter with every second.

How could there be a cottage in la Forêt when it had been forbidden to go there for time out of mind? It wasn't until a hailstone hit me on the head that I found my legs. Questions could be answered later. Right now, I needed to get out of the storm.

I dashed madly for the cottage, the wind pushing from behind. By the time I reached it, my hands were so cold and wet I couldn't work the latch, so I ended up kicking at the door. I was just on the point of raising my leg to try to kick it in when it opened. I lost my balance and somersaulted across the threshold, landing in a great puddle of water and mud in the middle of the floor.

"I believe it's customary to knock before you kick the door in," a voice said.

Then the door slammed behind me and I was staring up into the face of a young man I had never seen before.

# Chapter Eleven

HIS EYES WERE THE SAME COLOR AS THE branches of the evergreens, and were flecked with gold in a way that reminded me instantly of Oswald. Looking up into them was like gazing up into the Forest's canopy with the sun dappling down. His hair was muddy brown. He looked exasperated with me, to say the least.

"I didn't think anyone was here," I gasped. "I didn't think people lived in la Forêt. If I've hurt your home, I'm sorry."

"Yes, well," he said after a moment. He leaned back and stopped looming over me. "I suppose your haste was understandable. The storm really *is* remarkable. I've never seen such hailstones, have you?"

At this, he scurried to one of the windows and began to peer out, his irritation with me apparently completely forgotten. The look on his face was such a strange combination of studiousness and excitement, I half expected him to start making notes. A moment later, to my amazement, he pulled a quill, ink, and a small leather-bound book out of a knapsack at his feet, and did just that, not noticing when he dripped ink down the front of his shirt.

I had seen such hailstones, of course, and ones that were even larger. But since my unexpected companion seemed so excited about the size of the ones currently hurtling through the trees and thundering on the roof, I decided to keep quiet about it. At least one of us was enjoying the current situation. It seemed a shame to spoil it.

"Oh, and by the way, I don't live here," he went on. He made a notation in his book, then pressed his nose against the glass. I feared he'd decide to open the window in another moment. "This isn't my home. I've come to the Forest on a great quest."

He spoke those last two words as if they should be spelled entirely with capital letters, punctuating them by shutting his book with a snap. I tried in vain to think of a suitable reply.

"That's nice," I finally said.

He turned back then, his expression slightly crestfallen, and I realized he'd probably expected me to ask him what it was. A thing I most likely would have done, if I hadn't suddenly been feeling so out of sorts. It had taken all the courage I possessed to enter la Forêt, or at the very least, a whole lot of courage. While I hadn't been sure what to expect, I *had* expected to face it on my own. I might even have been looking forward to it, in a funny sort of way. A test of my inner strength, or something like that. Of my ability to be brave, to do what was right, even if that meant hardship and sacrifice.

Now here I was, in a cottage that shouldn't be there, with a companion who viewed a hailstorm as an opportunity for note-taking, claimed to be on a great quest, and yet somehow managed to look as if he might have trouble pulling on his boots in the morning. Not at all what I'd expected, to say the least.

*Oh, for heaven's sake, Aurore,* I chastised myself as I climbed soggily to my feet. *Oswald is right about you. You really are the most contrary girl alive. Anybody else would be happy to have discovered they're not alone, but not you. No, you're actually feeling cross because you haven't ended up all by yourself.*

"I don't suppose you're any good at fire building, are you?" the young man inquired suddenly. I realized then that, in spite of his enthusiasm for the hail, he was just as wet as I was.

"I did my best, but the truth is, I'm not very good at practical things. My hands never seem to know what to do, no matter how often they've been told how. I'm much more of a scholar, really." He attempted a cajoling smile. "You know, brains over brawn?"

"As long as my flint didn't get wet," I answered, and I unfastened my cloak and shook it out. It was heavy with water, but it had done its work well, for beneath it my knapsack was dry. I hung the cloak on a peg near the door, then turned, hands on hips, to take stock of the cottage.

Whoever had built it had definitely known what they were doing. The roof didn't leak. The fireplace stood in the cottage's very center, so that all the heat it generated would be trapped inside. I could see firewood stacked neatly to one side of the hearth, with a basket of kindling nearby.

"Someone must live here," I said finally. "It's too well kept to have been abandoned."

"I've been thinking the same thing." The young man nodded. "I hope whoever lives here isn't getting too wet."

"And that they don't mind that we came here to get dry. Well, let's see what I can do." I moved toward the fireplace, then stopped. Resting in front of it was something I hadn't noticed before. A sickly green rug with bumps as big as the coils of giant snakes.

"You'll want to keep an eye on that rug," my companion advised. "I walked across it when I first got here and it almost pitched me flat on my face. It seems to have a mind of its own."

*But that's not possible,* I thought. I knew where this rug was, or at least I knew where it belonged. Papa kept it in his study. I'd made it for him as a birthday gift shortly after I'd turned nine.

"Thanks for the warning," I said.

Carefully, I lifted the rug and moved it to one side. No doubt there was an explanation for its presence here, but it wouldn't do much good to think about it. I was unlikely to figure out what it was. Instead I concentrated on fire-building, a thing I was good at. The wood was well seasoned. It caught at once, and I soon had a bright blaze going.

"Oh, well done!" the young man exclaimed, and he put away his writing supplies and knelt down at my side. We stayed that way for a moment, both of us warming our hands. If it bothered him that it had taken me so little time to perform a task he'd claimed had defeated him, he didn't let it show. I could feel my irritation begin to fade away. It's hard to be cross with someone who isn't cross back, particularly when you're safe and warm in the bargain.

"What's your name?" I asked.

To my surprise, he reddened, as if my everyday question was cause for embarrassment. "I was afraid you were going to ask me that," he said. "Sooner or later, every new person I meet does. I don't suppose you'd like to take three guesses and choose the one you like the best?" He must have seen the astonished look on my face, because almost at once he said: "No, I didn't think so. Very well, if you must know, I'm called Prince Ironheart."

"What's wrong with that?" I asked. "It's a fine name. Strong and true."

"Yes, well, I'm afraid it's also something of a joke," he confessed. "I was dubbed that by my older brother in a moment of extreme annoyance. I mentioned I'm not very clever with my hands, didn't I? The truth is, I'm often downright clumsy. I once managed to drop his favorite sword in a way that caused it to splinter into exactly seven shards, after which it took the same number of days to put it back together again. As a matter of fact . . ."

He settled down cross-legged on the floor and his tone grew hushed and confidential, as if he was preparing to tell me a bedtime story.

"It was really quite a remarkable feat, if you stop to think about it. The royal mathematician and I did some computations later, and discovered that the odds against such a thing occurring were well over one in a hundred thousand. But it was after this that my brother started calling me Ironheart. He said my heart would have to be strong, since my arms so obviously aren't."

All of a sudden, I discovered I was liking Ironheart quite a bit better than I'd expected to, a thing I'm pretty sure had to do with a feeling of kinship inspired by the word *clumsy*.

"What's his name?" I asked. "Prince Smart-mouth?"

"No," Ironheart answered, his tone slightly troubled. "Actually, it's Prince Valiant. It suits him, which makes it even worse."

I settled down cross-legged myself and gave his knee a reassuring pat. "I don't think I like him."

"Oh, but you would," protested Ironheart. "Everybody does, except, perhaps, for Grandfather. Just between you and me, Grand-père thinks that Valiant is something of a prig. He told me so on the eighth day. You know—the one on which the incident with the sword could finally be considered over."

I laughed, my earlier irritation with his presence now completely forgotten. "I *know* I like your grandfather. But surely you must have a given name. A birth or christening name that you could use instead."

"Of course I do," he said. "It's Charles. But somehow, Ironheart just seemed to stick. I've grown so accustomed to it, if you called me Charles I'd probably look over my shoulder to see who was behind me."

"Well, I only have one name," I said. "And it's Aurore."

His expression brightened. "I wondered if it would be that. Or something like it. The second you took your cloak off, I was reminded of the sun coming up. And Aurore means *of the dawn*, doesn't it? I think it must be your hair. All that gold."

"You're right," I answered, resisting an impulse to pull my fingers through it to see if there were any snarls. It hadn't occurred to me until that moment to think about the way I looked. "Without it, I would have ended up named for my grandmother."

"What was her name?"

"Henriette-Hortense."

"Oh dear," Ironheart said involuntarily, then blushed. "That was rude, I'm sorry."

"Don't be," I said. "I agree entirely."

"Still," he said after a moment. "Even Henriette-Hortense is a proper name, not a joke like Ironheart. It's awful to know people are laughing at you, day in and day out."

Once again, he reminded me of Oswald. That was how his nickname of Prince Charming had gotten started, before he'd decided to make it his own.

"Why don't you make it true?" I asked. "Live up to your nickname and put them all to shame. *Become* Ironheart."

"How on earth would I do that?"

"You're the one with the big brain," I said. "Can't you figure something out?"

"I suppose I could," he said, though now his voice was doubtful. "I hadn't really considered that approach before. I'll have to think about it."

"What about this quest of yours? That should offer plenty of opportunities, don't you think?"

"You're right!" he exclaimed. "You're absolutely right! I wonder . . ." He broke off, his expression thoughtful.

"What is the quest, anyway?" I said, then had a terrible thought. "Not slaying a dragon, I hope."

"Oh, no," Ironheart replied at once. "Nothing like that." He paused. "Or, at least, I don't think so. There aren't a lot of details to go on, other than the basic ones. I mean, nobody knows much about the Forest, so there are a lot of unknowns."

"The quest," I prompted.

"Oh, yes. Well, it's really quite simple," he replied. "There's a beautiful princess sleeping in the heart of the Forest. I'm going to find her and wake her up."

# Chapter Twelve

IT WAS A GOOD THING I WAS ALREADY SITTING down, because if I hadn't been, I'd have probably fallen over.

*"What?"*

"There's a beautiful princess sleeping in the heart of the forest," Ironheart repeated obligingly. "I'm going to find her and wake her up."

"With what? The kiss of true love?"

Ironheart's green eyes grew enormous. "Wait a minute," he said. "How did you know?"

I put my head down in my hands. *This can't be happening. It just can't be,* I thought. Somehow, some version of my story had gotten all mixed up. Turned around. In fact, it had gotten so confused that I was actually in the same room with someone who wanted to come and rescue me from something that hadn't even happened yet.

*Just breathe deeply, Aurore,* I told myself. *Calm down. He can't be talking about you. He said the princess was beautiful, or had you forgotten? That would certainly seem to rule you out.* Nobody thought that I was beautiful, with the possible exception of

Nurse and Papa. Perhaps the other countries bordering la Forêt had their own tales to account for its strangeness.

"How do *you* know?" I asked.

Confusion flickered across Ironheart's face. "How do I know what?"

"How do you know there's a beautiful princess sleeping in the heart of the Forest?"

His expression cleared at once. "Oh, that. That's easy. Because Grand-père told me so. He's been telling me stories about her for as long as I can remember."

"Well how does *he* know, then?" I persisted. "How can he be so sure she's there? Has he seen her for himself?"

"Of course not!" Ironheart exclaimed. "Nobody goes into the Forest. It's been forbidden for time out of mind."

This was getting worse by the minute. "But—" I began.

Ironheart held up a hand, and I fell silent. "Do you know anyone you always believe?" he inquired. "Someone you trust with your heart, even though your mind occasionally warns you they might be pulling your leg?"

"I do, in fact," I replied, thinking once again of Oswald.

"Well, there you have it. That's what Grand-père is like. I don't know how he knows the story of the Sleeping Beauty. I just know I believe that he does."

He gazed into the fire for a moment.

"She's been sleeping in the heart of the forest almost for-ever. Longer than the memory of any man alive, save his, says

Grandfather. All that time, she's been waiting for someone to come along and bring her true love's kiss.

"Grand-père says that many men have tried to find the Sleeping Beauty, and all have failed. He says this is because they're like my brother Valiant. Handsome, strong, and brave, even reasonably intelligent. But nothing special. Nothing out of the ordinary. But Grand-père says the princess who sleeps in the heart of the Forest is so special she could never love an ordinary man. Therefore, the one who awakens her must be someone special also."

"And your grandfather thinks you're the one," I said.

"Actually," Ironheart confessed. "He's not my grandfather. He's my great-grandfather. Or maybe it's great-great. I can never remember. He really *is* incredibly old."

"But he's certain you're the one to break the spell," I insisted, at which Ironheart made a face.

"It is kind of far-fetched, isn't it? You don't have to tell me. I know."

"I didn't mean that."

"Well, I wouldn't blame you if you had," he said, his tone philosophical. "I know I'm not like most other princes. I've always known it. But Grand-père says that's what makes me the right one for this quest. He says being different is my strong point."

"What do you think?"

He fell silent again, gazing into the fire. While he was busy saying nothing, I busied myself watching the way the light played across his face. It was a good face, better than I'd originally given it credit for. Ordinary at first glance, but on second glance, far from ordinary.

On second glance, you noticed the stubbornness of the chin—a contrast to a mouth that, even when straight and serious, looked as if it was just waiting for its chance to smile. The cheekbones were determined, high and wide, but there was just a hint of sadness around those evergreen eyes. A face shaped by both love and adversity, I thought. But where neither held sway. They were balanced, point to point.

Once more, I was reminded of Oswald. For it came to me suddenly that this was how he might have looked, had his life contained the bedrocks I'd so recently learned he thought they lacked: Compassion. Acceptance. Love.

"I think I must believe I'm different," Ironheart said at last. "That I can be the one to break the spell. I've never really wanted to be like my brother, much as I love him. At the very least, I must want to find out whether or not what Grand-père says is true. Otherwise, I wouldn't have come."

"That's a good answer," I said. At which he looked at me and smiled.

"And that's a very nice answer. Thank you, Aurore. But what about you? What brings you to the Forest?"

I hesitated, suddenly fearful that he would think me a coward. "I guess you could say that I ran away from home."

"Oh," he said, and I could sense him hesitating, trying to decide whether or not to say more. "That must have been a difficult decision," he continued after a moment. "You don't strike me as someone who runs from her problems."

"I'm not, or at least not under ordinary circumstances," I said, more than a little grateful that this was his response. "But the circumstances were far from ordinary, so I did what I thought was best."

"In that case, I'm sure it was," said Ironheart. "What will you do now?"

I opened my mouth to answer, then closed it again. The truth, which I didn't particularly care to admit, was that I simply didn't know. Just getting to la Forêt had seemed so huge, I hadn't really thought much about what would happen after I arrived. I guess I thought it would become obvious once I got here.

"I'm not sure," I said at last. "At the time I set out, just getting here seemed like enough."

"Why don't you come with me?"

For one dazzling moment, I actually considered it. Now that I'd gotten used to his presence, I had to admit it was nice not to be alone. But I knew I couldn't do it. I had no idea what I would encounter in la Forêt. What fulfilling my destiny truly held in store. How could I go with Ironheart, possibly put him in great danger, when I hadn't even been willing to bring my horse along?

"I thought a quest was a thing you had to do by yourself," I hedged, not quite ready to say *no* outright.

"Not necessarily," he said. "Jason had the Argonauts."

"I'm not so sure that's such a great example," I commented. "Considering the way things turned out."

"Well—" He pondered for a moment, and suddenly I could see the lines of mischief deepen on either side of his mouth. "Hercules had the Labors."

I gave a snort of laughter. He was clever, I had to admit. "That's not the same thing and you know it."

"Well if you don't want to go you can just say so," Ironheart said, his tone growing offended. "Believe me, I've heard the word *no* before."

"I didn't say *no,*" I said. "I just didn't say *yes,* either. And stop trying to twist my words around and confuse me and trick me into going."

"I don't trick," he replied, his voice huffy. "I wheedle and cajole. Occasionally I manipulate, but I'm always very sneaky about it, so you wouldn't know it was happening until it was far too late."

In spite of myself, my lips twitched. "Thanks for the warning."

"Not at all."

We stared into the fire for a moment.

"I ran away because things were happening," I finally said quietly. "Horrible things, calamitous things. Things which could—would—have destroyed everything I loved. They were all my fault, all because of me. Coming to la Forêt was the only way I could think of to make them stop."

"I probably shouldn't say this," Ironheart said. "But don't you think that's a bit egotistical, Aurore? In my experience, things happen for reasons, that's true enough. But very few of them actually have to do with us even when we feel as if they do."

"You don't know anything about me!" I cried. "There are things inside me, Ironheart—spells. Cast upon me from almost the moment of my birth. One dark, the other light. One seeking my destruction, the other my salvation. They're the things that almost tore my people apart."

"And you as well, I think," Ironheart said quietly. "But the fact that you carry them inside you doesn't mean they *are* you, Aurore. Or that you're responsible for them."

"What difference does that make?" I asked, suddenly as tired as I could ever remember being. "I carry them with me wherever I go. That makes them mine."

"A great deal, I should think," he answered. "Do you have no will of your own? You say you know what the spells want— your destruction or your salvation. But what about what *you* want, Aurore?"

"I don't know what I want," I whispered, for suddenly, horribly, I realized it was true. "I don't know. I have never known."

"Then come with me until you do," he said simply. "Let the journey be a quest for us both."

All of a sudden, I wanted to say *yes*. Wanted it so much, I feared to say it, lest it be the same as taking the coward's way out.

"Let me sleep on it," I said. "I'll give you my answer in the morning."

"Fair enough."

At that, Ironheart got to his feet. "I don't know about you, but I'm starving. I do have food. Grand-père supervised my packing."

"Why didn't you just bring him along?"

"I would have," Ironheart acknowledged cheerfully as he retrieved his knapsack from beneath the window and carried it to the cottage's only table. "But he said he was too old. And furthermore that going into the Forest was my destiny, while his was to wait as he had always done. He said he'd been doing it so long he'd pretty much perfected the technique."

There was a pause. "I'll bet it drives your brother crazy when you do that," I finally said.

"When I do what?" he asked, but I could see the smile lurking around his mouth like a cat after a bird.

"Refuse to take offense when one is offered." I got to my feet, pulled my knife from its sheath, then strolled to the table and picked up a loaf of bread. Holding it against my chest, I began to slice. "I'm surprised he didn't name you Ironwill."

He began to hack at a hunk of cheese. "I suppose he might have, if it hadn't already been taken. That's what the people call Grand-père, because he's lived so long. They say it's his will

393

alone that's kept him alive for all these years. You'd like him, Aurore. He teases the same way you do, and he's quick-witted, just like you are."

"Don't," I said, as I finished slicing the bread and set down the loaf. "I said I'd think about it and I will. There's no need to wheedle. I keep my word."

"That was not a wheedle. It was an observation," said Ironheart. "When I wheedle, my voice gets kind of high and whiney. It's impossible to mistake a wheedle for anything else."

By now I was trying so hard not to laugh it was making my stomach hurt. It felt good, I realized suddenly.

"Are you always this impossible?"

Ironheart nodded cheerfully. "Almost always. It's better when I'm asleep. Unless I snore."

"You snore and I'm stuffing your cloak in your mouth."

He grinned. I grinned back. And suddenly, it came to me that I did know what I wanted, or at least a part of it. At least for now. I wanted more moments like this. Wanted a thing I had never really had, but hadn't missed until now.

A friend.

Even so, it wasn't until the middle of the night that I well and truly made up my mind. The hail had turned to a steady drumming of rain upon the roof not long after we'd eaten our cold supper, stirred up the fire, and spread our cloaks before it to dry. Then we'd parcelled out the blankets from the bed. I stayed in it, while Ironheart settled with his back to the fireplace.

But in spite of the weariness which seemed to come from nowhere, rising up to fill me like liquid in a cup, I could not sleep. The uncertainty of the next day had cast a pall over my rest. And not me alone, for, time and again, I heard Ironheart stir at his place by the fire.

"How did you know?" I said at last. I couldn't see him where he lay on the far side of the fireplace, and so I spoke to the embers' glow. "How did you know that this quest was the right thing to do?"

He answered at once, and I could tell by his voice that he'd been pondering this very question for a very long time. "It's hard to explain," he said, his voice as quiet as mine. "I guess because, even more than Grand-père's words, I felt the truth of it inside me. I hate to sound all epic and swashbuckling, but this is what I was meant to do. It's the thing that I was born for, Aurore."

I felt my whole body relax then, the tension and uncertainty streaming out of it. Hadn't I described my desire to discover life outside the palace walls in exactly the same way? And wasn't it that same desire which, for better or worse, had brought me here, to Ironheart and la Forêt?

Who was to say going with him wasn't my destiny, just as his had been to ask me? That our destinies weren't entwined?

"All right," I said. "I'll go."

"I'm glad," he answered.

After that, we both slept peacefully for the rest of the night and dreamed of nothing at all.

## Chapter Thirteen

AFTER THE STORM, IT HAD TURNED COLD DUR-
ing the night. So cold that the entire Forest seemed covered in
a single sheet of ice when we opened the door of the cottage
the next morning. It shimmered in the morning sun like spun
sugar on a child's birthday cake, snapping and crackling as we
walked upon it. Even the leaves and branches were covered in
a thin sheet of ice. Throughout la Forêt, nothing stirred. There
was not a single sound, save for the ones Ironheart and I made
ourselves.

After breakfasting, we tidied the cottage, determined to
leave it as much as we had found it as possible. Ironheart folded
blankets while I swept the hearth and brought in fresh wood
for the fire. I still hadn't solved the mystery of the hearth rug,
but I had resolved not to think about it. We shouldered our
packs, put on our cloaks, and stepped out the front door, closing it firmly behind us.

"How will we know which way to go?" Ironheart asked.

"That's easy enough," I said. "We continue on past the cottage."

"How do you know?"

"It only stands to reason," I said, as I began to circle around to the right of the cottage. The crunch of ice beneath my feet sounded like broken panes of glass. "I came upon it not long after I'd entered la Forêt. Therefore, the cottage must be on its outskirts and the heart of the Forest must be beyond it. That means, this way."

"Um . . . Aurore?"

I was squinting straight ahead, trying to see through the sudden dazzle of the sun. "What?"

"You might want to—that is, I hate to contradict you, but—"

I brushed tears from my cheeks. The glare had become so great, it was making my eyes water. *"What?"* I said again.

In answer, Ironheart simply stopped walking. And that was when I realized that we hadn't moved at all. Or that the cottage had moved right along with us, which would perhaps be a more precise way of describing it. For in spite of the fact that we'd taken enough steps to carry us clear along one side, as soon as I stopped walking too, I found myself standing by the front door. Right where we'd started. Instantly, the glare decreased, as if to reward us.

"Oh," I said. "Well, this is annoying."

"Do you think so?" Ironheart asked. He had that look on his face, the same as the one he'd worn when staring at the hailstones, or describing the calculations he'd made concerning his brother's broken-in-seven-pieces sword. I expected the notebook to come out of the knapsack at any second.

"When you stop to think about it, it's really quite fascinating. In fact, I think the odds might be somewhere around—"

The expression on my own face must have shown my frustration because he broke off abruptly, then added. "Though it is very inconvenient, of course."

"It's just that I don't care very much for games," I said, moving straight out from the cottage by several steps in what I considered to be the wrong direction. "Too sneaky. I much prefer it when things are straightforward. They don't have to be simple or easy, but they do have to be fair."

I put my hands on my hips and glared at the closest stand of trees. *Are you listening to me?* I shouted.

"Maybe we should just go back inside and rest for a day," Ironheart said, his tone a bit nervous now. "You don't seem to be feeling quite yourself, Aurore."

"I feel just fine," I answered. "This will all make sense in a minute." I took a few more steps. I was under the closest branches now.

"I know you're enchanted," I shouted up at the trees. "He knows it. I know it. We all know it, so you can just stop showing off. If you want us to go in a direction that doesn't make sense to anyone but you, that's fine. You're making all the rules, anyway. That's obvious. Though I could wish I didn't feel quite so much as if you were making them up as you went along."

No sooner had I uttered these words than a bright shaft of sunlight shot through the Forest canopy to illuminate the trees under which I was standing. It was a stand of aspens, their leaves as yellow as my hair. Their trunks stood close together, the branches entwined, as if the trees had stepped closer together during the long, cold night in an effort to keep warm. Their leaves were frozen solid.

I was pretty certain this particular group of trees hadn't been there the night before, though I suppose it is possible that I just didn't notice them in the storm.

Then the sun struck the leaves, and the shimmer of ice became a sparkle, and the sparkle became a shine. And then the shine became a dazzle so bright it hurt to look upon it. And that was the moment that the leaves burst forth like hundreds of yellow butterflies all breaking free of their cocoons at the same time. They fluttered in a breeze that was for them and them alone, for though I stood beneath the boughs, I felt no breath of air.

"Looks like we're going this way," I said. The way that made no sense at all. The one I would have sworn was back the way I had originally come. But it was plainly what the Forest wanted, and equally plain I was in no position to argue.

"Whatever you say," said Ironheart.

We walked for several hours as the Forest thawed and came to life around us. I probably don't need to tell you that the direction in which we traveled was the right one after all. About the time when the trees cast no shadows because the sun was directly overhead and the day was now very warm, we came to a stream and sat down beside it to rest our legs and eat our lunch.

Ironheart ate with great determination, though I could tell his mind wasn't on the meal. He shifted restlessly every few seconds, gazing around him, a furrow between his brows.

"What's the matter?" I finally asked. "Are you sitting on an anthill?"

"It doesn't make any sense," he announced.

I'm afraid I gave a very unprincesslike snort. "You aren't just *now* figuring that out are you?"

"I mean the stream," he said. "It doesn't make any sense. There aren't any streams flowing out of the Forest, at least not where I come from. Or into it, either."

"Nor where I come from," I said. "Maybe it's just inside of la Forêt."

"But that's the thing that doesn't make any sense," Ironheart said at once. "It's not the way things are supposed to work. A stream has to start someplace and go somewhere."

"I'm sure it does," I said. "It just does it all within the boundaries of the Forest."

"But—" Ironheart began.

"The stream makes as much sense as going the wrong direction to get where we're going," I interrupted.

"You have a point," he said after a moment. He eyed the stream, *that* expression on his face again. "I wonder what it tastes like."

"I'm not so sure that's a good idea," I said. "What if it's enchanted or something?"

At this, he gave a snort of his own. "It would have to be, wouldn't it? We're in an enchanted forest."

"You know what I mean," I said.

"Of course. But we're breathing the air already. We don't have much choice about that. How much more dangerous could it be to drink the water?"

"I don't know. That's the point."

I could tell the second he made up his mind. His face took on a look of determination and his chin jutted out. "I'm doing it," he said. "Don't try to stop me, Aurore."

"Why on earth would I do that?" I inquired. "You can make up your own mind. Just don't expect me to come and rescue you if you fall into a stupor or something. I have no intention of getting all wet, and besides, that water looks cold."

He clambered down the bank of the stream and lay on his stomach atop a large stone at its edge. Then he leaned out over the stream, dipped his cupped hands into the water, and brought them up to his mouth. Drops trickled through his fingers, sparkling bright and clear as stars.

"Well?" I called.

"It's good!" he said, rolling over onto his back. "You were right. It is very cold. But there's something else. A thing I've never tasted before. I'm not quite sure how to describe it."

"Stop trying to cajole me into tasting it myself," I said.

"That wasn't cajoling," he answered, pushing himself up onto his elbows. "That was tantalizing. There's a big difference. Couldn't you tell?"

"Either way, it's not going to work."

One eyebrow shot up. "You just keep right on thinking that, Aurore."

"That's not going to work either," I said, though, by this time, I'd started to laugh, which was just as good as admitting that he'd won. "Oh, all right," I said, getting up and marching down the bank to flop down at his side. I followed his example, gathering the stream water into my cupped hands to drink. I don't think I've ever felt anything so cold. But it slid down my throat as smoothly as honey.

"Oh," I said, after a moment. And then again, "Oh."

"That's just what I thought." Ironheart nodded. "It's like—"

"Like drinking from all the streams there ever were at once," I said, rolling over to gaze up at the sky. Like being able to hold the clear, pure essence of the very world itself within your hands, and then take it in with one long swallow. "I wonder if that's how the magic of this place works."

Ironheart sat up. "What?"

"Doesn't it seem to you that there's more of everything here?" I asked, sitting up also. "As if the Forest holds all the possibilities for everything all at once? Maybe that's why time is different here."

He was nodding vigorously even before I finished speaking.

"That's exactly how it seems to me," he said. "But what I wonder is this: Do we choose what we experience here, or does the Forest choose it for us?"

"My guess is that it's both," I answered slowly. "It definitely guided me to the cottage last night. And this morning, it wouldn't let us go in the direction we wanted. But since then, it's pretty much left us alone."

"I wonder why it cares where we go," Ironheart said. The frown was back between his eyes. "And whether it's taking us toward its heart or away from it."

"There's only one way to find out," I said. At which he nodded and got to his feet.

"Let's go."

# Chapter Fourteen

WE WALKED FOR DAYS, GENERALLY GOING THE way the Forest wanted us to go. Any time we tried to turn around, or choose an alternate path, the same thing happened as at the cottage: We ended up right back where we'd started. Finally, even I gave up trying to go do anything but travel in the direction the Forest wished. We could do nothing but trust the steps we took would bring us closer to our goal.

One day the trees through which we walked were comprised entirely of evergreens—pine and fir. The pine bows were heavy with fat, brown cones. Now and again, one would fall from its branch and land with a *thunk* upon the long needles that covered the floor of the Forest like a great green rug, never turning brown themselves at all. Delighted, as if the Forest had offered him a gift, Ironheart stuffed several of the cones into his knapsack, taking them out to sketch and make notations whenever we stopped.

There was the day we walked through an orchard of saplings so energetic we could actually see them grow. It was on this day that Ironheart stopped putting his quill, ink, and leather-bound book away in his knapsack. Instead he kept them out all the time, the book tucked under one arm or into the front of his breeches. His right ear soon became spattered with ink due to his habit of placing the quill there when not actually writing. It gave him a jaunty air, poking out from behind his ear like the feather of a new cap.

There was the day we crossed a great meadow without seeing any trees at all. Ironheart made notations about butterflies and picked wildflowers to press between the pages of his book. And, though the day was bright and clear, it was also the one in which I felt a shadow slowly begin to take shape in the back of my mind. In the depths of my heart.

*This isn't the way it's supposed to be,* I thought. Though *How can this be the way it's supposed to be?* is probably more precise. I had come to la Forêt expecting it to be dark and dangerous and terrible. Or at the very least to hold the possibility for those things inside it, as I held such things inside me. So far, with the exception of that first hailstorm, I'd seen nothing of them.

The longer I walked, the more certain I became. The current situation couldn't last for very much longer, because it just couldn't be right.

And as for Ironheart, he'd forgotten all about his beautiful sleeping princess, as far as I could tell. He hadn't mentioned her in days, seemingly content to simply ramble through the Forest making notes. Surely true love was a thing not so easily distracted. Though how he could actually *be* in love with a girl he'd never even met was a thing I still hadn't managed to figure out.

All in all, I was becoming what my nurse would have called *out of sorts*. So I suppose it was only reasonable that out-of-the-way things began to happen, for that is how the world works, or so I've always been told. Thinking about dark and troublesome things, wondering when they'll come to pay you a visit, turns out to be the very best way to call them to your side.

It all started when I picked the fight.

A thing I'm hardly proud to admit, but as I've promised to tell the truth, there's really no way to leave it out.

It happened on a day that started out much like any other, but turned out to be the one on which I decided that I'd simply had enough. The day of the never-ending apple orchard.

We came across it early in the morning of what I was pretty sure was our fifth day in the Forest. A number that felt significant, somehow. Hadn't it taken six steps to cross the boundary between la Forêt and the world I knew? Therefore, might it not make sense that it would take six days to reach its heart, as well? In which case, tomorrow could be eventful in ways that were impossible to predict.

Not that anything about la Forêt had been all that predictable so far.

The first trees we passed were all in bud. Aside from noting that they were different from the trees of the day before, I don't think even Ironheart thought all that much about them. The land through which we walked had grown hilly overnight—soft green rolls of earth with tiny valleys nestled like jewels in between them. A land like the gentle swells of the ocean, swells just high enough to hide what was beyond them. We couldn't see what was up ahead until we'd reached the top of each rise.

Shortly before noon, a strange sound began to fill our ears, a deep low buzzing. Ironheart lifted his head like a dog on a scent.

"What's that?" he inquired.

"How should I know?" I said, my tone already grumpy. I was getting tired of all this upping and downing. To me, it felt as if la Forêt was playing tricks again, when it knew quite well I wanted things to be clear and straightforward. "I can't see any farther ahead than you can, you know."

Ironheart glanced at me, a furrow between his brows. But I could tell that only about half of the frown was for me. The rest of his attention was already fixed on whatever lay beyond the next rise.

"Come on, let's go find out," he said.

"Wait a minute," I cautioned. "You don't—"

But by then, of course, he was off and running. I watched him top the rise in front of us, then stop dead, his hands hanging loosely at his sides. On a spurt of adrenaline, I followed him up, my hand reaching for the knife at my boot.

It was more apple orchard. But such an orchard as could exist only within the boundaries of la Forêt. Which, of course, is really just another way of saying, an apple orchard the likes of which I'd never seen before.

Below us, the land flattened out into the broadest valley we had seen that day. It was round, like an enormous bowl. The trees closest to us were all in bloom, their scent rising up to meet us, a great fragrant cloud so strong it was almost visible, and brushed with just the faintest hint of rose.

"They're bees," said Ironheart. For naturally it was they who were making the buzzing. I'd never seen so many before, not even among my father's orchards. So many they almost covered the blossoms.

But even this was not the most remarkable thing. More amazing still were the trees that stood in the very center of the bowl, for these were not in blossom. Even from a distance, we could see ripe fruit hanging from their boughs. They had been planted in a great pattern of diamonds, each comprised of trees bearing fruit of one color. Green. Red. Gold. It was like looking down on a tapestry made entirely of apple trees.

Beyond even these, at the bowl's far edge, were trees whose limbs were stark and bare, as if in the midst of winter. An entire season of growing in microcosm.

"I don't understand this place," I said.

Ironheart nodded, his expression sober, "Neither do I." Then the smile that never seemed to be far from his face burst out across it. "But I do know I want to find out if those apples taste as good as they look. Come on."

And so I followed him down.

The air among the blooming trees was so thick it made me

dizzy. The apples themselves, when we finally reached them, were so plump and ripe the juice all but burst from their skins as they hung upon the trees. Ironheart picked two of each kind and stowed them carefully in his knapsack. (Away from the pinecones, I assumed.) Then he plucked a golden one and held it up against my cheek.

"Look, Aurore. It matches your hair."

"Don't be silly," I said, but I took it from him anyway. I polished it absently against my shirt while I watched him dash into the trees the next diamond over, scouting until he'd found the biggest, reddest apple of them all. He devoured it in six enormous bites, the juice running down his chin. A look of wonder filled his face.

"It's like the water," he said. "More of what it is. I wonder how each color tastes different from the next."

"Try it and see," I said, and tossed the golden apple to him. As it arced through the air, it flashed in the sun, bright as a coin. This one he devoured in only four bites, as it was smaller than the one before.

"It tastes like honey warmed in the sun." And the green tasted of spring, or so he said. But, although Ironheart urged me to, I couldn't bring myself to eat a single bite. It was as if I feared that, if I did, I'd fall under some spell. Voluntarily put my hand in a trap. The beauty of the apple orchard had only increased my fears. You draw more flies with honey, or so I've always been told.

I did consent to let Ironheart stuff several more apples into my knapsack. In case I changed my mind later, he said. When I pointed out he had some of his own, he loftily explained that the ones in his pack were for scientific purposes, not for eating.

It was late in the day when we reached the outskirts of the orchard, the limbs of the barren trees on the rim looking like stiff, aching arms that stretched toward the darkening sky. By mutual consent, we halted. Beyond the orchard lay a great bank of mist. We could not see our way forward.

"I think we should stop here for the night," Ironheart said. "Find a place to make camp in the orchard. There's no sense blundering around in the dark."

"All right," I said. *Tomorrow, the sixth day will dawn,* I thought. A day I was pretty sure would prove to be significant, one way or another.

"Let's go back a little ways," Ironheart suggested suddenly. "I don't like the idea of camping on the edge of anything." He eyed the fogbank suspiciously. "It feels—I'm not quite sure— too exposed."

At this, I felt the tension that had been riding me all day ease a bit. *It isn't just me. He feels it too,* I thought.

"All right," I said again, as we began to make our way back toward the center of the orchard. It was well and truly dark now, a night with no moon, no stars. We stumbled along for a few more rows of trees. Then I heard Ironheart cry out, and then a *thud* as he hit the ground.

I had the knife out of my boot in the time it took to blink. "What is it?" I cried.

For a moment, I thought I heard him swearing under his breath. "Just my own big feet," he said after a moment. "Or big foot, I should say. And a gopher hole." In the dim light, I could see him stand up, and dust himself off. "I'm going to take it for a sign. This is far enough."

I slid the knife back into its sheath. "Over here," I said, walking closer to the nearest row of trees. "It's not so bumpy." Together, we shucked off our knapsacks and settled to the ground, wrapping ourselves in our cloaks. "Ironheart, I've been wondering something."

"Well, it's about time," he said. "A little longer and the suspense might have killed me. You've been brooding all day, Aurore."

"I have not either," I said, feeling a spurt of irritation. "Just because I don't treat every single day like it's a lark."

"You know perfectly well I don't do that," he said in a reasonable tone. A thing which caused a second spurt of irritation to shoot through my veins. There's nothing worse than being spoken to patiently when you're well and truly cross. It's enough to make even a grown person feel like a child.

"Stop trying to pick a fight, Aurore," Ironheart went on. "Tell me what it is you wonder instead."

"All right," I said. "Since you asked me: How will you know when we've reached the heart of the Forest? Do you even know what it looks like?"

"Not really," he admitted, and though his features were just a blur, I could imagine him making a self-deprecating face in the darkness. "I guess I just assumed it would be obvious. That there would be a castle or a bower or something. I don't think a beautiful princess would just be sleeping out in the open, do you?"

"What if there isn't a beautiful sleeping princess?" I asked. "What if she's not so beautiful, or she's wide awake, or somebody else got there first and she's gone?"

"No," he said at once. "She's going to be there, and I'm going to bring her the kiss of true love."

"But you can't *know* that," I protested. If I'd been standing up, it's likely I'd have stomped my foot. "You can't possibly know for sure."

"Yes, I can, Aurore."

"How?" I challenged.

"Because it's what I feel in my heart," Ironheart said, his tone telling me he thought this should be obvious. "My heart knows she's going to be there, even if my mind can't explain how."

"But can't you see how preposterous that is?" I said, suddenly appalled to realize I was fighting back an impulse to cry. How could he be so certain love would be waiting, when I wasn't certain of anything at all? "How can you love someone you've never even met? It can't even be love at first sight!"

"I don't have to meet her," he answered. "I've known her my whole life."

"Ironheart, you're talking about a story," I said, striving to make my own tone reasonable now. "A romantic fairy tale told to you by your grandfather. For all you know, he made it up to give you a purpose. Make you feel good about yourself. It's not the same as loving a real live human being."

"She's real to me," said Ironheart, his voice sharp. "And my grandfather never mentioned any fairies."

"All right," I said. "What does she look like?"

"What difference does that make?" exclaimed Ironheart. "What she looks like isn't important. I care about what's in her heart."

"But you can't *know* what's in her heart! That's my whole point!"

"I can, too," said Ironheart. "It's the match for what's in mine. Just because you don't feel that way about anybody doesn't mean I can't."

"It does so, because nobody can. And that's a terrible thing to say. You don't know anything about my feelings."

"I can so, and you asked for it," shot back Ironheart. "What's gotten into you today, Aurore? I'd have said the quest was going fine, until today."

"It's *not* a quest," I all but yelled, as I jumped to my feet. "It's a walk in the park. A quest is supposed to test your mettle, make you prove yourself. How many obstacles have we faced so far? How many challenges?"

"Counting you right this minute, you mean?"

"Ha ha. Very funny. Okay, answer me this: How many steps did it take you to get into the Forest?"

Even in the dark, I could see him drop his head into his hands. "What kind of a question is that? You think I was counting?"

I took a deep breath, striving for calm. "When I got close to the Forest," I said, "there was a ring around it, of dry grass. Sort like a moat without the water. As if it marked the place where the regular world ended and the Forest began. It seemed to me that it went all the way around it."

Ironheart lifted his head. "All right, yes," he said. "You're right. I remember. What about it?"

"How many steps did it take you to cross it?"

"What difference does that make?"

"Look, if you can't remember, just say so."

"All right, all right, let me think a minute." He took almost exactly sixty seconds to come up with his answer. I know because I counted. "Half a dozen. I remember because I thought it would take less. It didn't look that far, and my legs are kind of long."

"Six steps," I said. "That's the same number it took me. How many days have we been walking through the Forest?"

"Five," Ironheart answered promptly. "I know that because I've been taking notes, by the way. Which only goes to show they haven't been a waste of time."

There was another moment of silence. "Oh," he said. And then again, "Oh. So you think . . ."

"That tomorrow will be the day we reach the heart of the Forest."

"What's so bad about that?" he asked at once. "Isn't that what we've been trying to do all along? And how do you know it will be six days? Why not some multiple of six? Twelve? Eighteen? Twenty-four?"

"It's going to be six," I said.

"Oh, I see," he replied. "You mean you just *know.* In your heart."

"Something like that," I said.

"So you can do it but I can't, is that it?"

"Now who's trying to pick a fight?"

"I'm not picking a fight," Ironheart said, his tone so reasonable it made me want to kick something. "I'm defending myself. Just because I'm pointing out the flaws in your logic is no reason to start accusing me of things. There's no shame in being afraid, you know, Aurore. If you are, you should just say so."

"I am *not* afraid," I said. Though, of course that was the moment I realized how desperately I was. Afraid of what awaited me in the heart of the Forest. Afraid that it would be something shining, quick, and sharp. That had just one reason for its existence: to draw from me one bright drop of blood.

Whatever waited for me in the heart of la Forêt, I was sure it wasn't love. And suddenly, the thought that tomorrow Ironheart might embrace his happiness, while the only thing I embraced, fear, was more than I could bear.

"I'm finished with this conversation," I said. "I'm not talking to you anymore."

"Oh, for heaven's sake, Aurore!" Ironheart exclaimed. "Will you listen to yourself?"

I stomped to a tree a little ways away from the one under which he was sitting, desperately praying I didn't step right into another gopher hole. It's hard to be on your high horse when you're falling on your face. There, I sat down in a huff and put my back against the tree.

"Fine," Ironheart said. "If that's the way you want it. But don't blame me if you catch cold."

"I don't know why you bother to keep speaking," I said. "Nobody's paying attention to a word you say."

I heard him sigh. "Oh, go to sleep, Aurore. If you're not in a better mood tomorrow, I'm going on without you."

As I sat with my back against the rough bark of the apple tree, I wondered suddenly if that hadn't been exactly what I wanted all along.

That night, I dreamed of home.

At first I thought it was the nightmare, come to haunt me even within the confines of la Forêt. But, even from inside the dream, I knew that this was wrong. It was true the dreams began in much the same way, though instead of actually being in the palace, I was in the village below, moving toward it. The sense that I was searching for something I had lost was as strong as ever. But, in this dream, I knew I was myself. I was Aurore.

Instead it was the land around me which seemed to have changed, though at first the alterations were so subtle I hardly noticed. But gradually it came to me that, everywhere I looked, the colors seemed brighter than I remembered. The crops and livestock taller and fatter. The whitewash on the village cottages just a little more white. Prosperity and contentment had cast their mantles out across the land, gleaming satin cloaks of green and gold. Peace and happiness seemed to reign in every direction.

*The stewards have done well,* I thought.

And with this thought, I reached the palace and stopped. For I saw that the walls that had once kept it locked away from the world outside had been torn down, a thing I knew had long been a dream of Papa's. An elaborate wrought-iron gate marked the entrance to the palace grounds, but it stood wide open. A white rose and a red rose clambered up either side as if racing to embrace one another. Their scent circled around my head as I passed beneath them, heading for the kitchen garden.

It looked much as I remembered, save that it was more abundant, just as everything was. The paths between the rows of plants were broader, covered in nutshells that made cheerful cracking noises as I walked along. And beside each plant was a marker, telling what its name was. As if someone had anticipated the curiosity of all the little girls who had come after me, of royal birth or not.

Beside a plant with leaves mottled green and purple, I knelt down. I had no need to read the marker to know what it was. Not only did I remember for myself, but it seemed to me that I could hear my cousin's voice, clear as the peal of a church bell in the back of my mind.

*"That is sage, Aurore."*

*Sage,* which even as a child I had known meant *wise. You and your descendants have done well, Oswald,* I thought.

For surely the prosperity I saw all around me was my cousin's handiwork, proof positive that he had taken our final conversation straight into his heart. No other combination of things could have produced the peace and bounty I saw around me, for those things required both wisdom and love. And patience, also.

This was the world my departure had created. A future both shining and glorious. This was the gift I had given my people by holding my love for them safe and strong within my heart.

Yet even as this thought came to me, I began to weep, for suddenly I perceived that this bright and shining future held no place in it for me. There was no one left whom I had known and loved. And as my tears fell unchecked into the fertile earth, it seemed to me that, at long last, I understood the unhappiness that had always seemed to dwell inside my cousin Oswald.

Had he not been surrounded by all that he desired, yet been undesired in return? Rising each day to live in a world in which he knew he had no place. And so, just as she had spoken her spell first, so it seemed to me that Cousin Jane would have the last word now. For though Chantal's spell might save my life, it would doom me to live in a world which owed its very existence to the fact that I hadn't been in it. Like Oswald, I would be surrounded by others, yet always alone.

*"Aurore,"* I heard a voice say. *"You're dreaming. Wake up."*

There were hands upon my shoulders, shaking me. Then I felt myself pulled into a pair of arms. *"Don't weep, Aurore. I'm here,"* the voice said.

And at that, I woke up, and knew where I was. I was in la Forêt, at the base of an apple tree, held tightly in Ironheart's arms.

"I wasn't weeping," I said. "I never cry."

"Well, at least I know you're awake now," said Ironheart.

I tried to sit up, but he pushed my head back down against his chest. "Stop fussing," he said. "I've had enough conflict for one day. Just lie still, Aurore. Try relying on me for once. Think of it this way: I owe you for building five nights worth of fires."

Part of me was tempted to argue. I hated to seem weak, but he did have a point. Besides, the dream had left me shaking and Ironheart felt solid and warm.

"I'm sorry I was so disagreeable," I mumbled against his chest.

"I'm sorry you were too," said Ironheart. At this I tried to lift my head again, but he held it firmly in place with the back of one hand. "Shut up and go to sleep, Aurore. We can argue again in the morning, if you still want to."

And so I gave up and went to sleep in the shelter of his arms, my head pressed against the rhythm of his heart. All through the night, it seemed to me that it pounded out his name. One I was beginning to believe was his true one after all.

*Ironheart. Ironheart. Ironheart.*

# Chapter Fifteen

WHEN I AWOKE THE NEXT MORNING, I WAS alone. My head was resting on a great tree root instead of where I thought it would be, which was Ironheart's shoulder. I had a crick in my neck I was sure would remain for the rest of the day, a thing I certainly intended to mention in no uncertain terms.

Just as soon as I found him.

I stood up and stretched, then shouldered my knapsack and wrapped both cloaks around me. He'd left me his, which I had to admit was very considerate. The air was sharp, though the sky was clear even in the early morning. It was the kind of day Nurse always said reminded her of the one on which I had been born. A day like a beautiful wild animal with a glossy coat and a mouth full of teeth. The kind of day where anything could happen, so you'd better watch out.

The sixth day since I'd come to the Forest.

I found Ironheart standing at the very edge of the apple orchard, staring straight ahead and frowning.

"Oh, good, you're awake. Come and tell me what you make of this," he said as I moved to stand beside him.

I studied it.

"Whatever it is, it's green," I said. "And yes, thank you, I did sleep well. Except for the crick in my neck that I'm sure is all your fault. Good morning."

At this, he gave me his full attention, turning to me with a smile and slinging one arm around my shoulders. "Good morning, Aurore. I can see that it's green. But what else is it? That's what I really want to know."

We stared ahead in silence for a moment. "Well," I said. "It's obviously a hedge of some sort."

It was taller than either of us and extended in both directions as far as my eyes could see. Even from where we stood, some distance away, I could see that its branches were filled with both buds and thorns. As we watched, the sun struck the section closest to us, causing it to suddenly burst into bloom. Blossom after blossom of a pink as pale as the first flush of light in the sky.

"Roses," Ironheart exclaimed suddenly. "It's a hedge made of roses." I could tell by the sound of his voice that he was relieved. More than that, he was delighted. Roses and sleeping princesses were the sorts of things that almost always went together.

"It's in our way," I said, my own voice grumpy.

He chuckled. "How can it be in our way when we don't really know where we're going? Besides, I should think you'd be happy about something like this. You were the one who wanted a challenge."

I didn't have a particularly good answer for that remark, as he happened to be right, so I decided to ignore it. Instead, I took off his cloak and handed it to him.

"All right," I said. "Let's see if we can go around it."

After some debate about which direction to go, we went to the right and walked for several hours, the sun inching ever higher in the sky and the rose hedge blooming as we moved along it. There were white roses, then lavender, and then a gold that Ironheart said exactly matched the color of my hair. And finally a vivid red that reminded me of the fate that awaited me. The prick of a finger, followed by one bright drop of blood. As we walked along, we munched apples and the last of Ironheart's cheese, until the sight of the red roses made me lose my appetite.

"Do you suppose this was here last night?" Ironheart mused as we halted about midday. With the sun directly overhead, the rose hedge was a riot of color. "And we just couldn't see it because of the mist?"

I nodded. "It's too tall to have just sprung up overnight." I watched a branch move as if stretching in the sun, an action I swear made it taller. "Though, considering where we are, I suppose anything is possible."

Ironheart cocked his head. "I don't think it's just a boundary," he said. "I think there's something inside it."

"You mean your princess," I said.

He shrugged as if what I'd said wasn't important, but I saw that his face had colored. "Why not? You just said it yourself: Considering where we are, anything is possible."

"Well, if there is something inside, there has to be a way in," I said. "I don't think we can just climb over it."

"I've been thinking the same thing," Ironheart nodded. He fell silent, studying the hedge. "I wonder when we'll find it."

"Probably when the Forest wants us to," I said. Or when we wanted it enough. "Come on. Let's keep going."

We found it about an hour later, though the opening was so small we almost walked right by it.

"Ouch," I heard Ironheart suddenly exclaim. He stopped walking abruptly. A long branch of roses whose blossoms were the same color orange as the sun when it set had become entangled in the hood of his cloak. "Help me, will you please, Aurore?"

I eyed the branch, specifically, its thorns. They were small, but I knew better than to assume that meant they weren't sharp. I took off my pack, fished out my leather gloves, and pulled them on. A moment later, Ironheart was free, the branch bobbing above his head as if laughing at some secret joke.

"Thank you," Ironheart said, as he turned around. "I can't think why—" He stopped speaking as abruptly as he'd stopped walking, his eyes growing wide. I think I knew what it was before I even turned to follow his gaze.

Just below the branch that had snared his cloak there was a break in the hedge, so subtle that if I hadn't been staring straight at it, I would never have noticed. The hedge still continued as straight as ever, but one section was offset, as if it had taken a step backward. If you were careful and turned sideways, you'd be able to slip in between the two sections of hedge.

"What do you think?" asked Ironheart.

"I think it's what we've been waiting for," I said. Whether I was ready for it or not.

"I'll go first," said Ironheart.

He pulled his hood up over his head, gathered his cloak in close to his body, then stepped to the hedge, turned, and scooted sideways. A moment later, I heard his sharp intake of breath.

"Are you all right?" I called.

"I think you'd better come and see this," he said.

I followed his example. A moment later, I was standing by his side. In front of us was another series of hedges, moving off in different directions. Branching every which way like a series of corridors.

"It's a maze," I said.

"I knew it," Ironheart whispered, his eyes shining. "I knew there was more to that hedge than met the eye. We're almost there, Aurore. Can you feel it?"

*Oh yes,* I thought. I could feel my skin prickle, the way it did when danger approached. For, no matter how long it took to solve them, all mazes had one thing in common: They had a heart. And, in that moment, it seemed plain to me that the heart of the maze and the heart of the Forest were one and the same.

Now all we had to do was to find it.

# Chapter Sixteen

AS IT TURNED OUT, IT DIDN'T TAKE NEARLY AS long as I thought it might, which is the way things sometimes go. The anticipation takes longer than the actual event. In this case, it was as if even the Forest was in a hurry to get things over with, now that we'd gotten so close. Perhaps it feared that we would change our minds at the last moment. Decide to turn around and go back home instead of heading forward toward the goal.

Ironheart went first, insisting we go to the right as we had first thing that morning, his voice happy and excited when I asked him why. This wasn't a mysterious puzzle, like la Forêt itself. This was a puzzle he knew how to solve.

"Because that's the way a maze works," he said, as we reached the first intersection. Without hesitation, he moved to the right once more. "Or at least, some of them. The ones constructed the way this one is. I can tell just by looking at it. The royal gardener and I once made a series of studies."

We came to a second intersection and he turned right yet again, walking so close to the hedge he almost brushed it with his shoulder in spite of the ever present thorns. After that, the maze became more complex and he picked up the pace, weaving through a series of twists and turns so swiftly I practically had to jog to keep up.

"For heaven's sake," I said. "Whatever's waiting for us isn't going anywhere. Slow down."

"The hedge on our right is continuous," he called back over his shoulder, continuing his explanation of how he knew how to get where we were going. "There are no breaks in it anywhere. All we have to do is follow it, always keeping it *on* our right, and it will lead us to the maze's heart. It's really incredibly simple, once you know the trick."

I suppose I don't have to tell you that this was the moment that disaster struck. Never say a thing is simple, even if you know it is. Because as soon as you do, things get complicated. You might as well just come right out and invite something you'd rather not meet to rear its ugly head and bite you. Or in this case, scratch you, which is what happened next. As Ironheart turned back around, he turned a corner at the same time and one long cane of thorns, hidden by the turn in the maze, slashed across his face.

He gave a cry that had my heart leaping straight up into my throat. I sprinted toward him, already shucking off my knapsack.

"How bad is it? Let me see!" I said.

He had one hand—his left hand—pressed against the same side of his face. As if, even in wounding him, the maze had deliberately left his right side unimpaired. I could see bright drops of blood leaking out through his fingers—the same color as the blossoms covering the bushes all around us, as the thorns on the cane that even now arched above us, still quivering with the force of their contact.

"It's all right. I'm all right," he gasped.

"You're not all right," I insisted, dragging on his hand. "Ironheart, I can't help you if you won't let me see."

To my amazement, he jerked back. "Not yet," he snapped. "Not until we reach the heart."

"That's crazy," I said. "You're hurt. You have to let me help you *now.*" But I was talking to his back.

"When we reach the heart," he said again as he staggered off. "Not before that."

And so we completed our journey to the heart of the maze, the heart of the Forest, with Ironheart weaving like a drunkard and me trailing along behind him, following the bright drops of blood that slipped from his fingers and fell to the grass like so many scarlet bread crumbs. To this day, I can't tell you how long it took, though he was right about the way the maze worked, of course. After what seemed like endless twisting and turning, we rounded one final corner and there it was. I'm not sure quite what I'd expected. Something stately and royal, I suppose. Or at the very least something that reeked of storybook magic. A smooth square of perfectly green grass with a pavilion made of crystal in its very center and a fountain splashing water as clear as diamonds. Or perhaps a woodland glen inhabited by both a lion and a unicorn.

La Forêt being what it was, the thing it held within its heart was neither of those things. It was simply a garden, and a practical one at that, with herbs and vegetables planted in tidy rows. The only structure I could see was an old wooden potting shed. The closest thing to a fountain was a brick-lined well. And the only place where a princess might have slept for a hundred minutes, let alone a hundred years, was a bench with a flowered cushion for her head at one end. On the other end lay a straw hat with a bright blue ribbon tied around the crown, as if whoever tended this place had just taken it off and gone for a morning stroll.

But of the gardener herself, there was no sign.

"No," I heard Ironheart choke out. His steps faltered, and he came to a halt. *"No."*

My heart was knocking against my ribs so hard I thought it might break. With his sorrow, not with my own.

"Sit down," I said, putting my hands on his shoulders and pushing him downward. "Let me see your face."

His legs folded like a house of twigs, his hands flopping useless in his lap. "She's not here. She's not here, Aurore."

"Don't be ridiculous, of course she's here," I said, making my voice as brisk as I could. "You don't think a princess is going to sleep for a hundred years outside. She'd catch her death of cold long before her handsome prince could even set out, let alone arrive."

*Not so bad. It's not so bad,* I thought. Though it had bled fiercely during our sprint, most of the bleeding had stopped by now, and the wound had somehow missed his eye. It started midforehead, then slanted downward across the left side of his face. I was pretty sure the thing that had saved his eye had been the bridge of his nose. But the cut was deep, especially across his cheek, and would need to be cleansed and stitched.

"Sit there," I said. "I'll get some water from the well."

"No," he protested, trying to get to his feet. "I can't just sit here. I have to find her, Aurore."

"And so you will," I said. "But you can't do it looking like you've just been attacked by brigands. You want to bring her the kiss of true love, not scare her half to death. Wouldn't you say she's already been through enough?"

"You're right. Of course you're right," he said. "It's just—"

"Sit still," I commanded, making my voice as stern as I could. "The sooner you let me do this, the sooner you can get on with your quest."

But as I started to rise, he caught my hand. "She is here, isn't she? I will find her, won't I, Aurore?"

"Of course you will," I said, though I felt the pain of doubt close like a vise around my heart. "Isn't it the thing for which you were born?"

"That's right. It is," he said. And then he smiled, a thing that caused a sluggish line of blood to ooze from his cut at its deepest point.

"I'll be right back," I said. I made for the well. After

returning with most of a bucket of water, I knelt down beside him, then rummaged in my knapsack for my extra shirt and the healing supplies I had brought along.

"This will probably hurt," I said, as I used my knife to hack one of the sleeves off the shirt. "I'm sorry, but I don't think it can be helped."

Ironheart attempted a smile. "It's all right," he said. "Really, I'm tougher than I look."

I paused in the act of dunking the sleeve in the water and met his eyes. "No, you're not."

He opened his mouth to protest, then closed it again as he realized what I'd meant. "Thank you," he said. "I think that's about the nicest thing anybody's ever said to me, Aurore."

"Just don't let it go to your head," I remarked. "There's nothing worse than a man who thinks too well of himself."

Then swiftly I laid the damp cloth against his face while he was still chuckling. He jerked once, his eyes telling me he knew exactly what I'd done, then calmed. Carefully I washed the dried blood from his face, working slowly and patiently until I felt sure the wound was as clean as I could make it.

"I'm going to have to stitch your cheek," I said.

Somehow, he managed to make a face. "A thing you've no doubt done a million times before."

"A million and one," I said, as I deftly threaded my needle, grateful for the first time for Maman's insistence that I learn to use one properly.

He chuckled and reached one hand out to grasp mine at the wrist, holding it still. "I like you, Aurore. I just wanted to say that—before whatever else is going to happen happens."

"I like you, too," I replied.

"All right," he said. "Let's get this over with."

Though the first instance of needle going through flesh gave us both a bad moment, in a matter of minutes I was snipping off the thread and the deed was done. I wove the needle through the thigh of my right pant leg, desperate to get it out of my hands before they could begin to shake, then turned to dip a fresh piece of torn shirtsleeve into the bucket.

"Here, take this," I said, leaning forward to hand it over. "The water is cold. It will help keep the swelling down. Why don't you rest for just a moment before you—"

I felt a small, bright spear of pain, for all the world like the sting of a bee, shoot through my right hand as I sat back upon my heels and my hand brushed against my thigh. Turning it over, I could see something exactly in the center of the pad of my right forefinger.

One bright drop of blood.

My eyes dropped to where I'd tucked the needle into the top of my pants. *You great idiot, Aurore.* And so the fate I'd been waiting my whole life for was upon me, and of course I'd brought it on myself.

"Ouch," I said softly. And then, "I wonder what happens now?"

Ironheart took the cloth down from his face. "What is it? What's the matter, Aurore?"

There was urgency in his voice, I could hear it, but I could no longer seem to summon any sense of urgency myself. There was a strange sound filling my ears, a sound that somehow managed to sound like weeping beyond all hope of consolation and joyous shouting at the same time.

"There's something I need to tell you," I said.

"What is it?" he said, and I think I felt his hands upon my shoulders. "For the love of God, Aurore."

No longer able to answer, I looked up into his face, and, as I did so, for the very first time, I saw what and who it was I carried, strong and safe, inside my heart.

*Oh for heaven's sake,* I thought. *How on earth could I have missed a thing like that? I wish that I had said something, but I suppose it's too late now.*

Then my eyes went blind and my mind went blank. And in my ears, a sound like church bells ringing on a cold, clear dawn.

# Chapter Seventeen

I AWOKE TO A THING I'D NEVER FELT BEFORE. Something was moving across my face, fierce and demanding. And a voice was saying my name in exactly the same way. *"Aurore. Aurore."* Then I felt something touch my lips. Once. Twice. Then a third time, each with growing desperation, and realized what I felt were lips themselves. I was being kissed.

"For the love of God, don't leave me," the voice said. "Come back, Aurore."

"All right," I said, struggling to open my eyes. They didn't seem to want to obey my mind's instructions, as if they knew better than I that being closed was their proper position. A position they'd been in for a very long time.

"I can hear you. My ears still work. There's no need to shout."

Whoever held me made a strange sound and pressed me against his chest, rocking me back and forth the way you do a small child.

"I'm going to knock you senseless as soon as you're completely awake," he said.

At this I struggled to sit up, for it seemed to me it was a voice I knew. And no sooner had this thought occurred than

I opened my eyes. The sun was so dazzling that I immediately shut them again.

"Ironheart?"

"Well, who else would it be?" he asked, his tone more than a little aggrieved. "What on earth happened? You scared me to death, Aurore."

"You kissed me," I said, opening my eyes once more. They watered like anything, but this time I managed to keep them open. "Did you kiss me?"

"All right. Okay. Yes, I did," said Ironheart, and even through my watery eyes I could see the way his face colored.

"There's no need to get all bothered about it. The truth is, I sort of lost my head. One minute you were fine. The next you were saying all these things that didn't make any sense at all. Then you keeled right over. I've never seen anybody go as white and still as you did. I thought—that is—I was afraid that you were dead, or something."

"Not dead. Just sleeping. I was supposed to sleep for a hundred years," I said. And watched his mouth drop open.

"Well, it certainly *felt* like a hundred years," he said forcefully. "But that would mean—" He broke off, his eyes growing wide. "That would mean that you—that I . . . oh." He dropped his head down into his hands. "I don't understand any of this, Aurore."

"Neither do I," I said with a smile. "I do know one thing, though."

"What's that?"

"I want to go home."

"Sounds good to me," he said. "Do you suppose the Forest will let us go?"

"Your grandfather must have thought so," I said. "Otherwise, he never would have sent you on this quest."

"Good point," said Ironheart. And with that he stood up, pulling me with him. Supporting me when I swayed, as if my legs had forgotten their proper function. "Oh, my."

"What?" I asked. In answer, he simply turned me around, so that I faced back the way we'd come.

The maze was gone.

In its place were low-growing rose shrubs and wild clematis, scrambling over and through one another in great curving mounds. It was as if the maze had become an old woman, still beautiful, but bent, softened with time. Beyond the roses, the trees of la Forêt opened up to rolling pastureland. I could see the towers of a castle in the distance, their banners blowing bright against the sky.

"That's my father's castle," I said. And heard Ironheart make a sound.

"I was afraid you were going to say that," he said.

I turned in his arms to gaze up at him. "Why?"

"Because it's also the place where I grew up. This is getting stranger by the minute, Aurore."

"The sooner we get back, the better," I said.

"Right," Ironheart agreed at once. "Okay, off we go."

With that, he scooped me up into his arms and started down the hill toward the castle.

"Wait a minute!" I cried. "I'm not a sack of potatoes, in case you hadn't noticed. Put me down!"

"In a minute," he said. "And if you keep squirming like that, I'll throw you over my shoulder as if you *were* a sack of potatoes. You're still a little shaky on your feet. You just don't want to admit it. Let me help you for once, Aurore."

"You could have asked first," I grumbled, though I did stop squirming. The sentiment he'd expressed had been rather sweet.

"What for? All you would have done is to say no."

"I suppose you think you know me pretty well," I said.

"Well enough," said Ironheart with a smile.

We reached the bottom of the hill. The trees thinned out, and the pastureland began. After a few more moments of walking, we reached a road.

"Put me down, please," I said, and, at once, Ironheart obliged. As if he understood my desire to return home, if it was still home, on my own two feet. The same way I had left it behind.

"What do you suppose will happen when we get there?" I asked.

Ironheart reached down to take my hand. "I don't know. Would you rather go the other way? I suppose we could."

"No," I said swiftly, though I had to admit the offer was tempting. To put it from my mind I said, "No," once more. "I guess I just thought going home would be less mysterious than leaving it. Instead, it's more."

"I know exactly what you mean," Ironheart said, in such heartfelt agreement that I laughed in spite of myself, and suddenly, things didn't seem so bad anymore.

"I guess it's like taking medicine," I said. "The sooner you do it, the sooner you can get on to whatever comes next."

"Could be," Ironheart said. "Though I do hope it won't involve any throwing up."

"That's disgusting," I said. "Race you."

And with that, we were off.

# Chapter Eighteen

IT TOOK LESS TIME THAN I REMEMBERED TO get home from la Forêt.

Home.

Could I really still call it that? I wondered. When I was far from certain what was waiting for me there? A home is more than just a building, after all, even if that building is a castle.

*Stop thinking and just keep walking. You won't know if it's home until you get there, Aurore.*

The closer we got, the more settled the land around us became. What had once been open countryside was now dotted with prosperous farms. People stopped working in the fields as we passed by them, running to crowd around Ironheart. It was plain that his great quest was quite well known, a thing that soon caused people to crowd around me as well. By the time we reached the place where the castle gates stood open to all who wished to enter, we'd collected quite a throng. As we passed through them, farmers and townspeople streaming like a great living train behind us, a young man came out from the palace to meet us.

"You're back," he said to Ironheart. "You brought a girl with you." In both statements, the astonishment was plain in his voice.

"A princess," I said with a silent apology to both Maman and Ironheart. I knew it wasn't proper etiquette for me to speak first, but the truth was that the young man's tone irked me. He sounded so surprised. "And you must be Ironheart's brother, Valiant," I said, and watched surprise become bewilderment.

"That's right," he said. "How did you know?"

"From Ironheart's very accurate description," I said, not daring to look in Ironheart's direction, particularly when I heard him give a strangled snort.

"Grandfather wants to see you," Valiant blurted out. "He's in the audience chamber. The big one."

"Then we should go see him right away, don't you think?" I asked, giving him my very best smile. Still looking slightly bewildered, he stepped back. Ironheart and I mounted the palace steps and stepped across the threshold into the great hall, side by side.

"I think he means the royal audience chamber," Ironheart whispered as we bore left and climbed another set of stairs. "Though I can't think why Grand-père would be there. He never uses it, since he's not really a king."

"What do you mean he's not really a king?" I asked.

But any reply he might have made was cut off by a sudden

fanfare of trumpets so loud and jubilant I almost clapped my hands across my ears. In the next moment, the doors to the royal audience chamber were thrown wide open, leaving Ironheart and me no choice but to go right in.

*This is the very room in which I was christened,* I thought. So I suppose it only made sense that this was where my journey to and from la Forêt should end. Down the length of the room Ironheart and I walked side by side, while the townspeople and farmers crowded in behind us, jostling the courtiers who were already assembled, for all the world as if they'd known we were coming.

I could hear the rustle of silks as bows and curtsies were performed all around us. I never once turned my head. All my attention was focused on the man who sat at the far end of the room, at the base of the royal dais.

Not at their top, I instantly noticed. All that rested there were two empty thrones. My father's. My mother's. I blinked rapidly, desperate to hold back a sudden rush of tears. When my eyes were clear again, the old man and I were face-to-face, and a silence more absolute than any I had ever known had followed in my wake to fill the audience chamber.

He was the oldest man that I had ever seen. Though how old that actually was, I did not know. He sat straight and vigorous, hands resting lightly upon his knees. Hair as white as the first winter snowfall tumbled across his shoulders. The unadorned chair upon which he sat was made of dark red wood, polished until it gleamed like a ruby. Papa had given me a box made from the same kind of wood, the day I turned ten. What had he called it? Ah, yes. *Rosewood.*

And at this sudden memory I belatedly remembered my manners and sank into a curtsy, momentarily forgetting that I was wearing breeches and a shirt no doubt stained with Ironheart's blood.

"No," he said, in a clear voice. "No, you should not bow before me, Aurore."

"You know my name," I said, and, in my amazement, looked straight into his eyes. They were gray as a storm at sea, flecked with gold like unexpected sunlight. At the sight of them, my heart rolled over once within my chest and then lay still.

"Oswald."

He smiled then. A flash of teeth that had remained unchanged through all the years that lay between us. And now my heart reared up and then began to gallop like a horse.

"I promised that I would wait for you, did I not, little cousin?"

# Chapter Nineteen

WITHOUT WARNING, MY KNEES TURNED TO water and I sank to the floor at his feet.

*For heaven's sake, Aurore,* I thought. *Now is hardly the time to turn all mushy.* But by now a wild trembling had seized all my limbs. I could not have stood if my life depended on it.

"Valiant," Oswald said, his voice brisk. "Bring a chair for the princess Aurore."

This was done, and I was seated, with Ironheart standing beside me. Then my cousin reached to take my hand in his. And at this it seemed to me that he began to tremble also, though before his hands had been steady and sure.

"I'm sorry, Aurore," he said. "I should have realized that it would be a shock. It's just—"

"That you've been waiting for a hundred years," I filled in for him. I sat back, and he released my hand. I shook my head, hoping the action would convince my brain cells to function. "Even with all the magic there is around here, I still don't understand how any of this is possible."

"Many things are possible, if you desire them enough,"

my cousin said simply. At which my mind calmed and I remembered a thing I had forgotten.

"Ironwill," I said. "Isn't that what they call you?"

"Indeed, they do," said Oswald. "Iron seems to run in the family. Tell me, what do you make of my grandson?"

I answered without hesitation. "That although it may not have been the intention at the time, he is well-named also."

"Ah!" Oswald exclaimed. "I was hoping you would think so. You will marry him and live happily ever after, then," he said, but this time, his eyes slid away from mine. At my side, I felt Ironheart go perfectly still. And now, at last, the trembling in my body ceased and I understood my story's outcome. For what I held in my heart was as clear to me as a sudden glimpse of starlight on a cloudy night.

"I can't do that," I said softly. "If it pains either of you, I can only say that I am sorry."

Oswald's eyes jerked to mine. "But . . . ," he began.

I leaned forward just far enough to place my hands on his. "The answer is no, cousin. There are many things that I would do for you, that I *will* do," I said. "But this cannot be one of them. Though make no mistake, Ironheart is as fine a prince as any princess could wish for," I went on, raising my voice. "But to live happily ever after, there must be love, and true love at that."

"But . . . ," Oswald said again.

"Be quiet," I said firmly. "Or your iron will will have gained you nothing. I'm trying to say that it's *you* I love, Oswald."

And I leaned forward the rest of the way and pressed my

lips to his before he could try to get another word in edgewise.

I felt his hands come up to grasp me by the shoulders, as they'd done the night when I left home. The sound was in my ears again, the same I'd heard when I'd pricked my finger in the Forest. But now the weeping faded away, leaving only one pure voice, singing high and joyful. Then, even that grew silent as the kiss ended and I opened my eyes. There were tears in Oswald's. And extraordinary as this was, it still wasn't the greatest cause for amazement. For my cousin was transformed.

No longer old, but young.

His outward form once more matched the image of him I had carried in my heart for so very long. For this was what I had seen in the moment before my sleep began. It was Oswald I carried in my heart. And so it was that the words my godmother Chantal had uttered on the day of my christening at last made sense. The power of her magic had snatched me from death. But it was the power of my own love which would give me the life I wanted.

All around us, I could hear a great commotion among those assembled in the room. I kept my eyes on Oswald's. And so I knew the exact moment he saw himself reflected in them.

"Sweet heavens," he whispered. "Sweet merciful, mercurial Aurore. You are, and always have been, my strongest magic."

"Not me," I said. "Us. Together."

For who could deny, literally in the face of so much wonder, that love was the greatest magic of them all?

# Chapter Twenty

LATE THAT AFTERNOON, I WALKED IN THE GARDEN with Ironheart. The kitchen garden, to be exact. The same one in which I'd taken my first steps into the world, so long ago now. Oswald and I were to be married the next day, with as little pomp and as much celebration as possible. I suppose there were those who considered such haste unseemly. But then neither of us had ever cared very much what other people thought. And for ourselves, it seemed to us, in particular to Oswald, that the waiting we had already endured was more than long enough.

"Aurore," Ironheart said, as he folded his long form onto a bench beneath a row of orange trees. "Will you tell me something?"

"Of course I will," I said, as I sat down beside him. Indeed, I had a feeling I knew what was coming.

"If you hadn't known you loved Grand-père, do you think—that is—I've been wondering—"

"Of course I would have," I said.

He poked at the dirt with one booted foot. "Honestly?

You aren't just saying that to sort of soften the blow?"

"You can probably answer that one yourself," I said. "Does that sound like something I might do?"

He gave a snort of laughter before he could stop himself. "All right," he said. "You've convinced me. I hope you'll be very happy, Aurore."

I linked my arm through his. "As happy as I hope you'll be someday. Come on now, admit it. You don't really love me, either. Not in a happily ever after kind of way."

"Don't I?" he said, then heaved a great sigh. "All right, it's true, I don't." There was a small but potent silence. "I thought it would make me miserable to say that," he went on after a moment. "Instead I feel much better."

"Listening to your heart and telling the truth about it does that," I said.

He made a face. "You're not going to get all know-it-all on me, are you? Because if you are, I'm going to Grand-père right now and tell him he'd be much happier marrying you off to Valiant."

"Don't tell me *both* my grandsons want to steal my bride away from me," Oswald's voice said. And there he was, suddenly standing beside us.

Ironheart jumped, then shook his head. "Did you hear him coming?"

"No," I answered. "But then sneaking up on people always was one of his best talents. Very well," I said, smiling up at Oswald. "We won't tell you. I'll just choose the one I want and run away with him. We'll write when we get to wherever it is we're going."

"I'd like to see you try," said Oswald. "You couldn't bear to leave me again. You may as well just come right out and admit it, Aurore."

"Easy enough," I said. "Considering I never wanted to leave you in the first place."

I heard him catch his breath. And, just for a moment, he closed his eyes. When he opened them again, all I could see was gold. There was no gray in them at all.

"You have to warn me before you say things like that," he said. "You make me lose my balance, Aurore."

"That's just because you're so old," I said, as comfortingly as I could. "Here." I scooted over. "I think the bench is big enough for three. Come and sit down."

"Oh, no," said Ironheart, standing up just as Oswald slid into place beside me. "I may not be sensible like Valiant, but I know when three is one too many. Besides, I promised the royal fireworks-maker I'd help him get ready for tomorrow."

With that, he hurried off.

"I hope he doesn't blow us all sky high," Oswald said after a moment.

"It would make for a memorable occasion," I replied.

He chuckled, shifting to put one arm around me and ease my head down upon his shoulder.

"I'd say the occasion is quite memorable enough."

We sat for a moment, his fingers toying with the ends of my hair.

"Oswald," I finally said. "Will you tell me something?"

"All your life," he said.

At which I sat up straight. *"What?"*

"All your life," he repeated. "Isn't that what you wanted to know? How long I've loved you?"

"Well, yes, I suppose I did," I said. "But that wasn't what I was going to ask just now."

He gave a bark of laughter. "I tell you I've loved you since the day you were born, and you tell me you want to know something else. There's no one quite like you, is there, Aurore?"

"Well, if you don't want to tell me," I said. "If you *want* to have secrets . . ."

He laughed again. "No secrets. Not anymore. Tell me what it is you wish to know."

"Whom did you marry, since you promised it wouldn't be Marguerite de Renard? Did I know her?"

"Actually, you did," answered Oswald. "Her name was Mary."

"Mary," I repeated, while my mind frantically flipped through the faces of the courtiers' daughters I had known. Nothing. "Do you mean Mary the gardener's daughter?"

"The same," said Oswald. "Our wedding day was the first time your father told me I had made him proud."

"But not the last?"

"No, not the last," answered my cousin. "On the day he rode away, he called me *son*. Aurore—about your parents."

"It's all right," I said, laying one of my hands on top of his to silence him. "I think I know. They followed me, didn't they?"

Oswald nodded. "I don't think there's anything I could have done. They waited ten years. Long enough for your father to make certain the kingdom would be at peace—that the changes we both wished to make were going well. Actually now that I think about it, it was surprisingly easy. The only one who really made trouble was le Renard."

"What happened?" I asked.

"He raised an army and attacked the castle, *after* your father had saved him the trouble of knocking down the walls. It didn't do a bit of good. He still lost."

"And after that?"

"There were no more problems after that. His family left the country. No one was sorry to see them go."

"And Papa and Maman?"

"It was the strangest thing," said Oswald. "One day, I looked at your father and I knew he had made up his mind. The next, he and your mother were gone. He built them a cottage just inside the borders of la Forêt. Sometimes you could see it from the outside, sometimes not. I used to ride by as often as I could, but the trees had a funny habit of moving around."

"I saw the cottage," I said. "I took shelter in it my very first night. That's where I found Ironheart. There was one of my

451

rugs by the hearth. That really awful green one with the bumps as big as snakes."

"I remember it," said Oswald.

"It was a good place," I said. "It felt—happy—inside. Whatever the Forest holds for them, I think they are—or were—content. I will miss them, but I won't grieve for them. I don't think we were supposed to meet again. Not like you and I."

He reached to tuck a stray piece of hair back behind my ear. "Thank you for that," he said. "I love you, Aurore."

"Will you give me a gift, if I ask for it?" I said, and had the pleasure of watching his smile flash out.

"What a shameful brat you are," he said. "Very well. What?"

"I have given you my true love's kiss," I answered. "Don't you think it's time you gave me yours?"

"Past time," said my cousin.

And so he kissed me as I had him. Opening every single door inside his heart. And the kiss was like nothing I can describe. For in that moment, I both lost and gained myself.

I ceased to be Aurore and yet became her, too. For, with my heart joined with Oswald's, I became more of what I was. All the empty spaces within me filled to the brim, yet never overflowing. For true love always knows its own measure. And it is the measure of two hearts, combined.

Two hearts who need no other magic than what they hold inside them, for they have learned to beat as one.

# Epilogue

*(A FANCY WAY OF TYING UP LOOSE ENDS)*

THE WONDER OF MY REAPPEARANCE AND Oswald's transformation lasted for a year and a day, long enough for our first child to be born. Actually I suppose I should say our first children, for I bore two girls, so alike it would have been impossible to tell one from the other were it not for their eyes. One had eyes of gold flecked with silver; the other of silver flecked with gold. We named them Jane and Chantal.

Over the years, they were followed by many others, both girls and boys. All straight and fine as royal children are supposed to be. And every single one of them got to go outside as often as they desired.

Our youngest daughter is named Sage, just in case you want to know.

Not long after the birth of the twins, Valiant begged leave to depart. There were rumors of monsters ravaging distant lands. As those able to dispatch them are always in short supply, and high demand, we let him go. Not long after, he wrote from the very end of the world, to say he had dispatched a particularly horrible ogre. The people of that land were so grateful, they gave him the hand of their princess in marriage, and the kingship besides, the ogre's first despicable act having been to devour the old king, the princess's father.

Valiant's sensible, straightforward approach is much valued in the wilds at the edge of the world. He is there still, living happily ever after himself, as far as we know.

And what, you will ask, of Ironheart?

As his nature was not so straightforward as his brother's, so did the finding of his true love take a little more time. For several years, he lived with us in the palace, alternately delighting and terrifying the children with his strange and wonderful experiments, all the while filling many a leather-bound book with notes. Until the day that the king of the country just to the east sent word that he wished to build a new drawbridge and desired Ironheart's help.

While there, he rescued the king's only daughter, who turned out to be as scientifically minded as Ironheart was himself. A strange and unusual contraption she'd had specially constructed to allow her to hang suspended from trees, the better to pick their fruit, collapsed, causing her to fall and knock herself cold.

As the tree just happened to be an apple tree, and was moreover located in the heart of the maze the king had recently commissioned, and through which Ironheart just happened to be strolling, he decided perhaps he ought to give kissing the princess just one more try.

Though this failed to awaken her entirely, some water to

the temples soon completed the job. When the princess's first concern was not herself but her invention, Ironheart ventured to make several suggestions concerning the design. The speed with which the princess grasped all his concepts, to say nothing of the way she elaborated upon them on the spot, soon turned their chance encounter into the world's most unusual case of love at first sight. And so he awakened a princess with true love's kiss after all.

As a wedding gift, we gave them a vast tract of land bordering her father's kingdom, so that they could live surrounded on all sides by those who love them. Her name is Marianna. Their first child was a son, and they named him Oswald.

Once a year, on the anniversary of my christening, my Oswald and I go to la Forêt. There we spend the night on which I always had bad dreams, sleeping peacefully in the cottage. To this day, we have never seen its occupants. But we bring with us mementos of our family. A rug that Jane and Chantal braided together rests before the fireplace now. It's a lovely blue, the color of a summer sky. And it lies completely flat. The year after we brought it, we arrived at the cottage to find a bowl upon the table heaped with what can only be described as a fruit still-life.

Oswald and I haven't discussed it much, but what I believe is that my parents are alive inside of la Forêt and will be for as long as I live, for they were the others I kept strong and safe inside my heart. Whether they have grown old with the years, as Oswald did, or stayed young within the boundaries of the

Forest is a thing that I can never know, though I have my opinions. But I know that they are happy, because I am happy. And so I let that be enough.

People go into the Forest now, from time to time. But never more than a handful every year, and they never stay for long. Though it has ceased to be frightening, it is still mysterious, and most people find life mysterious enough without going to seek out more.

As to what happened to me there, is it possible to sleep for a hundred years in the blink of an eye? Perhaps it doesn't matter how long I actually slept, only how long I was gone. Which was certainly a hundred years, if Oswald's condition upon my return is anything to go by.

Let's see . . . what else?

Actually, nothing that I can think of. Which I think means my story has come full circle, curved around to its close. And, for once, the traditional way of ending a story is exactly the way the story of my own life turned out.

You know the words. Of course you do.

*And they lived happily ever after.*

# About the Author

After the sort of introverted childhood you would expect from a writer, Liz Braswell earned a degree in Egyptology at Brown University and then promptly spent the next ten years producing video games. Finally she caved in to fate and wrote *Snow* and *Rx* under the name Tracy Lynn, followed by The Nine Lives of Chloe King series under her real name, because by then the assassins hunting her were all dead. She also has short stories in *Geektastic: Stories from the Nerd Herd* and *Who Done It*, and a new series of reimagined fairy tales coming out, starting with *A Whole New World*—a retelling of *Aladdin*.

Liz lives in Brooklyn with a husband, two children, a cat, a part-time dog, three fish, and five coffee trees she insists will start producing beans any day. You can email her at me@lizbraswell.com or tweet @LizBraswell or, uh, tumble her here: lizbraswell.tumblr.com.

**Cameron Dokey's** favorite place to go is Once upon a Time. Her other titles in the series include *Golden, Sunlight and Shadow,* and *The Storyteller's Daughter.* Other Simon and Schuster endeavors include the Charmed books *Picture Perfect* and *Truth and Consequences; Here Be Monsters,* a book in the Buffy the Vampire Slayer series; and *The Summoned,* an Angel series title. Cameron lives in Seattle, Washington.